Rio Ł

THREE RIVERS TRILOGY, BOOK II

RIO BONITO

PRESTON LEWIS

WHEELER PUBLISHING
A part of Gale, a Cengage Company

LIBRARY OF CONGRESS CIP DATA ON FILE.
CATALOGUING IN PUBLICATION FOR THIS BOOK
IS AVAILABLE FROM THE LIBRARY OF CONGRESS.

ISBN-13: 978-1-4328-9121-3 (softcover alk. paper)

Published in 2022 by arrangement with Preston Lewis

Printed in the United States of America
1 2 3 4 5   26 25 24 23 22

For Harriet
the Love of My Life

CHAPTER 1

"Nothing good'll come from this," Wesley Bracken muttered as much to himself as to his approaching partner, Jace Cousins, astride his yellow dun. Bracken tossed a bag in the back of the wagon as he finished preparing for the trip to town. "Nothing good'll come from this," he repeated.

"You're looking at it all wrong, Wes," Cousins responded, a grin creasing his face as he shook his head in that easy manner that Wes coveted. As Cousins scratched the cleft in his chin, he nodded. "You and Sarafina'll spend a night in Lincoln's finest hotel —"

"The Wortley is the only hotel in town," Wes corrected.

"— and consequently the best hotel just as I said."

"I'm talking about the politics, Jace, and you know it. Nothing good'll come from the meeting."

"If our neighbor Bob Casey's got the guts to stand up against Lawrence G. Murphy and his company of outlaws, we need to back him."

"I'm for supporting him because Bob's been square with me from the day I arrived in this valley until now. Problem is, Bob plays politics straight as a wagon tongue. Murphy fancies himself as the biggest toad in the puddle. He won't cotton to Bob driving him out of the pond, no matter how scummy the water. And rumor has it that Governor Axtell and the Santa Fe Ring are behind Murphy's thievery."

"We've got to start somewhere, Wes, if we want to protect our place," Cousins answered. "What's it been, two years since you arrived in Lincoln County and a year since I joined you? Look at what you've built."

Wes paused and looked around the property, which straddled the Rio Ruidoso before it merged with the Rio Bonito. "We did it together, Jace."

"You've got fine breeding horses, two hundred head of cattle, a new home, a large barn, and crops in the ground with corn head-high. I've even got the old adobe for my bunkhouse. You got a wife and her boy you call your own. And you built that against all odds. Now we must band together with the decent among our neighbors, Mexican and Anglo, to protect what's ours."

"I'll fend for what's mine, Jace, but I don't see dipping my toes in the political scum as the answer to our problems. Politics has caused most of them to begin with."

"L.G. Murphy's behind the county's ills. The county convention allows decent Democrats to stand against him and make things right in Lincoln County. Since Bob Casey's willing to run against Murphy for party chairman, I say we support him."

Wes sighed and shook his head. "I'll ride every last mile with Bob Casey as good as he's treated me, but I can't say I'll like swimming in the muddy political pond to do it."

Cousins laughed. "That's the spirit, Wes. You keep talking that way, and they may forward your name to President Grant to succeed Sam Axtell as territorial governor."

"Sam Grant would never appoint this Confederate to any position. Even if he did, I'd decline because I want to build up the Mirror B as it's cost me too much already." Wes lowered his gaze and twisted away from Cousins, staring at the whitewashed cross beneath a towering cottonwood tree near the Ruidoso, where he had buried Luther, his last surviving brother. Luther had claimed this land for them both, but had taken to the bottle and then to the Horrell brothers, a mean Texas brood that had terrorized the Mexicans in the valley until Wes and Cousins had organized the Hispanics and other decent men of Lincoln County to drive them back to Texas.

"You did what you could for Luther," Jace said. "He brought it on himself getting mixed up with the Horrells and involving himself in some of their killings. They vowed to kill you and wound up killing him."

Wes brooded, angered at himself for failing to save his older brother. Even more, it tormented Wes that as Luther lay dying, he had denied him the handshake his sibling had so desperately desired as a sign of forgiveness for the wrongs Luther had committed while running with the Horrells. Wes stared at the wooden cross, knowing he had squandered his one chance to make things right with his oldest brother. Wes was the last of six Bracken brothers, two dying on the altar of the Confederacy, another bushwhacked in northwest Arkansas in the partisan aftermath of the war, and the remaining one hanged for stealing horses. The Bracken boys had little to show for their time on earth, and Wes intended to right the family name. The simplest way to avoid further damage to the Bracken legacy was to stay out of politics, even though he knew he must support Bob Casey, no matter how uncomfortable it made him.

Cousins gave Wes his moment of contemplation, lifting the black hat from his head and running his fingers through his wavy mop of brown hair. A tall, lean man, he sat easy in the saddle with a carefree demeanor, though his brown eyes broached no nonsense and his lips had a peculiar curl at the corners as if he was always smiling. His cleft chin matched the gap between his two front teeth when he smiled. "You want me to get Sarafina and the boy?"

Wes broke from his thoughts and stared up at his partner, his gray eyes steely from two years of fighting Murphy and his desperadoes just to build his ranch along the Ruidoso and provide for his family. "I'm waiting on Carlos to ride over to guard the horses while we're gone. I told him to be here at high sun."

Cousins nodded, plopped his hat back in place, and looked at the sky as they waited on Carlos, Sarafina's hotheaded kid brother, who had lived with his sister and her first husband, Bonifacio Zamora, in an adobe halfway between the Mirror B and San

Patricio upstream on the Ruidoso. Carlos begrudged Wes Bracken's mixed marriage to his sister, but relations seemed more peaceable when Carlos stayed on the Zamora place and farmed that land rather than living with Sarafina and Wes. "How's Carlos managing these days, Wes?"

Bracken snickered. "He runs hot and cold. Deep down he still resents me for marrying his sister, though he tolerates me for running the Horrells out of the county and making it easier on the Mexicans."

"You're the most respected Anglo among the county's Mexicans," Cousins offered.

"Not by Carlos. A lot of vinegar runs through his veins, but that's common in an eighteen-year-old, that and spending too much time in San Patricio, chasing the *señoritas.*"

"What do you expect in a young buck like Carlos?" Cousins asked, standing up in his stirrups and looking westward. "Here comes Carlos on his donkey."

Wes grinned. "I gave him Luther's chestnut and saddle, but I suspect he sold them for cash to spend on whiskey and *señoritas.* He resents that I don't give him another horse. One day I fear he'll sell my gift of Luther's Winchester and revolver. You can't trust the boy."

12

"I'll ride to the creek and water my horse so you and your brother-in-law can catch up on things." Jace laughed as he steered his dun toward the Ruidoso.

Wes watched Cousins ride away, then glanced upstream, spotting a rider angling for him. After checking the wagon bed to confirm he'd loaded everything, Bracken stepped from the team of mules and headed for the door of his new adobe home. The dwelling exceeded what he thought necessary, but Sarafina had wanted a larger house than she had ever lived in, asking for a parlor, a kitchen, a bedroom for her and her husband, and a separate room for her son, Luis. Wes insisted on a small office, but otherwise left it up to his wife. Grateful Hispanics from San Patricio and throughout the Ruidoso and Hondo Valleys had built the large adobe for the Brackens to thank Wes for driving the bigoted Horrells out of Lincoln County forever.

"Sarafina," Wes called as he walked inside, "are you ready?"

"*Sí,*" she answered, "and Luis, too." Sarafina emerged from the kitchen into the parlor, her full lips and her black eyes smiling from a perfectly proportioned face framed by raven hair that fell to her shoulders. Wearing a black skirt and a simple white blouse, just like she had worn the first time he ever saw her, Sarafina advanced slowly.

"Where's Luis?" Wes asked.

Sarafina stopped and the two-year-old lad emerged from behind Sarafina, grasping a handful of her skirt with one hand and a piece of a tortilla with the other. He grinned when he saw Wes, then released his mother's skirt and ambled toward his stepfather with the awkward gait of a newborn colt. Wes squatted and stretched out his arms as Luis ran into his grasp, giggling as Wes lifted him from the floor and raised him over his head. "That's my boy," Wes said, and Luis answered with a babble that was neither English nor Spanish and that only he could understand. "You ready for the trip to Lincoln, Luis?"

"He is," Sarafina said, "and it tickles me that Luis has taken to you."

Wes looked at his wife and motioned toward the door. "I promised I would care for you and your son, Sarafina."

"I know, but you didn't promise you would *love* Luis." Sarafina marched outside, spotting her approaching brother.

"He is part of you, Sarafina, and what you love, I do as well," he answered, following his wife into the sunshine.

"Does that include Carlos?" Sarafina asked as her brother stopped on the opposite side of the wagon and slid off his donkey.

Wes pursed his lips and shrugged. "I try, but he makes it difficult."

"He's headstrong," she replied. "Be patient with him."

"And he should tolerate me."

"Agreed, but he is not as wise as you." Sarafina turned to greet her brother. "Welcome, Carlos."

He answered with a thin-lipped scowl.

"What angers you this time?" she asked.

Her brother shrugged. "I must ride a donkey when fine horses are available from your husband." Carlos glared at Wes, his frigid gaze frightening Luis, who began to cry.

"Good to see you, too, Carlos," Wes replied, handing Luis to Sarafina.

Sarafina held Luis against her shoulder and patted his back, speaking softly to him as she tried to ease his fears. He wailed, whimpered, and finally cooed as Carlos led his donkey around the wagon and out of the boy's view.

"Carlos, you're welcome to stay in the house or in the old adobe where Jace bunks. You're to keep anyone from getting near

15

our horses. You brought your Winchester, didn't you?"

Carlos pointed to his saddleless donkey where the carbine was strapped to the animal's side by a loop of rope.

Wes led his brother-in-law around the side of the adobe and pointed to the corral where a dozen horses danced about, including the sorrel stallion Wes called Charlie, and the bay mare that had foaled a filly, the first horse birthed on the Mirror B. The bay mare had since foaled a colt that had the look of a strong runner. Through some shrewd horse-trading, Jace Cousins had expanded the herd with quality stock, making the Mirror B animals the best group in Lincoln County. Wes felt pride all the way to the bone every time he examined his horses.

"Your job, Carlos, is to guard the horses against thieves. I don't want you riding them or taking any of them to San Patricio. You'll get a dollar for your trouble when I return as long as you follow these instructions."

"*Sí,*" Carlos replied.

"Today's Saturday, but don't slip off to San Patricio. I'm depending on you to watch the horses. The convention starts tomorrow morning at nine o'clock. We should be home before nightfall after that. Any questions?"

Carlos nodded. "When do you leave?"

"Not soon enough for you, I suppose."

Carlos grinned. *"Sí!"*

Wes laughed as he turned around and headed back to the front of the house where Sarafina had calmed Luis, who wore a tiny hat that made him look like a bunny beneath a toadstool. Sarafina wore a bonnet and a smile, always excited to go to Lincoln. Wes took Luis and placed him in the wagon bed on a quilt he had laid out for the little one to take a nap. Then he helped his wife climb aboard before crawling into the spring seat beside her.

Jace Cousins steered his dun toward the wagon and doffed his hat at Carlos. *"Buenos dias,"* Cousins said, planting his headgear back atop his head. Turning to Bracken, he said, "I'm ready when you are."

As Wes untied the reins for the mule team, Cousins pulled his Henry rifle from the saddle scabbard and rested the barrel in the crook of his left arm.

"Do you really need the Henry, Jace?" Sarafina asked.

Cousins squinted and nodded. "As long as Jesse Evans is running free in Lincoln County, I never ride from our place unless

I'm prepared for anything Jesse might throw at me."

"There's a woman and child in the wagon, don't forget," Wes noted.

"I ain't that bad of a shot, Wes." Cousins touched his spur to the dun's flank and the gelding danced toward the confluence of the Rio Ruidoso and the Rio Bonito. Wes followed in the wagon as Sarafina nestled next to him, while Luis alternately played on the quilt or stood up and held onto the sideboard as he watched the country roll by.

Where the two streams joined to form the Rio Hondo, Wes turned his wagon to the northwest on the road to Lincoln, a dozen miles away. They followed the meandering trail along the Rio Bonito, which flowed between two mountain ranges that caressed the Bonito Valley with rough-hewn limestone arms. Outcroppings of rock pockmarked the peaks, and dark green splotches of piñon and gnarled juniper, all more bushes than trees, pimpled the slopes. Real trees grew along the Rio Bonito, the giant cottonwoods with their grayish-brown bark towering up to a hundred feet above the stream and the leaves still green in the midsummer heat of the last day of July. Among the cottonwoods stood willows, their leaves trembling in the dry afternoon breeze.

As they advanced toward Lincoln, Jace guided his dun alongside the wagon and visited with Wes and Sarafina, who stared at Cousins as she built up her courage and finally blurted out a question. "I have heard many speak of the evil man Jesse Evans, but why do you hate him?"

"You don't have to answer that, Jace."

"I figured you'd've told her by now, Wes."

Wes shook his head. "I've never told anyone, and you don't have to now."

"No, it's fine," Cousins said, turning to Sarafina. "Jesse and I grew up together and I thought we were friends, but he set me up to sell a dozen horses he had stolen. The law caught me and sent me to twenty-four months in a Texas prison because of it."

Sarafina's hand flew to her mouth. "I'm sorry for you and sorry I asked."

"Jesse Evans owes me two years of my life, and I intend to collect what I'm owed. I came near getting him last year in fighting the Horrells. I got two in his band, but missed him. That'll change one day."

They finished the journey in silence. As they approached the town from the east, the valley widened and the Rio Bonito drifted to the north side while the town strung out along the south side of the stream. A smattering of nondescript adobes and pole *jacales* stood haphazardly along the dusty street for at least three quarters of a mile. On the opposite end of town stood the imposing two-story building that served as the mercantile, saloon, and headquarters for Lawrence G. Murphy and his renegades. On the north side of the street just down the road from "the House," as Murphy's store was called, stood the Wortley Hotel, where Wes drew up the wagon and helped Sarafina and Luis out. While Wes checked in with proprietor Sam Wortley, Jace unloaded their belongings and left them by the door as all the rooms opened onto the porch either in front or on the sides of the building. Then Jace tied his dun to the rig and drove it behind the hotel where he would spend the night on his bedroll in the wagon bed to keep an eye on Bracken's team and his dun.

Wes escorted Sarafina and Luis to their room, then carried in their belongings.

"I hope I didn't embarrass Jace," Sarafina said. "I'll not spread gossip."

"He wouldn't have told you if he thought otherwise."

Sarafina fed Luis and then shared the cold tortillas and frijoles with her husband.

"What's the matter?" she asked. "Are you upset with me?"

"No, Sarafina."

"Then what's wrong?"

"I've got a bad feeling about Lincoln County politics and tomorrow."

CHAPTER 2

Together, Wes Bracken and Jace Cousins marched toward the throng of men gathering under the shade of a massive cottonwood tree standing sentinel beside the peaceful waters of the Rio Bonito, which flowed lazily eastward.

"I still don't like it," Wes said, stroking his bushy mustache he seldom trimmed to hide his emotions and conceal his wickedly chipped front tooth, compliments of a Yankee rifle butt to the face at Murfreesboro.

"That's why I brought my friend Henry," Jace replied, patting the barrel of his rifle.

The gathering reminded Wes of the religious services conducted by itinerant preachers back in northwest Arkansas before the war, less the women and children here, as this was serious business. Those calling themselves Democrats mingled in two groups, Murphy's men toward the stream and their opposition among the makeshift benches of weathered planks resting on empty kegs. Just as at the Ozark church gatherings, these attendees segregated themselves into sinners and believers. The sinners lingered confidently around the Irishman Lawrence G. Murphy, knowing their political clout would crush all opposition just as their boss's economic sway controlled the lives of most folks in the county. Opposite them stood the faithful, men who trusted that right would ultimately win out in a democracy. Robert Casey walked among this group of Anglos and Hispanics, their conversations whispered in both English and Spanish. Casey, a tall man with a full brown beard that showed streaks of gray, spotted Bracken and weaved his way through the crowd toward him. His whiskers cracked with a smile as he walked up, grabbed Wes's hand, and pumped it vigorously.

"I'm pleased to see you, Wes," Casey offered. "Knowing what you think about politics, I was uncertain if you'd attend."

"You've been too fine a neighbor for me not to offer my support, Bob."

Casey's grin stalled as he turned to Cousins and glimpsed the rifle cradled in the crook of his left arm.

23

"I brought Mr. Henry in case we needed his vote." Cousins patted the breech block.

"Such a faith in our democracy," Casey countered, then swatted Cousins's back. "Glad you came, Jace. We need all the support we can get to beat Murphy."

The banging of a gavel at the table in front of the benches ended the murmuring. "Gentlemen, gentlemen," cried a man in a black broad coat, starched shirt, and bow tie. "Everyone must sign our attendance sheet before we begin."

Wes studied the fellow he suspected was less than thirty years old, taking in his curly brown hair, his wide forehead that angled down to a narrow chin, and his beady eyes over thin lips and mouth. "Who is that?" Wes asked Casey.

"James J. Dolan. He's Murphy's new partner. Like Murphy he's a hotheaded Irishman that drinks too much and prays too little." Casey pointed to another man in a suit, a shorter fellow with a bush of back-swept dark hair over a high forehead and a drooping mustache that resembled a sickly, black caterpillar clinging to the top and sides of his mouth. "That's Alexander A. McSween, a Scotchman and a lawyer working for Murphy."

"Once I sign everyone in," announced

Dolan, "we'll call to order this convention of Lincoln County Democrats and attend our business."

Casey motioned for Bracken and Cousins to step in front of him as they marched to the table to add their names to the list. As they fell in line, Wes asked Casey about his wife.

"Ellen stayed home with the children," Casey answered. "She's opposed me getting into politics from the beginning, but I've told her if decent men such as us didn't take a stand, the corruption would continue. I even got here in time yesterday afternoon to visit the Murphy store and purchase five dollars' worth of goods on credit, just to show there was nothing personal. All the citizens of Lincoln County want is a fair shake and an honest exchange on what we buy and sell. How about Sarafina? How is she?"

"She's staying at the Wortley, but she wanted to take Luis to church," Wes said as he stepped up to the table, picked up the pencil, and signed his name under Dolan's suspicious eyes. "It's a shame we have to use the courthouse for worship and lack a priest to offer Mass."

Casey nodded his agreement. "Odd thing, though. I've heard tell that Murphy himself once studied for the priesthood back in the old country."

Wes shook his head. "Those teachings didn't take," he said, drawing a scowl and an admonition from Dolan.

"Move along, fellow," Dolan groused, "and don't be insulting the county chairman."

Handing the pencil to Cousins, Wes responded to Dolan, "We'll see if he remains in charge."

Jace took the writing implement and placed his Henry on the table, then wrote his name and scanned the list.

"Take your rifle and get out of the way, fellow," Dolan said. "We don't want any trouble."

Tossing the pencil down, Jace picked up his weapon. "No trouble here unless Jesse Evans shows up."

"Haven't seen him," Dolan answered. "Now move along."

After signing in, Casey retreated with Wes and Cousins to rejoin his allies, half of them white and the rest Hispanics, including Juan Patrón, a leader among his people and past clerk for Lincoln County, the largest in the nation. Once the last man left his signature or mark on the attendance roster, Dolan instructed delegates to find seats so business could begin.

"This shouldn't take long," Dolan announced as the men squeezed into their places on the benches, which accommodated half of the crowd. Other fellows stood on the perimeter or sat on the grass in front of the benches. Wes and Cousins remained standing at the edge of the gathering, their backs to the stream so they could watch for troublemakers that might join the crowd. Only after the delegates had quieted did Dolan speak.

"Mr. L.G. Murphy, our county chairman for the Democrat Party, delegated me to start this meeting and handle the first order of business, the election of our next county chairman." Dolan picked up the gavel and announced, "The floor is now open for nominations."

As Dolan spoke, Wes studied Murphy, a daunting man in demeanor if not stature, dressed in a black suit, clean linen shirt, and black cravat. His faded auburn hair was a receding flame on his pale forehead, and his closely trimmed red beard and mustache circling his dictatorial mouth sat his pallid cheeks afire. His pink nose suggested he had consumed more whiskey than proper, even for an Irishman.

"Murphy don't look that healthy," Cousins

27

observed.

"He's well enough to make our lives miserable," Wes responded.

"Do I hear a nomination for party chairman?" Dolan said.

Somebody on the crowd's perimeter nominated L.G. Murphy to continue in the position, but before anyone could second the recommendation, Juan Patrón shouted, "I nominate Robert Casey for chairman."

Wes and several other delegates seconded the nomination as Dolan looked as perplexed as a stage actor who had forgotten his lines. Dolan glanced from Patrón to the lawyer McSween to Murphy, who stalked the perimeter of the proceedings, his eyes burning with disgust, a frown fracturing the neatly trimmed goatee.

"Alex," said Dolan, "how do we handle this?"

The attorney McSween stood up and looked toward Murphy as he spoke to the crowd. "A nomination of Lawrence Murphy was made without opportunity for a second."

Murphy strode to the front table and slammed his fist against the wood. "I'm 'ere to second the nomination meself."

Looking from Murphy to McSween, who shrugged, Dolan said, "So be it!"

Instantly, Juan Patrón shouted out again, "I nominate Robert Casey for chairman of the Lincoln County Democrat Party."

"Second," Wes and several other men called in unison.

Dolan sighed, glancing from the crowd back to Murphy, whose face was flushed with anger, his nose even redder.

"Speeches," called Patrón. "Let them state their platforms so we can vote and move on with other business."

Dolan shrugged, uncertain what to do. McSween paled, torn between following the proper protocol or agreeing to Murphy's known but unstated demand.

"Speeches, speeches," chanted the crowd.

Disgusted, Dolan stared at the attendees. "Are there any more nominations?"

Murphy slammed his fist on the table once again. "There's already been one too many. Nominations are now closed."

"Speeches, speeches, speeches," the men continued.

Dolan looked to Murphy. "Comments?"

Murphy strode over to Dolan and yanked the gavel from his hand, then banged it against the table. "Ye best votes for Lawrence G. Murphy if ye knows what's best for ye and Lincoln County." Murphy glared at the delegates, his pale skin shading red with rage and resentment. He threw the gavel on the table and stepped back toward the Rio Bonito, folding his arms across his chest and glaring at Casey, daring him to offer remarks on his candidacy.

Cousins nudged Wes with his elbow. "Most honest political speech I ever heard."

Wes nodded as he watched his candidate move before the audience. Though challenging Murphy's dominance over Lincoln County's economy and politics was the right thing to do, Wes worried that it dirtied the reformer as much as the perpetrator. As Casey neared the front, he drew jeers and catcalls from backers of the House, who were as shocked as their boss by the uprising.

Casey nodded at his detractors, removed his hat, and smiled at his allies. "Gentlemen, I stand before you today not to threaten you, but to promise you a new day in Lincoln County. Rumors abound of the theft of public funds from the county by my opponent and his lackeys."

Murphy scowled as he unfolded his arms, wadded up his right hand into a fist, and pounded his left palm with it. His men hissed at Casey, who plowed ahead.

"Whether or not those stories are true, I can't say," Casey continued, "but I promise you I will back candidates on the Democrat ticket that will find out. If corruption is found, I'll support a slate of office seekers who will hold accountable those responsible for the misdeeds."

As Casey outlined his promises and his hopes for Lincoln County, Wes watched Murphy motion toward the back of the crowd. Glancing that direction, Wes saw Sheriff Ham Mills emerge from the throng and stride over to Murphy, who leaned over and whispered in his ear. Wes had always suspected Mills of doing Murphy's bidding under the guise of the law, and now their arrogant interaction in front of so many witnesses supported that suspicion.

Casey concluded his remarks with a plea for all honest men to give him a chance to put together a slate of candidates that would clean up Lincoln County. "We can redeem our county's lawless reputation if we elect men who will serve both the law and the people rather than enriching themselves on the backs of the rest of us."

Slipping his hat back atop his head, Casey garnered hearty applause as he retreated to his supporters. As Casey joined the crowd, Wes watched the sheriff slip away from Murphy's side and toward the clump of Murphy backers, wandering among them for a few moments, then grabbing a man's arm and leading him from the throng. Dressed in a worn green bib shirt and tattered denim britches, the man followed the sheriff toward Murphy's store. When Wes glanced Murphy's way, he saw the kingpin of Lincoln County corruption rocking back and forth on his heels, a slight smile creasing his face.

After Casey's speech, Dolan huddled with the attorney McSween, then returned to the table and picked up the gavel. "We'll take a voice vote," Dolan called. "All those in favor of Mr. Lawrence G. Murphy, so say."

Murphy's men yelled "aye," their enthusiasm outweighing their numbers.

"Now those backing Bob Casey so state your support."

Casey's backers, including Juan Patrón and all the Mexicans, shouted their approval for the nominee, easily outmatching Murphy's advocates.

Dolan nodded. "It's obvious. I declare L.G. Murphy the winner and the continuing chairman of the Democrat Party in Lincoln County."

Murphy's men cheered, and Casey's supporters booed. Wes shook his head, astonished at the blatant corruption. Jace, though, raised his Henry over his head and fired into the air. Some hotheads reached for their guns, while others backtracked from the crowd.

"My friend Henry wants an actual tally, not a voice count," Jace said, lowering the rifle.

"The decision's been declared," Dolan sputtered.

Jace lifted his rifle again. "We'll settle this by ballots or bullets. I'm fine either way."

Dolan looked at McSween, who drew Murphy's scowl as he consulted with the boss's store partner. While Dolan argued with the lawyer, he periodically glanced at Murphy, whose growing impatience became obvious as he kept tapping his boot against the ground. Finally, Dolan announced they would do a count.

"Supporters of Mr. Murphy stand on the west side of the table," Dolan instructed. "The rest of you stand on the east side."

The delegates parted, moving to their respective spots, confirming with the eye what the ear on the first vote would have settled with an honest broker. Dolan and McSween joined the Murphy adherents, but even then, the numbers still tilted to Casey. As a formality, Dolan did a count before he announced the results. Wes tallied the votes as well.

"Thirty-nine votes for Mr. Murphy and fifty-six for Casey," Dolan cried.

Jace nudged Wes. "Does that tally with your count?"

"He's down one from my count on Casey's side," Bracken responded.

"Perhaps he forgot to count Mr. Henry," Wes said as he patted the rifle barrel.

Murphy pushed his way through his backers and approached the table, grabbing it by the corner and throwing it over, scattering the sign-in sheets and the assorted other papers on top. "Ye might as well try to stop the waters of the Rio Bonito with a fork as oppose me," he spat. "And, ye 'ave a better chance of stopping the wind with a net than ye do of stopping me. Ye can 'ave yer say today, but I'll 'ave mine tomorrow and the day after that and the day after that." Murphy spun around and strode through his supporters, who moved aside, opening a path for him back to his store.

"Democracy at its finest," Jace said to Wes, drawing snickers from a few men standing nearby but not from Bracken.

Just as he had for the past two days, Wes felt an uneasiness in his gut, a suspicion that this would not end well. He watched Murphy's men slip in behind their boss and follow him to the street and most of them into his store.

Casey's followers began to pick up the scattered papers and right the table. Casey nodded. "Thank you everyone for your faith in me. Let's adjourn the meeting and take time for heads to cool off, then we can meet after lunch to decide on some honest candidates for the November ballot." The new county chairman walked among his supporters, shaking hands and expressing his gratitude for their votes. He thanked Juan Patrón profusely for convincing so many Hispanics to attend and support him.

Finishing with Patrón, Casey ambled over and slapped Jace Cousins on the back. "I don't know if I'd gotten elected without your rifle, Jace."

"Mr. Henry believes in fair play and democracy, even if it puts him at odds with Murphy and his gang," Jace answered.

Casey turned to Wes. "Juan Patrón tells me there's not an American in the county respected more by the Mexicans than you. Would you consider running for sheriff? It'd be good for Lincoln County and restore decent men's faith in our government."

Bracken wagged his head from side to side. "I've got a family to support and a ranch to build. Can't do that if I take on other people's problems in a county this big."

"I'm sorry you view it that way, Wes, but not surprised." Casey turned to Cousins. "What about you, Jace?"

Cousins laughed. "I've got a past that disqualifies me and a grudge that limits me."

"Sorry to hear that, but to show you there's no hard feelings, I'll buy you both lunch at the Wortley."

"Thanks, Bob, but I'll pass," Wes said. "I must get home to my horses." He turned to his partner. "Why don't you stay, Jace, and get a free meal?"

Cousins grinned. "Suits me! And, I'll stay here for the convention's afternoon session."

"You've got more politics in your blood than I do," Wes replied.

"Mr. Henry and I'll see you back at the place before dark."

The partners turned their separate ways, Jace to the Wortley for a meal and Wes to the squat adobe building that served as the courthouse and, on Sundays, as a chapel where the Catholics gathered for worship, even though they lacked a priest. Wes glanced over his shoulder and saw Cousins and Casey ambling toward the hotel. Though a hot meal would've rested well on his stomach, Wes avoided eating noon meals at the Wortley because many of Murphy's gang congregated there. Where his henchmen met, trouble followed.

As he neared the courthouse, Wes listened to the faithful singing "Holy God, We Praise Thy Name," some crooning in English, others in Spanish. Wes waited outside the door for the Mass to finish, watching the activities at the west end of town where the two-story Murphy store, said to be the biggest structure in New Mexico Territory, loomed over Lincoln, standing as an undeniable symbol of Murphy's clout.

When the singing stopped inside the chapel, Wes heard a parishioner offer a prayer, seeking strength and protection from the Almighty and pleading for peace and prosperity for Lincoln County. That might be possible, Wes thought, as long as politics didn't warp folks' outlook on their neighbors. The wooden door opened and men, women, and children began to emerge, smiling and wishing one another a good week on this first Sunday of August 1876. With fall and harvest season approaching, the worshippers had much to be thankful for, provided the violence that always seeped from the House let up in the coming days. With the election approaching in November and Casey taking a stand against Murphy, Wes doubted peace was on the horizon, despite the hopeful prayer.

Sarafina marched out, carrying Luis. She smiled at her husband, and Wes answered with a grin, especially after Luis twisted around and flung his arms at his stepfather, calling "Pie, Pie," which Wes took as the closest he could come to pronouncing padre. Wes kissed Sarafina on the cheek and took her son, holding him against his shoulder, but Luis fought that position, pushing himself away and wanting to sit on the crook of Bracken's strong arm and tug at his heavy mustache. Both boy and man laughed at the mischief as Wes placed his arm over Sarafina's shoulder and escorted her to the Wortley to pack and start the dozen-mile ride back home.

"I pray for a priest to make worship more meaningful," Sarafina said.

Wes agreed, then yanked Luis's hand from his mustache, drawing a cackle from the boy who wiggled his fingers free and attacked the whiskers with greater vigor. "What Lincoln County lacks in piety it makes up with an abundance of wickedness," he observed.

"*Al mal tiempo, buena cara,*" his wife chided.

"I'm trying to pick up your language, but

you stumped me, Sarafina. What's it mean?"

"Put a good face on the hard times."

"The only face that counts in Lincoln County belongs to L.G. Murphy. I've heard gossip that he studied for the priesthood in Ireland before he came here. If that's true, the lessons didn't take for he's behind too much mischief in these parts."

"No hay mal que por bien no venga," Sarafina replied.

"There's no bad, is that right?"

His wife nodded. "There's no bad from which something good doesn't come. See, you are learning my language."

"Not as well as you've picked up English."

When they reached the hotel, men lined up outside the door of the eating parlor, waiting for tables to open up inside.

"It may take you a while to pay," Sarafina noted.

"I settled up before the meeting. All you need to do is pack while I hitch up the team, and we'll be on our way." Wes offered Luis to his mother, but the little lad fought the transfer, grabbing hold of Wes's mustache and squawking before Wes jerked his head away from the boy's grasp. "His grip is strong. One day he's gonna yank my whiskers off," Wes said as he handed the boy to his wife, then stared at Sarafina.

"What is it?"

"You look beautiful in your Sunday dress."

Sarafina smiled. "*Gracias!* Now let me change into my traveling clothes."

They stepped upon the hotel porch and squeezed their way between the waiting diners to reach their room. After Wes unlocked the door and saw his wife safely inside with her son, he retreated toward the Rio Bonito to hitch up the mule team and begin the ride home. At the wagon, he unhobbled his two mules and harnessed them together, then hooked the leather straps to the single trees.

He climbed aboard, took the reins, and guided the team back to the hotel where he dismounted and headed for his room to gather his wife's belongings. As he stepped back out the door toting Sarafina's kit bag and Luis's bundle, Jace and Bob Casey worked their way out of the dining room. Spotting Wes, they walked over and offered to help him finish loading the wagon.

"There's not that much to do," Wes said.

"Wish you'd stay for the afternoon session and consider running for office," Casey said.

"I've had enough politics for one day," Wes answered.

Casey nodded. "I figured as much."

"I fear you've grabbed a wildcat by the tail, Bob, going up against Murphy."

Shaking his head, Casey argued otherwise. "With the right folks, we'll get Lincoln County straightened out and make it a decent place for everyone. To show there's no hard feelings, I'm visiting the House to repay my five-dollar debt and settle my account with Murphy."

"I'll go with you," Cousins offered.

"No need for that, Jace," Casey announced pointing to the weapon. "Your rifle might convey the wrong message about my intent."

"Suit yourself, Bob, but if you're not back in ten minutes my friend and I will visit the Murphy place."

"I'll be with him," Wes added.

Casey laughed "You boys are imagining things. It's just politics."

Wes shook his head. "It's more than politics. It's survival and prosperity."

Still chuckling, Casey started across the street for the store.

"He's got courage," Jace observed.

"Beyond that, he's too trusting." Wes watched him a moment, then turned to enter the room for a load to take to the wagon. "I'll see you this evening back at the ranch."

BLAM!

Wes heard the gunshot and spun around. He watched Casey stumble and collapse on the ground.

BLAM!

Wes saw Casey twitch on the ground, then searched the opposite side of the street as Jace lifted his rifle to his shoulder and fired, his bullet splatting against a waist-high adobe wall. Behind the low adobe barrier squatted a man with a smoking Winchester in his hands. Wes had seen this attacker earlier. The assassin wore a green bib shirt and tattered denim britches.

CHAPTER 3

Wes Bracken jerked his revolver from his holster and fired a wild shot toward the assailant, his aim thrown off by the scream behind him. He glanced around and spotted Sarafina standing in the door, holding her son. Wes darted to her.

"Get inside," he shouted. "Shut the door and hide on the floor."

His wide-eyed wife slammed the entry closed as Wes spun about, glimpsing Jace Cousins as he darted for the attacker, who zigzagged from the wall to a tree and then behind the Murphy store. Though Wes didn't know the sniper's name, he recognized him by his worn green bib shirt and his tattered trousers as the man Sheriff Ham Mills had escorted from the county convention.

Jace darted after the assailant, pausing at the corner of the store to poke his head around the back of the building before resuming the chase. Wes re-holstered his pistol and ran over to the injured county chairman, who lay sprawled on the dusty street, a wound in his left thigh and a bloody second gash to the face, the bullet entering at the left jawline and exiting above the right cheek. Dropping to his knees, Wes turned Casey's head to the side so blood could drain from his mouth. The wounded man tried to speak, but his jaw and tongue no longer worked together.

"We'll get you cared for, even if we have to take you to the doctor at Fort Stanton," Wes promised as others gathered around him.

"Eee . . . lll —" Casey gasped.

"Ellen! You want me to fetch your wife?"

Casey nodded and grimaced through bloody teeth.

Cousins raced up, out of breath. "He slipped . . . inside . . . Murphy's place," he panted. "I don't . . . know his . . . name."

"It was Will Wilson," shouted Juan Patrón. "He's a saddle tramp."

Wes stood up and stared at the House. "He's in there with the man that put him up to it."

"We got to . . . do something," Jace cried as he regained his breath.

"Nothing we can do about Wilson for the

moment if he's hiding behind Murphy and the sheriff, but enough folks saw him to identify him so we can file charges later. For now let's get Casey to a bed and send someone to Fort Stanton for the doctor." Wes stood and turned toward the Wortley.

"Bring him to my place," Patrón instructed as another man volunteered to make the ten-mile trip to the fort for medical help.

"I'll ride to Casey's Mill and let Ellen know so she can get here for him," Wes cried.

"I can get there faster on my horse," Jace offered.

"Stay here and see that Wilson gets arrested," Wes called as he maneuvered through the crowd and bolted to the hotel.

Sarafina screamed as he flung open the door, then crossed herself when she recognized her husband. He helped her and Luis from the floor. "We've got to ride to the Casey place and tell Ellen Bob's been shot. He needs her in Lincoln."

Wes sprinted to the wagon, gently lowering Luis into the back and turning around to help Sarafina into the spring seat. No sooner had she settled in than Wes plopped down beside her, grabbed the reins, and started the mule team at a trot for Casey's Mill.

The mules were strong and steady but not fleet of foot, more fixed for pulling a plow than a wagon. Bracken pushed the team as hard as he dared, and they made the trip faster than ever before in a wagon, but even so it seemed to take forever. When the mules reached the junction of the Rio Bonito with the Rio Ruidoso, Wes realized the animals were exhausted. He turned west toward his own home instead of Casey's Mill.

"Aren't you going to the mill?" Sarafina asked.

"The mules are spent. I'll make better time on Charlie than I can in the wagon."

In five minutes he pulled up in front of the Mirror B and his house. He jumped from the rig, helped Sarafina out, and left her to fetch Luis and unload their belongings. "Carlos can unhitch the wagon and tend the mules," he shouted as he sprinted around the house to the horse corral. What he found stunned him. The gate was open. The horses had disappeared. All of them!

"Carlos," he yelled. "Carlos, where are the horses?" He looked about, taking in the barn, the small adobe where Cousins bunked, the new house he had built for his young bride, and the fields by the river where an acre of corn grew. Nothing. "Carlos," he screamed again.

Receiving no reply, he yanked his pistol from his holster, held it above his head, and fired it into the air. "Carlos, Carlos."

Sarafina appeared around the corner of the house with Luis in her arms and fear on her face. "What's wrong?"

"The horses are missing. Carlos doesn't answer. I don't know what's going on."

Sarafina gasped and pointed to the barn. "There he is."

Wes spun around and spotted Carlos coming out of the barn, squinting at the daylight and twisting his head from side to side. Wes ran to Carlos. "What's happened?" he screamed.

Carlos held up his hand. *"Silencio,"* he murmured as he shook his head and rubbed at his eyes, then pinched the bridge of his nose.

As Wes waited for answers, he heard a whinny from the barn and watched the door move as his sorrel stallion nudged it open and came out saddled and dragging the reins on the ground. Wes bolted past the dazed Carlos for Charlie and the barn, hoping to find the other horses inside. He grabbed the stallion's reins and turned him around enough to step past him into the barn. A quick glance determined the barn was empty of everything except Carlos's donkey.

He led Charlie to Carlos, grabbed his young brother-in-law's shoulder, and shook him. "What happened, Carlos? Where are the horses?"

Carlos squished his eyes and mouth, then held up his hand. "Not so loud."

"Where are the horses, Carlos?" he asked in a volume barely louder than a whisper.

"Gone!"

"What do you mean, gone? Stolen?"

Carlos answered with a tentative nod.

"All of them, including the colt?"

The response came as a deep sigh.

"Which way did they go?"

Carlos pointed to the southwest.

"Are you sure?"

"Sí! Sí! Ahora déjame en paz."

"He says to leave him alone," Sarafina translated.

Nothing made sense to Bracken, and he lacked the time to figure it out. Wes had to inform Ellen of her husband's injury before tracking the thieves. He would make time then to work through the facts. The one thing he knew for certain: Carlos had failed in his job.

Wes grabbed the saddle horn, shoved his

boot in the stirrup, and climbed aboard Charlie. He noted that his saddle scabbard was empty, instructing Sarafina on what she needed to do. "Gather my Winchester carbine and a couple boxes of ammunition. Put enough jerky and tortillas in a sack for me to stay on the trail for four days. Get my bedroll and fill two canteens with water. Have them for me within the hour."

"Sí, mi esposo," Sarafina replied.

"One more thing," Wes demanded. "When Carlos sobers up, have him put the wagon in the barn and tend the team." Wes whistled Charlie into a trot and then a gallop as he started up the trail to Casey's Mill, five miles to the east. Astride the sorrel stallion, the distance flew by compared to the mules' progress. As he rode, he wondered how best to deliver the news to Ellen, and then he tried to decipher what had happened at the ranch in his absence.

Carlos had been drinking, that was obvious, but Wes didn't keep liquor around the place as whiskey was the devil's brew that had ruined his brother's life. So, Carlos had gone elsewhere to imbibe, likely San Patricio, and had left the horses unguarded. But why did the thieves leave Charlie as the sorrel stallion was the best animal among the herd? Then the muddle in his mind cleared.

Charlie wasn't stolen with the other horses because the stallion was in San Patricio when the thieves struck. Carlos had ridden him there to impress the *señoritas.* When would Carlos mature into the man he could be? At least now Bracken understood what had happened, though he wondered if Carlos were honest enough to admit it.

Those were issues to be resolved later. At the moment Wes had to deliver to Ellen the terrible news of her husband's shooting. The reality of that impending duty put a knot in his throat when he rounded a bend in the road and saw the mill where Casey ground corn and grain for folks, the adobe that served as a store in the front and the residence in the back, and four smaller buildings for the ranching operation that Robert Casey managed with the help of a few hands and his six children, ranging in age from eight to eighteen.

From afar, the place looked lifeless, but Wes remembered it was still Sunday afternoon when most Lincoln County families rested after a hard week of chores. Nearing the dwelling, Wes offered a shrill whistle, "Anybody home?" In a moment, the front door of the store opened and a fellow in britches and a work shirt slipped out with a slight limp, reminding Wes of Ellen's gait.

This fellow wore a hat tugged over his forehead almost to his eyebrows.

Wes reined up hard in front of the adobe and jumped out of the saddle, holding the reins and walking to the fellow. "I'm here to see Ellen Casey," he cried.

"You're looking at her, Wes Bracken. What's all the commotion about?"

Wes did a double take to make sure his eyes were not deceiving him.

Ellen recognized his confusion and explained. "When Bob's not around, I wear men's clothes so passing ne'er-do-wells will think there's men around and won't get any ideas of taking advantage of me and my girls."

"I'm sorry, Ellen."

"It's okay, Wes."

"No, I don't mean about that, but I'm sorry to have to tell you Bob's been shot."

Ellen gasped, her hand flying to her mouth. "I told him not to get involved in politics. How is he?"

"Holding on when I left," Wes replied, "but he wanted me to fetch you."

"Oh, goodness," she said, turning and screaming toward the house. "Boys, come here." Two Casey brothers appeared at the door.

"Yes, ma'am," said the older.

"Saddle up two horses for me and one of you because we're going to Lincoln."

"You dressed like that?" snickered the shorter of the boys.

"Your father's been shot. Get a move on it."

The pair dashed away.

"Who shot Bob?"

"Folks say his name is Will Wilson."

Ellen shook her head. "Bob hired Willie for a spell to cowboy, but he was lazy and didn't do what he was told. Bob had to let the saddle tramp go. Where'd he shoot Bob?"

"The thigh and the face."

"Oh, God, please let him live until I can get to him," she said. "I love that man."

"I'd ride with you, but the Mirror B was hit by horse thieves last night. I must track them down and retrieve our breeding stock before they escape to Mexico." He walked over and hugged Ellen. "I hope Bob pulls through."

She patted him on the back, broke the hug, and nodded. "Go do what you've got to do, and I'll go do what I can for Bob."

"Sorry I can't do more." Wes winced as he said that. He could — or should — accompany Ellen back to Lincoln, but he had his horses to retrieve.

"You've done plenty by getting word to me. You be watchful, especially if you don't know how many thieves you'll run into. We can't afford to lose any more honest men in Lincoln County." Ellen turned away and ran into the house. Though she had held her emotions while talking to Wes, he heard her sob as she disappeared inside.

Wes jumped in the saddle and started back for the Mirror B, putting Charlie into a lope as he knew not to tire out the horse since he remained uncertain how big a start the thieves had gotten on him. Ellen Casey's warning kept resonating in his mind. How many thieves would he face, if he ever caught up with them? He wished Jace Cousins could accompany him, but his partner had to ensure that Casey's attacker in Lincoln was brought to justice.

As he neared his place, Wes figured the theft occurred around dawn. Glancing at the afternoon sun, he estimated the bandits had a ten- to twelve-hour lead on him. However, their escape would be slowed by the male foal that lacked the endurance to travel as fast as the older horses, assuming the outlaws didn't just shoot the little one and leave him for the buzzards. That colt and the two-year-old filly that was the first foaled on the Mirror B would become the foundation stock for the ranch's future horse herd. Based on those two foals, Charlie was earning a twenty-five-dollar stud fee by the Lincoln County ranchers who knew good horse lines and could afford to improve their horses. If that colt and filly were lost, his plans would suffer a delay of five or more years.

As he neared the Mirror B, Wes understood his dreams of raising the best horses in New Mexico Territory depended upon recovering the herd intact. He slowed Charlie at the approach to the Rio Bonito and let the sorrel drink the cool waters. When the stallion had his fill, Wes shook the reins and his mount walked across the stream, then trotted down the trail toward home. As he got closer to the place, he observed the wagon still hitched in front of the house. Carlos was still fighting his hangover. Wes wondered why he had dealt with one drunk or another ever since he had arrived on the Rio Ruidoso. First, his brother Luther had taken to the bottle and squandered away their sibling partnership and his life. Now, his wife's brother was taking to liquor. Wes prayed that it was just a young man's curiosity rather than a craving for alcohol that led along the trail to addiction. Those were issues Wes planned to address later. For now, he had to recover the horses or his dreams became irrelevant.

Reaching the house, Wes dismounted, tied his horse to the wagon, and stepped inside. "Sarafina," he called, "I'm back." On the bench beside the door, he spotted his Winchester carbine, two boxes of bullets, the food sack, his bedroll, and his saddlebags, which he hadn't even mentioned. "All I'm missing is the canteens."

Sarafina bolted into the room from the kitchen. "Here they are," she said, offering them to her husband.

"That was thoughtful, getting my saddlebags."

Sarafina shook her head. "Carlos did that. He feels so bad for what happened."

"Nothing would've happened if he'd stayed here like I told him."

"Carlos said nothing about going anywhere."

"He rode Charlie to San Patricio. That's why the stallion wasn't stolen with the other horses." Wes picked up the saddlebags, lifted a flap, inserted the two boxes of ammunition, and tied the flap back. As he did, Carlos walked into the room, his gaze downcast. "You went to San Patricio, didn't you, Carlos?"

Carlos nodded without lifting his head.

Luis toddled in behind Carlos and grabbed his uncle's leg, wrapping his arms around his thigh. Carlos dropped his hand and patted Luis on his mop of black hair.

"I don't have time to discuss it now, Carlos. How many thieves were there?"

Carlos shrugged. "I was sleeping it off. Didn't hear."

"You stay here with your sister and nephew. Protect them better than you did the horses." Wes carried his Winchester and saddlebags outside, sliding the carbine in the boot and tying his saddlebags behind his saddle. He stepped toward the adobe to fetch the rest of his gear, but Sarafina emerged holding his food sack and canteens. Carlos followed with the bedroll, Luis toddling behind him.

Wes grabbed the canteens, hooking one over the saddle horn and tying the second and the burlap food sack to the saddlebags. Next, he took the bedroll and secured it behind the saddle. He turned to Sarafina. "Take the wagon to the barn and unhitch the mules if Carlos doesn't do it."

"Once my head clears, I'll do it," Carlos said. *"Déjame en paz!"*

"You watch out for my wife and son even if your head isn't clear."

Carlos lifted his head and glared at Wes's

eyes. "He's not your son."

Sarafina stomped her foot and crossed her arms across her breast. *"Carlos, eso es algo terrible que decir."*

After two years of marriage to Sarafina, Wes had picked up bits of her language, thinking she told her brother his comment was a terrible thing to say. Wes approached Sarafina, took her in his arms, kissing her square on the lips as much to antagonize Carlos as to bid goodbye to his wife. He broke from her. "It'll take me three or four days, maybe a full week. You can depend on Jace. When he returns, send Carlos home."

"Ten cuidado, mi esposo," she answered.

"I'll be careful, and I'll bring back our horses."

Wes turned from his wife, untied Charlie from the wagon, mounted the sorrel, and rode out to the corral where he picked up the tracks and crossed the Ruidoso, following it west before turning south through a trail that meandered through the foothills. While the hoofprints by the Ruidoso showed the animals had been run, by the time the thieves turned into the mountains, the tracks indicated the horses had walked, except for a few occasions when the distance between hoof falls suggested they had trotted for a short distance, not uncommon for

57

horses that spooked easily in unfamiliar territory.

The best Wes could determine from the number of horse tracks was that only one or maybe two men had stolen his herd or at least still accompanied it. Wes liked those odds. Once he had a good grasp of the trail and what he was facing, he put Charlie in a trot and worked to gain on the rustlers before dark. He rode until darkness obscured the trail, then pitched a cold camp, eating the jerky and tortillas Sarafina had packed for him. Come morning he was up before dawn and back on the trail at the first rays of sunshine, pushing Charlie as hard as possible without fatiguing him, generally moving at a trot.

Just after high sun, Wes glimpsed in the distance his quarry, a carefree or confident outlaw who never glanced over his shoulder. Wes made a quick count and determined all of his horses were there, including the new colt and the two-year-old filly. Now that he had the thief in sight, he slowed his pace, waiting for the right terrain to work to his advantage so he might surprise the thief and reclaim his horses.

He trailed them for an hour until they came to a long narrow solitary mountain that split the trail. Wes wanted to get ahead of the thief and approach him from the south so it would not appear that he had been trailing the bandit from the north. As the main trail forked to the east, the rustler headed that direction and once he advanced out of sight, Wes kicked Charlie in the flank and sent him racing around the mountain's western perimeter. He pushed Charlie as hard as he could over a faint trail for two-and-a-half miles until the mountain tapered away, and the western route merged with the eastern trail the bandit had taken with the Mirror B horses. Wes looked to the south and found no sign of the thief, so he prepared to meet the fellow and take back his horses. He pulled his six-gun from his holster and checked the load, down two shells. Wes quickly extracted the two hulls and replaced them with bullets from his cartridge belt. Returning the handgun to his side, he yanked his Winchester from the scabbard, then checked the load. It was full. He rested the barrel of the carbine on his left arm, then turned on the trail and headed for the thief.

Though Wes expected to spot him, he failed to see the rustler for several minutes. At first he feared the rustler had turned off the trail or even gotten ahead of him, though he didn't understand how that was possible as he observed no fresh tracks to show the animals had passed. About a mile from where he turned down the trail, he spotted the bandit's horses grazing on the sparse yellow grass of late summer. At first, he didn't spot the outlaw. Wes tensed, fearing an ambush. He had identified but one man when he spotted the horses, but had he missed another? Even if he had, he didn't spot the solitary bandit until the trail jogged away from the slopes. Then Wes glimpsed his quarry sitting on the ground in the shade of a rock.

The thief sat eating, unworried by the approaching rider or a guilty conscience. As Wes neared, the man — more boy than adult actually — stood up and grinned. He wore a broad-brimmed hat and a wide smile that accentuated his two front teeth. He finished a piece of jerky and moved toward the trail.

"Howdy, friend," the rustler called, not a hint of fear in his voice. "Care for some lunch? Jerky's all I got, but I'll share it with you in exchange for a little company."

Wes studied the fellow, deciding he'd seen him somewhere, but couldn't place him.

"Sit and jaw for a while, friend. My name's Billy Bonney, though some folks call me Kid."

CHAPTER 4

Wes Bracken studied Bonney with a hard gaze, and the thief neither wilted nor trembled at the examination. "Nice looking bunch of horses. You got a bill of sale?"

Bonney grinned and strode toward Wes, smiling with each step. "Nope! They're stolen."

"Why'd you steal them?"

"Didn't say I stole 'em, just that they were stolen," the kid grinned even wider. "I took them from the thieves that stole them. Now I'm looking for the owner."

"That's me. My name's Wes Bracken."

"Then it looks like I'm in luck and my job's complete."

"Tell me, Bonney," Wes continued, disarmed by Bonney's incessant grin and the tall tale he was making up to alibi for his thievery, "how many rustlers did you take them from?"

"Six of them, mean fellows everyone,

including Jesse Evans. He was behind the theft."

"How is it, Bonney, that I've been tracking my horses for parts of two days and saw no sign of other men on horseback? Just my missing horses and your dappled gray is all I observed. How do you explain that, Bonney?"

"They rode light and didn't leave tracks, Mr. Bracken."

Wes snickered. "You understand horse thieves get hanged around here, don't you?"

Bonny chuckled. "I tried to hang them but I only had one rope, and I couldn't find a tree limb big enough to hold the six of them. I give you my word on it."

Shaking his head, Wes begrudgingly admired Billy's ability to spin a tale, even when they both knew it was as false as Satan's witness. "Is your word any good, Bonney?"

"I'd say it's as good as anybody else's in Lincoln County, but we'd both feel better if you slipped your Winchester back in the scabbard so we can visit a little more over a strip of jerky." Bonney shrugged. "Besides, you're not quick enough to use it before I plugged you." Bonney walked to the rock where he had been sitting.

Wes slid the carbine in its saddle sheath

and dismounted, leading Charlie to a patch of yellow grass to graze and hobbling him.

The Kid nodded when he saw the Winchester in its place.

"Something bothers me, Bonney," Wes said.

"Shoot, Mr. Bracken, but call me Billy."

"You were heading the wrong direction if you planned to return them to the owner. How do you explain that?"

"I was taking the long route for the scenery."

"Call me, Wes."

"Okay, Wes." Bonney closed the gap between them and offered his right hand to Bracken.

Wes accepted his courtesy and shook his hand, disbelieving that he was befriending a horse thief, but something about Billy Bonney fascinated him. Maybe it was the Kid's naïveté or the ease, confidence, and humor with which he made up a story. He was one of those rare thieves with the talent to pick your pocket and seem sympathetic when he told you how sorry he was that you were broke. "Well, where do we go from here, Billy?"

"I reckon to your place, Wes. I figure you'll need an additional hand to get them back safely. So, I'll ride with you for a couple dollars and make sure no one steals them again."

"That's mighty big of you, Billy, and I'll pay you a dollar for your effort as long as we take the shortest route back home."

"You're the boss, so whatever you say, Wes."

Bracken studied him. "Why is it I've got the feeling we've met before?"

Bonney grinned. "You refused me a job a spell back."

Wes shook his head. "Don't recall."

"It was on your wedding day. We met on the road between San Patricio and Casey's Mill. I asked for work, but you had other things on your mind that day and sent me away."

"Vaguely I recall it," Wes answered as he untied the string around the food sack and pulled out a pile of tortillas wrapped in a red kerchief. He offered Bonney a tortilla, and the Kid took two.

"I might say you caused me to turn bad." The Kid rolled up his two tortillas and took a bite off the end.

"How's that, Billy?"

"I couldn't find honest work so I started running with Jesse Evans and his gang for a while, but they were too mean for me. I did what I did to eat. They did it for pure meanness. My momma taught me better than that." He chomped down on the rolled tortillas.

"What did your momma say about stealing horses?"

Bonney choked and coughed out his latest bite. Then he grinned. "You're not much on forgetting or forgiving."

"I swear, Billy, you could charm the stripe off a skunk, and he'd never think of spraying you despite the theft."

"A quick wit's as important as a fast gun in these parts." Bonney offered his bucktoothed grin with a wink. "And, I'm quick with both of them."

"Then let's finish our lunch, mount up, and return to the Mirror B."

Bonney nodded his agreement.

Wes swallowed his final bite and unhobbled his sorrel, returning the hobbles to his saddlebags. He couldn't believe he was turning his back on an armed horse thief he'd caught with his animals, but the Kid exuded a mesmerizing charisma well advanced for his few years. When he secured the flap on the saddlebags, he mounted and watched Bonney glide over to his gray and mount with fluid-like grace. The Kid had a smooth way of talking, walking, and riding, as if he didn't have a worry in the world or a pang of conscience for anything he'd ever done, save for consorting with Jesse Evans. Quickly, they rounded up the horses and started moving them north toward the Rio Ruidoso and the Mirror B. As they began their return journey, Wes focused on the colt that was still less than a year old.

Bonney noted Wes's gaze. "Don't worry about the little one. I took it easy on all of them so I wouldn't ruin him. He's got fine lines. He takes after your stallion there. Is he the sire?"

"Yes, sir. I'm planning on breeding the best horse outfit in New Mexico Territory."

"Then you need to keep a better watch on your place so fellows with lesser scruples than me won't steal your horse."

"Now let me ask you another question. How'd you decide I wouldn't hang you when I found you with my horses?"

"You weren't carrying a rope."

Wes laughed. "Then how'd you know I wouldn't shoot you."

"You followed me for a couple hours. Yeah, I saw you back there. You never tried to position yourself to shoot me in the back. I figure you rode around the mountain to approach me head-on, making me think you weren't tailing me, but I knew for miles you were on my trail. I can trust a man that goes to so much trouble rather than bushwhacking a fellow."

Bonney impressed Wes with his humor and observations as they rode through a parched landscape that needed rain. They passed splotches of piñon and gnarled juniper, each more bush than tree, as the trail meandered among cholla and ocotillo with spindly arms that waved in the breeze to the rough-hewn mountains. Everything looked thirsty.

If words had been precipitation, Bonney would've flooded the entire region as he prattled on about his young years and the trouble he'd encountered, some of it brought on by his own actions, but much of it falling upon him due to circumstances. He told of losing his mother and shooting a man who had darkened her memory. Bonney spoke hardest of Jesse Evans, a man whose soul was darker than Satan's heart.

"Did Jesse Evans ever mention a fellow named Jace Cousins?" Wes asked.

"He did, Wes. He did indeed. Many times, in fact. Said Cousins had followed him from Texas to kill him. Even said he'd pay a hundred dollars to any man that would kill Cousins and bring him his scalp. Most of the men who rode with Jesse would've gladly killed Cousins, though all were squeamish about scalping him."

"Jace is my partner," Wes announced.

"Then that explains why Jesse avoided passing your place unless it was necessary. Evans is working for L.G. Murphy now. Did you know that?"

"I'm not surprised. Murphy's behind most of the problems in Lincoln County."

"Him and his partner, Jimmy Dolan, who's just as crooked and a lot meaner," Bonney offered. "Murphy blusters and bluffs but has others do his killing."

Wes nodded, recalling Bob Casey's shooting by Willie Wilson. Though he might never prove it in a court of law, Wes knew Murphy had instructed the sheriff to have Bob shot. His own guilt washed over him as Wes felt he should never have abandoned Ellen to retrieve his horses. He promised himself to make amends to her.

"There's rumors floating about that Murphy's bad sick and dying. As for Dolan," Bonney continued, "he's mean enough to do his own killing. He and Murphy are not the caliber of men I want to draw wages from."

"Why don't you get a job with John Chisum? He's always looking for hands."

"I tried, but he refused to hire me after he heard I'd ridden with Jesse Evans. Small operators like yourself can't afford to take on cowboys."

"You ever thought of leaving the territory, moving someplace else?"

Bonney laughed. "I had a few run-ins with the law in Arizona. I can't go back there. Texans are too mean. Colorado's too cold. Besides, I enjoy the *señoritas* around here, and they like me."

Wes rode with Bonney and listened to his stories until dusk, their pace slowed only by the endurance of the colt as Wes avoided pushing him. Wes remained eager to get back home and find out how Bob Casey was doing, though he feared he already knew the answer.

As Bracken dismounted and hobbled Charlie to make camp for the night, Bonney rode off, saying he would come back in a spell, though Wes figured the Kid planned to disappear in the darkness and never return. Several minutes later while he was gathering what wood he could find for a fire, Wes heard a gunshot. Uncertain what it meant, he dumped his load of kindling and retreated to his stallion to fetch his carbine and wait in case Bonney had encountered trouble or was bringing it back with him. After about ten minutes, Wes heard an approaching horse.

"Hello, Wes," cried Bonney's familiar voice. "I'm coming in with supper."

Wes exhaled a slow breath, wanting to trust Bonney but uncertain whether to believe a man who had stolen his horses and lied about it to boot. Wes watched as a horse and rider took shape in the darkness. As they drew nearer, he made out the Kid holding a rabbit by the legs.

"We'll have meat for supper," Bonney announced, as he dropped the carcass on the ground and dismounted.

"I've gathered enough wood for a fire," Wes replied, retreating to his stallion to return his carbine to the scabbard.

"That's better than eating it raw," Bonney laughed.

Wes unsaddled his mount and placed his gear on the ground, then piled the wood and kindling into a stack.

As Bonney skinned and gutted the rabbit with a knife he pulled from his boot, Wes extracted a tin of matches from his pants pocket and flicked a match to life. He touched the flame to a handful of dry grass he had shoved under the kindling and wood, watching the fire take hold.

"The fire won't last long, no more wood than we found," Wes said as he strode to his gear, grabbed the food sack, and retrieved his hunting knife from his saddlebags.

Bonney sliced the carcass down the spine and offered Wes his half. "Get started."

Wes impaled his ration on his knife, squatted by the fire and thrust the meat into the flames. Shortly, the Kid joined him, crouching by the fire to roast the meat. They cooked the flesh as long as possible without burning their fingers. When their meat was crispy on the outside, they pulled their knives away, blew on the sizzling meal to cool it, then took a bite. "Good supper," Wes said. He opened the burlap bag of food Sarafina had prepared for him and pulled out the cloth full of tortillas. He offered them to Bonney, who took a pair and alternated bites of tortilla with chunks of rabbit meat. They quickly devoured their meal, which they washed down with healthy swigs of water from their canteens.

After they finished, both men laid out their bedding and retired and slept as best they could on the rocky, uneven ground. The pair arose before dawn, though they didn't say much, just gathering their gear, saddling their mounts, unhobbling them, mounting and riding away while enjoying the early morning cool as they drove the horses back toward the Mirror B.

When the sun rose, Wes took strips of

jerky and a pair of tortillas from the burlap food bag and tossed the sack to Bonney, who caught it with a cat-quick motion and grinned. "Thanks," he said.

"Eat all you want, Billy. We should reach my place right after noon so Sarafina can fix us lunch."

Bonney still talked, but instead of himself, he asked about Bracken and his life. Though it was not something Wes would normally share with new acquaintances, he felt at ease telling the Kid about growing up in northern Arkansas before the War Between the States, joining in the rebellion and surviving the animosities and retributions that followed the downfall of the Confederacy. Bracken's combat experiences intrigued Bonney the most.

"What's it like being in battle and having hundreds shoot at you?"

"Soldier life is long spells of tedium and boredom interrupted by short flashes of terror and shock."

"Did you ever get wounded?"

Wes shook his head. "I was lucky mostly. I never got shot, though I had many near misses, bullets going through my hat or my coat, but never drawing blood. Worst I was hurt was in hand-to-hand fighting at Murfreesboro, where I took a Yankee rifle butt to the jaw. It left me with a damaged front tooth."

"I never noticed."

"That's why I wear a bushy mustache to hide it." Wes turned to Bonney and smiled, exposing the chipped and discolored tooth.

"I'd rather have your damaged tooth than these buck teeth," Billy answered. "There's no way I can hide them. I've been called everything from 'Bucky' to 'Trap Mouth' to 'Rock Biter.' It was no fun when I was younger, but it's amazing how the insults stopped when I started carrying a Colt forty-five."

"A gun can't solve everything."

"Maybe not, but it does stop a bushel of nonsense."

With Bonney's jabbering and his recurring questions about experiencing combat, the time passed quickly for Wes, and around noon they emerged from the mountains and hills into the valley east of San Patricio, two miles from home. Wes turned the horses toward the Mirror B, passing the Zamora place where Carlos worked the land from his modest adobe. Wes saw no sign of Carlos or his donkey as they followed the Ruidoso, then crossed it, stopping long enough for all the animals to quench their thirst with the stream's cool waters.

When they started again, Wes said, "We're near my place."

Bonney grinned. "I know."

Wes nodded as that comment represented a tacit admission that Bonney had indeed stolen his horses despite the denials, but he just shook his head at his young companion and remained amused at his audacious charm.

"I asked you this a while back," Bonney said, "but I need honest work and want to know if you can hire me."

Wes looked at Bonney. "Things are too tight to pay you more than the dollar I promised, though you're welcome to stay a day or two and eat with us. I'm sure my partner could benefit from picking your brain about Jesse Evans and what he's up to."

"What did Jesse do to him?"

"Let just say Jace got set up and punished for stealing horses that Jesse had taken. Jace can give you details if he's so inclined."

Bonney snickered. "Sounds like Jesse conned your partner just as he did me. I told you he was a snake."

Wes grinned. "Jesse's not the only one that's been doing a little conning."

The Kid's lips widened, exposing his buck teeth. "Now who might that be?"

"We both know, Billy, now, don't we?"

Both riders laughed, understanding they had delivered a pointed message without having to state any offensive facts.

Nearing home, Wes saw smoke coming from the kitchen chimney so he expected he and Bonney would have a hot lunch. Wes turned the horses toward the corral where Cousins's yellow dun and Carlos's gray donkey watched their approach. Bonney rode ahead and dismounted at the fence, lifting the latch and pushing the gate open for the horses to trot inside. After the young colt followed the rest in, Bonney closed and latched the gate, then tied his gray to a corner post.

As Wes dismounted, he heard a shout from the house and turned to see Sarafina running out, wiping her hands on her apron as she approached. Wes strode toward her and wrapped his arms around her as she flung herself into his embrace.

"You are back and safe with the horses," she said. "I missed you."

He kissed her and she returned the affection, as if no one else watched.

Bonney cleared his throat.

At the noise, Wes snickered and released his wife. Turning to Bonney, he introduced his wife. "This is Sarafina."

"I'm Billy Bonney. I helped your husband recover the stolen horses. He'd never made it without my help." The bucktoothed thief looked at Wes with a cocky grin.

"Yep," Wes answered, "none of this would've happened had not our new friend gotten involved."

Bonney rocked on his heels with a smile as big as the sun until he looked toward the house. Exiting from the back door and walking side by side came Jace Cousins and Carlos. Bonney's grin soured like milk in sunlight.

Wes caught the change in demeanor and wondered if Bonney had encountered Jace under different, less pleasant circumstances. Jace's expression never changed, but Carlos's face darkened with a frown and unexplained doubt that Wes detected in his uncertain eyes.

"Glad you're back safe," Jace said. "It's been a rough few days."

"Casey?"

Jace nodded. "We buried him yesterday afternoon on the Casey place."

Wes exhaled a long, deep breath. "Did Ellen get to him in time?"

"She had a dozen hours with him, though he didn't say much with the jaw wound. Ellen was holding his hand when he passed on." As Cousins provided details, Carlos stopped and drew a comment from Bonney.

"No digas nada," Bonney told Carlos. *"Ya te he explicado todo. Nadie necesita no más."*

Wes was trying to listen to Jace's explanation of Casey's demise and still understand what Bonney was saying despite his own limited fluency with Spanish. Wes thought Bonney had told Carlos not to say anything as he had taken care of all the necessary explanations.

Cousins continued updating Wes on the Casey murder. "Enough folks saw the shooting that the sheriff had to arrest Wilson. The biggest blasphemy of all is that Murphy presided over Casey's burial, something about him having studied for the priesthood in his youth. Even so, he looked weak and sickly, not boisterous like at the convention. Gossip's also going around saying Murphy paid Wilson five hundred dollars to kill Casey."

"Wouldn't surprise me," Wes answered. "Remember at the Democrat gathering when Murphy called the sheriff over and whispered in his ear?"

Jace nodded.

"After that, I saw Sheriff Mills visiting with Wilson and walking to the store with him. I suspect that's when the offer was extended," Wes explained.

"And now Wilson will have to spend that money on a lawyer." Jace replied. "Now tell me how you recovered the horses."

Wes turned to Bonney, then back to Cousins. "Easiest job I ever had because Billy Bonney here did all the dangerous work." Wes winked at Jace, who answered with a slight nod. "It seems young Bonney here surprised Jesse Evans and five members of his gang and reclaimed the horses so he might find their rightful owner."

Bonney nodded. "Only thing that kept me from hanging the horse thieves was I never found a tree limb strong enough to hold them all."

Wes watched Carlos, who looked as perplexed as a kitten with two tails.

"I'd like to catch up with Jesse Evans one day," Jace noted.

"Then you might want to visit with Billy here. He rode with Jesse's boys for a spell; says Jesse's running from you."

Cousins shrugged. "He's not running, just waiting for a time when he can shoot me in the back." With that he walked over to Bonney, threw his arm around the horse thief's shoulder, and steered him toward the barn. "Come along, Billy. You and I've got a few things to discuss."

Wes stared at Carlos. "You know Billy Bonney, don't you, Carlos?"

Carlos shrugged. "Time for me to get back to my place." He marched past Wes and into the corral to cut out his donkey for the ride home.

"Don't you plan to finish your meal, Carlos?" Sarafina asked.

"Not today," he responded.

Wes put his arm around Sarafina's shoulder and accompanied her toward their home. "I'll eat whatever you've cooked, but after that I must ride to the Casey place and offer my condolences to Ellen." In the kitchen Sarafina served Wes a bowl of stew, and he explained what really happened with the horses and that the Kid was the thief. More perplexing than that, though he didn't tell this to Sarafina, was that Bonney and Carlos somehow knew each other. Carlos may have even looked the other way when Bonney took the horses.

After finishing his quick lunch, Wes strode to the corral, untied Charlie from the fence post, and mounted him, angling by the barn where he reined up. "Jace, you still there?"

"Me and Billy," he answered.

"I've got a question for you, Jace."

"And I've got one for you." Moments later the barn door swung open and Cousins marched out, holding up two empty whiskey bottles for Wes's inspection. "Have you been drinking on the side?"

"Why would I hide my drinking in the barn if I wanted to imbibe?"

Jace shrugged and tossed the bottles aside. "What is it you needed to know?"

"I'm heading to see Ellen Casey. Anything I need to tell her?"

"Nothing comes to mind, Wes."

"Then I'll see you before dark." Wes headed Charlie toward Casey's Mill and dreaded the conversation he knew he must have with Ellen. Nothing he could say would ease her grief or bring back Robert Casey. Finally reaching the place, he pointed Charlie to the store where he tied his sorrel and dismounted. Toward the Rio Hondo, he saw the mound of freshly turned dirt where Casey rested forever.

He entered the store, a bell on the door jingling as he went inside. Momentarily, Ellen came in from the storeroom, again wearing a man's attire. She looked at Wes and her lips quivered, then she began to sob.

"I'm sorry, Ellen." He walked over and hugged her.

"I know," she answered. "I may never wear a dress again, but at least I got to hold his hand and comfort him before he died, thanks to you. Did you get your horses back?"

"I did, and I plan to settle my account here in a few days. I figure the money'll come in handy for a while." He broke his hug and stared into her eyes, swimming in bewilderment.

"It would," she sobbed. "Things are tight for sure."

"I'll be in next week to pay off my debt," Wes assured her. "I promise I'll help you stay afloat. And, Ellen, I'll make you one more vow."

"What's that, Wes?"

"That your husband's murderer will get the justice he deserves, even if we have to burn the House to the ground."

CHAPTER 5

Justice moved slowly in Lincoln County. Though a grand jury had indicted Will Wilson for murder two weeks after the shooting, the trial was scheduled two months later in mid-October when the circuit judge could come to Lincoln to preside over the proceedings. Wes Bracken and Jace Cousins were pulling ears of corn and tossing them in the back of the wagon for shucking and storing in the corncrib for horse feed the afternoon that Billy Bonney rode up with the news. Bonney grinned and shook his head as he guided his dappled gray toward the Mirror B partners.

"Howdy, boys," he called. "Don't let me stop you from your chores."

"Get off your gelding and help us," Jace suggested. "A little work would do you good, make an honest man out of you."

"You can't rustle corn, now, can you, Billy?" Wes added.

"Not unless it's in a jug, but who'd want to steal anything of yours, Wes Bracken?"

"Only the dumbest critter around," Wes replied.

Bonney grinned. "I bet he'd be a handsome devil, though."

"What brings you by, Billy?" Jace asked. "It's past lunch and hours until supper. I suspect you only like us for Sarafina's cooking."

"I've brought information. Willie Wilson goes on trial next Wednesday for murdering your neighbor. They posted a notice on the courthouse door. I thought you'd want to know."

"We're obliged, and we'll be there. How about you?"

Bonney shrugged. "Courtrooms make me nervous, putting your fate in the hands of twelve other men when justice is always skewed in Lincoln County. No, sir, I plan on staying away from lawmen, judges, and juries."

"Have you stayed away from Jesse Evans?" Cousins asked. "He's a snake that can get you sent to a courtroom or prison. I can attest to that firsthand."

"I don't care to run with him ever again, not after he stole Wes's horses."

"Speaking of that theft, Billy, I've got a

83

question. After you and I got back with the horses, Jace found two empty whiskey bottles in the barn. He didn't drink them, nor did I. You have any idea how they got there?"

Billy cocked his head and shrugged. "I don't keep up with other folks' drinking."

"Not even Carlos's?" Wes asked.

The Kid grinned.

"I suspect Carlos rode my stallion to the San Patricio cantina, and someone bought a couple bottles to bring back to the place, figuring Carlos'd get drunk and pass out, making it easier to steal my horses."

"That sounds just like something that Jesse Evans would do. You just can't trust the fellow." Bonney touched the brim of his hat with his trigger finger. "Boys, I'm riding on."

"Thanks for the trial news, Billy," Wes said. "We'll see you down the trail one day."

"Or at Sarafina's table," Cousins corrected with a laugh.

"*Adiós,*" the Kid replied, turning his gray around and heading up the Ruidoso toward Carlos's adobe and San Patricio.

Bonney remained a vagabond, Wes thought, always looking for work and never finding it. When he did get hired, he never held the job for long. The Kid survived on his abundant charm and his quick wit.

By contrast Lawrence G. Murphy lacked charisma. Murphy and Bonney might both be crooks, but the Kid's dishonesty, wrong though it might be, arose as a survival instinct. And, he was likable. As for Murphy he thrived on the power his corruption brought. No sooner had Casey been buried than the next day Murphy called another meeting of the Lincoln County Democrat Party and had himself voted chairman. After what happened to Bob Casey, Murphy ran unopposed and was unanimously elected by his cronies. Those who had previously voiced opposition to Murphy decided it was safest to keep their mouths shut and to stay home. Wes wondered how Murphy intended to play his hand at Wilson's trial.

Arising earlier than usual the day of the tribunal, Wes and Jace ate Sarafina's breakfast of fried bacon, tortillas, and eggs, which she had collected from her hens. Once they emptied their plates, they grabbed their weapons and bedrolls, then marched to the barn where they saddled the sorrel and dun for the ride into Lincoln. They led their horses back to the house where Cousins held their reins so Wes could say goodbye to his wife and little Luis.

The partners followed the Ruidoso east,

then turned northwest at the Rio Bonito on the road to Lincoln where they joined a dozen other parties either on horseback or in wagons for the journey to the county seat and the trial. Horses lined the hitching posts by the courthouse on the south side of the dusty street that was Lincoln's only road. Wes counted thirteen parked wagons near the low-slung adobe building that should have been the seat of justice in Lincoln County, but was in fact just another tool of L.G. Murphy and his machine.

Bracken and Cousins dismounted and hobbled their horses, then made their way inside. Men and a sprinkling of women, including Ellen Casey, who sat on the front row behind the table occupied by the district attorney, squeezed together on the spectator benches. On the opposite side of the room stood Murphy behind the defendant, the defendant's lawyer, and Sheriff Ham Mills. When the lawyer turned, Wes recognized Alexander McSween, who had served as Murphy's legal counsel at the Democrat convention. Wes studied the county's political and economic kingpin, deciding the rumors about Murphy's health had been true, his eyes listless and his suit fitting loosely over his frame, as if he had lost significant weight. Unable to find seats, Wes and Jace moved to the side and leaned against the cool adobe wall. Moments later, Juan Patrón spotted them and marched over.

"Glad to see you both," Patrón said. "We owe this to Bob Casey."

"This should be a conviction," Wes noted, "but justice is rigged in Lincoln County."

Patrón lifted his arm in despair. "Who knows? Word is the prosecutor and the judge are cronies of Murphy and Dolan. The prosecutor is William L. Rynerson out of Las Cruces. The judge is Warren Bristol, who lives in Mesilla. He's a Republican appointed to his judgeship by President Grant. You know Alex McSween, Wilson's attorney."

Wes replied. "I don't care for anyone that does Murphy's dirty work."

Patrón scratched his head. "Alex doesn't practice criminal law, generally handling contracts and real estate cases."

Wes laughed. "That tells me Wilson will be convicted for the wrong reason, not because he's guilty but because Murphy wants him silenced."

Sheriff Mills rose from his seat beside the defendant. "Everyone please rise for the honorable Warren H. Bristol, presiding judge."

Patrón nodded his farewell to Bracken and Cousins, then made his way back to his bench seat. When everyone arose, the prosecutor towered over the crowd, standing at least six-feet-six inches, maybe taller, with an unruly black beard beneath penetrating eyes and a high forehead. The judge entered the courtroom from a side door. He was a short man with graying hair neatly trimmed because there was so little of it above his brow, what remained being consigned to the sides and back of his head. His face tapered into a narrow chin with a close-cropped salt-and-pepper goatee. His gray eyes, his most striking feature, bulged behind thick wire-rimmed glasses.

The judge instructed everyone to take their seats, then began the preliminaries in the matter of the Territory of New Mexico versus Will Wilson. He asked if the prosecution was ready to proceed, receiving an affirmative response, then turned to the defense with the same question. Before he answered, Alex McSween leaned back in his chair and whispered something to Murphy. Only after Murphy nodded did McSween announce he was prepared to move forward. At that point Bristol called in the jury and twelve men squeezed into their box.

Rynerson opened the proceedings, standing up and in a booming voice explaining the territory's intention to prove that Will Wilson did willfully and maliciously gun down Robert Casey on the first Sunday of August with said victim passing into eternity the next day. When given his opportunity to rebut the charges against his client, McSween stood up and spoke softly that his client was innocent of the accusations, though he offered no proof.

Though Wes wanted to see Wilson hanged, he at least deserved a fair trial rather than this sham of a legal proceeding. The prosecution called four witnesses, all claiming to have seen the shooting. Odd thing was, the quartet sworn in to testify were Murphy cronies, men Wes had seen at the political convention the morning of the shooting. Neither he nor Cousins had been subpoenaed to testify, and they were the only ones who returned fire. Jace had chased Wilson into the back of Murphy's store.

As a defense attorney, McSween looked as lost as a sinner in church, especially when he cross-examined those on the witness stand. He never challenged if they had witnessed the ambush or if they had been instructed on their testimony. With Murphy sitting right behind him and the county boss often leaning forward to whisper something to him, McSween was tethered to Murphy's script for the trial.

The accused Wilson sat at the defense table dull-eyed and quiet, his head bobbing from side to side as if he were drowsy and trying to stay awake. Wes suspected Wilson had been drugged so he would not disrupt the House's plan, even if it resulted in his conviction and hanging. When Rynerson rested the prosecution, McSween arose and asked the judge to dismiss the charges as the prosecution had failed to prove the case. His bug eyes widening behind his thick glasses, Bristol banged his gavel and denied the motion.

McSween then said that the only witness who could prove the accusations wrong was the deceased himself, Robert Casey, because he would've known who shot him. Jace looked at Wes and rolled his eyes. Justice in this court was not only blind but also deaf, dumb, and stupid, Wes decided, especially after McSween opted not to call any defense witnesses, merely stating that Casey had owed Wilson wages and was driven by economic desperation to confront the victim for his pay. All in the room, save for Wilson himself, understood the defendant's fate was preordained.

After McSween made his closing remarks,

Rynerson stood and towered over McSween as he retreated to his seat. Rynerson countered McSween's argument, proclaiming the defense's contention of innocence had been disproved by four of Lincoln's finest citizens, drawing snickers from many in the crowd opposed to Murphy, his men, and his ways. The district attorney asked the jury for a conviction so the killer could be hanged.

"Only when men like Will Wilson are made to pay for their crimes will law and order come to Lincoln County," Rynerson concluded. "Justice today will father justice tomorrow and forevermore in Lincoln County."

Half the men in the jury nodded in agreement, and Wes anticipated the verdict before the jurors ever left the jury box to deliberate. Judge Bristol gave them their instructions and dismissed them to do their civic duty. After the jurors departed and Bristol exited to his quarters, many spectators headed outside for some fresh air or a smoke. Wes lingered, knowing this jury would make a quick decision. Ten minutes later Judge Bristol returned to his seat, and the jurors made their way back into the courtroom.

When Judge Bristol asked if the jury had

reached a verdict, the foreman indicated they had. Bristol next instructed Wilson to stand. He arose awkwardly, McSween and Sheriff Mills rising with him to hold his arms and steady him on his feet. Wes suspected Wilson's weak knees resulted more from him being drugged than nerves or a true awareness of his impending fate.

"How do you find the defendant?" Bristol asked the foreman.

"We the jury by a unanimous vote find the defendant guilty as charged."

Several people cheered while Ellen Casey sobbed with relief that her husband's murderer had received the justice he deserved.

"Order," Bristol called, banging his gavel against the bench. Then he turned to the defendant, and pronounced punishment. "Being found guilty of murder as charged, I hereby sentence Will Wilson to be hanged two months from today. Furthermore, having inspected the jail for Lincoln County, I find it inadequate and insecure for the proper incarceration of this convicted murderer. I further order that he be delivered to Fort Stanton and turned over to military authorities to be held in the Army stockade until the morning of his execution when he is to be returned to the sheriff of Lincoln County for hanging at high noon." Bristol banged his gavel. "This court is adjourned," he called, then stood up and exited the room. As the sheriff escorted Wilson from the courtroom, Wes made his way to Ellen, who stood wiping tears from her eyes with a lace handkerchief.

"How are you doing, Ellen?" Wes asked.

"Better now that Bob's killer will be hanged." She held up the kerchief for Wes to see. "Bob gave me this hankie last Christmas. It's the last gift he ever gave me." Her lips quivered as she fought her emotions.

Wes took her hand and squeezed it. "I'm sorry, Ellen. I'll help you any way I can."

"Me, too," echoed Cousins, who joined Wes and the widow.

"I'm managing okay for now," she said, "still trying to get a handle on the store, the mill, the ranch, and the cattle. Bob kept so much in his head that it's hard to figure out what he owns and what he owes. Several men and his supplier are hitting me up for debts they claim, but I can't prove it one way or another."

"I'm sorry, Ellen," Wes said, releasing her hand.

"Besides that, I don't have enough money to settle these claims, if they are genuine. Wes, you're the only one that's come in and settled your account with cash. Some think now that Bob's gone, they need not pay off their debts to the store, but they sure believe we should fork up what he owes. As overseer of his estate, I've got to sort that out, manage the business, and still provide for my children."

"It's a burden, I'm sure," Wes consoled.

"On top of that, Murphy's been sending his nasty partner Dolan out to collect money, saying Bob opened an account at their store and made five dollars' worth of purchases. You can't trust what the House says or does."

Wes nodded. "Your husband did buy five dollars in goods on credit the morning of the convention as a good-faith showing that he harbored no hard feelings against Murphy."

"Fact is," Jace interjected, "that was where Bob was going when he was ambushed. He saw how poorly Murphy had taken the defeat and decided it best to settle up. He was shot before he got there, so there's likely a five-dollar debt in his name."

"I don't have the money and even if I did, I couldn't face Murphy with all the rumors flying he was behind Bob's killing."

Wes nodded. "Don't worry about it, Ellen. Before I leave town, I'll go to the House and settle the account for you. No sense in letting them add to your worries."

"God bless you, Wesley Bracken. You're a decent man. Thank you both for coming to the trial. I felt better knowing there were a few honest men among this bunch of thieves."

Wes hugged her. "You head on back to your place, and we'll take care of this with the Murphy store."

Jace shook her hand, then exited the courtroom with Bracken. Once outside and beyond hearing range, Cousins turned to Wes. "You got five dollars on you?"

"Two at most," Wes answered. "I was counting on you for the other three."

"I've got one, maybe one and a half, but that's all," Jace replied.

"I intend to pay the debt in full when I visit Murphy."

As they discussed their dilemma, Juan Patrón approached. "Bob Casey's death will be avenged after all," he said. "I feared otherwise since word has it Murphy put him up to it. I figured he would protect his hired murderer."

Wes cocked his head and smiled. "Murphy just wants to shut Wilson up now that he's done the House's bidding."

Patrón grimaced. "I never thought of that."

"It's a possibility," Wes said. "Now I've got a favor to ask of you. Could you lend me two dollars?"

Patrón whistled. "I don't carry that kind of money, not on these streets. I got some at my place, though. What do you need it for?"

"Bob Casey died in debt to the House, five dollars to be exact," Wes said.

"Bob never would've bought a thing from Murphy," Patrón said emphatically.

"He did it as a gesture of goodwill to Murphy before the county convention," Wes said.

Jace added, "He was on his way to clear his account when Wilson shot him."

"Between Jace and me, we have three dollars," Wes said, "so we just need two more."

Patrón nodded. "Follow me to the house, and I'll contribute my part."

"It's a loan, Juan, not a gift," Wes said. "I'll repay you, likely this afternoon."

The three men turned east from the courthouse and walked behind the Montaño store toward Patrón's home. The Hispanic led them to his front door where he had them wait. He returned momentarily with a cigar box. Patrón opened the lid, counting out three dollars and handing them to Wes.

"I only need two," Wes said.

"Take them all. I owe it to Bob."

"*Gracias,*" Wes said. "Now it's time to face that den of snakes." He spun around and headed for the courthouse, Jace behind him. They unhobbled their horses and mounted for the ride to Murphy's store on the west end of town, their destination looming over the street like a sinister castle.

At the store they dismounted and tied their horses among the others at the hitching rack. Wes explained the layout of the store, the front door opening up on the mercantile itself. The door on the east side of the room led to the offices and the stairs to the second floor. A door on the west end of the merchandise room opened into a saloon. Jace yanked his Henry rifle out of its scabbard and slid his fingers into the lever and carried the weapon at his side as he stepped up on the porch behind Wes, who shoved open the door and strode inside, Jace following him in.

The front room overflowed with overpriced goods that Murphy sold to the locals when they could afford them or added them to their account when they couldn't so that most people in Lincoln County were in debt to the House. The clerk looked up from behind the counter, and Wes recognized Murphy's new partner, James J. Dolan, whose breath smelled of whiskey and whose narrow eyes reflected anger.

"What do you want?" he scowled, then rubbed the thin mustache beneath the nose he lifted in the air.

"We're here to see L.G. Murphy," Wes responded.

"He's busy. Doesn't have time for riffraff like you."

Jace smiled, stepped up beside Wes, and laid the barrel of his Henry across the counter so it pointed at Dolan's chest. "Mr. Henry thinks your boss can find the time to visit with us."

"We're here to pay off a debt," Wes said.

"You've never done business with us, Bracken."

"Mr. Henry's growing impatient," Jace said.

Dolan studied Cousins, his eyes widening when he realized Jace was serious. "I'll fetch Mr. Murphy."

"No!" Jace shouted. "You call him to the counter."

Dolan swallowed hard, the veins throbbing in his neck. "Mr. Murphy, you're needed at the front," he called.

Moments later, the owner approached the room, stopping in the doorway when he saw Bracken and Cousins.

"Get outta 'ere, the both of ye," he shouted. "Meself don't do business with yer kind."

Jace lifted his carbine from the counter so Murphy could see the rifle pointed at his nose.

Murphy's attitude softened. "What be yer business?"

"I'm here to pay off a debt," Wes answered.

"Ye don't owes me a red cent, Wes Bracken, because meself never deals with yer kind."

"It's not for me," Wes replied. "I'm here on behalf of Ellen Casey to pay off the account of Bob Casey, who charged five dollars to his good name the Sunday morning of the county convention." Wes counted out five dollars from his pocket and offered the money to Murphy.

Dolan looked from the cash to Murphy to Bracken again. "I need papers proving you represent Mr. Casey and his estate," Dolan said. "Without that, I can't accept your payment."

Wes shook his head. "Then transfer the debt to a new account in my name, and I'll pay that one off."

"Can't do it without the legal papers," Dolan reiterated.

"Don't have time for the legal details,"

Wes argued.

"Sure ye do," bellowed Murphy. "Check out the saloon. Judge Bristol and District Attorney Rynerson are 'aving drinks on the 'ouse. Perhaps they can help ye."

Wes suspected from the beginning that Murphy and now Dolan would never give in on settling Casey's debt. Now his suspicions stood confirmed. Still, he slapped the money on the counter. "Bob Casey's account is paid up. Everyone knows you had Casey killed."

Murphy's eyes narrowed and his gaunt cheeks flushed. "Ye best watch yer accusations."

"The morning of the convention when you realized you would lose the election, you called Sheriff Ham Mills to your side in front of God and everybody. That's when you told him to assassinate Casey."

"Ye be digging yer own grave, with yer baseless charges. Yer a man without 'onor."

"Then I saw the sheriff talk to Willie Wilson. An hour later, Wilson ambushes Casey. How many decent men have you put in Lincoln County graves, Murphy?"

"Not enough," Murphy spat. "Meself be looking at two more that needs an early burial."

"You're not man enough to do your own

killing, Murphy," Wes challenged.

"Ye don't 'ave to do yer own killing when ye got the money to 'ire others to do it for ye."

"Let's go, Jace. We're making no progress here." Wes pointed to the money on the counter. "Casey's debt has been repaid in full."

"Not without the appropriate legal authority approving it," Dolan called.

Wes and Jace backed out of the store and off the porch, watching the door as they untied their horses and mounted, then riding across the street to the Wortley.

"I've got enough of our money left to buy us lunch before we head home," Wes offered.

"Fine with me," Jace replied. They tied their horses behind the Wortley so as not to draw undue attention to their mounts, then headed inside.

Sam Wortley greeted them. "It's been a while since you've eaten with us, Wes."

"You draw too many men from across the street," Wes responded, pointing to the House.

Wortley shrugged. "They keep me in business." He pointed to a table in the corner and the two men tracked that way, telling Wortley they'd have the special written on

the chalkboard of fried steak, boiled potatoes, canned tomatoes, and cornbread. They
ate their meal quickly, paid for their fare,
and thanked Wortley for his hospitality.

When they exited, both men froze on the
porch, their hands reaching for their revolvers. Coming up the walk from the street
strode Jesse Evans.

Chapter 6

Everyone froze. Wes counted Jesse Evans and five other hard cases staring at him with squinting, malevolent eyes. All six gang members inched their hands closer to their sidearms as Wes studied Jesse, taking in his reddish-brown hair, his wide gaze, his broad face, and the stubble on his cheeks. His features and clothes were dirty from too much time on the trail and too little in bathtubs. While his outfit and those of his men were coated with layers of dust, their weapons were clean and glistening with oil.

Wes gauged his opponents until Jesse grinned.

"This is not the place to settle things, fellas," he said. "Too many witnesses." He lifted his finger and waved it at them. "But if the Mirror B boys wanna fight, let's start the party."

Jace took a step until he stood shoulder to shoulder with Wes, then spoke. "You always were braver when you outnumbered your prey."

"Well, howdy, Jace. You wouldn't want to do something that would send you back to the penitentiary, would you?"

"I did nothing to begin with deserving of prison other than accept the word of one I thought was a friend."

Evans shrugged. "It's you that's the convicted horse thief, not me, Jace. You ought to be guilty of murder as well from the last time I ran into you. How many months ago was it?"

"When Wes ran the Horrells out of Lincoln County, I took out after you, figuring the more skunks we scared back to Texas the better the county would smell." Jace studied each of the six men before him. "If you recall that day, Jesse, the odds were the same then as now, three to one. By the time I was done I'd evened the odds, but you turned tail and ran like a skunk with a yellow stripe down his back."

"No, Jace," Evans replied, "I did the decent thing and left to find a shovel so I could bury Clem and Ansel. They were decent boys that didn't deserve killing."

"Nobody that rides with you for long, Jesse, is decent," Jace shot back.

"Hell, Jace, half of Lincoln County's rode

with me for a spell over the years." Evans paused and pointed to Wes. "Even Bracken there's ridden with me, Clem, and Ansel against the Mes Brothers. Ask Bracken there."

"Circumstances dictated our brief alliance," Wes responded.

"We were doing John Chisum's dirty work for him so he wouldn't get his hands soiled," Jesse answered.

"And you were stealing Chisum's cattle while drawing his wages, Jesse."

Evans shrugged and grinned. "He wasn't paying enough."

"His wages were fair, Jesse."

"Speaking of fair, Wes, it ain't right that you've been spreading a rumor that me and the boys stole your horses."

"I never said that to anyone, Jesse."

"That's not what I hear," Evans continued. "Heard it from several people you said we stole your horses, and you only got them back after a running gun battle near the Rio Feliz."

Jace shook his head and laughed. "So you don't like being falsely accused, do you, Jesse? Try spending two years in prison for a horse theft you didn't commit."

"You needed a better lawyer, Jace. Don't blame me for that. Now if you Mirror B boys will step aside, we're hungry and want to eat. But believe me, these matters aren't settled. One day we'll catch you away from witnesses and resolve our differences for good." Evans scowled at Bracken. "Or perhaps we'll drop by your ranch one evening, Bracken, and shoot it out, then afterward have a little fun with your greaser wife."

Rage surging through his veins, Wes stepped forward, but Jace grabbed his arm and held him. "He's trying to rile you, Wes."

Jesse laughed. "Now let us pass."

Jace yanked on Wes's arm and pulled him down the porch so Jesse and his gang could walk inside the eatery. After the last one passed and the door closed behind them, Wes and Jace backed away, then turned and trotted to their horses. Quickly untying their mounts, they climbed aboard their animals and galloped toward the Rio Bonito before turning east toward home. They circled back to the road on the far side of town.

"Jesse's a patient cuss," Jace said when they had traveled far enough outside Lincoln that they could slow their mounts to a walk. "He wants you to make a mistake so he can kill us and claim self-defense."

"Justice being what it is in Lincoln County, that's what the court would decide

106

anyway if he ever came to trial."

"Yep, you've got it all figured out."

"I want to check on Sarafina and Luis when we get home, then ride over to see Carlos. He's been scarce since he let Bonney steal our horses. I need to warn him about the threats Evans made against Sarafina."

"You do that, Wes, and I'll look after the place and your family."

"Thanks, Jace."

"Just know that one day, I may take off and hunt Jesse down like the rabid mongrel he is."

"I understand," Wes replied.

As they reached the confluence of the Bonito and the Ruidoso, they turned southwest and rode toward home. Wes fought the urge to gallop ahead to check on Sarafina and Luis. When the place finally came fully into view, everything seemed in order, smoke coming from the kitchen chimney, the horses in the corral, the yellowing fields undisturbed, and the chickens ambling about and pecking at the ground around the henhouse.

Wes rode up to the house, jumped off his horse, and tossed his reins to Cousins, who climbed easily out of the saddle as his partner strode inside.

"Sarafina," Wes shouted, "I'm home." He walked through the parlor to the kitchen where she sat feeding Luis a bowl of corn mush.

She smiled at him as he walked to her side and planted a kiss on her cheek. Luis reached up to him, and Wes tickled the little fellow under the chin, drawing a giggle before the toddler spit up a spoonful of the yellow mush.

"Are you okay, Sarafina?"

"Sure," she replied. "Why would I be otherwise?"

"I just missed you," he said, opting not to tell her of the threat from Jesse Evans.

"Let me finish feeding Luis, *mi esposo,* and I will prepare you and Jace a fine dinner. How did the trial go?"

"Quick and predictable. Wilson was convicted and sentenced to hang in two months. I saw Ellen Casey. She was relieved at the verdict but overwhelmed with keeping Casey's place going and supporting her children."

Sarafina stopped feeding Luis and studied her husband. "Something's bothering you. I can see it in your eyes. What is it?"

"Nothing. It's been a long, tiring day, and I still need to visit Carlos."

His wife lifted her right eyebrow. "Something is wrong, *mi esposo,* for you haven't thought about him in weeks, ever since the horses were stolen."

Wes shrugged. "We'll talk later because I must visit Carlos so I can return before dark." He kissed her again on the cheek and quickly retraced his steps so he would not have to answer any more questions. As he closed the door behind him, he squinted and licked his lips.

"You look like you've got something on your mind, Wes," Jace noted.

Wes bit his lip and nodded. "I've been thinking we could use a watchdog to guard the place."

"You may be right," Jace said as he offered the sorrel's reins to Wes. "When you can do without me for a few days, I'll see what I can find, though I might have to go to Roswell or Mesilla to find the right one."

"As long as you bring back a solid watchdog, I don't care," Wes replied as he grabbed the saddle horn and pulled himself atop Charlie. "Depending on how moody Carlos is — I can never tell about that boy — it may be dark when I return."

"Don't worry, Wes, I'll shoot and ask questions later."

Wes snickered. "That's not what I had in mind."

"Doesn't matter, Wes. You deserved a good laugh. Glad I could help."

Wes turned his horse toward the Zamora place and Carlos. He didn't push Charlie, just let him move at his own pace because Wes needed time to think. The politics of Lincoln County roiled with treachery. Murphy controlled things in the western half of the county while John Chisum, with the vast rangeland he claimed, called the shots in the eastern portion. The cattleman was a better man than Murphy, but fate had placed Bracken and his family in Murphy's domain. The small ranchers throughout the county despised Chisum for his dominance and ability to sell beef in quantities that lowered the price for the little guy trying to make a living for himself and his kin. The small farmers throughout the region loathed Murphy because his political contacts helped him set the values the growers received for their products, and if they bought supplies at his exorbitant prices, they destined themselves forever to subservience to him and his associates. Bracken wanted to be his own man, not to get caught up in the politics that had killed Bob Casey, nor to side with any faction and abandon his principles.

Over the two years he had been in Lincoln County, Wes admired the Mexicans because they seemed to avoid many — though not all — of the entanglements that the Americans got involved in. He knew his marriage to Sarafina, though questioned by some at the time of their betrothal, and his willingness to stand up for what was right, regardless of the race of the participants, had put him in good standing with the Hispanic community. Since the wedding, his biggest challenge had been Carlos, whose emotions changed like the weather. Sure, he was young, but Wes knew he had potential if he matured, and if he did so quickly. A childish prank could get a man of any age killed in Lincoln County, something Carlos failed to understand.

As Wes approached the Zamora place, he saw smoke arising from the chimney and spotted Carlos's donkey in the corral along with a dappled gray. Wes recognized Bonney's mount and wondered what mischief the Kid was up to. Even more worrisome was how Bonney might influence Carlos, who remained at an impressionable age where tomfoolery and fun seemed more rewarding than hard work and boredom.

"Hello, Carlos," Wes called.

Receiving no response, Bracken rode over to the corral, tied his horse to a fence post, then slipped to the modest adobe that had been home to Carlos, Sarafina, and her first husband. Approaching warily, he heard the voices of Bonney and Carlos, but they were high-pitched and strained, their words interrupted by giggles and mumbles. Wes stepped to the door, knocked. and slid to the side so the thick wall stood between him and the occupants. The conversation died.

"*¿Quién es?*" Carlos called out.

"It's the bogey man," Bonney cried.

He and Carlos both giggled at his joke.

"It's Wes Bracken," he announced. "I'm coming in."

Without stepping in front of the door he pushed it, waited a moment, and entered the room. With all the shutters closed the interior was engulfed in the shadows of late afternoon, only a few burning embers in the fireplace and a shaft of light from the open door illuminating the interior. For a moment, Wes missed the two young men, but he was looking high, and they were lying low, sitting on the earthen floor, their backs propped up against the adobe wall.

Finally, Carlos spoke. "*Es el diablo mismo.*"

"Yes," Bonney answered, "it is the devil himself. He goes by the name of Wes Bracken."

Both fellows giggled as Wes moved around

the room, looking for a candle. Finding one, he stuck it in the fireplace until the wick touched a glowing ember and took to fire.

Wes grabbed a stool and placed it between Bonney and Carlos, tilting the candle to drop a dollop of wax in the middle of the seat. He pushed the candle into the melted wax, then glanced at Bonney and Carlos in the glow of the flame. Between them lay the problem, two whiskey bottles, their contents drained.

Disgusted, Wes retrieved another stool and sat it at the feet of the pair who kept jabbering, partly in Spanish, partly in English, and greatly in gibberish that only they could understand. Even if they didn't comprehend each other's words, they still giggled.

"I came to talk serious business, boys."

"Fire," his brother-in-law gulped, "away."

"You've been spreading rumors, Billy."

"Day . . . and . . . night," he responded, then hiccupped.

Both boys chuckled.

Deciding conversation was useless, Wes considered heading back to the Mirror B until he spotted two buckets in the corner. Thinking it worth a try, he arose from his stool, grabbed a bucket with each hand, and marched out the door, turning toward the Ruidoso. A pail of cold October stream water over their heads might sober them up enough that he could converse with them. The closer he got to the brook's noisy waters, the more he grinned about his plan.

At the stream's edge he moved from rock to rock until he stood on a large one in the middle of the Ruidoso and dipped his pails full of frigid water. Heavy though the buckets were, they were a delight to carry since he knew he would enjoy dousing the two drunks. He marched from the stream to the adobe and strode inside.

"El diablo ha vuelto," Carlos joked, both he and Bonney oblivious to the freight Wes carried.

"Well, boys, I'm about to give you a splash of hell," Wes advised them, lowering one bucket to the floor. He took the other pail to Carlos, who looked up as he turned the container upside down over his head.

Carlos spat, sputtered, and screamed, flinging drops of frigid water at the devil he imagined towering over him.

Bonney erupted in laughter for a moment, then seemed confused by the drops that had splattered on him. Switching his empty bucket for a full one, Wes carried it to Billy and emptied it on his head. Bonney yelled and cursed, instinctively reaching for his gun, but Wes was prepared and stomped on his wrist with his boot. Bonney yelped profanity.

With Bonney's gun hand pinned to the floor, Wes bent over and extracted the revolver from his holster and tossed the pistol out the front door, leaving Bonney to rub the soreness out of his hand and forearm. Gradually, the two imbibers shook their heads and made some sense out of the muddle puddle the whiskey had left in their brains.

"What was that about?" Carlos demanded. "You can't come in my house and do that."

"I can and I did, Carlos. I've got serious matters to discuss."

Bonney wobbled his head and slapped at his holster, confused and panicked about his missing pistol. "Where's my gun," he cried, grimacing at the pain bouncing around in his brain.

Slowly, Carlos tried to stand up, but he stumbled and knocked over the stool, sending the candle rolling across the floor and extinguishing the flame. *"¿Qué esta pasando?"* Carlos cried.

"I'll tell you what's happening, Carlos. You're drunk."

Bonney struggled to his feet and staggered about the room, mumbling "Where's my gun? Where's my gun?"

Wes grabbed Bonney by his shirt and shook him. "Get over there with Carlos." Wes shoved him that way. "I lost a brother to alcohol so don't you boys expect sympathy from me."

The two grimaced and shut their eyes, then wiggled their heads from side to side.

"Carlos, I came to tell you there's been threats to your sister by Jesse Evans and his gang."

"That don't have nothing to do with me," Bonney said.

Wes grabbed Bonney by the shirt again and shook him. "The hell it doesn't. I ran into Jesse Evans today in town. He accused me of spreading stories that he and his gang had stolen my horses. You're the one that started that rumor."

"I's only funning, that's all," Bonney said.

"Pranks and rumors can get a fellow killed in Lincoln County. You have put me and my family in danger."

"I didn't mean nothing by it," he pleaded.

"Don't you ever come by my place for a meal again unless you promise to stop spreading lies about me, my family, and our ranch." Wes turned to his brother-in-law. "And, Carlos, don't you come to visit your sister and your nephew if you've been drinking."

"We was just having a good time," Carlos said. "That's all."

"Remember my warning because I'll not tolerate any more mischief from either of you. Too many people could be hurt as a result." Wes glowered at the two, then turned and strode out to the corral. He untied Charlie, mounted the stallion, and headed for home at a trot, anxious to be with Sarafina and Luis so he could offer his protection. When he reached the Mirror B, he rode to the barn and tended his sorrel before entering the house through the kitchen door. Jace sat at the table finishing his supper while Sarafina peppered him with questions about the day in Lincoln as she knew something had gone wrong.

His partner looked up from his bowl of chili and wagged a half-eaten tortilla at his partner. "Glad you're back. How'd it go with Carlos?"

Wes greeted Sarafina with a kiss on the cheek, then grimaced. "Not well. Bonney was there. Both were drunk. Don't know that they'll remember a thing I said. I told them not to stop here for a meal again until they apologized and started acting like men instead of kids."

Sarafina stomped her foot on the hard-packed floor and planted her balled fists

117

upon her slender hips. "What is all this trouble?"

Jace scooted his chair back from the table, leaning over and sopping up the dregs of his chili with the tortilla remains, shoving it in his mouth, chewing fast, and swallowing hard. "I didn't tell her anything, Wes, though she tried to pry it from me. I'll head to my bunk and let you explain what you want." He took a last swig of coffee and charged out the back door for his adobe. "See you in the morning."

As soon as Jace exited, Sarafina turned to her husband. "Tell me everything."

Wes nodded and motioned for her to take a seat at the table. He began by explaining the trial and verdict, before he detailed his effort to pay off the Casey debt at Murphy's store. As he finished describing the encounter with Jesse Evans and his gang, Sarafina sat wide-eyed and scared, nervously tugging at strands of her raven hair. Wes explained that he had visited Carlos to tell him of the intimidation so he would watch out for his sister and nephew if he saw anything suspicious.

When Wes finished explaining the threats and the dangers, Sarafina arose and silently slipped to the corner fireplace where the pot of chili simmered over glowing embers.

She dipped him a bowl of chili and placed it before him on the table. His wife returned with a handful of tortillas and a cup of coffee, then retrieved Luis, who was squawking in his bed. She sat beside Wes, trying to calm the boy by patting his back as she bounced him on her knee. After Wes finished his supper and Sarafina had comforted Luis enough to sleep, they retired to their bed to wake up to a new and different day — one like the dozens more that would follow — when they had to stay vigilant against the threats stated and implied to their lives and well-being. Wes wondered if Sarafina should start wearing men's clothes — like Ellen Casey had — to disguise her gender to passersby.

From that day on, everyone took extra precautions, especially after word came that one of Murphy's henchmen had shot Juan Patrón, seriously wounding him. The attacker, John H. Riley, a pal of James J. Dolan, had plugged Patrón in the back, the bullet coming narrowly close to his spine and exiting out his abdomen. Riley had claimed self-defense, reporting that Patrón had been cursing and bad-mouthing him incessantly, and the district attorney accepted his assertion since Patrón was expected to die. Most folks in Lincoln knew better as Patrón seldom spewed profanity. The people also understood — though they never said it where eavesdroppers might hear — that Patrón was attacked because he had not only supported Casey for Democrat county chairman but also had convinced other Mexicans to do so as well.

Chapter 7

In the ensuing weeks, whenever Wes and Jace handled chores, they took their long weapons with them, always keeping them within reach. There was corn to shuck, cattle to check, horses to tend, eggs to collect, a cow to milk, hay to cut and dry, vegetables to pick, and water to tote. One day passed, then another and another until they all ran together. The first freeze came, killing the remnants of the garden and announcing winter's approach.

During those tense days, Carlos never stopped by, nor did Bonney drop in for a free meal. The Mirror B partners managed the place, seldom leaving unless Wes visited Casey's Mill to check on Ellen or purchase supplies, always paying with cash rather than buying on credit. Ellen was just getting by, able to pay only a single hand to manage the operation and relying on her two oldest sons to help her hang on. True to his promise, Jace left for three days to purchase a watchdog. He came home not with one but two mongrels he named "Nip" and "Tuck." The canine pair adapted to guarding the property, barking and howling when strangers passed by on the road, much less approached the house, though Nip had to be broken of killing chickens. Despite the threats, no one attacked the place, though on three nights over the ensuing two months the dogs went berserk. After each incident, Wes and Jace searched for the cause, once finding unexplained horse tracks, another time discovering sign of a black bear, and on the other occasion coming up empty on a possible cause.

Each passing day brought Lincoln County closer to the hanging of Willie Wilson. When that execution date arrived, Wes hitched the mule team to the wagon and left for Lincoln, Jace riding his dun. Wes drove the rig with Charlie saddled and tied to the tailgate. Sarafina complained that Luis was too small to attend the execution, but Wes countered that it was unsafe to leave mother and child alone at home, even with Nip and Tuck standing guard, unless Sarafina learned to use weapons.

The trip to see a man die was a solemn one on a chilly December morning. Sarafina kept Luis in her lap, bundled in blankets, fretting that her son might be terrified by the hanging. They arrived in Lincoln around noon, just as the escort of cavalrymen brought Wilson back from the Fort Stanton stockade where he had been imprisoned since the trial. Wes pulled his wagon to the side of the road opposite the courthouse to let other wagons and riders pass and to watch the prisoner exchange, as he didn't trust Murphy, Dolan, or anything to do with the House. The gallows stood ominously to the west of the courthouse, a cheap pine coffin resting on the ground near the foot of the scaffold. The coatless Wilson, shivering in the cool winter breeze that washed over the Rio Bonito Valley, wore the same green bib shirt and worn britches that he had been wearing when he shot Bob Casey and when he was sentenced to hang.

At the courthouse, the lanky lieutenant leading the dozen buffalo soldiers of the Ninth Cavalry halted his procession and ordered his soldiers to dismount. Then the troopers formed a circle around Wilson and two helped the bound prisoner down from his Army mule. At that point, Sheriff Ham Mills emerged from the courthouse, a double-barreled shotgun cradled in his arms, followed by L.G. Murphy, whose frame appeared thinner than at the trial. Rumors that he was seriously sick must be true, Wes thought, as he watched the sheriff escort the murderer Wilson inside.

After the court door closed, Wes nudged his wagon forward, making a wide swing across the street and driving to a line of wagons and carts parked by the clearing where the execution would occur. Jace dismounted and tied his horse beside Charlie, accepting a folded tortilla filled with frijoles for lunch. Wes and Sarafina remained in the wagon seat, finishing their meal while the rambunctious Luis played in the wagon bed. Other families brought their meals as well. It would've been a festive occasion for the folks of Lincoln, save for the ultimate purpose of the gathering.

After the men finished their second tortilla, Wes jumped down from the wagon and offered to help Sarafina, but she declined. "I'm hoping Luis will wear out and take a nap before the hanging. I'll stay with him."

Wes nodded and expected the little one would tire out, but the longer Luis heard the noises and watched the activities from over the sideboards, the more he squawked and cried to get out and join the fun. When Wes spotted Ellen Casey arriving in her wagon with her family, he walked over to greet them. He helped the widow from her rig, her somber demeanor reflected in the black dress she wore.

"Good to see you in a dress again, Ellen."

"Thank you, but I'll be back in shirt and trousers tomorrow doing a man's work again."

Wes took and squeezed her hand. "I'm sorry I haven't been by your place in a spell."

Ellen nodded. "I've heard about the threats to you and your family. I don't blame you." She turned from the gallows and released a heavy breath. "Let's end this so we can get on with our lives." She gathered her children and marched toward the scaffold. Several men took off their hats as she passed.

Spotting Juan Patrón on a stool near the corner of the courthouse, Wes and Jace strode over to greet him. Though he looked pale from his gunshot ordeal, he smiled and welcomed them, asking their pardon for him remaining seated.

"Tell me the cuss words you threw at Riley," Cousins teased.

Patrón grinned. "Profanity is the domain of the ignorant," he said. "I'm not ignorant like Murphy and his men."

"What do you think about this?" Wes said,

sweeping his hand toward the gathering crowd and the gallows.

"I'll be surprised if they hang him, as reptilian as Murphy is."

Jace shook his head. "Reptilian? Is that a fancy cuss word?"

Patrón laughed. "It means like a reptile or a snake."

"What else is bothering you, Juan?" Wes asked.

"I'm switching to Republican. Can't stay in a party that shoots its own in the back. With Hayes winning the presidency in the November election, maybe we can get federal attention here to clean up Lincoln County next year, once he takes office."

"It's politics," Wes said. "Little difference between the two parties other than which one of them gets the most graft."

Jace grinned at Patrón. "My partner doesn't think much of politics or politicians."

"Maybe Jace could make a politician with his slick tongue, but leave me out of it. I'll let you two discuss political affairs as I need to find my wife." Excusing himself and glancing at the wagon, Wes realized that Sarafina had disappeared, likely giving in to Luis's desires to play amongst the crowd. It took him a minute to find her and the boy, but he glimpsed them on the other side of the scaffold where Luis ran and giggled near the pine coffin. Wes chuckled when Luis picked up a stone and tossed it at the casket.

As the fateful moment approached, a throng congregated at the foot of the gallows and waited for the condemned to make his appearance. With the time nearing, the cavalry lieutenant led his dozen soldiers, each carrying a carbine propped on his shoulder, to the scaffold and positioned them around the wooden skeleton of the same pine of the coffin's making.

When noon arrived, the courthouse door opened and Wilson marched out, followed by the sheriff, Murphy, and a priest who had ridden up from Mesilla for the occasion. Oddly, Wes thought, Wilson now wore a coat over his original clothing. The murderer wouldn't need a coat where he was going. As people realized the procession of death had begun, they fell silent and watched, men removing their hats and women crossing themselves as the condemned man passed, his eyes widening as each stride brought him closer to the gallows and his mortality. Reaching the steps to the scaffold platform, the priest climbed the thirteen rungs first, then Wilson, followed by the sheriff and Murphy last.

"What's Murphy doing up there?" Wes asked Jace. "He has no authority over this?"

"Must be up to something," Jace answered.

Wes glanced for Sarafina and saw her keeping Luis occupied near the coffin. Next he turned his attention back to the scaffold where the four men had taken their positions on the platform, Wilson standing on the trapdoor, the priest to his right, Murphy to his left, and Sheriff Mills positioning himself in front of the other three.

As the padre blessed the condemned man, Murphy bound his hands and feet, then took the new rope and began to open the hangman's noose wide enough to slip it over Wilson's head.

"By the authority of the Territorial Court of New Mexico," Mills called out to the crowd, "I, Sheriff Alexander Hamilton Mills, am hereby authorized to execute William Wilson for the crime of murder of Robert Casey, a lawful resident of Lincoln County, New Mexico Territory."

Murphy struggled, adjusting the noose, and when he backed away, Wes realized something was amiss. The hangman's knot, rather than resting behind one of Wilson's ears, was centered behind his head. After Murphy nodded to Mills, he backed from

Wilson to the trapdoor lever.

Mills addressed the condemned. "Do you have any last words?"

Wilson nodded. "I was put up to this by —"

"No!" Murphy shouted and yanked the lever.

The trapdoor flung open. Wilson dropped and gasped for air as the stiff rope bit into his neck. Wilson kicked, thrashed, and fell still as the crowd viewed in silence, except for Luis, whose giggles trickled over the hush as he threw stones to amuse himself. For five minutes the body swayed from the end of the noose, the only noise being the whispers of the spectators and Luis's continued laughter. Sheriff Mills stepped to the front of the platform and addressed the throng. "In accordance with the laws of the Territory of New Mexico and by order of the territorial court, this execution has now been completed as directed by law and this proceeding is ended." At that announcement, the cavalry lieutenant ordered his men to march back to the courthouse and their mounts. On the platform, Murphy waved for a dozen of his cronies, and they swarmed the scaffold, four men climbing the steps up to Murphy and the other eight retreating beneath the gallows to retrieve the body.

Though most in the crowd remained curious about what Wilson had planned to say before Murphy yanked the lever, they kept it to themselves, not wanting anyone to know that they suspected the gaunt Irishman had a hand in both Casey's and Wilson's deaths. As the three hundred began to break up, Wes and Jace lingered to offer final condolences to Ellen Casey. Wes motioned for Sarafina to join them, and she grabbed Luis and took him flailing and screaming over to her husband's side as Murphy's men toted the body to the coffin and laid Wilson's remains inside.

As Wes and his wife stepped up to Ellen for a final goodbye, Sarafina lowered Luis to the ground, giving into his tantrum for the sake of propriety in wishing the widow Casey the best now that her husband's killer had been executed. Sarafina approached Mrs. Casey.

Ellen smiled at her. "I remember when my boys had fits like that. Your boy'll outgrow it." She clenched her lips, stepped to Sarafina, and threw her arms around her. "Cherish your husband, Sarafina," she said. "You never realize you could lose him in an instant."

Releasing Sarafina, who at once looked

for Luis, Ellen grabbed Wes's arm. "Thank you for what you did for Bob and all you've done for me and the family now."

"We'll do what we can, Ellen," Wes promised. "Call on us if you need anything."

As Wes stepped aside for Jace to offer his best wishes to the widow, he glanced around for Sarafina and saw her chasing Luis, who was dashing toward the pine coffin where three of Murphy's men squatted beside the box, fiddling with the lid.

Sarafina shouted, *"Alto, Luis, alto."*

Hearing his mother, Luis looked over his shoulder, stumbled, and ran headlong into one of the men placing the cover on the coffin, knocking him off balance. The lid slipped from their hands and fell into the box as Sarafina arrived to pluck her crying son from the ground. She picked him up, glanced in the coffin, and gasped.

Sarafina screamed, *"Los muertos han vuelto a la vida!"* She cradled her son and dashed toward Wes. "The dead has come to life!" Luis wailed louder, frightened by his mother's cry.

Wes ran to his wife, grabbing her shoulders. "What's wrong?"

Bewilderment flooded her face. "He's come back to life, the dead one. His eyes blinked. He gasped for breath."

Believing his wife must surely be mistaken, Wes jumped around her and dashed toward the coffin where six of Murphy's men hastily tried to nail the casket shut. "Remove the lid and back away," Wes shouted. The fellows ignored him until he pulled his pistol and coldcocked one with the barrel of his Colt.

"You heard what he said, boys, so scatter," Jace commanded.

Wes peeked over his shoulder and saw Cousins leveling his rifle at the fellows.

"Me and Mr. Henry are here to help, Wes. Attend your business."

Wiggling his revolver at the other pallbearers, Wes walked to the pine casket, lifted a corner of the cover, and forced free the shallow nails the attendants had started. The deceased fluttered his eyes and heaved for air. He wasn't dead, but he wasn't fully alive either.

Wes turned to Cousins. "Sarafina was right. He's alive. Keep these boys covered." He bent and slipped his hand under Wilson's neck and tried to raise him, but the murderer's body was too stiff to lift with a single hand. After holstering his revolver, Wes grabbed the coat by the lapels and pulled the body up. Wilson moaned. Wes propped him up against the side of the coffin and unbuttoned the coat, sliding it off one arm and yanking it down the other to reveal a metal contraption strapped to his body.

"Watch it, Wes," Jace warned, "here comes the sheriff."

Wes looked around, surprised to see a hundred or more men gathered about him, many with guns drawn.

Sheriff Mills barged through the spectators. "What's going on?" he demanded.

"More Lincoln County chicanery, Sheriff," Wes answered as he yanked Wilson up enough from the pine box for everyone to see the metal frame strapped to his back. At the top of the frame was a metal ring. When Murphy had secured the noose, he had tied it to the ring so that the iron contraption carried the weight of the fall rather than Wilson's neck.

When the spectators realized the execution had been a sham, they chanted. "Hang him again! Hang him again!"

"Back away, Bracken," Mills ordered.

"You back off, Sheriff," countered Cousins. "If shooting starts, you'll die first, Mills."

Murphy pushed his way into the circle. "What's 'appened?" he shouted.

"You dealt justice a crooked hand," Wes

133

answered, aiming his gun at the store owner's heart. "If any firing starts, I'm killing you first. It's time to re-hang Wilson."

"Hang him again! Hang him again!" chanted the crowd.

Wes scanned the throng and realized they outnumbered the sheriff and Murphy's men.

"Ye can't 'ang 'im again. Ye're breaking the law, ye are," Murphy shouted, but he had as much chance of stopping the mob as he did stopping ocean waves with a fork or the wind with a net, as Wes recalled the political kingpin's words at the county convention.

"We've hung him as the law required," Mills shouted. "We can't hang him again."

"The court's order," Jace reminded the lawman, "was to hang him until dead. He ain't dead."

"Hang him again! Hang him again!" cried the mob, four men advancing from the crowd and yanking Wilson to his feet.

"It'll be a lynching if you do," Mills cried, "and I'll arrest every one of you."

"Ye 'eard 'im. Ye'll be 'eld for murder," Murphy shouted.

"Shut up, Murphy," Wes ordered.

"You, too, Sheriff," Jace said.

The four men attending Wilson stripped

off the coat and unbuckled the straps that held the metal harness in place. When the last band was loosened, the iron contraption fell to the ground. The quartet looked to Wes for instructions. When he nodded, the four men began to tug and carry Wilson back to the scaffold. Twice he stumbled and collapsed, and two other men assisted until they reached the thirteen steps to the platform. They grabbed Wilson by the arms and legs and toted him up the stairs. Beneath the gallows, three men pushed up the trapdoor, snapping it in place and re-setting the drop lever.

"Whoever pulls the lever's guilty of murder," Mills shouted. "I'll identify who did it and arrest him after this."

"No you won't," Jace cried, walking over to the sheriff and slamming the stock of his rifle into the sheriff's cheek. The lawman melted into a heap of unconscious flesh at Jace's feet.

"Ye'll pay for this ye will," Murphy threatened until Jace walked over with the butt of his gun ready to strike the jaw of Lincoln County's lead political steer. Murphy cowered as Cousins came within reach.

Jace drew back the Henry ready to strike Murphy, then hesitated and sighed. "I can't coldcock an old man," he said, lowering his weapon. He pondered the situation, then yanked the rifle skyward. "The hell I can't," he said, and slammed the carbine butt into Murphy's pale, goateed jaw. The store owner collapsed to the ground, proving he was as mortal as any other man at the day's proceedings.

By the time Wes moved his gaze from the frail form of L.G. Murphy on the soil to the gallows, one attendant had tightened the noose around Wilson's neck and secured it behind his left ear while two more men held him up, his knees wobbling, though Wes was uncertain if it was from nerves or the foggy state of mind that surely had muddled his brain. Two other men pulled the slack out of the rope and tied it to one of the upright planks that supported the crossbeam. The men holding Wilson stepped back, and the condemned man slumped forward an inch until the rope was taut. "Are you ready?" a man at the lever called to Wes.

"No, not yet," Wes cried, waving his gun at the throng. "As many of you men as possible climb up there with him and screen whoever pulls the lever so the law won't know." Wes counted fifteen men bolting up the stairs and surrounding the others, milling around until the lever clicked and the trapdoor fell away. Wilson plunged through the hole, his neck snapping and his head tilting at an awkward angle toward the noose. This time no one questioned that justice had been served. The men on the platform removed their hats and covered their faces as they exited the scaffold and melded into the crowd that once again started to thin as spectators left individually or in groups.

Ellen Casey walked over and hugged Wes as he slipped his revolver back in his holster. "Thank you," she whispered in his ear and turned to usher her brood back to the wagon for the ride back to the mill.

Juan Patrón approached Wes, grinning widely.

"You're the happiest Republican I've ever seen, Juan."

"*Sí,*" he responded. "The man you slugged by the coffin is the one that shot me in the back." Patrón paused. "A rumor I picked up while waiting for the second hanging is that Alex McSween is quitting as Murphy's lawyer. He might become an ally we can call on."

Wes cocked his head and spat. "Not me. Any man that'd work as long as he did for Murphy's got larceny in his heart. I'd trust Murphy before I would him."

"Perhaps, but McSween and Murphy are

fighting over ten thousand dollars in insurance money. Murphy says it's his while McSween's claiming most of it for the expenses it took him to collect it from a New York insurance company."

"They remind me of rats squabbling over a piece of rotten cheese; everybody comes out of the tussle smelling bad," Wes responded.

Jace pushed the brim of his hat up with the barrel of his gun. "Wes is not too fond of politicians and their ilk."

"Speaking of their type," Wes pointed toward Murphy still cold on the ground and being attended by James J. Dolan. "There's two rats."

Just beyond them, Ham Mills groaned and stirred, trying to arise, first crawling on his hands and knees, then pushing himself to his feet and staggering toward the courthouse.

Dolan stood up and strode over to Wes, Jace, and Patrón. "Who did this?"

"He tripped and fell," Jace replied. "He's getting old and sickly and can't walk like he once did. I tried to help him, I did, even offered him Mr. Henry for a crutch, but he kissed my carbine before he kissed the ground."

"You Mirror B boys'll get what's coming

to you for this," Dolan threatened. "You may think you have friends and allies in Lincoln County, but if you don't have L.G. Murphy on your side, all those folks don't matter."

"John Chisum would disagree with you, Dolan," Wes replied.

"Chisum ain't close enough to be of any help to you and Jace Cousins when Jesse Evans and his men come-a-calling. Remember that, Wes Bracken."

CHAPTER 8

The threats of James J. Dolan shrouded the Mirror B like the low-hanging December clouds that enveloped the Hondo Valley and spat sleet and snow equally upon the righteous and the sinful, the latter outnumbering the former in Lincoln County. In the weeks that followed the execution, Wes Bracken and Jace Cousins hurried to prepare for winter's frigid embrace, cutting and bundling hay, plowing the garden plot to await the spring planting, running the horses for exercise, driving the cattle closer to the ranch house to watch them, chopping firewood, securing the henhouse to discourage hungry winter predators as well as Nip from consuming a chicken dinner, and training Nip and Tuck to announce human predators, starting with Jesse Evans.

Wherever they went, even when handling chores around the new adobe or Wes's bunkhouse, both men carried their long arms and seldom walked within fifty feet of each other so they might protect one another's back in case of an attack. Sarafina worked as much as possible about the place, but she tired easily. Though she still made meals, she fixed the easiest vittles she could and ate what she could, sometimes failing to keep it down. Wes offered to take Sarafina to the doctor at Fort Stanton, but she adamantly refused his suggestion, saying she feared the Murphy-Dolan bunch more than she did her malady. She said she expected her situation to clear up by Christmas day and until then little Luis would be her doctor, his antics and needs always bringing a smile to her face even when she was exhausted.

Though Wes worried over his wife's fatigue, he still had plenty to do before he felt ready for winter's onslaught, including purchasing final supplies and materials such as lumber to build a winter shelter for Nip and Tuck. A week before Christmas, Wes hitched up the mules to the wagon and prepared to head to Casey's store to make his acquisitions, including gifts for Sarafina and Luis. Leaving his wife and boy in the warmth of their house and under Jace's protection, Wes grabbed his coat, hat, and carbine and started the five-mile ride to the

Casey place. The brisk breeze slapped his cheeks with its frigid fingers, and occasional slivers of sleet stung his nose as he headed east past the crossing where the Bonito merged with the Ruidoso to form the Rio Hondo. Few ventured out in the freezing weather, and that was why Wes chose this chilly day for his trip. The fewer folks on the road, the less likely he was to encounter Jesse Evans or any of Murphy's other henchmen. Even so, he remained as attentive to his surroundings as a hungry hawk on the wing. Much of the way, he mulled what to do about Carlos, hoping his brother-in-law would come hat in hand to apologize for his drunkenness. But Carlos could give a jackass lessons in obstinacy, and Wes wondered if he should make the first move at reconciliation as Christmas neared.

Reaching Casey's store, with the wind howling down the valley, Wes secured his team, jumped from his wagon, and scurried inside, startling Ellen as he opened the door and slammed it behind him to block the stiff breeze.

Ellen, again wearing men's clothing, jerked her hand to her mouth in surprise, letting it fall to her side when she recognized Wes.

"I didn't hear you come up," Ellen apologized. "So good to see you, Wes. I've been worried about you and your family with all the threats from Murphy and Dolan's bunch."

"How are you getting by, Ellen?"

Pointing to her attire, she grimaced. "I'm still here, but I'm running scared. Murphy's wanted this place ever since Bob built the mill and added all the improvements, especially the store. I can't afford to buy more goods because I don't have the money. You're the only one that pays cash. The wholesaler Spiegelberg Brothers out of Santa Fe says Bob owes almost three hundred dollars, and I doubt I can repay that. I have one hand plus my boys to manage Bob's four hundred head of cattle and there's no market for them in Lincoln County that John Chisum or L.G. Murphy don't control."

"I've got cash, Ellen," Wes offered. "Not much, but it'll help once I buy a few things for Christmas."

"If everybody paid cash like you, Wes, I might make it, but most everyone else buys on credit or barters. I'm at wits' end to figure what to do. I'm considering moving back to Texas and giving up this land that Bob loved so."

"I'll help any way I can, Ellen," Wes

answered as he unbuttoned his coat and surveyed the shelves and tables that he had never seen so bare of goods. The meager selection proved Ellen had reason to worry. He studied the shelf behind the counter where Casey had always displayed his ammunition for sale. Not a carton of cartridges was visible.

Ellen watched Wes inspect the goods. "It's pathetic, I know, but I have little to offer."

"I was hoping to find something for Sarafina's and Luis's Christmas," Wes said.

"I've got yellow ribbon that would look nice in Sarafina's hair and a tin whistle that Luis would enjoy, though I suspect the rest of you might tire of it quickly. And I've a supply of rock candies you could share. What about for yourself and Jace Cousins?"

"Something practical, but I see you're out of ammunition for our carbines and revolvers."

"Seems everybody's interested in cartridges," Ellen responded. "That's why I hid them and I'm glad I did. Jesse Evans and his boys dropped in last week, wanting to buy every bullet I had in the place."

Wes felt his back stiffen and his jaw clench. He did not realize Jesse and his gang had been so close.

"I could've used the cash," Ellen said,

"but not tainted money like those thieves and murderers carry." She smirked. "I told them you bought every cartridge in the store so maybe they'd think twice about attacking your place."

Coughing, then laughing, Wes sputtered. "I wouldn't want to play cards with you, Ellen, not with that poker face. I'll buy all the ammunition I can afford."

"You're not buying a single bullet from me," Ellen responded, plopping her hands on her hips. "I'm giving you every bullet we don't need here at the mill. It's my Christmas gift to you for seeing Bob's murderer hanged and for paying cash for your purchases. I could sell the cartridges, but I can't trust the other folks in Lincoln County not to use them for mischief."

Wes thanked Ellen, gave her a hug, and made his selections: ten candles for forty cents, three bars of soap for seventy-five cents, two yards of yellow ribbon for sixty cents, a tin whistle for a dime, three tins of sardines for a dollar fifty, a pound of sugar for fifty cents, five pounds of coffee for two-fifty, a quart can of molasses for a dollar, a dozen tins of matches for a dollar twenty, and a pound of rock candy for a dollar.

Ellen totaled up his purchases with a pencil on the worn countertop. "It comes to nine dollars and fifty-five cents."

After counting out eleven dollars from the dozen in his pocket, he pushed the bills toward Ellen. "You keep the difference as a Christmas gift from Sarafina, Luis, and me."

She placed his purchases in a burlap bag, tied the top with twine, and handed the sack to Wes. "You load that up, and I'll retrieve the ammunition."

Wes started for the door, stopped, and turned around. "You got any scrap lumber here? I need to make a shelter for my dogs."

"Can't say, Wes. Just go down by the mill and the barn. You're welcome to whatever you can find."

He toted the bag to the wagon and dropped it in the back, then headed inside. Ellen was loading two more burlap bags with boxes of cartridges she retrieved from beneath the counter. "That's it," she finally said as she tied the mouth of each bag shut. "You must carry these. They're too heavy for me."

Wes grabbed the two sacks by the neck and carried them outside, glad to be well provisioned with ammunition. He dropped one bag beside the wagon and hefted the other into the back. Wes picked up the second and wrestled it beneath the seat next to his carbine. He retreated inside to wish

Ellen a merry Christmas and thank her for the cartridges.

"What does it say about Lincoln County," Ellen asked, "that I'm giving you ammunition to celebrate the birth of the Prince of Peace?"

"Maybe eighteen seventy-seven will turn out better for us all," Wes offered.

"We've been in New Mexico Territory for over seven years and each one's been worse than the last," Ellen said, her words trailing off in defeat.

"Maybe next year will be better for your family and the rest of us." He smiled and strode to the exit, emerging into the brisk breeze that spit raindrops at him as he closed the door. After climbing in the wagon, he started the team toward the barn and mill, finding and loading enough lumber to make a decent shelter for the dogs, then headed back home. He whistled his approach to the house, drawing the growls of Nip and Tuck, who raced out to drive him away before recognizing his scent and the team. The two dogs spun around and escorted Wes and his rig back home.

Jace came out to greet him and help him unload the burlap sacks, grabbing one and yanking it by the neck. "Damn!" he cried. "What have you got in here, an anvil?"

"Cartridges," he replied. "Ellen gave me every spare carton of ammo she had, figuring we'd be able to use it in the coming days."

"I hope one of those bullets has Jesse Evans's name on it."

"As for Jesse, Ellen said he dropped by the store last week, offering to buy her ammunition." Wes laughed as he retrieved his carbine and the sack of cartridges beneath the wagon seat. "Spunky gal that she is, she told him she'd already sold it all to us."

Jace laughed. "Perhaps that's why Jesse hasn't attacked us yet."

The two partners walked into the house together, each carrying a sack of ammunition to the kitchen where Sarafina worked on supper in the corner fireplace. She looked up, surprised. "What have you got that is so heavy?" she asked as Luis ambled into the room and grabbed Wes around the leg, hugging him.

"It's not Christmas gifts," Wes answered as he tried to keep from tripping or hurting Luis as he edged to the table and dropped the bag atop it. "It's bullets."

Sarafina's eyes showed disappointment as Jace placed his sack beside Wes's.

"Don't you worry, Sarafina," interjected Jace. "I've got something for you and for

Luis, even if Wes doesn't."

Wes spun around and rolled his eyes at Jace. "Thanks, partner. That's what she needs to hear. Why don't you bring in the final sack from the wagon, then take the rig to the barn and tend to the team?"

"I was thinking the same thing, Wes. And another thing I've been wondering about is Carlos. We haven't heard from him for a spell. Do you want me to ride over and check on him?"

"That would please me," Sarafina said. *"Extrañé a mi hermano."*

"I know you've missed your brother, but he could've visited us anytime," Wes replied.

"The trip would give me a chance to run my dun, get him a little exercise before the weather gets worse."

Jace left husband and wife in the kitchen while Luis stuck like a tick to Wes's leg, laughing every time his stepfather would shake it.

"You're good with Luis," Sarafina observed. "I wish it were the same with Carlos."

Wes thought of telling Sarafina that her brother was headstrong and destined for a fall if he didn't handle his temper better, but decided not to challenge his wife's feelings for her sibling. Jace came back with the last burlap sack and offered it to Wes, who unloaded the five pounds of coffee, the pound of sugar, the quart of molasses, and the dozen tins of matches. He held back the ten candles, three bars of soap, the trio of sardine tins, the yellow ribbon, the tin whistle, and the rock candy for Christmas day. He unwrapped Luis from his leg, then picked up the burlap bag to remove from the kitchen and hide.

"The bag's not empty. What are you hiding?" Sarafina teased.

Shaking his head, Wes said, "It's your Christmas, and you know it."

"When you return, I must talk with you," Sarafina said.

He carried the sack of gifts plus the two with ammunition into his small office, leaving it in the corner for Christmas day.

When he returned to the kitchen, Sarafina lingered at the table, holding Luis, who reached for Wes with both arms. Wes sat in the chair beside his wife, plopped the boy on his knee, and bounced him up and down, drawing great peals of laughter from the little fellow. From outside came a whistle from Jace as well as the sound of his galloping horse on the way to Carlos's place.

Sarafina smiled. "I must talk to you, *mi esposo.*"

"Go ahead," Wes said, paying more attention to the giggling Luis than her.

"No," Sarafina answered. "You must look at me, if I am to speak. I do not begrudge you for the time you spend with my son."

"Our son," Wes reminded her.

"Yes," she answered, "and next year he will have company."

Wes shook his head. "I don't want Carlos living here. He creates too much tension."

A smile cracked Sarafina's face. "You do not understand, do you, *mi esposo?*"

He stopped shaking Luis on his knee and pondered Sarafina's question. "I reckon not."

"Though I wanted to wait until Christmas, I can no longer hold my excitement, *mi esposo. Estoy con un niño.* I am with child."

For a moment her words failed to penetrate his understanding. Then he realized he would be a father.

"You mean Luis will have a little brother?"

"Or a little sister," Sarafina reminded him.

Wes placed Luis on the floor, arose, and grabbed Sarafina, lifting his wife from her chair and hugging her before releasing his grip. "I didn't hurt you, did I?"

"No, silly," she replied. "I tire easily and my stomach is sometimes queasy but otherwise I am okay."

Wes leaned over and kissed her. "We will have our own son, you and me!"

"It could be a girl," Sarafina reminded him.

"Either way, that's wonderful news, Sarafina," Wes said, releasing her, then motioning for her to sit back down. "You rest since you're doing everything for two now."

Uncertain how to express his pleasure, Wes talked about building a cradle from scrap lumber he brought back from Casey's Mill or taking her to visit Ellen and share the news. A thousand thoughts ran through his mind, as Sarafina stood up and returned to the corner fireplace to finish the tortillas and frijoles she had started for supper.

Within the hour, Jace came back, a frown upon his face. As he entered the kitchen, Wes strode to greet him. "I'm gonna be a father," he announced.

"I know," Jace replied. "Sarafina's been tired and queasy in the morning. I figured it had to be a baby that was sapping her energy."

"You should've told me," Wes countered.

"Why, Wes? I thought you was smart enough to figure it out. Guess I was wrong." He grabbed Wes's hand and shook it firmly. "Congratulations, even if you are the last to know."

Sarafina stepped to Cousins. "What about my brother?"

The merriment stopped.

"I can't say, Sarafina. He wasn't there. It looked as if he had abandoned the place. No fire or embers in the fireplace like you would expect if he was around. I looked around before dusk, but found nothing, not him, not his donkey, nothing."

Sarafina's demeanor clouded with concern.

"Might be he's been staying in San Patricio, finding a *señorita* to cook his meals and feed him," Wes offered.

"We should've checked on him before now. He's little more than a boy, Carlos is. I am so worried." She turned back to the fireplace, squatting before the tin sheet where she cooked her tortillas, and stirred the clay vessel holding the frijoles.

"Tomorrow, Sarafina, I will take you to his place and to San Patricio to see what we can find out, but you must understand he thinks he's a man."

The joy that had sprouted with Sarafina's announcement of the forthcoming birth had washed away with the news of Carlos's absence. They ate in silence except for the babbling of Luis, who sat proudly in his mother's lap, tearing off little pieces of tortilla and dipping them in the frijoles before shoving the bites in his mouth.

After supper they all retired, all lost in their thoughts about Carlos. Come morning, Wes arose early and hitched up the team, hoping to ease Sarafina's anxiety over her lost brother so it would not worry her to the detriment of the child growing within her. The weather remained cloudy and cold, but Sarafina bundled herself and Luis in the thickest clothes they had, then cocooned themselves in wool blankets once Wes helped them into the wagon. He pulled himself aboard after checking that his Winchester was nearby.

"You sure you don't want me to go along?" Jace asked. "Mr. Henry could come in handy, Wes."

"You watch the Mirror B and the horses, Jace. We'll make a quick run no further than San Patricio and return as soon as we can." He rattled the reins and the mules started up the road toward Carlos's place, never encountering another person on the way. At his brother-in-law's adobe, Wes whistled his arrival and called for Carlos. The only answer was the shrill of the wind. No smoke wafted from the chimney and no donkey wandered the corral. The place appeared just as Jace had seen it, abandoned and forlorn.

He pulled up to the front, tied the lines to the mules and jumped down, quickly approaching the house and pushing the door open. Entering the house, he found the corner fireplace cold. Carlos had never had much and even less remained in the dwelling. His coat and hat were missing as was his bedding and the Winchester '73 that Wes had given him. Wes stepped outside, closed the door and turned to his wife. "He's gone, Sarafina, and it appears he's taken his belongings."

"I can't believe he left without telling us. Maybe he's in San Patricio."

Though he doubted it, Wes nodded and climbed back into the wagon for the short ride to the little Mexican enclave. As they rode into the village, they passed the cemetery where Sarafina's first husband was buried. "We'll stop on the way out of town," Wes told his wife.

"Gracias," she replied.

They spent a half hour in the village asking the few people outside if they knew of Carlos's whereabouts. The Mexicans were cordial but lacked any information. At one of the town's two cantinas, Wes roused the proprietor and asked if he had seen Carlos.

155

"No en cinco o seis días," the owner answered.

Wes asked for clues where Carlos had gone and if he had left with anyone.

"Se fue con Billy el Niño."

"¿Adónde?" Wes asked, trying to decide where Carlos and Bonney went.

The heavyset proprietor shrugged. *"Dónde había más señoritas y licor más barato."*

"Gracias," Wes said, figuring that it sounded about right that Bonney and Carlos would go where there were more girls and cheaper liquor. *"Buenos dias."* Wes tipped his hat at the proprietor and exited the cantina.

Back at the wagon, he climbed in beside Sarafina, who was holding Luis to her bosom to keep him warm. "Carlos was spotted with Billy Bonney a week ago and hasn't been seen since." Sarafina nodded, but said nothing more. Wes turned the rig around and drove back through San Patricio, stopping on the village outskirts so Sarafina could visit the grave of Bonifacio Zamora, her first husband. Wes helped his wife and Luis from the wagon and watched as they moved reverently among the wooden crosses and occasional stone markers that identified the last resting place of Sarafina's people. Sarafina lowered her and Zamora's son to the ground, knelt, and crossed herself before leaning over and kissing the white cross. She held Luis's hand and explained to him that his father was buried at this spot. Too young to understand, Luis walked over and kissed the wooden marker as he had seen his mother do. Sarafina arose, picked up Luis, and marched back to the wagon, never looking at Wes, who suspected she was hiding her tears.

Wes took Luis and boosted him up onto the seat before turning to help Sarafina into the wagon. He strode around to the other side, stepped on a spoke of the front wheel, and crawled into place, taking the reins and starting the wagon back toward the Mirror B after a trip that was as fruitless as Wes had expected. "I'm sorry," he said as they drove away. She said nothing. Wes could only guess she was emotional over visiting her late husband's grave and concerned about Carlos's safety. They rode wordlessly back home, and Sarafina seemed distracted or queasy, Wes unable to determine if it was from her pregnancy or from worry over Carlos's fate.

A pall fell over Sarafina for the next six days, even as she prepared for their modest Christmas celebration. Jace cut a sapling about three feet tall and stood it up in the parlor's corner, decorating it with stars, crosses, and ovals he sliced from tin cans he found around the place. Wes built the shelter for Nip and Tuck from the scrap lumber he had brought back from Casey's Mill. Then he spent time in his little room sorting out the ammunition bequeathed to him by Ellen Casey. He totaled more than fifty cartons of cartridges for various weapons, including bullets that would work in his Winchester carbine, Jace's Henry rifle, and both of their Colt revolvers. Even if some of the ammunition did not fit their weapons, at least the cartridges wouldn't fall into the hands of those that might use them against the Mirror B. He divided out the presents for everyone, ready to offer the meager gifts to Luis, Sarafina, and Jace.

On Christmas eve, Sarafina emerged from the melancholy she had experienced after Carlos's disappearance. Or, maybe it was the knowledge that her body was showing signs of the baby within her. Wes never knew, just leaving her to find herself and deal with the emotions until her former persona returned.

They went to bed early as the winter winds howled through the valley. Come morning, Jace came to the adobe from his bunkhouse, carrying his Henry rifle in one hand and a burlap sack in the other. As he was up before Wes and Sarafina, he added wood to the fireplace in the kitchen and the one in the front room, warming the house for Wes's family. He started a pot of coffee and settled into a chair by the table waiting for the brew to boil. Wes soon joined him, and they enjoyed their cups together, reminiscing about Christmases when they were kids.

As they laughed, Sarafina came into the kitchen, yawning and smiling. "Merry Christmas," she said.

Then Nip and Tuck took to barking outside.

As the two dogs snarled, Jace grabbed his Henry and ran to the front door while Wes raced to his office to get his Winchester. Jace cracked the door and made out two approaching riders in the early morning gloom. Wes scurried beside Jace, looking over his shoulder.

"Dammit," Jace whispered. "It'd be just like Jesse Evans and his gang to attack us on Christmas morning."

"Nothing surprises me in Lincoln County," Wes replied.

Jace nodded. "I'll slip out the back door and make sure no one's approaching from the rear. If not, I'll slide around to the side of the house so we can shoot them from two angles. Count to thirty and ask them who they are and what's their business."

Jace slipped away while Wes edged closer to the door and peeked through the crack. He counted to thirty, then called out to the visitors. "State your name and business."

"We come as friends," answered a voice distorted by the winds.

"I still don't know your names."

"Billy Bonney and friend," came the voice again. "And tell your fellow at the corner of the house not to shoot. If he does, it'll be the last mistake he ever makes."

"Ease off, Jace," Wes called.

"You sure you can trust him?" Jace asked.

"Sure he can," Bonney answered for Wes. "I'm the most trustworthy fellow in Lincoln County. Just call your dogs off."

Wes whistled. "Nip, Tuck, behave."

Jace called the dogs, too, and led them around to the back of the house as Bonney and his friend dismounted.

Bonney took his carbine from his saddle and untied something hanging from the saddle horn. He stepped toward the door, his accomplice sliding in behind him.

Unnerved that the fellow kept hiding behind Bonney, Wes called, "Identify your friend."

"You know him," Bonney said, stepping aside.

A shy smile across his lips, Carlos walked into Wes's view.

CHAPTER 9

"Carlos!" Sarafina screamed and brushed past her husband, running out into the frigid air to hug her brother. "You're safe," she cried. "My prayers have been answered." She grabbed her sibling and yanked him inside by the arm, drawing a grin from Bonney.

As Carlos strode in, Wes noted that he was wearing a gun belt and revolver.

Bonney held up a turkey gobbler by the legs. "Christmas dinner! I'll even clean it for us."

"Let me get my coat," Wes replied, "and I'll help with that and getting your mounts in the barn." He closed the door, fetched his jacket, pulled it around him, and buttoned it before grabbing his hat, tugging it tight. He exited into the cold, quickly closing the house behind him. He shook his head as he joined Jace and Bonney. He stared at the two horses. "Last I knew,

Carlos was riding a donkey."

The Kid grinned. "I've instructed him in horse-trading, just as you taught me a grave lesson the last time we visited."

"Like what, Billy? You were too intoxicated to remember." Wes grabbed the reins of Carlos's gelding, realizing the animal lacked a saddle.

"How can I help?" Jace asked.

Bonney offered his reins to Cousins. "If you'll tend my horse, I'll clean our turkey." The Kid turned to Wes. "You taught me never to get so drunk that I'd let another man take my pistol. It took me half an hour to find my revolver outside the door where you threw it."

"Why's Carlos wearing a pistol now?" Wes asked.

"Anybody that rides with me should be armed," Bonney explained, "especially when we are returning stolen horses to their owners. Some fellows might get the wrong idea, just as you did a while back." The Kid grinned widely. "Let me dress this turkey, and then we'll talk, as I've got news for you." He turned to Cousins. "Mind if I feed the innards to the dogs?"

Jace hesitated. "One of them has an appetite for poultry, killing a hen or two. Not sure it's a good idea."

"It's Christmas," Bonney countered. "Give the dogs a fine dinner for a change."

Shrugging, Jace nodded. "Go ahead." He and Wes headed to the barn while Bonney veered off toward the stream to clean the turkey.

"Do you trust him?" Cousins asked Wes as they opened the barn door and led the two animals inside where they kept their breeding stock to protect them from the weather.

Wes stopped and contemplated for a moment. "I like him as there's something in his easygoing ways and that bucktoothed smile, but I can't say that I trust him. I'm worried that Carlos has taken to riding with him. Could mean trouble for them both."

"You worry too much, Wes."

They tied the two geldings in a stall and checked on their breeding stock before retreating outside into the wintry air. By the Rio Ruidoso Bonney had plucked and gutted the turkey, leaving the offal on the ground for Nip and Tuck to gobble up.

"Do you think Bonney's feeding the hounds to keep them from barking next time he rides up?" Jace asked.

"You worry too much," Wes echoed Jace, drawing a laugh.

The partners waited for Bonney to catch

up with them, then escorted him and the turkey to the house.

"Now your dogs like me," Bonney said. "What's their names?"

"Nip and Tuck," Jace responded.

"What news do you bring from Lincoln?" Wes wanted to know.

Bonney grinned. "The sheriff's left the county."

"Ham Mills?" Wes asked.

"That's the one," Bonney replied. "Gossip has it that Murphy was furious about Willie Wilson's hanging as he'd planned to spirit Wilson out of the county. Murphy blamed Mills for botching the execution and not removing the coffin before Wilson was discovered alive. The rumor going around is that Murphy had a prisoner in jail killed to set up the sheriff for the fellow's death. Rather than face contrived murder charges, Mills ran off."

"Who'll replace him?" Jace asked.

"Word has it William Brady'll be the next sheriff," Bonney answered. "He's been sheriff before and is Murphy's pal. So, nothing'll change in Lincoln County."

"That's a shame," Wes responded.

"There's something else I came to tell you boys. Jesse Evans has been making threats about attacking your place as soon as the weather clears."

"That could be tomorrow or two months from now," Wes said as much to himself as his companions.

"Jimmy Dolan's been putting him up to it, so they say," Bonney continued. "Word of mouth is Dolan hates you. Seems to me, Wes, you're just not that likable a fellow."

"We don't all have your charm, Billy," Wes responded.

They marched to the back of the house and entered through the kitchen door, welcoming the warmth and the smiles of Sarafina and Carlos. Luis sat at the table still trying to rub the sleep from his eyes.

Bonney lifted the dressed turkey for everyone to see, and Sarafina jumped from her chair and motioned for him to place the bird on the griddle she used to cook tortillas. Wes stared at Sarafina, glad that Carlos had reappeared in her life, if only briefly, as Bonney was too much of a vagabond to stay at one place too long. If Carlos had given up farming to ride with Billy Bonney, he faced an uncertain and precarious future.

Sarafina offered everyone cold tortillas for breakfast. When her guests finished, Sarafina herded them into the front room, Wes excusing himself to go into his office and fetch the burlap bag of gifts. He placed the bag by the modest tree and returned to the kitchen to bring in two chairs, offering one to Sarafina and sitting beside her in the other as Bonney, Carlos, and Jace seated themselves on stools. Sarafina smiled constantly at Carlos. *"Lo que se perdió ahora se encuentra,"* she said. "What was lost now is found."

As Carlos nodded at his sister, Wes studied his brother-in-law, uncertain how to deal with him. As Wes pondered, Jace interrupted his thoughts.

"Since this is your home, Wes, you need to say a few words before we hand out gifts," Jace reminded him.

Wes acquiesced. "It is a pleasant surprise to have two guests join our family on this special day and provide us with a turkey."

"You're welcome," answered Bonney.

"It's a season of giving, and Sarafina has already given me a great gift," Wes began, staring at Carlos as he spoke. "She's let me know she is with child."

Carlos's smile soured. He scowled at his Anglo brother-in-law.

Wes turned to Sarafina, who grimaced as she looked at her brother. "We are *all* happy at this gift from God, *aren't we,* Carlos?"

Her brother played deaf.

"Aren't we, Carlos?" she said more emphatically.

Offering but a slight nod, Carlos turned his gaze toward Bonney, who tendered his congratulations. "That's about as good news as any of us ever get in Lincoln County."

Wes picked up his burlap sack and untied the neck, slipping his hand inside and pulling out the three tins of sardines. He had planned to share them with Sarafina and Jace, but with the unexpected guests he decided instead to give his and his wife's tins to Carlos and Bonney. He tossed a tin to Jace, another to Bonney, and the third to Carlos. "Merry Christmas."

Bonney grinned. "Obliged, but we didn't bring you anything."

"You brought the turkey and news," Wes replied. "That's plenty."

Jace thanked his partner, stood up, and stepped to the modest tree. From behind it he pulled a stick horse. "I made this one for our little vaquero," he said as he offered it to Luis, who reluctantly took it, looking at his mother for directions.

"It's a horse, Luis. You can ride it, but first thank Uncle Jace," Sarafina said.

The two-year-old stepped toward Jace, lowered his head, and stared at the floor. *"Gracias,"* he offered.

"You're welcome, little one. Now ride your horse." Luis looked confused, so Jace slipped the toy from between his fingers and put it between his legs. "Giddyup," Jace called and began to walk by the tree astride the gift. Luis looked up, grinned, grabbed the stick horse, lifted a leg over it, and galloped around the room, his smile growing wider with each step.

Jace stepped to the tree, squatted, and picked up something else, which he hid behind his back as he walked over to Sarafina. He extended his arm, and Sarafina took a hand mirror from his fingers. "That's for including me at your table and washing my clothes when they need it."

"*Gracias,* Jace," Sarafina responded.

He nodded. "If you don't mind, I like Uncle Jace better."

Sarafina smiled. "*Gracias,* Uncle Jace."

Wes shoved his hand back in the burlap bag and extracted a bundle of candles, offering them to Sarafina. "These will provide more light for you." Next he pulled out the soap bars, offering the first to Sarafina, tossing the second to Jace, and keeping the third for himself. "Sorry, fellows, but I don't have enough to go round, though you both could use more baths," he said to Bonney and Carlos.

The Kid snickered, but Carlos glared at him.

Reaching back in the burlap sack, Wes took out the bag of rock candy. "This is for everyone," he announced, offering it to Sarafina, who took a piece for herself and Luis, then passed it to Jace, who shared it with their two visitors.

As they distributed the candy, Wes extracted another gift. "I fear this may be a mistake, but it was the only thing they had at Casey's for a toy." He displayed the tin whistle.

Jace recognized it. "I'm glad to be sleeping in the bunkhouse."

Wes grabbed Luis on his next pass around the room and offered him the toy. Luis shook his head. Wes put the toy to his lips and blew. "Threeeet, threeeet," trilled the whistle. Luis's eyes widened. Grabbing the toy, he shoved it to his mouth. "Threeeet, threeeet, threeeet," he blew, then grinned and kicked his stick horse into another gallop, blowing on his whistle as he ran.

Sarafina shook her head. "He likes it. I'm not sure about the rest of us."

Wes pulled the yellow ribbon from the burlap sack and offered it to his wife. "I thought this would look nice in your hair." As she took the gift, she let her fingers linger on his, squeezing them softly and lifting the band to her raven locks. Wes saw her eyes glistening and knew his gesture touched her. Sarafina ran her fingers through her black hair, lifted the back, and slid the yellow band under her tresses, tying it atop her head.

"Gracias, mi esposo," she said when she finished straightening the bow.

They visited for a half hour while Luis scurried around the parlor, riding his stick horse and tooting on the whistle. Saying she must fix their dinner, Sarafina arose. When she disappeared into the next room, Wes turned to Bonney.

"What more do you know about Jesse?" he asked.

"Just that Dolan wants him to attack your place as soon as he can. Rumor has it Murphy's too sick to run things anymore. Supposedly, bowel cancer is eating him up."

Jace stood up and paced back and forth in front of Wes, turning to his partner. "All we're doing is waiting on them to move against us. We've been looking over our shoulders ever since the hanging, Wes. We know it's coming. Either we can stay here and wait, or we can go looking for him and settle it on our terms." Jace pounded his fist in his open palm.

Wes hesitated. "I've got a family to consider."

Bonney stood up between the two men. "I'm with Jace on this. I'd trust a rattlesnake before I would Jesse Evans."

Wes paced back and forth in the room as Luis continued to ride his stick horse and blow on his tin whistle. Wes picked him up and carried him to the kitchen, leaving him with his momma. When he returned to the parlor, Carlos announced, "I'll defend my sister and nephew with everything I've got."

Catching the omission of his name, Wes pinched the bridge of his nose. He had a responsibility to his wife, his stepson, and the new baby. "We can't bargain with the devil."

Jace stepped over and threw his arm over Wes's shoulder. "I'm with you, partner, as long as you're against Jesse. I couldn't stomach you riding with him."

"You think differently when you've got a family to protect," Wes answered. He turned to Bonney and Carlos. "I wish I had the money to hire you both to work the place, especially the cattle, and provide some extra eyes and guns in case of trouble."

"I'm riding with Billy," Carlos said. "It's better than farming."

"You haven't farmed in quite a spell," Jace said.

Wes looked at Bonney, then his brother-in-law. "You could get by farming the place you abandoned, Carlos. Billy could work, too. You'd have shelter through the winter and spring."

"I'm done digging in dirt," Carlos said. "Billy's showed me life can be more fun than working fields."

"You won't earn a living returning stolen horses to their owners." Wes eyed Billy.

The Kid grinned. "We make more money when we don't find the rightful owner, but I may be near lining up something for Carlos and me."

"It better not be a job with the House," Wes warned.

"No, sir, it's not," Bonney replied. "There's a new man with money in Lincoln, a young Englishman, looking to start a ranch, maybe even open a store and a bank."

"The House won't go for that," Wes answered.

"That's not stopping him from trying. His name's John Henry Tunstall. He's partnering up with the lawyer McSween."

Wes's enthusiasm for Tunstall's plans died with the mention of the lawyer. "Alex

McSween worked for L.G. Murphy awhile, doing the House's dirty work with a pen and paper instead of a gun. I don't trust McSween or any man partnering with him."

Bonney shrugged. "If Tunstall purchases land and cattle, he'll be looking for hands. Word has it he'll pay a dollar a day to his hires."

"A partnership with McSween will just lead to trouble," Wes answered.

Jace laughed. "Everything leads to trouble in Lincoln County."

Wes looked from Jace to Bonney and Carlos. "You two understand that if Tunstall hires you, he's wanting your guns more than your experience working cattle."

"Makes no difference to me, as long as I get paid," Bonney responded.

"I ride with Billy," Carlos added.

"You boys need to be careful you don't dig a hole you can't climb out of," Wes warned.

Bonney laughed. "It don't matter how deep the hole is as long as I can shoot my way out of it."

Luis scampered back into the room on his stick horse, though Sarafina must have taken the tin whistle away as he no longer tooted it. His mother entered after him. "I have our dinner ready," she said as she moved to retrieve the two kitchen chairs. Wes and Bonney headed her off and each grabbed a seat, following her into the kitchen. Jace grabbed a pair of stools from the parlor and followed the others.

Sarafina had a platter of sliced turkey she had roasted over the fire, bowls of boiled corn and frijoles, plus the customary tortillas. Sarafina grabbed Luis and took the stick horse away from him, placing it in the corner. She lifted her son and stepped to the table where the men stood. When she nodded at her husband, Wes bowed his head and blessed the food and the occasion. After the amen, Wes motioned for their guests to sit and help themselves first. Bonney and Carlos filled their plates, then Wes and Jace as Sarafina fed Luis pieces of turkey she had cut to cool. She served her plate, smiling at how much everyone enjoyed the meal. When the men had polished off the turkey, corn, and frijoles, Sarafina put Luis down and fetched the tin of molasses her husband had bought at Casey's store. To finish the meal with a sweet, she offered tortillas with molasses, again drawing compliments from her diners. When they finished, Sarafina fetched a dishpan, but before she could fill it with hot water from the kettle in the fireplace, Wes sent her to the front room with Carlos.

"Visit with your brother," he said, taking the pad from her hand and emptying the kettle in the dishpan. Wes picked up a rag and began to scrub the utensils and dishes.

Bonney laughed. "You'd make some ol' boy a good wife, the way you handle a dishrag!"

"Do me a favor, Kid. Go see what the weather's doing, will you?" Wes asked.

Smirking, Bonney answered, "Whatever you say, ma'am."

"You help him, Jace, and let me know what you think. Something's gnawing at me."

The two men stepped outside, taking their time before returning ten minutes later.

"It's clearing off," Bonney reported.

"Sun's breaking through the clouds, and it's warming up," Jace added. "We should have four hours of strong sun with the temperatures rising. What's been bothering you?"

Wes bit his lip and cocked his head. "Billy said Jesse and his gang were planning to attack our place soon as the weather broke. Why wait? The mist and fog we've been having in the mornings would make it easier to disappear after an assault. It makes little sense."

"That's what I heard," Bonney interjected.

"I believe you, Billy," Wes said, "but I can't figure out why."

"They didn't want to freeze their butts off in the attack," Bonney offered.

"Maybe they were stalling Dolan," Jace suggested "and never intended to raid us."

Wes twisted his head from side to side. "That doesn't sound like Jesse."

"You're right," Jace acknowledged.

Wes gave up trying to figure out the devious plans of the House and Evans. "Let's visit with Carlos and Sarafina," he suggested.

"I'll join you in a moment," Jace said, exiting out the back door.

Bonney accompanied Wes into the front room, each carrying a chair from the kitchen. They plopped their chairs on the floor opposite Carlos and Sarafina, Wes sitting down normally while Bonney turned the chair away from the siblings, straddled the seat, propped his arms on the back, and rested his chin on his shirtsleeves. Luis purred as he walked around the room astride his stick horse, though it was clear he was growing tired even if his mount wasn't.

When Jace returned, he brought in a third seat and a well-worn black book Wes suspected to be a Bible. "I thought I might read the Christmas story," Jace offered.

"I didn't know you was a religious man," Wes commented.

Jace managed a small shrug. "I had two years where I had plenty of time to read. The Bible was the only thing I had to pass the time and keep me sane, though I admit I'm more of an Old Testament than a New Testament fellow, at least until I get Jesse Evans. Once he's dead, perhaps the New Testament will make more sense to me like the passage, 'vengeance is mine; saith the Lord.' "

Sarafina called for Luis to come to her chair, and he rode over. She gently lifted him from the toy and held him in her lap. He rested his head against his mother's bosom as Jace Cousins began to read from the second chapter of Luke: "And Joseph also went up from Galilee, out of the city of Nazareth, into Judaea, unto the city of David, which is called Bethlehem; . . . to be taxed with Mary his espoused wife, being great with child. And so it was, that, while they were there, the days were accomplished that she should be delivered. And she brought forth her firstborn son, and wrapped him in swaddling clothes, and laid him in a manger; because there was no room for them in the inn." Next Jace read of the shepherds in the field and the multitude of heavenly hosts proclaiming, Glory to God in the highest, and on earth peace and goodwill toward men.

Everyone listened reverently, lost in their thoughts of Christmases past. When Jace completed his reading and closed his Bible, Wes said, "Amen," the others echoing his word as he turned to Bonney and Carlos, "After hearing that, I'm obliged to offer you boys a place at the inn. Carlos, you can sleep in our house and, Billy, you can bunk with Jace in the bunkhouse."

"Sounds fine by me," Bonney replied. Carlos went along with whatever Billy wanted.

"Good then, unsaddle your horses," Wes said.

"Carlos doesn't own a saddle, and I'm leaving mine where it is so we can head out early tomorrow for Lincoln to see if Tunstall's decided whether he'll be hiring hands," Billy answered.

They visited until darkness set in; then Carlos and Bonney retreated to the barn to collect their bedrolls and returned to their assigned quarters. Wes took the sleeping Luis from his wife's arms and carried him to his bed, gently placing him down and

179

leaving the stick horse by his side while Sarafina drew the blanket over him.

Sarafina took her husband's arm and pulled him to their bed, kissing him on the cheek. "Thank you for a wonderful Christmas. The greatest gift was seeing Carlos again."

"I worry about him running around with Bonney," Wes replied as they prepared for bed.

"He thinks he's a man," Sarafina responded, "though we know he's not. We must trust God to protect Carlos."

Wes retired with his wife, and they slept soundly until an hour before dawn when Nip and Tuck began to bark, howl, and growl. The noise took a moment to register. Wes shook himself awake, thinking the dogs must've encountered a varmint.

Suddenly, a gunshot exploded outside, then another.

Wes rolled out of bed and scampered into his office where he had left his pistol and Winchester. After slapping the gun belt around his union suit and buckling it at the waist, he grabbed his Winchester and raced to the front door, cracking it and firing blindly at his attackers.

A gunshot answered him and a bullet thudded into the door.

Carlos rushed to Wes's side, his Winchester in his hands. "What is it?" he cried.

"I don't know," Wes called as he fired off another shot.

Next a flurry of shots sounded from the bunkhouse toward the assailants.

"Come out and fight in the open, Jace Cousins," called a voice Wes recognized as belonging to Jesse Evans.

Wes flung open the door, stepped outside, and fired three shots, sending the horsemen riding. Wes counted five horses.

Jace came running from the barn. "Let's saddle up and get them."

"I've got a bad feeling about this," Wes replied.

They heard other horses trotting over from the barn.

"Don't shoot," cried Bonney, reining up hard in front of Wes and Jace, plus Carlos, who had stepped out with them. Billy tossed Carlos his reins. "Come on," he cried, "let's get them."

"Watch out for an ambush," Wes warned as Carlos clambered atop his gelding and started after Bonney, who rode like a cat with his tail on fire.

"I'll saddle up to help," Jace volunteered.

Wes grabbed his arm. "No, get a carton of

cartridges for Mr. Henry. We're staying here."

CHAPTER 10

As Jace Cousins raced for more ammunition, Wes retreated to his bedroom, tossing his Winchester on the bed, removing his gun belt from around his union suit, and pulling on his britches and shirt, then tugging his boots over his sockless feet. He slid into his coat.

Sarafina ran into the room, cradling Luis in her arms. "What is it?" she gasped.

"Not sure," Wes replied, buckling his holster back on, "but you stay in here with Luis. If you hear gunfire, drop to the floor and remain there until I tell you otherwise."

Reclaiming his Winchester, he scurried into his office and got a carton of cartridges he stuck in his coat pocket. As he emerged into the front room, Jace rejoined him.

"It sounded too obvious," Wes explained. "Jesse identifying himself and trying to bait us to leave the house. Let's take positions outside, you by the bunkhouse and me by the barn. Bird whistle if you spot something."

Jace nodded. "I'll shoot and ask questions later." He raced through the kitchen and out the back.

Wes headed for the front door, sticking his head out to survey the surroundings. Seeing nothing, he sprinted to the corncrib, taking up a position behind it so he could watch both the barn and the road. He waited and fidgeted, uncertain if his intuition had been right, fearful that the Kid and Carlos had ridden into an ambush intended for him and Cousins. Time dissolved into the darkness, and Wes no longer could differentiate between seconds and minutes. As the sky behind the eastern mountain ridges began to pinken, Wes observed twin pinpoints of light approaching along the road. At first Wes feared he was hallucinating, but the lights gradually grew bigger and bounced as they neared, as if they were being carried on horseback.

Wes exhaled slowly, distinguishing in the glow of the torches two men astride their mounts. Suddenly, it made sense. The attackers intended to torch the place. The earlier assault on the house was a ruse to draw Wes and Jace away so these arsonists could set fire to the buildings with no regard for the lives of Sarafina and Luis. These Murphy men had waited for the cloud cover to break and the moisture to evaporate so the buildings would burn easier. Wes whistled softly toward Jace. "Threet-threet! Threet-threet!"

Cousins answered. "Threet-threea! Threet-threea!"

Wes moved in a crouch from the corncrib to the corner of the barn, dropped to a knee, and lifted the Winchester to his shoulder. Inside the shelter, the horses, catching a whiff of flame and danger, stamped and whinnied. Anger boiled over in him like an untended coffee pot over a fire. These men sought to harm his family and destroy everything he had built. Wes had tried to do it the honest way, but Lincoln County worked against what was right and righteous.

Onward came the two riders. Wes fought the temptation to fire, but he wanted them near enough to make a sure shot, but the closer they approached, the greater the risk that one of their torches might reach the barn and set it ablaze. Wes waited and inhaled deeply, hoping Jace held his shots until he could shoot first.

The men rode within fifty yards of the barn.

Wes debated whether to maim or kill. He'd had enough killing back in the war, but these men were threatening his family and his livelihood.

Twenty-five yards.

Wes leveled his Winchester at the nearest one, aiming for the shoulder of the arm that carried the torch. His finger slid over the trigger.

Twenty yards.

Wes squeezed the trigger. The carbine exploded. The closest rider screamed, dropping his torch and grabbing his shoulder. "Ambush," he shouted.

The second rider jerked his horse to a stop. Another shot pierced the early morning air as Jace fired his rifle. His target crumpled over in the saddle, releasing the flaming shaft that scorched his mount's forelegs as the fire fell to the ground. The animal reared in the air when Jace squeezed off two more shots. The gelding bawled as bullets thudded into its hide.

As the wounded arsonist spun his mount around, Wes followed his target with the sight of his Winchester and fired again. The man screamed, grabbing his leg as the terrified horse dashed for safety. Wes fired another shot, but the attacker hunkered low over the saddle as his horse took a crooked course back to the road.

Jace raced from his position toward the flickering torches that marked the closest spot the two assailants had come to the barn. Wes watched him fire one, two, three shots at the retreating attackers as they disappeared into the long shadows of dawn in the Ruidoso Valley.

"If he doesn't die," Jace shouted, "mine'll wake up with a bellyache in the morning. Fear I hurt his horse as well."

Wes jumped up from his knee and sprinted with his partner toward the torches, which had set a patch of dry vegetation to smoldering. Each man grabbed a torch from the ground and stomped out the tiny flames licking at the yellow grass.

"Best I could tell, I got mine in the shoulder and the thigh," Wes explained, inspecting the soil to confirm the sparks had been smothered. Certain the fire had been extinguished, Wes and Jace walked to the stream and doused the burning rags at the end of the torches.

"How do you think Carlos and Bonney made out, Wes?"

"Bonney's cagey. He'll manage as will Carlos, if he stays with the Kid."

They lifted the scorched shafts from the water and started back to the house.

"How'd you know the first attack was a ruse?"

"Just instinct. Something wasn't right with Jesse identifying himself and calling you out. He's more of a back-shooter. Now we need to find Bonney and Carlos."

Cousins nodded. "I've heard no gunshots from that direction."

"I figure they didn't want to make a stand within hearing range of the Mirror B. I suspect they led Bonney and Carlos well past San Patricio."

"Maybe so. I think I'll saddle my dun and check downriver to see if either of our attackers fell on the road. After that I'll ride to San Patricio and look for the Kid and Carlos."

Wes nodded. "Let me check on my family, then I'll join you."

The men parted, Wes jogging to the house and Jace stepping inside the barn. Wes opened the front door and entered, propping his Winchester by the entrance.

"Sarafina," he called, "the shooting's over."

As he marched into the bedroom, his wife arose from the floor, trembling and holding her whimpering son. *"¿Estás bien, mi esposo?"* she asked.

"I am fine, Sarafina. So is Jace."

"Gracias a Dios," his wife answered, putting Luis on the bed and stepping across the room into Wes's arms. *"¿Cuándo terminará?"* she asked. "When will it ever end?"

Wes hugged his wife. "One day, Sarafina, it will conclude but only God knows when that day will come."

She began to cry. "I hoped the *diablos* would stop picking on me once I married an Anglo, but they are as vicious to their own kind as they are to my people," Sarafina gasped. "And Carlos? What about Carlos?"

"I don't know. Jace and I will find him."

Sarafina broke from his grasp. "Then go, go now and find him."

"Bonney'll watch out for Carlos."

"Perhaps, but you will protect him. Please go." She motioned toward the front as she turned her attention to Luis, fidgeting on the bed.

Wes hesitated to leave Sarafina and Luis alone, should Jesse Evans double back, but decided that was impossible with Bonney on the outlaw's tail. Wes marched off, grabbing his Winchester and heading for the barn where he saddled Charlie and reloaded his carbine before shoving it in its saddle scabbard. He led the stallion out of the shelter, looking around at his breeding

189

stock, which had calmed since the attack. It angered him that his enemies would burn his barn and kill his horses without a single pang of conscience.

The light of early morning began to brighten the sky as Wes climbed atop Charlie and headed for the road. Ever alert, he scanned the countryside for any place that assassins might hide, then turned to the east toward Casey's Mill. A half mile down the road, he met Jace holding something in front of him. From the size of the object, Wes first thought it was the body of an attacker, but as he got closer, he realized his load lacked legs and arms. As Jace neared, Wes realized he was balancing a saddle between his stomach and the dun's head.

Wes drew back the reins on Charlie and waited in the road for his partner to join him.

Jace nodded. "Sorry to say my bullets killed one horse, but the attackers escaped." He pointed to the tack. "I stripped this from the carcass, thinking Carlos might use it instead of riding bareback."

"We'll drop it off at the corral, then find Carlos," Wes suggested.

They retreated to the barn where Jace draped the saddle over the top rail of the adjoining fence. After that, they started at a trot toward San Patricio. Townsfolk were just rising when Wes and Jace passed through. They moved at a steady lope, making the best time they could without exhausting their horses. When they were beyond the village, the sun cleared the mountains and the sunlight invigorated their ride, warming their muscles and improving their spirits, though the farther they rode the more concerned they became of the fate of Bonney and Carlos.

"We were lucky," Wes told Jace, "they were with us. Jesse must've thought we were chasing him."

"Bonney and Carlos saved our place and maybe even our lives," Jace responded.

The two partners covered a couple miles with no sight or sound of Bonney and Carlos until they rounded a bend in the road and spotted three riders a half mile away approaching at a canter. Both men reached for their long guns until Wes recognized Bonney's gray and Carlos's brown gelding, but not the mount of the stranger riding with them.

Wes pushed his carbine back in its scabbard, though Jace removed his Henry and held it against his thigh as the trio approached. Wes and Jace brought their mounts to a stop in the middle of the road as the three neared.

Bonney grinned and yelled. "You boys took your sweet time joining us. Fact is, you missed the dance."

"You look none the worse for the encounter," Wes replied. "Was it Jesse Evans?"

The Kid nodded. "Him and three others. They planned to ambush you, but when they realized it was me and Carlos, they were as confused as an Indian at a spelling bee, finally apologizing for shooting at us." Bonney laughed.

Jace lifted his Henry and waved it toward Carlos. "We found you a saddle."

"He manages okay bareback," Billy answered.

Carlos nodded. "I learned it from living with the Apaches for a spell."

Wes leaned toward the stranger. "Who's your friend, Billy?"

"Dick Brewer's his name. He bought the old Horrell place. Heard the commotion and came out to check on things. He sided with us after realizing we were up against Jesse Evans and his gang."

Wes turned to the stranger. "I'm Wes Bracken, and this is Jace Cousins. We run the Mirror B on the other side of San Patricio."

"Pleased to meet you," Brewer said, doffing his hat and revealing a mop of curly black hair over a serious face with no-nonsense blue eyes, a narrow nose, and thin lips. "I've heard you're honest men."

Jace laughed. "Wes more so than me."

Brewer grinned. "You're showing your honesty already, Jace."

Wes nodded. "It's difficult to stay honest in Lincoln County."

"Then tell me," Bonney interrupted, "what took you so long to come for us?"

"Wes had a hunch that the attack was a decoy to draw us away from the ranch before a second attack," Jace explained. "Wes was right."

"Two men with torches rode up five or ten minutes after you left," Wes said. "They headed for the barn, planning to burn us out. We sent them scurrying back to momma, both with extra bullet lead in them."

"My aim was off," Jace admitted, "but I killed one of their horses. That's where I got you a saddle, Carlos."

"Gracias," he answered, "but a dead man's saddle is cursed."

"I nicked him, Carlos, so I wouldn't jinx your new tack."

Bonney nodded. "That was mighty thoughtful of you, Jace, saving Carlos time and money for a new saddle. Next time you shoot a fella, though, take his wallet for me. I'm down to my last tail feather until someone gives me work."

Jace grinned. "I'll keep that in mind, especially if I plug Jesse Evans, but don't hold off taking a job on my account."

Brewer reined his horse closer to Wes and Jace. "Word has it that this new Englishman John Tunstall in Lincoln plans to start ranching and is looking for land and cattle to buy. He'll be touring the county inspecting suitable property."

"Is it true he's partnering with the lawyer McSween?" Wes asked.

"That's what I've been told," Brewer replied. "They're even planning on opening up a bank and challenging Murphy straight up with a new store."

Wes nodded, but held his estimation of Alex McSween as Brewer must make his own judgment. Any man that once did Murphy's bidding, even if only briefly, was not to be trusted.

"I'll hear Tunstall out," Brewer concluded, "and find out if there's anything in it for me as long as it's honest work."

"I'm not like you," Bonney said, "I'll take any kind of job, honest or not."

Brewer turned to the Kid, scratched his

chin, and nodded. "Here's what I'll do, Bonney. I saw how you handled a weapon against Jesse Evans. I'll hire you at two bits a day to do chores and provide an extra gun around my place. That comes to seven fifty a month in U.S. dollars."

"What about Carlos?" Billy asked.

"That's stretching my resources as is," Brewer answered. "No offense, Carlos."

"It's both of us or neither of us," Billy responded.

Carlos smiled.

"I'll do it if Carlos will accept a bit a day," Brewer countered. "That comes out to three dollars and seventy-five cents a month."

Bonney turned to Carlos. "What do you say? Remember your gun handling is not as experienced as mine."

Exhaling, Carlos finally nodded. "*Sí*, once I get my saddle."

Brewer maneuvered his horse next to Bonney and shook the Kid's hand, then moved over to Carlos and repeated the gesture. He looked to Wes and Jace. "Gentlemen, I best check on my place to make sure Jesse Evans didn't backtrack and hit my ranch or steal any of my stock." Brewer turned to his new hands. "You two come by this evening. You'll start work in the morning." He touched his trigger finger to the brim of his

195

hat and started home.

As Wes watched him ride away, Jace noted, "Brewer seems like a decent fellow."

"We'll see what happens if he ties in with McSween," Wes cautioned.

The four headed back to the Mirror B, passing San Patricio and the small adobe and plot Carlos had abandoned. When they reached home, Sarafina cautiously poked her head out the front door as they approached.

"It's us," cried Wes. "Nothing to worry over." He aimed his sorrel toward the house while Jace led Bonney and Carlos to the barn where they had left the salvaged saddle. Wes dismounted and stepped to Sarafina as she emerged from the adobe. "We're all well, including Carlos."

Sarafina awkwardly hugged her husband. "I feared you were more Texas *diablos*," she explained.

"Everything is fine. A small rancher the other side of San Patricio even offered Bonney and Carlos a job." He patted her stomach and realized she was shivering. "You must step inside where it's warmer. Don't want you to take cold. Got to keep our next son warm."

When his wife entered the house and closed the door, Wes grabbed Charlie's reins and led the stallion to the barn where Carlos was cinching the gift saddle on his horse. *"Gracias, gracias,"* he said to Cousins, who stood amused at Carlos's delight.

"Hell, Jace," Bonney started, "why don't you shoot ol' John Chisum for me and give me his cattle herd? Then I wouldn't need to work for Dick Brewer."

Jace could only shake his head. "Why didn't you plug Jesse for me earlier this morning?"

"Carlos and I got off a couple shots before they realized we weren't you and Wes. They called a halt to the firing, even offered their regrets for starting something with the wrong folks. When Brewer rode up, they got on their horses and rode away. Besides that, Jesse Evans knows I'm a deadlier shot than he is."

Wes unsaddled his sorrel, then watered him and pitch-forked hay in the trough for him to eat. When Wes exited the barn, he observed Bonney and Carlos mounting their horses for the trip back to Brewer's place.

Wes walked over to them both, extending his hand, grasping theirs, and shaking them. "You two saved our home this morning because they thought you were me and Jace. They would've burned us out had we not been here, maybe even hurt Sarafina and

Luis. *Gracias.*"

Bonney flashed a bucktoothed grin. "Hey, we got a saddle from it and a fine Christmas dinner."

Wes turned to Carlos. "Don't let Billy get you into any trouble."

His brother-in-law laughed. "No trouble with Billy Bonney, only fun."

Jace shook his head. "Fun gets you in more trouble than anything else. Remember that, Carlos."

"Before you leave, Carlos, drop by the house and tell Sarafina goodbye. She worries about you."

The two young men turned their mounts and started west, stopping only for Carlos to run in and offer his farewell to his sister.

Wes and Jace watched them ride away. "You think they'll stay out of trouble, Wes?"

"Nope. Carlos is too hotheaded and Billy is too fun-loving. The combination is bound to create problems for them and even us."

Jace laughed. "We've got enough troubles of our own."

The two men retired to the house, exhausted from the day's encounters and skittish over what the days to come would bring. For a week they handled their winter chores undisturbed. Then on the second day of the New Year, a lone rider turned off the road and headed for the adobe. He wore a long black coat with a matching felt hat, pulled low over his brow. Wes was chopping wood when Nip and Tuck took to howling and growling. He picked up his Winchester resting against the woodpile and started for the front of his dwelling.

"Hello the house," the rider called as Wes rounded the corner.

"Afternoon," Wes said, startling the man who had missed his approach. "How can I help?"

The stranger lifted his left hand to his chest and pulled back the long coat to reveal a badge on his frock coat. Releasing the cloth, the rider removed his hat. "I'm William Brady, the new sheriff of Lincoln County. Might you be Wes Bracken or Jace Cousins?"

"I'm Bracken."

"I'm Cousins," said Jace, approaching from the barn.

The fellow nodded. "I was sworn in yesterday as sheriff and I'm following up on a complaint of a week ago, the day after Christmas. Some riders report ya'll shot them while they were riding along the road. They say you killed one of their horses and meant to kill them. I spotted a horse carcass back up the trail. So I know there's a touch of truth to the story." Brady ran his fingers through his thick black hair, which hung over his ears and accentuated a high brow, thin eyebrows, narrow eyes, and a broad mustache.

"We were defending our home against attackers," Wes replied. "The two we shot tried to burn down our place, starting with the barn."

"Why didn't you report it to the law?" Brady asked, replacing his hat atop his head.

Jace stepped toward the sheriff. "From what we heard, Sheriff Ham Mills resigned and left town. There was no one to notify until you were sworn in."

"On top of that," Wes said, "these were Jesse Evans's men. Everybody knows what a scoundrel he is, but the law ignores him because he hides behind Murphy, Dolan, and the House."

"How about you, Brady? Do you hide behind the House?" Jace asked.

The sheriff slapped his left breast. "I wear a badge. I don't hide behind anybody."

"We don't deny shooting the horse and the two riders, but we were defending what was ours, our family and our property," Wes answered.

"It's no matter to me," Brady replied, "being it happened before my term, but I'm

200

warning you that you will be held account-able by me for any future shootings on or off your place. That's not a threat, just fact. Now I'll leave you to your business." The sheriff tipped his hat, then turned back up the trail to the road and headed west toward San Patricio.

Jace glanced at Wes. "What do you think? Murphy man or not?"

"Bonney said he was a House man, but like everything else in Lincoln County, you can't be sure if he represents the law or the outlaws."

Jace shook his head. "Odds have it the outlaws as there's more of them."

For the next two weeks, the Mirror B partners continued their chores, undis-turbed by company until a buggy turned off the road and headed straight for their house, drawing the attention of Nip and Tuck, who announced the visitors' arrival. Wes and Jace had saddled up and were about to ride off and check on their cattle when the carriage pulled up in front of the adobe.

Wes and Jace directed their mounts toward their guests and rode over, commanding the dogs to hush. As he neared the conveyance, Wes recognized Alexander McSween, the one-time L.G. Murphy attorney. He assumed the fellow with him was the Englishman everyone had been talking about for so many weeks because the fellow's attire seemed prissier than was common in New Mexico Territory.

"Good morning, gentlemen," the lawyer announced. "I wonder if we might take a moment of your time?"

"You already have," Jace replied, drawing a grin from Wes.

As stiff as a double-starched shirt, McSween found no humor in Cousins's remark. "I'm Alex McSween, attorney at law, and with me is John Henry Tunstall, British investor and philanthropist."

The Englishman tipped his hat at them. "Good day, chaps."

Wes nodded, taking in the Englishman, who was much younger than he had expected, early twenties at the most. Tunstall had light upswept hair and a thin matching mustache that barely showed up over his pale skin. He had long, effeminate fingers and a smile as phony as a politician's promise.

"We'd like to discuss some land investment possibilities," McSween continued.

Law or outlaw? Wes wondered about his visitors.

Chapter 11

Alexander McSween swept his hand toward the front door of the house. "Might we step inside to discuss business?" he asked.

"This is fine where we are," Wes answered. "We have work to do."

"You are the proprietors rather than hired hands, are you not?" McSween spoke with condescension as he looked from Bracken to Cousins and back.

"Around here, we are everything," Wes responded.

"You are?" asked the Englishman.

"Wesley Bracken is my name, and this is Jace Cousins. We run the Mirror B."

"A fine parcel of property it is," Tunstall observed. "Well-watered, nice improvements. Mr. McSween is my solicitor —"

"What's he soliciting?" Cousins interrupted.

"Ahem," McSween sniffed, lifting his arrogant nose in the air. "Solicitor is an

English term for a civil lawyer."

Jace sneered. "Never realized there was such a thing as a civil lawyer. The only solicitors I've ever dealt with have been rude and vulgar."

"Gentlemen," Tunstall said. "I'm willing to make a substantial offer to you for your place. What was it, the Reflecting Glass B?"

"The Mirror B," Wes corrected.

"Ah, yes, the Mirror B," the Englishman said.

"We're not interested in selling," Wes shot back.

"Mr. Tunstall can make it worth your while," McSween answered, "as he comes from a monied family in England."

"Doesn't matter if he's Queen Victoria herself, that holds no sway with us," Wes replied.

"No offense to your queen, Mr. Tunstall, as I'm sure she's quite the sage hen," Jace offered.

The Englishman removed his bowler and scratched his head.

"It's cowboy slang for a woman," McSween explained to his client, then turned back to Wes and Jace.

"If you're not interested in selling to Mr. Tunstall, might you consider claiming property that he might buy from you?"

Wes shrugged. "What are you talking about?"

"There's legislation before Congress now — the Desert Land Act it's called — that should pass in a matter of weeks. It allows citizens to claim 640 acres of desert land if they intend to irrigate it and reclaim it for farm use. There's no residency requirement. You file on it in your name for two bits an acre. After three years you'd owe a dollar an acre to keep the property or sell it to my client, once you've proved your claim."

"Sounds like a shady scheme," Wes replied

"It wouldn't cost you a thing," McSween countered. "Mr. Tunstall would cover all costs."

"Such legal shenanigans could cost me my good name," Wes replied.

McSween turned to Tunstall. "We are wasting our time with these two. Perhaps we should check out some of the Casey land along the Rio Feliz. It's farther from Lincoln, but comparable for raising cattle, though not as good farmland as here in the Ruidoso Valley."

"The widow Casey might be interested in selling," Wes offered, thinking such a sale might ease her financial bind.

Laughing, the attorney responded, "The Caseys never filed on most of the land they claim and what they filed on has unpaid taxes. Their land's there for the taking, regardless of what the widow thinks or does."

Jace looked at Wes, shaking his head and scowling at the attorney. "Have you no sense of decency?"

"The law's the law," McSween shot back.

"Even when outlaws are behind it," Wes answered.

The lawyer shook his index finger at Wes's nose. "One day you'll regret not taking advantage of Mr. Tunstall's generous offer."

"What offer?" Wes shot back. "To buy our land, the land we've invested so much sweat and blood in? To claim land in our names to turn over to him?"

"Mr. Tunstall is backed by his father's extensive wealth. Murphy's empire is crumbling. He's dying of cancer, and he owes more money than he'll ever repay. Mr. Tunstall is here to fill the void when Murphy's kingdom collapses. He's starting a store to compete with the House and opening a bank. We've even talked with John Chisum about joining us in that venture, uniting the east and west halves of the county through the bank. In a year or two, Mr. Tunstall will collect half or more of every dollar spent in Lincoln County. You can join our side or stay with Murphy, but you'll reap what you sow in the coming months."

"The only side we are on is our own side," Wes shot back. "Now get off of our property."

Tunstall offered a smug grin as he placed his bowler atop his head. "Good day, chaps."

McSween swatted the rump of his horse with the buggy whip, and the conveyance lurched forward as the vehicle aimed for the road, Nip and Tuck chasing the visitors away.

Wes and Jace sat in their saddles, neither of them hushing the dogs as they barked and howled at the vehicle until it turned toward San Patricio.

"If that doesn't beat all," Jace said, "the arrogance of those fellows."

"Just more vultures fighting over the carcass of Lincoln County," Wes answered. "Even if Murphy is as bad off physically and financially as McSween says, I don't see Dolan lying down and rolling over for those two."

Jace scratched his chin. "It surprises me about John Chisum throwing in with these boys. He always struck me as a loner, looking out for himself and his empire, never for others."

Wes shrugged. "McSween may have been

lying. Maybe Chisum fears this Desert Land Act, since open range makes up most of his grassland. A hundred claims on land he runs but possesses no title to would eat a huge bite out of his domain. I'm more worried for Ellen Casey than I am John Chisum. Sounds like McSween and Tunstall aim to take advantage of her."

Jace whistled, and Nip and Tuck trotted back to the house, proud that they had driven the interlopers away.

Wes watched until the buggy disappeared, then turned to Jace. "Let's check our cattle. After that, I'll visit the widow Casey."

The two partners spent the rest of the day making sure their cattle hadn't strayed too far from the place. Wes and Jace remained ever alert that Jesse Evans was still hunting them, so they carried their long weapons at the ready. If they were surprised, they could return fire quickly. Wes hoped the failed ambush and arson attack had sent a message to the Evans gang that the Mirror B partners would fight back, though Wes understood much of their success belonged to the unplanned visit of Bonney and Carlos.

Two days later, Wes saddled up for a morning ride to the Casey place to inform Ellen about his disconcerting conversation with McSween and Tunstall. He entered the store to find her wearing men's clothing and still distraught over hers and her children's future.

"It's been hard," Ellen informed Wes. "Money's even tighter."

Taking off his hat, Wes looked around the store, the shelves depleted of goods. "I hope you earned money from sales."

"Very little," she replied. "Most people still buy on credit, and I'd sooner give it to them than let it wind up in Murphy's hands."

"That's what I came to talk to you about."

"What's Murphy planning now?" the widow asked.

"It's not Murphy or the House this time," Wes informed her. "There's a new fellow in town, an Englishman named John Henry Tunstall. He and the lawyer Alex McSween are sounding as if they plan to drive Murphy out of business and start a store so they can swindle folks with overpriced goods of their own."

"I don't stand a chance," Ellen said, her voice dripping with resignation.

"It gets worse, Ellen."

"Oh, goodness, no," she said, her hand flying to her mouth.

"This Tunstall fellow intends to get into

ranching. He's been looking at property and says there's overdue taxes on your land. They've got an eye to claiming your land for themselves."

She waved her arms in frustration, then dropped them helplessly to her side. "Maybe I should take the family back to Texas. People can't pay me what they owe, and I don't have a tail feather left to pay my taxes."

Rolling the brim of his hat in his fingers, Wes grimaced. "I'd buy your store and mill if I had the money, but I can't afford it, Ellen."

She lowered her chin and stared at the floor. "There's nobody I'd rather sell it to than you, Wes Bracken, but most honest folks in Lincoln County are cattle-poor. Best we can determine, I've got four hundred or so cattle, but with every market controlled by Murphy or Chisum, nobody'll buy 'em, especially when they can steal them." Ellen began to cry. "What am I gonna do, Wes; what am I gonna do?"

Wes stepped to Ellen and patted her shoulder, uncertain how to ease her worry and calm her fears. He felt as helpless as a cowhand without a lariat. "No one's certain how things will work out, Ellen. We just play our hands with the cards we're dealt."

Ellen's shoulders drooped, and she let out a long sigh. "I ask myself why God dealt me a bad hand, losing Bob and all his dreams. Now I may lose everything because of taxes I can't pay, and men I've never met scheming to steal what Bob built for his family."

His mind awhirl, Wes offered no answers as problems always outweighed solutions in Lincoln County. "You're stretched thin enough as is, Ellen. Letting go of the Rio Feliz land will simplify things for you so you can hold on to your store, mill, and property in the Hondo Valley."

"But what of my cattle? They need grazing land. I can't afford to lose the livestock because they'll bring money most anyplace save Lincoln County."

Considering the options, Wes said, "You can run your cattle with mine. Jace and I will keep them with ours, and you can let go of the Rio Feliz property, as it'll be taken from you for taxes anyway. After that you focus on maintaining your Hondo holdings."

"You'd do that for me?"

"Why sure, Ellen. We're neighbors. I remember all Bob did for me when I first arrived in Lincoln County. I'll add your four hundred to my two hundred head."

"Won't that stretch your winter grass?"

"We'll make do, Ellen. Don't you worry."

She leaned over and hugged Bracken. "Thank you, Wes."

When he broke from her embrace, he smiled. "There is some good news I'll share with you."

"I need some uplifting news for a change."

Wes grinned. "You're the first one I've told this outside of family, but Sarafina's gonna have a baby."

A wave of joy rolled over Ellen's face. "That's wonderful, Wes. When?"

"The best we can figure, the baby'll come in July sometime."

"I'm delighted, Wes. It'll be nice for little Luis to have a playmate. I brought six young'uns into this world, and I'll be glad to midwife yours. That's the least I can do for you tending my herd."

Wes nodded. "That would be appreciated. I may need your two older boys and your hand to help me round up your cattle. I fear leaving Sarafina alone without me or Jace there."

"She's welcome to stay with us."

"She'd enjoy that, but I've had so many threats, I can't leave the place unguarded as they've already tried to burn it down."

"Lincoln County," Ellen sighed. "There's more evil here than in the devil's workshop."

Ellen escorted him to the door and bid him farewell. Wes asked Ellen to send her lone cowhand and two oldest sons to his house in three days for the ride south to the Rio Feliz to drive the Casey cattle to his place to protect them from the schemes of Murphy and Dolan or McSween and Tunstall.

Back at the Mirror B, Wes extended Ellen's congratulations to Sarafina upon her pregnancy, then huddled with Jace Cousins to apprise him of the plan for managing the Casey cattle. Wes and Jace argued over who should remain home and who should accompany the Casey crew, settling the dispute with a coin flip. Jace called heads, but it came up tails so Wes was slotted to lead the expedition.

"I still think you ought to stay here with your wife, Sarafina being with child," Jace lamented.

"Your Henry has a longer range than my carbine, and that'll put my mind at ease you'll protect her in my absence," Wes responded.

At sunrise on departure day, Nip and Tuck took to barking and howling as three riders approached from the east. Wes, who had taken his cup of coffee outside to await their arrival, smiled. He appreciated their early start as it showed they — likely with prodding from Ellen — understood another man's time was valuable. Wes called off his dogs and pointed for the riders to meet him at the barn. He stepped back inside, gave Sarafina his cup and a kiss, then turned to Cousins. "Take good care of her and Luis."

"I can still go in your place, Wes," Jace offered.

"We settled it fair and square. I've got to pull my weight around here. It was me that agreed to do this."

"It'll be freezing out there this time of year when you could have a warm bed with Sarafina. My bed's always cold, whether I'm in the bunkhouse or on the ground."

"Time's a wasting," Wes offered, kissing Sarafina a final time, grabbing his carbine, and trotting out to the barn, where Charlie was saddled and ready to ride.

In the dim light of dawn, Wes inspected his cowhands as he introduced himself. "You boys had much experience working cattle?"

"I'm more of a mill hand, grinding corn rather than chasing cows," said the oldest rider. "I go by Buck."

Wes estimated Buck was in his thirties as he turned to the two younger hands, neither of whom appeared to be two decades old.

214

"You boys must be Ellen's sons."

"Two of them," replied the older one. "I'm Will, and I'm seventeen."

"My name's Adam, but everyone calls me Add," said the other boy. "I'm fifteen."

"Pleased to meet you," Wes answered. "You've both got some of your father's features. Have you done much cowboying?"

"We've ridden out before," said Will, "but others did the hard work."

Wes nodded. "You'll pick it up. It's common sense, though cattle have cow sense, which takes a while to grow accustomed to. I'll give you lessons along the way."

Wes retreated inside the barn to fetch Charlie. Once he slid his Winchester in its scabbard, Wes glanced at the breeding stock, then led his sorrel outside. After he closed the barn door, he mounted Charlie, and they started toward San Patricio before cutting off the main road along the trail that Wes had followed chasing Bonney when he stole Wes's horses.

After they hit the trail, where they were less likely to encounter any enemies, Wes began to explain the basics of rounding up and herding cattle. His three pupils listened until the cold wind picked up and made it harder to understand. Each rider drew his coat around tighter and snugged down his hat as they rode south by southeast toward the head of the Rio Feliz, some thirty miles distant. Like most streams in southeast New Mexico Territory, the Feliz fed into the Pecos River, though well below where the Rio Hondo emptied into it.

It took a day to reach the place where Wes found the bulk of the Casey herd. Along the route, they rounded up more than fifty strays with Casey's brand burned in their hide. As dusk approached, they pitched a cold camp, it being too windy to start a fire. Wes ate tortillas Sarafina had wrapped around mashed red beans while the three others split a can of sardines and a few crackers. They slept as best they could with the chilly ground beneath them, the frigid air above them, and not enough cover between earth and sky.

Come morning they ate what was left from their supper and began to round up the cattle, which were as much as five miles distant from their camp. By the end of light, Wes estimated they had accounted for three hundred and sixty of the Casey herd. With the wind and weather continuing their assault on those foolish enough to be outside, the four drovers spent another uncomfortable night wrapped in their bedrolls. Everyone was eager to get moving the next morning to see if the activity would erase the cold and stiffness from their bodies.

"I prefer milling to cowboying," Buck said as he saddled up.

The Casey boys never complained, realizing their future depended on keeping what remained of their late father's cattle. Once Wes and his crew mounted, they whistled and yelled, getting the lethargic longhorns moving toward the north and their new home. The animals moved stiffly and reluctantly at first, warmed up later, and by afternoon marched at a steady pace, making good time for the four hands, who were inexperienced at driving cattle into a strong blast of frigid northern wind.

By midafternoon, as they neared the last line of mountains before the trail opened onto the Ruidoso Valley, Wes spotted three riders approaching from the north. At first he failed to identify the riders as they wore thick coats with their hats pulled low over their foreheads. As the trio moved toward them, Wes pulled his Winchester from its scabbard and rested its barrel across his saddle. Wes recognized a dappled gray that resembled Billy Bonney's horse, but in Lincoln County a man should always be careful. Someone might've stolen the Kid's horse, or he could've traded it for another one.

Wes twisted around in his saddle, issuing orders to his three hands. "Keep the cattle moving while I check out the riders," he instructed them, nudging his horse into a lope and riding out to inquire about their business. As they came within fifty yards, Wes watched the rider on the gray lift his head and smile, his buck teeth unmistakable, even from that distance. It was Billy Bonney. Recognizing Carlos and Dick Brewer with the Kid, Wes slid his Winchester back in its scabbard and removed his hat, waving it at his acquaintances, glad to greet them rather than Murphy-Dolan men.

As they came within speaking range, Bonney pushed the brim of his hat up with his left hand and grinned even wider. "Taken up rustling, have you?"

"Just returning them to their rightful owner," Wes answered.

Billy laughed. "I've heard that story before, and we both know it *is* a story."

"Afternoon, Dick," Wes offered. "And how are you doing, Carlos?"

Both men nodded their acknowledgment.

"What brings you this way?" Wes asked.

Brewer reined up opposite Wes. "The

Englishman's hired me to manage his ranch."

"He's hired us, too," Billy interjected. "Paying us a dollar a day."

Wes shrugged. "Didn't know he had a ranch."

"He's looking at taking over ranchland along the Rio Feliz," Brewer continued.

"Whose land?" Wes asked.

"McSween instructed me not to say."

"Who are you working for, the Englishman or the lawyer?"

"Tunstall, but McSween gives him legal advice."

Wes released a deep breath, frustrated that Tunstall with McSween's advice was aiming to take over Casey's land. He twisted in his saddle, looking for the Casey boys, hoping they had been too far away to hear. Thankful that Will and Add were on the opposite side of the herd from him, Wes turned to Brewer. "You boys've hitched your wagon to a crooked team of jackasses."

"At least we ain't hooked up with the Murphy-Dolan bunch," Brewer defended. "They're proven crooks."

"And he's paying us a dollar a day," Bonney repeated.

"*Sí,*" echoed Carlos.

"Has he paid you yet?" Wes asked.

Bonney and Carlos looked at each other, then the Kid spoke. "We just started."

"When he pays you, tell me," Wes continued. "Tunstall's dreaming too big to pay small fry like the two of you."

"You don't know him," Billy responded.

"I've met Tunstall and talked to him long enough to get the measure of the man," Wes answered. "McSween worked a spell for Murphy. That tells me all I need to know about his integrity. I'm telling you, you can't trust either McSween or Tunstall."

"We've got to trust someone to survive," Brewer said.

"Trust yourself," Wes shot back. "That's the only person you can believe in here in Lincoln County."

The approach of the herd distracted Brewer, who never answered, instead studying the passing cattle. "Is that Bob Casey's brand on their flank?" he asked.

Wes realized it was trouble to acknowledge the cattle's owner, but he could not deny the obvious. "Yep. I'm managing the Casey cattle until the widow Casey decides what to do with them. Don't want them stolen either."

"That's good to know they're safe," Brewer answered. "What's the count?"

Wes decided Brewer was fishing for information, likely for Tunstall and McSween. He shorted the herd. "We started out with two hundred and nine, though a few more have joined the herd since we began."

Brewer reached inside his coat and fumbled around for a moment, pulling out a folded sheet of paper and a stubby pencil. He scribbled a note and stuck the paper back in his pocket with information Wes suspected would get back to Tunstall and McSween.

"Good to see you, Wes," Brewer said, "but we need to ride on to the Feliz." He pulled his hat down and nudged his horse forward.

Bonney rode by. "Be sure those cattle get back to their rightful owner."

"Make sure Tunstall pays you," Wes responded.

Carlos offered nothing but a guttural grunt as he passed.

"Thanks, Carlos," Wes responded. "I'll tell Sarafina you send your love."

Wes turned his horse and watched the trio ride toward the Rio Feliz. Then he aimed Charlie north and caught up with the herd and his hands for the final leg of the journey home. When he reached the boundary of his place, he and his crew drove the herd southeast to join the Mirror B cattle. After that he sent the Casey boys and Buck home and reported to the house, greeting Sarafina with a kiss and a report of seeing Carlos.

"I worry over him," Sarafina replied. "How is he?"

"He sends his love," Wes answered, drawing a smile from his wife. He patted Sarafina's stomach. "How are you two doing?"

"Better, now that you are back."

Wes smiled. "Let me find Jace and discuss a little business with him."

"He told me he'd be in the barn," she replied.

Wes found Jace feeding the breeding stock and reported on the drive's success, the encounter with Brewer, and his suspicions that Tunstall and McSween were up to no good.

Three weeks later as the cold hand of February gripped Lincoln County his fears were confirmed when a galloping rider approached the house, sending Nip and Tuck into a fretful bout of barking and growling. Undeterred, the rider raced to the adobe and reined up hard as Wes emerged, Winchester in hand. Wes recognized the oldest Casey boy astride his gelding, waving a sheet of paper at Wes.

"What is it, Will?"

"Mother wanted me to show you this," he shouted, leaning over in his saddle and handing it to Wes.

Unfolding the paper, Wes saw a writ of attachment issued by Lincoln County to claim all the Casey cattle until they were sold to pay off outstanding debts to creditors.

"Mother says the sheriff will be coming over to take the cattle. She wanted to make sure you didn't get hurt trying to defend our cattle."

Damn Tunstall and McSween, Wes thought, then reconsidered. If the creditor was the county for land taxes, officials would claim the land and sell it at auction, rather than the cattle. Bob Casey didn't owe anyone in Lincoln County as most of his patrons owed him. The only ones who might hold outstanding debts were the suppliers in Santa Fe, but they were ignorant of the cattle. Too, Tunstall and McSween lacked sway with the county as Murphy's henchmen ran it.

"It makes little sense," Wes told Will Casey, "unless L.G. Murphy is behind this. Tell your mother we'll do what we can with your cattle."

"I will," the Casey boy said, then turned his horse and galloped away.

Wes wondered how to keep the promise he made to the Casey boy and his mother.

CHAPTER 12

Two days later right after lunch when Wes Bracken was chopping firewood behind the house, the barking of Nip and Tuck announced the approach of five riders. Wes grabbed his Winchester propped up against the adobe and went around the front to confront his visitors. By his stiff-backed saddle posture, the frock coat, and the black hair tumbling from beneath his hat, Wes recognized Sheriff Brady, though he questioned why he needed four men to assist him. Wes whistled to settle the dogs, and they trotted back to Bracken, still growling at the riders.

As the lawman neared, Jace Cousins walked over from the barn where he had been feeding the horses. He toted his rifle and a smile. "What did you do this time, Wes?"

"Nothing but chores and minding my own affairs, Jace."

"That can get a man in big trouble in Lincoln County."

Brady reined up in front of the two and doffed his hat. "Afternoon, gents." He replaced his hat and reached inside his coat pocket. "I'm here on official business."

"Why, Sheriff, I'm surprised," Jace said. "I kinda figured you came out on this chilly February day for a game of checkers."

Brady scowled as he pulled folded papers from his coat and offered the documents to Wes. "This is a writ of attachment for the Casey cattle. I'm told they're running with your herd."

"Where'd you hear that, Sheriff?" Wes asked.

"That's neither here nor there, Bracken. I'm simply doing what the court ordered."

"What court?"

"District court in Mesilla."

"On what grounds were the cattle attached?"

"Bob Casey, God rest his soul, owed the Murphy store considerable money. Mr. Murphy's trying to collect what's due him."

Angered at the lie, Wes stepped toward the sheriff before Cousins grabbed his arm and held him. Wes shook loose, lifted his hand, and pointed it at Brady's nose. "Bob Casey didn't do business with the House.

Before the Democrat county convention, he bought five dollars' worth of goods as a gesture of goodwill at the outcome of the party elections. Casey was returning to the House to pay his debt when Willie Wilson shot him, likely at Murphy's behest."

"Take it up with the court, Bracken," the sheriff replied. "I'm here to herd the cattle to Lincoln until an auction is scheduled, and Casey's debts made good with the House. Where are you pasturing the beeves? I'm after two hundred and nine head."

Wes hesitated for a moment, knowing he had returned with over three hundred and fifty beeves, until he recalled telling Brewer the same number as the sheriff quoted. "They're scattered on my place. It'll take a few days to round them up."

Jace stepped between Wes and the lawman. "Why don't you let us gather the herd and drive them to Lincoln for you, Sheriff? There's no sense in you and your hands working in this weather when we can do it for you. It'd break my heart if you fellas took cold and died on us."

Brady scratched his goatee. "No funny business, Wes?"

"What about if I simplify things," Wes replied. "I left five dollars with Murphy weeks ago to pay the debt. Do you understand this is a fraud over a mere five dollars?"

"That's the judge's decision, not mine. If you care to ride to Mesilla and work it out, so be it, but I'm simply doing my job until I'm told otherwise by the court."

"This is wrong, Sheriff."

"I do what the court tells me," Brady replied.

"And what Murphy orders you to do," Wes shot back.

Brady scowled. "Drive the cattle to my place east of town by the end of the week. I'll keep them there until the auction." The sheriff yanked the reins on his horse and turned him around toward the road, followed by his four deputies.

"Always nice to see you, Sheriff," Jace called out, then snickered as he looked to Wes. "There's over three hundred and fifty head."

Wes nodded as he watched Brady and his men retreat. "That's the number I told Brewer when we met him on the trail with Bonney and Carlos. He made a note of it and told Tunstall."

"Don't tell me Tunstall and Murphy are helping each other out."

"Nothing would surprise me, Jace. Everything's so rotten in Lincoln County that alliances shift out of greed."

"How do you root out corruption, if both sides are crooked?" Jace asked.

"You don't let them taint you," Wes answered.

"Hell, Wes, you can't breathe Lincoln County air without getting tainted."

"We're wasting time talking," Wes said. "I'll ride to Casey's Mill with the news. After I get back, we'll figure out what's best for us and start rounding up the cattle in the morning. We'll have two days to get them to Brady's place by his deadline. Once that's done, I intend to visit L.G. Murphy again."

Two hundred and nine head of cattle, their hooves kicking up a cloud of dust, headed up the road to Lincoln, Wes Bracken and Jace Cousins herding them west. Though uncomfortable leaving Sarafina alone, Wes risked it to deliver the cattle to Brady and keep his promise to Ellen Casey. The partners had split the Casey beeves into two smaller herds, the one that had been attached and a second of a hundred and forty head. Eleven of the group they had returned from the Rio Feliz had either died or wandered off. The smaller herd Wes and Jace drove to the Casey place to pasture nearer home in case the widow decided to take her family and belongings back to Texas and family there.

Along the trail to Lincoln, the cattle bellowed and bawled, tired of being driven anywhere in the frigid air of late February. Four miles shy of Lincoln the herd approached the place Wes believed to belong to Sheriff William Brady. He allowed the animals to graze while he turned Charlie off the road toward the modest adobe. Reaching the place, he reined up an easy distance from the dwelling so as not to appear threatening.

"Hello the house," he called.

In a moment the wooden door cracked, then slowly opened. A Mexican woman with a red kerchief draped over her hair poked her head out.

"*¿Es esta la casa del señor Brady?*" Wes asked.

"*Sí,*" she answered.

"*Me dijo que llevara este ganado a su rancho,*" Wes explained.

She slipped out of the door and gestured behind the house. "*Arrea el ganado en esa dirección,*" she instructed. "*Se lo diré a mi esposo cuando regrese. Está en Lincoln.*"

"*Gracias,*" Wes answered. "We will drive them north of the house and look for your husband in Lincoln." He touched the brim of the hat and returned to the herd, thinking he and Brady had one thing in common — a Mexican wife — but little else.

Back at the road he yelled to Jace with instructions where to push the herd.

Jace waved his hat over his head to show that he understood, then whistled and started the beeves moving to their new home. After a half hour, Wes and Jace situated the animals to their satisfaction and headed toward Lincoln with Wes planning to confirm delivery of the cattle with the sheriff and then visit Murphy.

A mile from Lincoln, Wes and Jace tensed as seven riders approached from town. Jace pulled his Henry rifle from the scabbard and rode with it at his side to be less conspicuous than carrying it across his chest.

Wes reached for his Winchester, relaxing when he recognized the lead rider by his lanky frame and oversized ears, his thin face held together by a thick mustache and dark piercing eyes. "Don't worry, Jace. It's John Chisum."

A grin cracked Chisum's handsome, leathery countenance as he approached. He lifted his hand and the riders behind him stopped in the road, awaiting Bracken and

Cousins to reach him. Wes and Jace tugged on the reins and drew their horses to a stop to converse with the cattleman who ran the eastern half of Lincoln County.

"It's Wes Bracken, if my memory serves me right," Chisum said, then stared at Cousins. "I've seen the face before but I don't recollect your friend's name."

"This is Jace Cousins. He's my partner on the Mirror B. You saw him awhile back when we drove the Horrells across your place and out of New Mexico Territory."

"Maybe so, Wes."

"Glad to meet you, Mr. Chisum," Jace said, tipping his hat at the rancher.

"What brings you to Lincoln, Mr. Chisum?" Wes asked.

"Meeting with Alex McSween and John Tunstall," Chisum announced. "They've got big dreams for Lincoln."

Wes felt his lips tighten, then he spoke carefully. "I'm uncertain I trust either of those fellows and their visions for the county."

Chisum offered a queer look as if he'd been sucking on a lemon, then grinned. "I don't know that I do either, but they're willing to take on the House and that's enough for me."

"Not me," Wes answered.

"Alex is gonna construct a fine dwelling, and John is planning to start a store to compete with the House. Fact is, we've even talked about starting a bank, hoping to build up the county rather than tear it down like Murphy's done for years."

"I hope you're right, Mr. Chisum."

"Wes has a skeptical view of mankind." Jace grinned. "He distrusts lawyers and liars."

Chisum cocked his head at Cousins. "And you offer a more benevolent view of mankind?"

"Once you get past Jesse Evans, folks aren't so bad."

This time Chisum's face soured like he'd eaten a whole crate of lemons. He hawked and spit out the bile on the side of the trail. "Jesse Evans has been rustling my cattle left and right. I can't believe I ever let such a dishonest man work for me. I gather you and he share a dislike for each other."

"I've vowed to kill him," Jace replied, "and he's vowed the same for me."

"Is that why you're carrying your rifle at your side?"

"Just being cautious," Jace answered. "You never know who you're gonna meet around Lincoln."

Chisum nodded. "He's been working

south and east of here, stealing cattle and either adding them to Murphy's herd or re-branding and selling them to ranchers in the Seven Rivers area. He likes that part of Lincoln County because it's closer to Mexico where he takes stolen horses to sell."

"That's good information, Mr. Chisum," Jace said, sliding his Henry back in its saddle boot.

"One more thing, Jace," the cowman continued. "If you kill him, come to see me and bring the hull of the cartridge that sends him to hell. I'll give you a replacement bullet and a hundred-dollar reward for your contribution to the betterment of mankind."

Jace looked at his partner. "Mr. Chisum pays better than you do."

"He can afford to," Wes replied, turning to the cattleman. "I need to ask a favor."

"I'll consider it as long as it doesn't cost me money."

"Shouldn't," Wes said. "The widow Casey is considering returning to Texas."

Chisum nodded. "A shame about her losing Bob. He was a decent man."

"She may be driving her husband's herd if she leaves Lincoln County, and I'm requesting safe passage for her family and cattle across your land, just as you provided for the Horrells, even though they didn't deserve it, when we drove them out of the territory."

"I'd be glad to help her, Wes."

"It might be a sudden move, Mr. Chisum."

"That won't matter. I'll spread the word among my foremen, and we'll see she gets safe passage to Texas."

"Obliged," Wes replied. "Ellen deserves a little kindness for a change." He tipped his hat to the cowman. "We've got business to attend to in Lincoln so we best be riding."

Chisum nodded. "Good luck to you both and especially you, Jace Cousins, in your quest to improve mankind for us all."

"It'd be my pleasure." Jace grinned as he passed the cattleman.

Wes laughed. "You're a smooth talker."

"Unlike you, I certainly knew better than to tell him he was establishing a bank with a pair of crooks in Tunstall and McSween."

Wes could only shake his head. "I was telling the truth."

"Sometimes, Wes, you're too truthful. You don't have to say it for it to be true."

"That's the problem with Lincoln County. Folks haven't spoken up."

Jace twisted his head from side to side. "Bob Casey spoke up and he's dead. You need to hold your tongue so you make fewer enemies."

"You've got plenty of enemies and making more all the time."

Jace nodded with such vigor it was obvious he was proud of his foes. "That's true, but I don't have a pretty wife and boy with another one on the way. You've got more to live for than I do. Think about that."

"I will, but I intend to do what's right."

"Who knows right from wrong in Lincoln County?" Jace replied as they approached the outskirts of town and its scattered buildings, which were strung out like a necklace of dingy brown pearls on both sides of the road.

The two riders headed for the sheriff's office, a grimy, low-slung adobe marked by a faded sign. Wes and Jace dismounted and walked inside, surprising Brady at his desk. Wes took in the dark office, lit only by a corner fireplace and what light could seep in through the waxed brown paper that served as a flimsy window. In the corner opposite the hearth was a hole in the ground six feet in diameter and eight deep.

Jace walked over and looked into the pit. "What you got here, Sheriff, a wishing well?"

"It's where we keep our prisoners awaiting trial," Brady answered, arising from his desk.

"What happened?" Jace asked. "Did Murphy steal all the county tax money so you couldn't afford a jail with iron bars?"

Wes shook his head. "You talk about me keeping my tongue."

Jace smiled. "I'm better at giving others advice than taking my own."

Brady stepped around the desk. "Did you bring the cattle?"

"Two hundred and nine head," Wes answered. "We left them with your wife."

"Maria," he said.

"She didn't give her name, but told us to drive them north of the house."

Brady nodded. "That's what I told her."

"Now I need a receipt."

"Can't do it until I've counted them myself. I'll do that this evening before dark."

"Can I trust you?"

"You better well trust me because I'm the closest thing to the law around."

Jace interrupted, pointing to the pit. "Sheriff, that's the oddest jail I've ever seen. A fellow that tries to dig out of that one's only making a bigger jail and saving tax money."

"You boys need to head back home," Brady said. "Your business is done here."

"Not quite," Wes answered. "I intend to visit L.G. Murphy, and I want you to go along."

Brady swallowed hard. "No need for me to accompany you."

"I intend to repay a debt, Sheriff, and I need a witness."

"No trouble then, Bracken?"

"I'm not starting any. That's why I need you there."

Brady looked from Bracken to Cousins. "You promise no trouble?"

"You promise me a receipt for the Casey cattle?"

The sheriff nodded and motioned them to the door.

They strode out of the building ahead of Brady and mounted as the sheriff walked around the back of the building to get his horse. He joined the Mirror B men and rode with them west down the street, passing the Wortley Hotel on the right and approaching the House on their left.

A dozen horses stood at the hitching rack out front, and they added theirs to the bunch, as Jace studied each animal.

"Looking for Jesse Evans's mount?"

Jace nodded as he dismounted. "Maybe he's elsewhere in Lincoln County like Chisum said, but I prefer to be careful. I don't recognize it unless he's switched or stolen horses." Cousins reached for his rifle stock.

Wes shook his head as he slid out of the saddle. "Leave the Henry with your dun. This visit is for Ellen Casey."

The two men stepped up on the plank porch and awaited Brady, whose slow pace suggested he was not interested in accompanying them inside. He dismounted, hitched up his gun belt, strode on the porch, took a deep breath, and opened the entry, allowing Bracken and Cousins to walk in ahead of him.

As soon as Wes entered, he saw James J. Dolan standing behind a counter littered with overpriced goods and foodstuffs. Another door to the right opened up into Murphy's saloon. Jace took a position there to make sure none of Murphy's men interfered with Bracken. Dolan stared in disbelief that Wes had dared enter the House. "I'm here to see L.G. Murphy," Wes told him.

"He's not well, and he's not taking visitors," Dolan replied, turning to Brady. "Why'd you bring these two here, Sheriff?"

"They said they wanted to settle a debt with the store," Brady replied.

"I know the books," Dolan replied. "They've never bought a thing here so they don't have an account."

"Get Murphy," Wes demanded.

"I tell you he's sick," Dolan replied.

Jace interrupted. "If he is, he's taking his medicine in the back of the saloon." Jace pointed to a table in the far corner.

Wes strode over to his partner, then stared between the other saloon patrons and saw him seated with his back to the corner, eyeing Wes and Jace. Murphy nursed a whiskey bottle. Wes moved past Jace through the door and into the saloon, several men stopping their drinking and gambling as he passed. Murphy stared with dull, blank eyes, seeming at first not to recognize him as Wes approached.

Dolan bolted after Wes, and Jace after Dolan. "Leave him alone," Dolan said. "He's not well."

In Wes's view, Murphy appeared sick, his eyes lifeless, his cheeks sunken, his body gaunt, and his senses dulled by pain or liquor so much that he did not comprehend the commotion that was approaching on him. Dolan reached Wes and grabbed his arm, trying to pull him away from his boss.

"Leave him alone," Dolan cried, until Jace yanked him away from Wes.

"I'm here to settle a debt, Murphy, and pay you the money you're owed. I paid you once, but I'm paying you again, this time with the sheriff as a witness," Wes shouted.

Murphy shook his head, running his fingers through the auburn hair that had once matched his fiery temperament. He looked up with bewildered eyes that slowly focused on Wes. "Ye be Wes Bracken, and ye're always up to no good."

"I'm here to repay a debt," Wes replied, "give you money you're owed."

"Money? Go ahead and ye pay me now."

"You remember Robert Casey?"

Murphy nodded as a sneer clouded his face. " 'e was a competitor. Ran a store and tried to get elected county chairman. 'e died trying, 'e did."

"He bought five dollars of goods from you on credit the day of the county convention. He was coming to repay you when you had him killed."

Dolan screamed, "Murphy didn't have anybody killed."

"I'm here to settle Casey's debt so you have no reason to attach his widow's cattle. I repaid your five dollars the last time I was here, but I'm doing it again so the sheriff can verify it," Wes barked.

Murphy's hands flew to his ears, as if the shouting rattled around in his brain. He shook his head. "Pay meself, and ye be gone, Wes Bracken."

Wes shoved his fingers in his britches pocket and pulled out five greenbacks, counting them out one at a time and slapping them on the table in front of Murphy.

"One dollar!"

The store owner grimaced at the noise.

"Two dollars!"

Jace jerked Dolan around and pointed to Brady standing in the doorway. "The sheriff is a witness that Casey's debt is being repaid."

"Three dollars!"

"Quit yer screaming," Murphy pleaded.

"Four dollars!"

Murphy held his hands up to his ears to block out the sound.

"Five dollars!" Wes said, banging the table with his fist as he slapped the final bill atop its predecessors.

Murphy's whiskey bottle tumbled over, and the store owner snatched at it but knocked it over the edge of the table, spilling the amber liquid before the bottle shattered on the floor.

"Bob Casey's debt has been paid in full," Wes shouted for everyone to hear. He motioned toward Brady. "You want to count the payment, Sheriff?"

Brady waved away the offer as Murphy

picked up the bills, looking at them as if he still didn't understand.

Dolan broke free from Jace and jumped toward Bracken, his fingers knotting into fists. "He's dying," Dolan cried, "and doesn't deserve to be intimidated by the likes of you two."

"Murphy's done worse than intimidate folks for years in Lincoln County," Wes shot back. "He's had them killed."

"That's a lie," Dolan answered. "He never was a vigilante like you and Cousins, lynching Willie Wilson. Ya'll hung him on the streets of Lincoln." He lifted his fist to strike Wes.

Cousins yanked his pistol from his holster and shoved it in Dolan's back. "I wouldn't do that, Dolan," Jace coughed, "or you'll be sicker quicker than old Murphy there."

Dolan lowered his fists.

"Now that Casey's debt is paid, you best release the attachment on his widow's cattle," Wes demanded.

Dolan smirked. "This changes nothing. It's in the hands of the court now in Mesilla. You must get the judge's approval for these five dollars to matter. Ain't that right, Sheriff?"

Brady nodded. "That's a fact."

"There's something else you need to

242

understand," Dolan sneered.

"What's that?" Wes asked.

"Mr. Murphy's sold me the store. By this time next month, it'll be J.J. Dolan and Company so you better stay on my good side if you want any future in Lincoln County and by gawd that's a fact," Dolan announced.

Wes shoved the storekeeper aside and marched past the sheriff and out of the room, as Jace backed out with his gun still pointed at Dolan.

"You'll both be sorry," Dolan screamed. "Jesse Evans hasn't forgotten the debt he owes you, Cousins." Dolan stomped his boots on the floor. "Bracken, I'll make sure he adds you to his list."

CHAPTER 13

February turned to March on the Mirror B and winter faded as the promise of spring budded throughout the Ruidoso Valley. But even as the land paled with a thin film of green along the Rio Ruidoso and with the assurance that winter's harshness was receding, the threats of the Murphy-Dolan allies hovered over the valley. Every ranch chore or pleasure brought the dark thought that enemies with grudges might be lurking to settle past grievances. Wes Bracken and Jace Cousins spent their time prepping the fields for spring planting, breeding Charlie with Mirror B mares or the horses of owners willing to pay the twenty-five-dollar stud fee, checking their cattle and the balance of the Casey herd, and clearing the land of winter debris, such as the broken limbs from the cottonwoods beside the stream.

Wes fretted over the auction of the cattle attached by the sheriff, but the sale remained unscheduled. When he mentioned his bewilderment over the delay, Jace told him it was better that the cattle were consuming Brady's grass rather than that of the Mirror B. Jace always offered a sunnier perspective on most issues confronting the Mirror B and Lincoln County. At first the wait bothered Wes, but he came to appreciate the postponement because he anticipated the widow Casey would leave the county after the sale. He preferred Ellen to remain nearby until Sarafina delivered their first child as Ellen could serve as the midwife. The best he and his wife could figure, they expected the baby to come in July. By March Sarafina was showing and by April her bulging belly could not be missed beneath the loose clothes she wore.

Even after they planted corn, alfalfa, and garden vegetables in April, the livestock sale never came. At first Wes suspected Murphy was behind the delay, likely coordinating with the court in Mesilla, a hundred and fifty miles distant, how to best dispose of the herd to benefit the House and the politicians. Then the Irishman left Lincoln for the hospital in Fort Stanton, folks gossiping he might never return to town. Rumors circulated that Murphy had sold the store to Dolan without revealing the actual debts he owed to his suppliers and others. It turned out Murphy was as good at draining his own pocketbook as he was those of the citizens of Lincoln County. If Murphy was indeed broke, Wes delighted in knowing the Irishman had shortchanged his partner just as he had his customers. The longer the auction was postponed, the more perplexed Wes grew. Though Wes and Jace avoided Lincoln after the encounter with Murphy and Dolan, they paid Juan Patrón to watch the postings at the courthouse for the auction or for other county news. Patrón updated them on the progress of McSween's new adobe house and Tunstall's store, not as big as the House but well fortified with thick adobe walls and iron shutters to protect the windows from gunfire. Patrón also purchased meager supplies for the Brackens in the Montaño store as Ellen Casey's store had long been depleted.

When May came, the crops sprouted and the heifers calved. Wes and Jace spent their time hoeing and irrigating their fields as well as branding their new calves, estimating their herd had grown by a quarter over the preceding twelve months. Sometimes in the evening when he thought it safe, Wes walked with Sarafina along the Rio Ruidoso, allowing Luis to throw rocks in the stream or chase the cottonwood seed that dropped from the branches and floated on the silky white threads that gave the tree its moniker. They talked of the coming baby and agreed that if it were a boy, Wes would name him, and if it were a girl, Sarafina would decide.

In the middle of the month, Juan Patrón came over from Lincoln with news that the auction date was posted at the courthouse with the sale scheduled for noon the last Friday of May. Patrón reported that tensions had only worsened in Lincoln with Dolan running the House. As the pressures of the House's debt weighed on the new owner, he turned more hotheaded than Murphy had ever been. Just the week before, the furious Dolan had shot and killed a Mexican employed by the House. The poor fellow had angered Dolan with an innocuous comment and had died as a result. The store owner had claimed self defense, and the sheriff had let him walk away without arresting him. After all, Hiraldo Jaramillo had committed the unpardonable sin of being a Mexican and questioning the authority of his Irish boss. Patrón said the weight of the debt Dolan had assumed from Murphy and the impending opening of the Tunstall store terrified the new owner because he feared his monopoly over Lincoln

County was ending.

Then Patrón announced an arrangement that worried Bracken. Until the new mercantile was completed, John Henry Tunstall would stay at Patrón's house.

"I don't trust Tunstall any more than I do Dolan," Wes told Patrón.

He shrugged. "Tunstall's not James J. Dolan, and he's paying me for room and board. That's good enough for me."

"Maybe so, but Tunstall's bad for Lincoln County. He's as greedy as the House from my talks with him. Now that we know the date of the auction, Juan, there's no need for you to make your weekly trips to update us."

"Are you upset I'm taking Tunstall in? He's naïve about his opposition. He thinks he can outsmart them. Perhaps he can," Patrón offered.

"But they can damn sure outshoot him," Wes answered, grasping his hand and thanking him for his support since the impounding of the Casey cattle. "Just make sure when the shooting starts you're not in the line of fire."

Patrón nodded and returned to Lincoln. In late May Carlos and Bonney visited the Mirror B on their way to Lincoln, stopping for an hour at lunch, while Brewer rode on to meet with Tunstall in town. Carlos was torn, delighted to see Sarafina but angered at her condition as it proved his sister would birth Bracken's child. Bonney remained as lighthearted as always, he and Jace bantering at the table.

"Tell me, Billy," Wes asked, "have you returned any more stolen horses to their rightful owners?"

Bonney snickered. "Not since I've gotten a job, I haven't."

"Then tell me," Wes continued, "has Tunstall paid you your dollar-a-day wages?"

Bonney coughed on a bite of tortilla. "He's been slow, I admit, but he's sinking money into his new store. Once it's up and running, he'll take business away from the House, and he'll be making money hand over fist. He's also filed on land along the Rio Feliz to run cattle. He'll be taking on John Chisum, too, before he's through."

Wes fluttered his head in disagreement. "Tunstall lacks the experience of a cattleman like Chisum, nor does he have the vicious streak of a Murphy or a Dolan, though he's equally greedy. You're only asking for trouble if you hitch your team to his wagon and do the heavy pulling for him. He doesn't have a lick of prairie sense in him."

Bonney shrugged. "That's why he hired Brewer and me."

"And me, too," Carlos echoed.

Wes grinned. "Jimmy Dolan won't stand for losing business once the store opens."

"Nothing he can do about it," Bonney responded.

"Except kill him like Murphy ambushed Bob Casey," Wes shot back.

"Please," Sarafina interrupted, "let's not talk Lincoln County politics anymore. It's frightening enough to live it without having to hear it at the table."

After lunch, Bonney and Carlos continued their journey to Lincoln. Wes knew they were heading for the auction, figuring to have a herd to drive back to the Rio Feliz and the land Tunstall had filed on through surrogate owners under the Desert Land Act. The next morning, Wes arose early to take Sarafina and Luis to stay with Ellen Casey, then returned to the Mirror B and accompanied Jace to Lincoln in time to attend the noon auction. Their long guns in the crooks of their arms, Wes and Jace rode toward town, ever alert for Jesse Evans or any of Dolan's other crooked associates. They encountered a few riders, mostly Mexicans, on the road but no trouble, arriving at the courthouse a half hour before the scheduled auction.

A quarter before noon Patrón arrived with Tunstall and McSween. Dick Brewer, Billy Bonney, and Carlos walked up behind them. Patrón, Brewer, Bonney, and even Carlos greeted Wes and Jace, but Tunstall and McSween remained aloof, standing to the side and whispering to each other. Five minutes until midday, James J. Dolan showed up with a dozen of his henchmen, whose grim demeanors told Bracken these men intended to intimidate potential bidders.

Dolan sauntered up to Tunstall, shoving his finger at the Englishman's nose. "You come to bid on the cattle?"

McSween stepped between the two store owners. "That is my client's business, not yours."

"Everything's my affair in Lincoln County," Dolan replied, pointing down the street toward the building under construction. "As much money as the Englishman's throwing into this new store, he can't afford to buy cattle."

"My client," McSween answered, "has adequate resources for anything he cares to purchase in Lincoln County."

"If he's not careful," Dolan shot back, "he'll buy a bigger load of trouble than he can afford." As he spoke, his men edged toward Tunstall and McSween.

No sooner had they done that, than Brewer, Bonney, and Carlos stepped in behind their boss. Brewer and Carlos watched with nervous eyes, though Bonney merely grinned.

Wes grabbed Jace's arm and tugged it. "This ain't our fight."

Jace nodded and the two partners backed away to let the factions settle it, though the threats were more bluff and bluster than blood and thunder. As the rival groups faced each other, Wes wondered why Dolan even bothered to attend the auction. Murphy had never deigned to buy cattle when so many were available to steal, and Dolan had followed that larcenous practice, at least that was the rumor.

Promptly at noon, Sheriff William Brady emerged from the courthouse and read the legal notice authorizing the sale of two hundred and nine head of cattle to repay debts of the late Robert Casey to L.G. Murphy and Company and its successor, J.J. Dolan and Company. Under the authorization, the purchaser must pay cash to the county, which would distribute the proceeds to cover the balance owed. Bile rose in Wes's throat that this auction had arisen over a five-dollar debt that he had repaid twice, a debt intended as a gesture of goodwill.

As soon as Brady opened the bidding, Dolan shouted out fifty cents a head. McSween offered a dollar on behalf of his client. Dolan upped the bid to two dollars apiece. Tugging at his mustache while wondering if the rumors were false about Dolan's poor cash flow, Wes finally realized Dolan never intended to buy what he could steal on the hoof anywhere in Lincoln County. Dolan was bidding merely to up the price and drain Tunstall's bankroll as much as possible.

The cost kept inching up, McSween offering three fifty and then Dolan four. McSween fidgeted after that bid, then whispered to Tunstall, who nodded. McSween then offered four fifty and Dolan countered at five fifty a head. This time, the Englishman hesitated, clenching his jaw and grimacing at McSween, who offered his advice.

"Going once," Brady cried. "Going twice."

"Six dollars," shouted Tunstall, drawing a glare from McSween.

Brady looked to Dolan, who wagged his head and his hand that he was through bidding.

"Going once, going twice, sold," Brady

called, receiving a smattering of applause from the spectators not associated with Dolan and the House. The sheriff took a pencil and pad from his pocket and calculated the cost. "That comes to twelve hundred and fifty-four dollars by my figuring."

Tunstall nodded. "That's right."

"Payment's due now," Brady called.

Even at over twelve hundred dollars, Wes knew Tunstall had purchased a bargain, getting the cattle at likely a fourth of their value. The Englishman had achieved his goal, becoming a cattleman. So too had Dolan succeeded by bidding up the cost. The Englishman was in over his head and didn't know it. Wes wondered if the lawyer McSween was smart enough to realize it or if he was just playing Tunstall to drain into his own pockets as much of the Englishman's family wealth as possible. Only time would provide the answer. As the Englishman and the lawyer entered the courthouse to complete the purchase, Wes and Jace said goodbye to Brewer, Bonney, and Carlos.

The Kid shot Wes a bucktoothed grin. "You'll see us later today when we drive the cattle by the Mirror B," he offered.

Wes cocked his eyes at Bonney. "Tell me something, Kid. How is it that Tunstall has plenty of cash to buy a line of cattle, but not enough to pay you?"

"When our payday comes, it'll be a big one, Wes. You just wait and see."

"I'm waiting, Billy."

Brewer defended Tunstall. "We're taking a herd of the Englishman's horses and mules to my place as he's thinking about selling them. When that's done, I'm sure he'll give us our due."

"What about the cattle?" Wes wanted to know.

"After we deliver the horses and mules, we'll drive the Englishman's cattle to his new place on the Rio Feliz."

"Don't you mean Ellen Casey's spread and cattle, Dick?" Wes asked.

Brewer shrugged. "Not now. They belong to Tunstall fair and square."

"Maybe square, but not fair," Wes answered. "One other thing, don't stop at our place when you move the cattle."

Wes turned around and marched away, Cousins joining him at the horses. They mounted and rode toward home.

"What's bothering you?" Jace asked.

"It ain't right, the Englishman taking Ellen's cattle."

"What do you plan to do about it?"

"I'll do something. I just don't know when."

Jace responded with a low whistle. "You intend to rustle the cattle, don't you?"

Wes reined up Charlie and turned to look at his partner. "As Bonney would say, I'm just returning them to their rightful owner."

As May became June and summer's heat bore down on the Mirror B, Sarafina was so bloated with pregnancy she waddled around the house, tiring at her chores and resting more as the impending birth approached.

June rolled over into July and Sarafina waited anxiously each day for the moment that the little one would join them. Wes fretted as well as the first day of the month passed, then another and another until they all ran together in his mind. On the morning of the twenty-eighth day of July, Sarafina picked up Luis, grimacing and quickly lowering her son to the floor before patting her belly. Stepping to the back door, she yelled for Wes. "Come quick, *mi esposo,* my time is near!"

Wes ran from the garden to her, then whistled to Jace in the corral as he was exercising the horses. He pointed to his wife's belly and Jace waved that he understood. He ran to the corral fence, climbing over it and racing inside the barn as Wes bolted to his wife. As he escorted Sarafina past the bewildered Luis to their bed, Wes heard Jace galloping away to the Casey place to bring back Ellen. Wes helped Sarafina on the bedding as Luis walked up beside her, his lip trembling.

"No te preocupes, pequeña," Sarafina said, patting him on the head. "Do not worry, little one. Soon you will have a playmate." She grimaced and moaned as a set of contractions rippled across her belly.

Wes found a towel and began to daub at the perspiration that pimpled on her forehead. Wes had helped Sarafina birth Luis, though only because her husband had been killed going for assistance. Even with that experience, Wes felt helpless trying to bring his own child into the world. Time dragged as he awaited Jace's return, and relief washed over him as he detected the jingle of the trace chains of an approaching wagon. He recognized the whistle of Jace, who had returned with Ellen.

"Hurry, hurry," Wes cried.

Ellen burst into the bedroom carrying a carpetbag and a canteen of water. Wes greeted her, pleased she was wearing a dress rather than a man's outfit as she had done so often since her husband's death. "You look nice, Ellen," he offered.

She shook her head. "If I'm gonna help a

woman, I should dress like one. Didn't seem right to be in men's clothing for a birth. Now get out of here. If I need something, I'll call."

Wes nodded, scooped up Luis, and headed out front to visit with Jace.

"You nervous, poppa?" Jace asked.

"I've never had my own child before."

"Let me tend my horse and Ellen's team, then we can wait in the bunkhouse. Might be easier on us, including the boy there. It'll scare him if he hears his mother screaming."

Wes nodded and strode to the bunkhouse. The day wore on with no word from Ellen. Twilight came and then darkness, Wes and Jace passing the time by amusing Luis until he fell asleep and then playing cards by candlelight.

After midnight, the card players heard a gunshot and a distant yelp. Though Jace had brought his Henry from the barn, Wes had left his carbine in the house. He rushed from the bunkhouse and sprinted for the kitchen door, bursting inside and finding his Winchester.

Surprised at the noise, Ellen rushed into the room to see Wes fingering his Winchester. "You startled me," she said.

"Gunshot," he replied. "Don't know who

258

fired it."

"It won't be long now," Ellen reassured him, returning to her charge.

Wes slipped outside, angered that on this evening, the night of the birth of his first child, his enemies would attack the Mirror B. He slid to the front of the house, peering into the darkness, looking for any assailants. "Jace," he cried, "do you see anything?"

"Nothing," he answered. "I'll check the barn and make sure no one's hiding there."

As Wes studied the perimeter of the place, he found it odd that Nip and Tuck had not raised a ruckus over a visitor. He whistled, then called, "Nip, Tuck." One dog trotted up from the road before the second one, ambling and whimpering. Unable to distinguish them in the dark, Wes patted the first, deciding it was Tuck. Nip whined as he approached, close enough for Wes to reach out to stroke his head. The dog flinched as Wes rubbed a damp spot on Nip's neck. As Wes removed his hand, he felt a stickiness between his fingers. He lifted them to his face and sniffed at his flesh, which smelled of dog hair, sweat, and blood. Someone had shot Nip. Was it a night rider thinking Nip was a wolf or was it an assailant trying to kill the dogs and draw Wes into an ambush? On edge, Wes gritted his teeth at the sound of a wail. His senses so strained over the threat from the road, it took a moment for him to realize the scream came from inside the house instead of the trail. The cry came again from newborn lungs, and Wes realized he was a father. He stepped to the front door and cracked it open.

"Is everything fine, Ellen?" he called.

"It's a boy, Wes!"

Wes smiled. "Is Sarafina okay?"

"She's fine," Ellen answered, "just exhausted and sleepy. Is all well out there?"

"Can't say."

"You take care of yourself, Wes, you and Jace."

Wes eased the door shut, calling to Jace. "Any problems your way?"

"Nothing out here that I can see, and the horses aren't fretting like they hear anything."

"Somebody shot Nip," he called.

"Bad?"

"Can't tell. Will have to wait until dawn to check him. Ellen tells me I've got a boy."

"Congratulations, Wes. I'll look around the place so you can meet your son."

"Not until sunrise, and we can see," Wes replied. "I'm staying out here so no one can slip up and ambush us."

Wes spent the night looking out for whoever had fired the shot that wounded Nip. He visited the bunkhouse twice to check on Luis, who remained asleep on Jace's bed. Neither Wes nor Jace ever spotted another soul, and Wes thought it might have been either an accidental shooting or a subtle message that the gunman would return. As the sky lightened behind the mountains and the cover of darkness receded in the valley, Wes and Jace scouted the land around the place without finding a sign of the assailant. Spotting Nip lying beside the front door, Wes squatted to check the watchdog. He found a grazing bullet wound over Nip's right shoulder and a mass of hair matted with dried blood. "We'll tend you later," Wes said, patting the animal on the head. "First, I want to meet my new son."

Wes marched around to the back, informing Jace he was leaving the sentry duty to him, then entered the kitchen, placing his carbine on the table and taking a pitcher of water to the washbasin and dumping it in so he could clean his hands of Nip's blood before meeting his son. He soaped, lathered, and rinsed, then grabbed a towel to dry his hands before tossing it aside and running into the bedroom. Wes found Ellen asleep in a chair in the corner and Sarafina on the bed still drowsy, but holding a bundle

261

against her bosom. Wes walked over and picked up the baby and gazed upon him for the first time, examining his shock of black hair, his black eyes, his button nose, and his tiny fingers clasped in a fist. Sarafina smiled as she realized her husband held their boy. Wes bent and kissed her on the cheek. "Thank you for giving our son life," Wes whispered.

"What will we call him?"

"He is a son of Lincoln County," Wes answered. "I will name him for two men buried in Lincoln County soil, Robert Casey and my brother. He will be Robert Luther Bracken."

Sarafina smiled. "I will call him 'Roberto,' " she said as Wes returned her son to her arms. She kissed him and offered the baby nourishment at her breast. "He will grow up to be a fine man like his father."

July became August and Nip healed from the bullet graze to the shoulder, though it left a purple scar where the projectile had skimmed his hide. Wes never determined the reason for the attack, writing it off as a rider thinking his dog was a wolf. September brought fall to the valley as the leaves began to color and the cornstalks yellowed. The autumn chores multiplied as everyone except the boy and the baby prepared for winter. Wes relished watching Roberto grow and become more attentive to the world around him. Somehow Sarafina nursed the baby, kept Luis busy, and managed her household tasks. Wes handled the outdoor chores closest to the house while Jace covered those farther away, checking on the cattle, branding any calves they missed earlier in the year, and keeping count on the herd. Since Roberto's birth, Wes strayed from the place only twice, both times to see Ellen Casey, who thanked him each time for naming his son after her late husband. The widow had decided to return to Texas as soon as the weight of fall tasks fell on everyone so fewer enemies might come after her. Wes told Ellen to have her wagon packed and her family ready to move on short notice, if she stood any chance of getting her lost cattle back. She promised she would. Wes returned home to Sarafina and the boys, facing six weeks of chores to prepare everything for the cold season.

Jace took one day to drive the wagon to Lincoln to buy what supplies he could at the Montaño store, but goods were scarce or pricey. Jace passed, and admired, the well-stocked shelves of the Tunstall store, but ignored it for his business. Dolan's men had so intimidated anyone that approached the store that Tunstall drew but a handful of customers and none of them regulars. Jace reported to Wes that Juan Patrón rejoiced after Tunstall moved into quarters in the rear of his store, but remained angry that Tunstall had made no payment for room and board.

"Word'll get around that the Englishman doesn't pay his debts," Wes told Jace, "and nobody'll do business with him anymore. Dolan's boys won't have to scare his customers away."

The day after Cousins returned from Lincoln, he left early to check on the cattle. Midmorning, Wes was milking the cow when Nip and Tuck cut loose a great cry, running toward the road before retreating, barking, and howling as eight men turned down the path to the house. Wes jumped up, knocking the milk pail over, then grabbed his Winchester and dashed from the barn to the kitchen door, yelling as he spurt past for Sarafina to take the boys in the bedroom and stay low if she heard gunfire. He slipped to the front door and cracked it enough to see the approaching men, all cradling long guns in their arms.

Wes bit his lip as he recognized Jesse

Evans in the lead. If ever a man needed killing, it was Evans, but that would be suicide
for him and his family. Wes grimaced and
hoped for the best.

CHAPTER 14

"That's the barrel of a Winchester sticking out the door, not a Henry rifle," Jesse Evans called. "Come on out, Wes Bracken. We mean you no harm." He spat at the barking Nip and Tuck. "You might call off your dogs."

Bracken whistled, and the hounds' snarling turned to low growls. "State your business, Jesse. And don't think Jace doesn't have his Henry sighted on your chest as we speak," Wes bluffed.

Evans leaned forward over his bay gelding's neck, trying to see inside the house. Rising, he slid his carbine in the scabbard under his left leg. "I hold nothing against you, Wes, or even Jace Cousins."

"That's a lie, Jesse. Your boss Dolan carries a grudge, and he's told me you'd be calling."

"Dolan's a hotheaded Irishman," Jesse replied. "Jimmy's always spouting off until he cools down or gets sober. He understands you're not the threat that the Englishman is. Join with us in fighting Tunstall, and bygones will be bygones."

Wes waved his carbine barrel at Jesse. "I'm not taking sides with Dolan or Tunstall, so why don't you move on?"

"If you don't take a side, Wes, you're against everybody."

"So be it," Wes answered. "I don't care for the Irish or the English in this."

"You're a stubborn man, Wes, one that doesn't know what's best for him."

"I'm trying to do what's right."

Jesse laughed. "There's no right or wrong in Lincoln County, just the strong and the dead." He twisted in his saddle enough to point to the men behind him. "These boys can fight and win. Come out and show your face because you'll run into them again."

Wes hesitated, lowering his rifle to his chest, opening the door, and stepping outside. "Hold your fire, Jace," he yelled, continuing his bluff.

"Yeah, Jace," shouted Evans. "Come on out and meet the boys."

"Get on with it," Wes said. "We've got chores to finish."

Evans started down the line of men backing him up and introduced them as Buck

Morton, Frank Baker, Tom Hill, George Davis, Jim McDaniels, Indian Segovia and Bob Martin. They stared at Wes with hard eyes and grim demeanors. "Last chance to throw in with us, Wes," Jesse offered with a smile on his face."

"I'm my own man," Wes answered.

"Bad decision," Jesse said. "We'll ride back by this evening, and we'll fire our guns so you'll know it's us. Watch us when we pass. You'll see what's in store for you and your place."

"Get moving, Jesse. I'm done talking."

Jesse nodded and twisted in his saddle. "Okay, boys, you heard the man. Let's ride on so we can make a call on Dick Brewer's place."

Nip and Tuck barked as the riders spun around and retreated up the trail to the road to San Patricio and Brewer's place. Wes watched until they disappeared toward San Patricio. He stepped in the house to comfort Sarafina. He found her seated in the corner on the floor, holding Roberto to her bosom and playing with Luis.

"My prayers have been answered," Sarafina said when she saw her husband.

Wes helped her to her feet and picked up Luis, carrying him to the kitchen. "Everything's fine." He kissed her cheek, then lowered Luis to the floor and returned outside to finish milking. Wes spent the rest of the day pulling corn ears and waiting on Jace to come home. His partner returned an hour before dusk, so Wes related the visit of Jesse Evans and his boys along with their implied threats. As the daylight dimmed, Wes and Jace heard gunfire up the road from San Patricio. Both men grabbed their long guns and marched outside, picking up the sounds of galloping hooves. Sure enough, Jesse and his gang had returned, driving thirty horses and mules. Wes understood the implied threat Jesse had made to his place. Now his herd stood at risk.

"Think those are Brewer's animals?" Jace asked.

"His and the Englishman's," Wes replied, then clapped his hands. "This is what I've needed since the auction."

"What are you talking about, Wes?"

"The Casey cattle."

"Huh?" Perplexed, Jace tugged on his ear.

"Those are Brewer's and Tunstall's horses. Brewer'll have to recover them. That'll give us a chance to ride to the Rio Feliz and reclaim Ellen's beeves stolen from her at the auction."

"Damn," Jace replied. "What are you trying to do, Wes? Get me thrown in prison again?"

"I'm living up to the promise I made Ellen. It ain't right her losing two hundred head because of a five-dollar debt to Murphy. One of us needs to inform Ellen Casey that she should start for Texas first thing in the morning with what belongings she can manage and with the cattle we mixed with our herd. Tell Ellen to have her boys sort her cattle from ours and start for Texas."

"I'll get the word to Ellen and her brood," Jace offered. "You gather supplies for our trip."

Wes nodded. "We'll leave before dawn tomorrow."

Bracken and Cousins started for San Patricio an hour before sunrise and passed through the village while it still slept, before turning south through the mountains along the trail where Wes had first met Billy Bonney. Wes regretted leaving Sarafina and the boys alone, but he figured it safer than normal since he knew Jesse Evans and his ilk were likely headed northeast toward Fort Sumner or Tascosa in the Texas Panhandle. Normally Evans sold his stolen mounts around El Paso or in Mexico, but Wes speculated he was going against old habits to give Brewer the slip. Had Evans started the animals through rangeland, they would've been easier to track. Instead, he drove them along the road, making their tracks indecipherable until they cut off the road for their ultimate destination.

Wes led Jace down the trail to the Rio Feliz, eating tortillas for breakfast and sipping water from their canteens to quench their thirsts. Midmorning they saw in the distance three men approaching, one on a dappled gray that Wes recognized as the Kid's mount.

Bonney waved his hat and started at a trot toward them, Brewer and Carlos quickly catching up with him. Wes and Jace drew back on their reins, stopping their mounts to await Tunstall's hands.

"This is turning out better than I imagined," Wes said softly.

Jace nodded. "I won't know how it works out until I'm certain I won't return to prison."

Brewer stopped his horse in front of Wes's sorrel.

Before he could speak, Wes addressed him. "Bad news, Dick. Jesse Evans and his boys hit your place last night and stole your horses and mules."

"Dammit," said Brewer.

"They raced them by our place," Jace offered. "They were headed east toward Roswell."

"I figure they were hoping to disguise their trail for as long as they could before heading toward Fort Sumner or Tascosa," Wes added.

"They usually head south for Mexico," Bonney countered.

"That's what I've heard," Wes said, "but you had as good a herd of horses as any except ours in Lincoln County, and they'll bring a better price up north than they will down south."

Brewer cursed.

"They've got twelve hours or more on you," Jace added.

"We can catch them," Billy said, "if we keep our horses at a lope and don't ruin them."

"Seven others were riding with Evans," Wes offered.

Brewer released a deep sigh, then nodded. "Obliged for the information. Are you coming with us?"

"Our mounts are worn out. We'd only slow your progress," Wes said. "I hope you catch them and your horses." Wes turned to his brother-in-law. "Be careful, Carlos. These are dangerous men."

"Gracias," he replied.

"What about me?" Billy asked.

"You don't need to be careful, Billy, because you're too ornery to care," Wes answered.

Bonney tipped his hat as Brewer put his horse into a lope. The Kid and Carlos started after their foreman. Wes and Jace sat in their saddles, watching the trio disappear into the terrain, only the wisp of dust thrown up by their horses' hooves marking their location.

"You feel bad about windying them?" Jace asked.

"Not when they're doing Tunstall's work," he replied. "Let's find the Casey cattle and get them back to Ellen."

They moved southeast until they reached the Rio Feliz, then followed its course — Wes on the north side of the river and Jace on the south — northeast toward the Pecos River. They gathered the occasional stray with the Casey brand on its flank, then in the middle of the afternoon when the sun hung like a furnace in the western sky they found the bulk of the Casey cattle watering along the Rio Feliz.

Wes did a quick estimate of the herd and realized those stock and the dozen strays they had picked up totaled more than the two hundred and nine belonging to Ellen Casey. "There's more cattle here than the Caseys are due. Rather than separate them now, I say we run them all to Chisum's place, cutting out any we can as we ride."

Jace eyed his partner and shook his head. "I can taste prison slop already."

"I'm trying to do what's right, Jace."

Scratching his chin, Cousins sighed. "It's a damn shame that by rustling cattle we believe we're in the right."

"That's Lincoln County!"

"Okay then," Jace replied, tugging his hat snug over his forehead, "let's go. The sooner I'm done with this, the sooner I'll get out of prison."

Wes laughed, and they began to drive the cattle into a compact herd, forcing them to drink their fill of water as Wes intended to drive them straight through to Chisum's range as fast as they could. Once they reached the cowman's grassland, they would have protection, if Chisum lived up to his promise to give Ellen and her cattle safe passage to the Texas border. With the beeves watered, Wes and Jace started them moving northeast. The Mirror B men pushed them hard while they had light, then slowed the pace and covered another five miles by moonlight before bedding the beeves and themselves for the night. Arising an hour before dawn, Bracken and Cousins saddled up and resumed their drive.

Barely had the sun topped the horizon, sending long shadows across the landscape, when Wes spotted four riders approaching from the east. "We've got company," he called to Jace.

"I noticed," Jace answered, pulling his Henry rifle from its scabbard. Wes nudged Charlie in the flank and trotted out to meet the quartet, the four men reining up to wait for him. A fellow with a patch over his left eye nudged his horse a step ahead of the other mounts.

"Morning, friend," the cowboy said. "What brings you to Mr. Chisum's land?"

Wes smiled, glad to be on the cattleman's range. "I'm Wes Bracken. Mr. Chisum promised safe passage across his property for the widow Ellen Casey and her herd. These are her cattle, at least most of them. We didn't have time to separate them because we needed to catch her before she reached the Texas line."

The fellow pointed toward Cousins. "Who's the fellow with the Henry rifle?"

"That's Jace Cousins. He's my partner on the Mirror B."

"I'm Claude Tinsley, Mr. Chisum's fore-

275

man over this section of the ranch. He mentioned the Casey woman and her cattle might cross the ranch, but he said nothing about them coming in two groups."

"These were pastured on a different range," Wes explained. "She needed to leave her place fast because of threats to her and her family from the House."

Tinsley nodded. "Before we let you pass, I want my hands to check the brands on the cattle and cull out those that don't have the Casey brand. After that we'll help drive them to Roswell where the Casey family is staying outside of town on the Pecos." As the foreman twisted around in his saddle, he ordered the trio behind him to sort the Casey cattle from the others. The cowboys trotted to the herd and inspected the brands.

Seeing the Chisum hands working the cattle, Jace put his rifle back in its scabbard and turned his yellow dun toward Wes and the range boss. Wes introduced the two.

Tinsley studied Cousins. "You're the fellow that's hunting Jesse Evans, right?"

"Part of the time I am," Jace answered.

"I hope you get him," Tinsley said. "That'd solve many problems for Mr. Chisum."

"Jesse's known for making more enemies

than friends." Jace lifted his hat and wiped the perspiration from his brow with the sleeve of his shirt. "It's the same everywhere he's been."

"You must go a ways back with Jesse," Tinsley observed.

"We had run-ins in Texas," Jace replied as one of the Chisum hands rode up to his foreman. "He took something from me, and I intend to make him pay for it."

The cowhand leaned over in the saddle, cupped his hand over his mouth, and whispered toward Tinsley, who nodded twice, then looked to Wes and Jace.

"My man says thirty-three of the cattle have Mr. Chisum's long rail brand on them and another seventy-two with various brands from the Seven Rivers ranches."

"Take what's Chisum's and do what you want with the rest," Wes replied.

"You sure you fellows aren't rustlers?"

"The cattle were stolen from the widow Ellen Casey. Looks to me like the thieves added stock from other owners along the way."

"You may be right," Tinsley responded. "We'll take Mr. Chisum's cattle and add the other odd-branded animals to our herd."

"Now who's rustling cattle?" Jace interjected.

A laugh pried its way out of the foreman's lips. "The Seven Rivers ranchers steal plenty of stock from Mr. Chisum." Tinsley pointed to Cousins. "Didn't your partner say Jesse Evans took something from him, and he intended to make him pay for it? No difference here."

"Lincoln County," Jace said.

"Yep," Wes agreed.

Once the Casey cattle were cut from the others, two of the hands drove the Chisum and Seven Rivers stock to the east while Tinsley and the remaining hand helped push the widow's beeves on toward Roswell, circling south of the small town and joining up with the Casey family at their camp along the west bank of the Pecos.

When Ellen Casey spotted Wes and the cattle behind him, she bounced up from her camp stool and ran out to greet him. "Thank God you're safe, Wesley Bracken. And you got our cows. I can't believe it."

"Most of them," Wes replied. "We're three shy of two hundred so we lost a dozen, but it's the best we could do." He dismounted and hugged the widow, grabbing her shoulders and holding her back to inspect her. "You look great, Ellen, in your dress."

"I hated to leave poor old Bob in a grave, Wes, but I tell you the farther I get from

278

Lincoln the better I feel. I'm not worried somebody's trying to kill me every day. Starting over in Texas is better than staying in Lincoln County, and the cattle are money on the hoof, something that can get me started back in Texas."

"I'm glad for you, Ellen. Wish it could've turned out different for Bob and the rest of you, as you were fine neighbors. I'd never have made it without your help when I first arrived on the Ruidoso."

"Join us for supper, Wes, would you? You and Jace?"

"Sure, Ellen, but let me help Jace and Chisum's men get your animals settled with your others. When that's done, we can visit."

Wes climbed atop his sorrel and rode away to attend to the cattle. He joined Jace in driving the cattle to the river to drink. Wes inspected the waters, which were lazy and shallow, then directed Charlie to the crossing where the waters reached a foot up the sorrel's strong legs. He let Charlie drink all he wanted. Once the cattle had filled on water, Wes and Jace drove them from the riverbed and up the gentle slope that led to the other cattle, where Wes spotted Will and Add Casey keeping watch over the expanding herd. Wes joined Jace to return to the Casey camp. They dismounted, tended their horses, and unfurled their bedrolls before joining Ellen, her two daughters, and her two younger sons at the campfire.

"It's not much," she said of the supper fare, "but it's the best I got, biscuits and roasting ears." She lifted the lid from a Dutch oven and forked out two biscuits apiece on the tin plates her daughter Lily held. Ellen picked up a pair of tongs and stuck the iron into the coals, extracting from the embers one and then a second ear of corn still in the shucks. She added a roasting ear to each tin plate and Lily offered the tinware to Wes and Jace, who sat on the ground by the fire and shucked and silked the corn, pitching the refuse in the fire. They ate supper, relishing the taste of a hot meal after the last two days of eating stale tortillas smeared with refried beans.

Ellen pulled up her stool and sat opposite her former neighbors. "You want more?"

Wes did, but he looked at a frowning Lily and realized Ellen had yet to feed her family. "Maybe later, after you've fed your brood." Lily smiled, and Wes confirmed he had made the right decision as Ellen arose and fixed plates for herself and her offspring. Wes saw two remaining ears of corn by the fire and knew that those were for Add and Will. He placed his plate on the ground to his side and stretched his arms. "I'm plenty full, Ellen."

Jace glared at him with still hungry eyes as if he was crazy.

"Hope there's enough left for Will and Add," Wes continued, drawing a nod from Jace that now he understood.

Ellen nodded. "There's plenty. We've learned to eat light since we lost Bob."

"We still wish things had turned out better for you," Wes offered.

The widow sighed. "Me, too."

Wes saw her eyes glisten. "I wish we could've done more for you."

"You did more than anyone else. I can't tolerate living in fear the rest of my life in Lincoln County. Texas may be a hard place, but it's still safer than Lincoln County."

"Perhaps all the mean Texans moved to New Mexico Territory," Jace joked.

Ellen smiled. "You may be from Texas, Jace, but you're not callous like other Texans." She set her plate on the ground and arose from her stool. "I've something for you both," she said, as she walked toward one of her wagons. She stood on the spoke of a front wheel and reached beneath the wagon seat, pulling out a canvas bag with a closed flap. Ellen flipped back the canvas cover and stuck her hand inside, extracting a thick envelope. She dropped the bag and stepped down from the wheel, returning to Wes and offering him the packet.

"It's papers on my place," she said. "I didn't want the House to take over the land that Bob built and irrigated with his blood and sweat, so I signed the place over to the two of you. Ash Upson over in Roswell notarized the bill of sale."

"But we didn't pay you anything, Ellen," Wes said.

"We owe you something," Jace added.

"You recovered my cattle," she replied, "that was the best I could hope for as I can sell the cattle in Texas and make enough for a fresh start. There's still a few goods left in the store if no one's plundered it. And, there's tools in the outbuildings, and the mill, which may help you."

Never before had Wes felt so beholden to a person. "How can I repay you? There must be something."

"Two things," Ellen replied, "and one you've already done."

"What?" Wes asked.

"You named your boy Robert. It would've touched my husband that you thought enough of him to brand your son with his name."

"He was an honest man," Wes answered.

"And so are you, Wes."

"What else can we do?" Jace asked.

"Keep Bob's grave looking pretty, not overgrown with weeds," Ellen said as she dabbed at her eyes. "If you prosper, one day you can buy him a stone like he deserves rather than the wooden marker we planted at his head."

Wes arose, handing Jace the bill of sale and stepping to Ellen. He hugged her, not knowing what else to do.

"We'll buy him a stone," Jace said, shoving the papers in his pants pocket and walking to Ellen. "I promise we'll purchase a tombstone." When Wes released her, Jace wrapped his arms around her as well and thanked her again.

"We'll be leaving early in the morning, Ellen," Wes informed her. "We left Sarafina, Luis, and little Robert alone, and I must check on them."

Ellen nodded. "I understand you must take care of Robert and your family. You go ahead. I hope one day our paths cross again when you are the wealthiest man in Lincoln County. From the first day, you've always been the most honest fellow I knew."

"And good luck to you and the rest of your family," Wes said. "I'd never survived my first months in Lincoln County without you."

"Nor me these last weeks without you." She turned and walked to the wagon, crying softly.

Come morning, Wes and Jace arose, saddled up, and started the fifty-mile journey to the Mirror B. Wes thought he should stop by John Chisum's South Spring Ranch headquarters south of Roswell, but he remained eager to check on his family. West of Roswell, Wes patted his shirt pocket, then his britches pockets, looking frantically at Jace.

"Did I give you the bill of sale to the Casey place?" Wes asked, bewilderment shadowing his face, even in the soft early morning light. "I'm certain I did and you put them in your pants pocket."

Cousins stuck his hand in one pocket, removed his knife and kerchief, then pulled the lining inside out.

"Dammit," Wes said, "we must backtrack and find where we dropped the papers."

"You worry too much, Wes," Jace said, stuffing the lining back in his pocket, then inserting his knife and kerchief inside. "The papers'll turn up."

Panicked, Wes twisted in his saddle and looked back down the trail. "How do you know we'll find them?"

"Because they're in my saddlebags. I put them there for safekeeping this morning when I saddled up." Jace laughed. "Sure had you going."

"I oughta shoot you for that."

"Join the list of men that want to do that," Jace replied. "Not a one has hit me yet." He kicked his horse into a trot and jogged ahead of Wes as they tried to make as good time as they could without ruining their mounts, both the sorrel and the dun having had a hard few days since they left the Mirror B.

Toward dusk as they neared the mouth to the Hondo Valley, Jace pointed out six men and a herd of horses approaching from the north. Both Wes and Jace pulled their long guns from their saddle scabbards to ward off any threats. One rider lifted his hat and waved. Wes recognized the dappled gray that Billy Bonney favored. He next discerned Carlos and Dick Brewer along with him, but it took him longer to identify the other three. When he did, he rubbed his eyes and looked again.

"I'm not believing what I'm seeing," Wes informed Jace.

"And what's that?"

"That looks like Brewer recovered his

stolen horses. And unless my eyes deceive me, Brewer, Bonney, and Carlos are riding with Jesse Evans and a pair of his gang like they were long-lost pals!"

CHAPTER 15

Wes shook his head in disbelief. The nearer the band and the stolen horses came, the more jovial the riders appeared. Wes recognized Jesse Evans and thought the other two were the ones Evans had introduced as Tom Hill and Frank Baker. The three outlaws rode with their hands and reins resting on their saddle horns, while Brewer, Bonney, and Carlos held their lines closer to their waists. The horse thieves grinned as Bonney talked and gestured with his right hand. Brewer remained stoic, as if annoyed by the banter. Carlos rode behind the others, keeping the riderless horses bunched together and moving.

The approaching party angled toward the road so their path would intersect with that of the Mirror B riders. As the band neared, Wes saw the reason that Jesse and his comrades rode stiffly in the saddle — their hands were tied to their saddle horns. Bonney kept up his banter, badgering the captives and laughing at his own comments. Even as a prisoner, Jesse sat cocky in his saddle with all the confidence in the world and a grin slathered across his face.

As was his habit, Jace pulled his Henry from his scabbard. The levity on Evans's lips died the moment he saw the rifle appear. As best he could with tied hands, Evans tugged on the reins, slowing his bay until Bonney's gray passed him and screened him from Jace's view. Jesse's swagger drained from his face.

Brewer hailed the Mirror B boys. "We got our horses and three of the scoundrels that stole them."

Wes and Jace pulled up their mounts to await the caravan. When Jace realized the rustlers' hands were bound to their saddle horns, he slid his Henry back in his scabbard. Taking note that his predator had put away his long gun, Evans regained his swagger and nudged his bay beside the Kid's horse.

"Well, if it isn't my old pal Jace Cousins," Evans called, grinning like a man on the way to a brothel rather than jail. "If you'd have your pals untie me, I'd gladly shake your hand, Jace."

"I ought to shoot you," Jace replied.

"This is the best chance you'll ever get."

Brewer twisted in his saddle. "Shut up, Jesse."

Evans spoke past Brewer. "Wes Bracken," he called, "this is your chance to make amends with the House. Free us, and we'll not bother your place anymore as Tom Hill and Frank Baker are my witnesses. Ain't that true, boys?"

His accomplices nodded. "Jesse's right," Hill said.

"Not a more trustworthy man in Lincoln County," Baker added, then laughed.

"Give us a hand, Wes, and we'd be forever obliged," Jesse offered.

"Shut up," Brewer screamed.

"I'm not choosing sides," Wes answered.

"We'd never caught them," Brewer said to Bracken, "if you hadn't ridden out to alert us."

Wes grimaced, knowing Brewer had given away his role in the capture.

"Well, well," observed Jesse, his grin replaced by a sneer, "it appears you've chosen a side after all. You should've kept your word and minded your own business, Wes Bracken."

Jace yanked his Henry from the scabbard and lifted it to his shoulder, aiming at Evans's nose. "I can't speak for my partner,

289

Jesse, but I'm on any side but yours. Open your mouth again, and I'll put another hole in your head so you'll whistle when the wind blows."

The air seeped out of Jesse's bluster, and the Kid mocked him. "Jesse struts about in big pants until the shooting starts. Once lead begins flying, he puts on girl britches."

"Shut up, Kid," Jesse scowled.

"Ah, ah, Jesse," Jace said, wagging the gun barrel at his face.

Wes turned to Brewer. "How'd you catch them?"

"We trailed them out of the valley to the north. They stayed a night in a box canyon while five of them rode off to the east to see if they could steal horses from Chisum. We jumped them before dawn the next morning. Billy slipped into their camp and took their rifles. Damndest thing I'd ever seen. Then he woke them one at a time with a gun barrel to the nose and convinced them to hand over their sidearms. Never fired a shot."

"That's a fact," Bonney added. "I even offered to give them their pistols back if they'd shoot it out with me. The cowards declined my offer."

"We've seen you shoot, Kid," said Jesse.

"So you think I'm that fast, Jesse."

"Can't say about speed, but you're a curly wolf that shows no fear," Jesse said. "Start riding with us rather than running around with these herders."

"Ah, ah, Jesse," Jace interrupted, "you've said enough for this evening. If I hear another word out of you, I'll put a bullet in your ear so even you won't know what you're saying."

"You're a big man, Jace, when your quarry can't fight back."

BOOM! The Henry rifle exploded with fire and brimstone.

"Damn," Jesse cried, yanking at the saddle horn, but his bound hands didn't budge. "That stung."

"Must've been a wasp," Jace said as he levered the smoking hull from the chamber of his rifle.

Wes glanced at Jesse, who struggled to keep his horse from bolting, and spotted a trickle of blood from a nick at the top of his left ear.

"Now shut up, Jesse, or your right ear is next."

Jesse gritted his teeth as he shook his head to fight the pain.

"That was a damn good shot," Bonney said.

"Not really, boys. I was aiming at his

nose," Jace replied as he lowered his smoking rifle.

Brewer shook his head. "We've been riding with Billy's prattle and Jesse's threats for more miles than I care to remember. I think we'll bed down for the night. Want to join us?"

"I'll pass. I've got to get home and check on Sarafina and the boys. Besides that, I'm staying neutral in this dispute, wherever it's headed."

"Too late, Bracken," Jesse shouted. "We see where you two stand. We won't forget."

"You'll be in jail for a spell," Jace said.

"Maybe so, but it won't be two years in the pokey. Hell, I doubt it'll even be two days before I'm free. Perhaps I'll come calling at your place, say hello to the little meskin wife, and those half-breed boys."

"Come on, Wes, let's get out of here," Jace said. "I'm tired of this skunk and the stink he raises everywhere he goes."

Wes nodded. "Fine by me." He touched the brim of his hat at Brewer and rode over to Carlos, inviting him to visit Sarafina whenever he got a chance. "She enjoys seeing you, and the boys need time with their uncle."

His brother-in-law shrugged. "Another day."

Wes turned and rode to catch up with Cousins, wondering what it would take to crack Carlos's shell.

The last remnants of daylight disappeared as they entered the Rio Hondo Valley, riding west along the trail. Occasionally, they detected the rippling waters of the Ruidoso as it meandered toward the Pecos or the hoot of an owl out of its perch to find food. They passed isolated houses with the dim light of tallow candles flickering through solitary windows. They rode by Casey's Mill, which was little more than a hulking shadow up the rise.

"I can't believe that place is ours," Jace said.

"Me neither, and I'm not sure what we should do with it."

They reached the Mirror B around midnight and to their delight Nip and Tuck raised a commotion that shattered the night air. Wes whistled and the dogs calmed. He spotted the flicker of a candle through the front window by the door.

"It's us, Sarafina," Wes called. "We're back safe."

The door flung open, and Wes saw his wife run out in her nightgown. He jumped from his horse and caught her in his arms.

"Is everything okay?" she cried.

Jace nudged his dun over by Charlie and picked up the reins. "I'll care for your horse, Wes. Grab your carbine."

Wes released Sarafina and twisted around to take his Winchester, then he escorted his wife inside and closed the door behind them.

"Did you find the cattle?"

"We did, and we saw Carlos, who sends his best."

"I wish he'd visit."

"I invited him, but he's never accepted that you married me. And now that we have a son of our own, Carlos is even more torn."

Sarafina sighed. "I chose you for my husband. Carlos should accept that. He runs around with that Bonney boy and other Anglos. There's no difference."

"There is in his mind," Wes replied, taking her hand. "Let's check on the boys and head to bed. It's been a long, tiring week."

Sarafina leaned into her husband's chest. "I'd like that."

Wes smiled as he ran his fingers through her raven hair. "One more question. Do you know how to shoot a gun?"

"What a strange thing to ask."

"Though an important one."

"No," she answered.

"I must teach you," Wes said, feeling her body tremble at his answer.

The next morning, Wes and Jace, both pleased with how Sarafina had managed necessary chores in their absence, resumed their tasks to prepare for winter, always wearing their sidearms and carrying their long guns as they chopped wood, bundled hay, pulled corn from yellowing stalks, plowed up the dying remnants of their garden, and tended to the horses, giving them time to run and water along the Rio Ruidoso. In the evenings when the light had faded too much to work outside, Wes began teaching Sarafina how to handle a spare pistol of his and his Winchester, starting with empty weapons and instructing her how to load, cock, aim, and fire the guns. She resisted at first, despite her husband's informing her of the threats to her well-being, but when Wes explained that any hazard to her represented a risk to her sons, Sarafina became a focused student. After two evenings of instructions, Wes took her outside after sunrise while the boys still slept and gave her live practice with a dozen rounds in both the pistol and the carbine. As they finished her initial lesson with live ammunition, Nip and Tuck started a commotion that could only mean visitors were approaching.

Wes looked toward the road and spotted three riders driving a herd of horses. "Your practice might come in handy if these men bring trouble."

"I doubt that I could ever shoot another person," Sarafina said, her hand shaking as she offered the pistol to her husband to reload.

Wes pulled cartridges from his gun belt and filled the cylinder on Sarafina's revolver, all the time watching the approaching horsemen until he recognized the dappled gray of Billy Bonney. "You won't have to shoot anybody, Sarafina. It's Carlos with Brewer and Bonney." As he handed Sarafina the loaded pistol, Wes whistled at the dogs, and they barked a few more times before turning and retreating to Wes.

Jace emerged from the barn, carrying his Henry as he studied the visitors.

"It's friends Brewer and Bonney," Wes called to his partner.

Jace nodded, turned around, and reentered the barn, emerging with his rifle in one hand and a pail of milk in the other. His trail converged with Wes and Sarafina's as they stepped out to greet their guests. The riders, though, circled around the barn and drove the horses to the stream to water, then returned to Wes, Sarafina, and Jace.

Brewer tipped his hat as they neared while Bonney offered a bucktoothed grin and a wave. Carlos merely nodded.

"Carlos, me alegro de verte," Sarafina shouted, lifting the pistol to wave.

Bonney laughed. "If you're so glad to see him, why are you threatening him with your revolver?"

"Lo siento," she apologized as she lowered the pistol to her side.

"After the threats from Jesse Evans," Wes explained, "I thought I'd show her how to use a gun for protection."

Brewer reined up in front of Wes. "Jesse's in jail with Hill and Baker."

"Likely not for long," Bonney interjected as he stopped his horse beside Brewer's.

Carlos rode past his companions to Sarafina. He leaned over in the saddle and kissed her on the cheek. *"¿Cómo están mi hermana y sus hijos?"*

Smiling, she nodded. "I am fine, and the boys are sleeping. If you can stay, I'll fix breakfast for everyone."

"Thank you, ma'am," Brewer said, tipping his hat, "but we've no time to tarry. We've got to get our horses back to the Rio Feliz and check on Tunstall's cattle."

Jace glanced at Wes, then stared at Brewer and nodded. "No telling how far those cattle have strayed as long as you've been gone."

"That's what worries me, what with the Seven Rivers ranchers rustling beeves and Chisum's hands taking what they want."

"Yep," Jace answered. "Those cattle could be in Texas by now."

Brewer grimaced at the comment. "That concerns me, but be forewarned, Jesse Evans is still threatening your family, Wes. Jimmy Dolan's working to get Jesse and his companions out of jail, but he's strapped for bail money."

Lifting the pail of milk, Jace said, "Care to drink to Jesse's threats?"

Bonney laughed. "We need something with more kick to it."

"Thanks for the offer, Jace," Brewer grinned, "but we must be riding."

Cousins lowered the bucket.

"Obliged for warning us about Jesse's threats," Wes responded. "We'll be careful."

Carlos leaned over in his saddle and kissed his sister again. *"Adiós,"* he said. He turned to Wes, offering a slight, tight-lipped nod to his brother-in-law.

Wes tipped his hat as the trio turned back to the stream where the horses watered and nibbled on the yellowing grass along the bank. As the three drove the herd from the Rio Ruidoso toward the road, Jace looked at his partner. "Think they'll find their cattle, Wes?"

"Not unless they ride all the way to Texas."

"How you gonna explain it, Wes, if they come back asking questions?"

Wes laughed. "I'll tell them you did it, Jace! What else?"

Sarafina swatted her husband on the shoulder. "That's not nice," she scolded.

"Or, honest," Jace added. "I was only following your orders."

Both men grinned, though Sarafina saw little humor in their banter. "I must check on the boys," she said, handing Wes her revolver and walking toward the house.

Jace took a step toward the barn, but Wes grabbed his arm. "Hold on a moment."

When Sarafina slipped inside the adobe, Wes released Jace's arm. "I'm worried about her and the boys if Jesse's gang attacks."

Exhaling a deep breath, Jace nodded. "I am too. Any idea what to do?"

"I've thought of moving her to the Casey place, her and the boys, but we can't abandon this place or they'll destroy it and wipe out all our hard work."

"We might move at night when we'd be less likely to be spotted," Jace countered.

"Think she'd be safe there by herself?"

Wes shrugged. "Can't say for sure."

"Nothing's certain in Lincoln County," Jace answered.

For four days Wes and Jace pondered what was safest for Sarafina, Luis, and Roberto. Every stratagem carried a risk to the Bracken family and the Mirror B. Wes realized Sarafina was more worried than normal because she prayed for protection two or three times a day. On the fourth day, Jace saddled his dun and rode over to the Casey place to check on it.

Before noon and after Jace departed, the dogs took to barking and announcing an approaching guest. Wes, who had gone inside the house for lunch, grabbed his carbine and burst out the front door. Why did it always work out that trouble arose when you were least prepared to respond? Wes had no answer other than the carbine in his hand, the grit in his craw, and the determination to protect his wife and boys.

A lone rider approached from San Patricio to the west. Wes studied the man and recognized Dick Brewer. Wes relaxed and stepped away from the house to greet Brewer. As the rider approached, Wes doffed his hat and nodded. "Welcome back, Dick.

Sorry you didn't bring Bonney and Carlos with you."

"Billy's too glib, and Carlos carries a chip on his shoulder against you, Wes, so I thought I ought to visit alone, just you and me. Not them and not Cousins."

"Jace is gone. You're in time for lunch. We can talk while we eat, if you'd join us."

Brewer eyed Wes and shook his head. "Not today, likely never. I don't eat with cattle rustlers, Wes."

Wes clenched his jaw and glared at Brewer. "That's a serious allegation, Dick."

"We tracked Tunstall's cattle to Chisum's spread, Bonney, Carlos, and me. I visited with Chisum's range foreman, Claude Tinsley, I believe his name was."

"That's him," Wes confirmed.

"He said Chisum had given you safe passage across his land all the way to Texas with Tunstall's cattle."

"They were Ellen Casey's cattle, Dick."

"So you admit stealing them, do you?"

"I recovered Bob Casey's cattle for his widow."

"Something didn't seem right when we encountered you on the trail when we were taking Evans, Hill, and Baker to jail. The previous time we ran into you we were heading the opposite direction. I tried to figure it out, but I'd never taken you for a cattle thief." Brewer spat at the ground in front of Wes's boots. "John Henry Tunstall purchased them at a legal county auction for failure to pay taxes."

"That's untrue, Dick. The county attached them on orders of L.G. Murphy over a five-dollar debt Bob Casey was on his way to repay the day the House assassinated him. I repaid the loan twice with five dollars from my own pocket, but the county didn't release the cattle. Your boss understood there was questionable title to the livestock, but he bought them anyway. He's no better than the House."

Brewer flinched. "You should've let the courts settle this, Wes, instead of taking what was Tunstall's."

"The courts are crooked in New Mexico Territory. You know that, Dick. Honest men are few and far between here. You understand that. Tell me this about your boss, Dick. He had enough money to buy the Casey cattle at a fourth of their value, but has he paid you, Bonney, or Carlos yet?" By Brewer's hesitation, Wes could confirm Tunstall still held their wages. "Well, has he, Dick? Let's get everything on the table."

Brewer lowered his head, sighed, then tightened his lips. Finally, he shrugged, at first avoiding Wes's gaze before looking him square in the eyes. "He's stretched tight, what with opening his store, trying to attract customers scared of retribution from Dolan, and buying more cattle."

"An honest man pays his hands," Wes replied. "An honest man doesn't take Alex McSween for a partner. I bet the lawyer gets paid regular."

"Maybe so, maybe not, Wes. I don't know." Brewer paused and shook his head. "What I know is that our boss is behind in settling our wages. His cattle in my charge were stolen by a man I took to be one of the few honest men around. Jesse and his boys are threatening me."

"They've threatened me and Jace as well, not to mention my wife and boys."

"Sheriff Brady's in Dolan's pocket, doing whatever he wants, and most of us have nowhere to turn to get things straight."

"What you can do, Dick, is unhitch your wagon from Tunstall and McSween. Cut your losses while you can. Tunstall wants to control business in the county, same as the House. McSween is an opportunist. He'll ride whatever horse can make him the richest the fastest. And both of them will let other people do their fighting — and their dying."

Brewer sat in the saddle, the fingers of his rein hand tapping the saddle horn.

Wes paused, allowing Brewer to state his thoughts, but he kept them to himself. "You're still welcome to eat with us, Dick."

Brewer shook his head and sighed. "Not today and not tomorrow, likely never again."

"Sorry you see it that way, Dick. Next time we meet, though, are we friend or foe?"

Shrugging, Brewer pulled back on the reins and turned his horse toward the road. "I don't know, Wes, I just don't know." He never looked back over his shoulder.

"One more thing, Dick," Wes called. "It was my idea to take the Casey cattle. Jace rode with me because I ordered him to. He followed my orders against his will."

Brewer lifted his left arm to acknowledge he had heard the defense of Cousins.

Wes watched Brewer disappear down the road toward San Patricio. When he started for the door, he saw Sarafina standing in the doorway, staring at him.

"You are so sad, my husband," she said, stepping outside, the sunlight glistening off of her black hair. "Do you want to talk?"

"Not now," Wes replied. "Maybe at supper after Jace returns." He put his arm around Sarafina's waist and escorted her back into the house to the kitchen where

Luis sat in a chair eating a tortilla smeared with mashed frijoles. Propping his carbine against the wall, Wes approached the table.

Luis smiled at Wes as he enjoyed his lunch. Wes longed for a life as carefree as that of his adopted son, but existence in Lincoln County took a heavy toll on a man's peace of mind. Luis lifted his hand, offering Wes a bite of the tortilla. Wes bent over his chair and nibbled at the orb, chewing it with an exaggerated movement of the jaw, drawing a laugh from the little boy. Wes sat at his place at the table as Sarafina served his plate and placed it before him. As he started to eat the tortilla smeared with beans, Sarafina returned with a cup of coffee and eased into the chair beside him, silently patting his thigh. Wes appreciated how his wife had learned to read him and give him time to think things through, even if there were no answers for every question.

Sarafina remained by his side until the baby squawked in the bedroom. She excused herself to tend Roberto. Before she returned, Wes finished his plate, drained his cup, and arose, stepping to the corner to fetch his carbine. He headed outside to attend to more chores, though his mind was not in it. He went to the barn and let the horses out into the corral where he could watch them run about, the antics of the frisky colts drawing a sliver of a smile across his otherwise serious face.

Two hours before dusk, he heard a whistle from the road and watched Nip and Tuck charge up the trail to greet Jace and his yellow dun. His partner was as carefree as ever, greeting the dogs and turning toward the corral. Grim-lipped, Wes nodded as Jace dismounted and tied the reins to a fence post.

Stepping beside Bracken, Jace draped his arms over the top rail of the fence and smiled at the three colts frolicking among the other mounts. He turned to Wes, who felt his inquiring gaze. "I've seen more joy at funerals than I see in you, Wes."

"A man tries to do what's right, and it just blows up in his face."

"It's not you. It's Lincoln County," Jace replied.

"Whatever it is, I made us another enemy today."

"Before you're done doing what's right all the time, you won't have a single friend in the territory, save for me. Who was it?"

"Dick Brewer and possibly Billy Bonney and even Carlos."

Cousins whistled. "Fill me in."

CHAPTER 16

The crisp chill of autumn settled over the Rio Ruidoso as the leaves of the cottonwoods turned as golden as the dreams of Wes Bracken for the Mirror B. He had come to New Mexico Territory seeking peace away from the postwar troubles of Arkansas. Wes had found little tranquility. He had wanted to raise fine horses on a good piece of land and hoped to find a loving wife and start a family. Wes had discovered the land and met the woman, but he had not found peace, not when he had to carry his carbine wherever he went or when he had to look over his shoulder while doing the innumerable chores necessary to make the ranch a success.

As he cleaned the main irrigation ditch that fed his garden and hayfield, Wes worried that succeeding was no longer as important as surviving the undercurrents of the crooked politics that flowed through

Lincoln County. He raked out the debris that had collected in the *acequia.* Cousins worked behind him, shoveling out the sediment from a season of watering crops.

"You ain't been yourself for the last week," Jace observed as he straightened and pushed the blade of his tool into the soft earth. He placed his hands at the top of the handle and rested his chin on them. "I'll not do another lick of work until you tell me why you're sulked up like a bullfrog."

Wes shook his head. "Talking won't get this ditch cleaned."

"And sulking doesn't clear your mind, Wes. It's Brewer, isn't it?"

"I reckon. Getting the Casey cattle back for Ellen was the right thing, but it put Brewer in a bind."

"But Tunstall's no better than Murphy and Dolan. You've said that yourself."

"That's the devil of it, Jace. We're all tainted in Lincoln County."

Nip and Tuck ran from behind the barn and began howling. A distant gunshot cracked the air before Cousins could answer, then another and another. Both men looked at each other and tossed aside their tools, sprinting for the cottonwood tree where they had propped their long guns. Instantly, they heard the thunder of pounding hooves and the shouts of men. The hounds raced toward the road barking and growling. Wes and Jace grabbed their weapons and darted to the house, ready to defend it against whatever threat galloped their way.

Nearing the adobe, Wes saw what must have been thirty riders making the turn from the road onto Mirror B property. The hounds had never seen so many riders and snarled as the horsemen headed their way. Reaching the kitchen door, Wes recognized Jesse Evans in the lead. He bolted inside, Jace right behind him.

"Take cover in the bedroom, Sarafina," Wes shouted. "Keep the boys on the floor." He scampered into the parlor, opening the door, his Winchester at the ready.

Jace grabbed his arm and yanked him back. "You've got a family to think of, Wes. Give me cover from the window."

Wes hesitated until Cousins shoved him out of the way and stepped into the doorway, lifting his Henry to his shoulder.

"I want Jesse," Jace said with a laugh. "You take the rest."

The riders fired in the air as they raced toward the house.

Jace pointed his rifle at the sky and fired, levering the smoking hull from the chamber.

"That's close enough," he cried.

The riders slowed their steeds and halted fifty yards in front of the place as Nip and Tuck went crazy.

Evans raised his pistol skyward and fired. "We're celebrating my release from jail."

"How's your ear, Jesse?" responded Jace. "Come any closer, and I'll nick your other one, assuming my aim's steady and I don't put a hole in your forehead."

Evans laughed. "My boys provided me bail. I wanted to let you know because we'll be back to settle our score."

Jace shook his head and whispered to Wes, "I oughta shoot him now, but there'd be too many to fend off if I did."

Wes nodded. "The odds are against us."

Jace laughed. "Nothing's in our favor in Lincoln County." He waved his Henry at Evans. "Now git along, Jesse, 'cause if there's any more shooting, I'll plug you first."

Evans cackled. "You'd die quick if you did."

"But I'd die with a smile on my face knowing I'd sent you to hell," Jace shot back.

Evans laughed and turned to his gang. "Time to go, boys," he cried. "We'll stay longer on our next visit. Take care, Jace. You, too, Wes Bracken. You haven't seen the last of us yet." He yanked the reins on his horse and spun him around for the road. His men chased after him.

Jace stepped outside, followed by Wes, both watching them head toward San Patricio.

"Think it's a trick, Jace, and they'll be back?"

"Don't think so. The boys must've broke him out of jail so they won't linger in case the law comes after them, but you never can tell with a snake like Jesse." Cousins scratched his chin as the gang disappeared. "I doubt they'd double back, but why take a chance. I'm gonna tail them for a spell as I'm tired of cleaning irrigation ditches."

"Perhaps I should go with you," Wes offered.

"No, sir. You stay here and watch out for your wife and boys while I saddle up."

"Let me do something for you, Jace."

"Get me a box or two of rifle cartridges, will you? I might need them."

By dusk Wes fretted. Cousins had not returned from his foolhardy adventure. What chance did one man have against thirty? Wes should never have let him pursue Jesse's men. After putting the boys to bed and kissing Sarafina good night, Wes slipped on his coat, grabbed his carbine, and eased outside into the brisk evening air. Nip and Tuck came over and sniffed at his boots as he paced around the house, looking for unseen threats spawned more from his imagination than reality. He crept out to the barn to check on the horses and the milk cow. He took the milking stool and carried it back outside, dropping it at the corner of the corral where he could see the road and the approaches to the house. Wes sat down and placed the Winchester across his thighs. Nip and Tuck rested on either side of him as Wes leaned back against a fence post. He reached out and stroked the dogs' heads and ears, something to keep him busy as the time dragged.

Wes waited two hours beneath the sliver of a moon that rose in the cloudless skies over the mountains that paralleled the Rio Ruidoso. Though tired, he was too anxious over Jace's fate to doze off and sat there stroking the hounds' necks. The hounds remained as content as Wes was nervous. Then the dogs' muscles tightened, and Nip and Tuck stood looking toward the west. They had sniffed something. Wes picked up the Winchester, sliding his forefinger against the trigger and his other fingers in the lever.

Slowly, Wes stood up as Nip and Tuck stepped away, their ears erect. They offered a low growl, lifted their heads, and trotted away. Wes released his breath and lowered the Winchester to his side. It had to be Jace.

In a moment he detected a shadow turning off the road toward the barn. By the posture of the man in the saddle, Wes recognized Cousins. "Jace, I'm over here by the fence."

"You didn't have to wait up for me, Wes. I'm a big boy."

Wes laughed. "Was too nervous to sleep, especially if Jesse and his boys backtracked."

"No, sir, they had other folks to pester, mostly the fine folks of San Patricio. They shot up the village and rode on. Best I could tell, no one was hurt, but everyone was terrified when I reached town. They feared I was with the gang, but I told 'em I was your friend, and they calmed down because they respect you, Wes."

"I've always tried to treat them as the decent folks they are." Wes picked up the stool.

"Jesse and his boys sure didn't show them any respect, nor Dick Brewer's place." Jace slid out of the saddle, his boots hitting the ground with a thud.

"Is Dick okay?"

Jace took the dun's reins and led the animal inside the barn. "Don't think Dick was home, but they shot up the place and burned his barn. Would've burned his home if it weren't adobe."

"It'll burn if they fire the roof," Wes answered as he followed Jace into the barn, quickly shutting the door to keep Nick and Tuck out.

"Jesse's not that smart."

"He's just mean." Wes stuck his hand in his britches pocket and pulled out a tin of matches. "Let me strike a match."

"I don't need any light," Jace answered, rubbing his right cheek with his hand.

"You'll get done faster, if you can see." Wes flicked the tip of the match with his thumbnail, and it flared to life, spewing sulfurous fumes as a ball of light replaced the dark.

Jace pivoted away from Wes, catching him by surprise. Something was wrong, Wes thought as he stepped to his partner, who twisted around, hiding his face. Wes grabbed Jace's shoulder and pulled him about. Jace covered his right cheek with his hand as the match peaked and dimmed.

"Move your hand, Jace."

Cousins hesitated.

"I've got a full tin of matches so I'm

314

gonna see what's the matter."

Jace lowered his hand. In the fading glow of the dying match, Wes saw for an instant Jace's blood-smeared cheek with a red gash under the cheekbone. The match died, and darkness enveloped both men.

"Nothing but a scratch," Jace explained, turning to his dun and releasing the saddle.

"What's the story? Anybody else hurt?"

Cousins hesitated. "I followed Jesse's boys from our place to San Patricio to Brewer's spread and on up the valley, keeping out of sight until they camped for the night."

"They spotted you?"

"No, sir. I hobbled my horse in the trees a mile or more from their camp and slipped up on them once they had unsaddled and staked their horses. I figured I'd end my vendetta with Jesse right there. I didn't want him hurting your family, and that's where it was heading."

"Go on."

Jace nodded. "They built a big fire for supper and warmth, and I slipped up on them, taking cover among the rocks. I waited for Jesse to get near the fire where I could see him good, thinking I had time for two shots to kill him. I fired once and hit somebody, but I don't know that it was Jesse. Before I fired my second shot, one of them shot blindly into the rocks. It must've ricocheted off the boulders or kicked up a piece of rock that creased my cheek. That's all. Didn't expect I'd have to explain it to you as I figured you'd be in bed by now."

"Did they give chase?"

"No. They never spotted me as they fired everywhere. I slipped back to my horse and stayed off the road for an hour. They never came after me, though I kinda wish they had. I'd like to end it with Jesse."

"Did they recognize you?"

"They never saw me. It was a lucky shot that they even scratched me. I know I got one of them, though I'm uncertain it was Jesse. Not sure if my second bullet hit anything."

"I'm grateful, Jace, for you thinking of me and my family."

"I'm tired of looking over my shoulder like I'm a wanted man. I served time for a crime that was Jesse's doing, and I've grown weary of having to be on the lookout for him."

"You think they might backtrack on us?"

"I got the idea they were headed for the Mescalero Reservation, though I can't prove it."

"Proof of anything is scarce in Lincoln County," Wes answered.

"What do you want me to tell Sarafina

about my cheek?"

"Tell her you ran into a low-hanging limb when you were hiding from the Evans gang."

Jace laughed. "I'm not that bad of a horseman."

"Nor that good of a liar, Jace, but it will have to do."

The scab on Jace's cheek had given way to a pink slash across his flesh in the ten days following his attack on the Jesse Evans gang. The weather remained cold for a week, then warmed up for three days. Few travelers traversed the road, and the only unusual activity was the passing of a troop of cavalry from Fort Stanton riding up the Ruidoso Valley toward San Patricio. Jace stayed close to the Mirror B so no one might pry about the new scar on his cheek. If anyone turned from the road to the house, Jace found work in the barn or elsewhere out of sight. When a fellow in a buckboard aimed for the house, Jace called Wes. "We've got company!"

Nip and Tuck took to growling, but Wes whistled at them and they hushed. "It's Juan Patrón. We can trust him, Jace."

"You're the only man I trust in Lincoln County. I'll take the dogs and see if we can scare up a rabbit. Here, Tuck! Here, Nip!" he called, ambling off toward the stream with the hounds eagerly following him.

Wes wiped his hands on his britches and walked out to meet the visitor, one of the few men he felt he could trust in Lincoln County.

Juan Patrón waved his hat when he spotted Wes and rattled the lines so his horse pranced up to the house. "*Buenos dias,* Wesley," Patrón called.

"What brings you to the Mirror B?"

Patrón tied the reins to the buckboard's foot rail and jumped from the seat, offering his hand to Wes. The men shook hands warmly. "I needed to get out of Lincoln."

"Don't tell me you've switched parties again."

"I tell you, Wesley, I don't know what to do. Murphy and Dolan are crooked Democrats and the lawyer McSween is a mean Republican. His wife is even meaner. She's one of those — what to you call them? — suffragettes. That notion that women should be allowed to vote has seeped down from Colorado. What's this world coming to?"

Wes slapped Patrón on the back. "I'm less concerned about the world than I am Lincoln County."

"Well, I worried about you when I learned Jesse's gang attacked your place."

"It was more of a threat than an attack,

but they promised to return and settle scores."

"You knew his men busted him from jail, didn't you?"

"That's what we gathered."

"Word has it they shot up San Patricio and Brewer's place before someone ambushed them that night, killing two of them," Patrón continued.

"You don't say, Juan?"

"That's a fact. They think Brewer did it after he saw they'd burned his barn."

"Was Jesse Evans killed?"

"No! Jesse reminds me of an old tomcat with nine lives. He and his gang stole fifty or so mules and horses from the Mescalero Reservation so soldiers are out looking for him now. I hope they chase him out of Lincoln County. We'd be better off if they did."

"That explains the cavalry we saw riding by last week." Wes waved his hand toward the door. "Why don't we go inside and visit?"

"Suits me," Patrón replied, and they stepped into the house.

"We've company," Wes called.

Sarafina walked into the parlor, smiling at her guest. "Most visitors want to shoot us," she said, "so it touches my heart to see a friendly face. Come in the kitchen. I'll warm

319

up the coffee."

Patrón and Wes followed her and took seats at the table. Sarafina brought over two tin cups and sat them in front of her husband and Patrón. Luis ambled into the kitchen until he saw Patrón, then ran to his momma and hid behind her skirt. Patrón made pleasant talk with Luis and Sarafina in Spanish until he convinced Luis he wouldn't bite the boy.

When Sarafina poured hot coffee in the cups, Patrón turned to Wes and updated him on the latest news from Lincoln, starting with Jesse's escape from the jail while Sheriff Brady stood there and watched, never lifting a finger or a gun to fend off the attackers. Next the audacious gang rode along the street shooting up the town, laughing the whole time.

"I'm surprised Dolan didn't get them out earlier since Jesse and his boys do so much of the dirty work for the House," Wes noted.

Patrón shrugged. "Jimmy Dolan has his own problems. Supposedly, the House is broke, and Murphy pulled a fast one on Dolan, selling him the enterprise without sharing the actual books that showed him thousands of dollars in debt."

"No honor among thieves, as the saying goes," Wes added.

"And no bigger thieves than those two. Now Dolan's claiming that Alex McSween defrauded the House while the lawyer was working for Murphy."

"Like I said, no honor among thieves."

Patrón took a sip of coffee, letting it linger in his mouth before swallowing the hot liquid. "Now McSween's set up his legal office in Tunstall's store and the Englishman lives in a back room. The two of them have partnered with John Chisum in the Lincoln County Bank, which operates out of the store."

"I'm sorry to hear Chisum got involved with the lawyer and the Englishman," Wes said. "I thought he was a better judge of character than that."

"Mr. Chisum is for anything that'll damage the House. Murphy and Dolan have stolen too many of his cattle over the years to fulfill contracts with the Indian agency and Fort Stanton."

"But when you wallow with hogs, you smell like them, too," Wes responded.

Patrón drained his coffee cup, nodding. "Those hogs, though, are hurting the House. Since opening his store, Tunstall has slowly taken business from Dolan, not because the prices were any cheaper but because the customers didn't feel threatened dealing with the Englishman's people, as they did with the crooks Dolan and Murphy hired. Losing business is putting more strains on the House. We're headed for an explosion, Wes. Things can't keep going this way without bloodshed." Patrón toyed with his empty cup.

Wes studied Patrón, taking in a slight twitch of his eyes and his fingers tapping on the tin cup. "There's something else, Juan. You didn't come out here simply to share Lincoln gossip."

Patrón swallowed hard and nodded. "Tunstall's been spreading word that you stole his cattle and that you are working for the House."

"I work for myself and my family, nobody else," Wes replied. "The Englishman's hands aren't any cleaner than anybody else's in Lincoln County. I didn't steal those cattle, Juan. I just returned them to their rightful owner. Those were Ellen Casey's cattle. Everybody knows that and everybody knows the House rigged the facts so the county could claim them over a mere five-dollar debt to Murphy, a debt I repaid twice." Wes felt his cheeks heating with anger as he clenched his fists.

"Everyone knows who those cattle belonged to," Patrón replied. "I thought you needed to hear what was being said."

"It's time I called on the Englishman," Wes responded.

Though always uncomfortable leaving Sarafina alone with the boys, Wes Bracken calculated Jesse Evans would be less of a threat with the cavalry on his trail. Too, his wife could now handle a pistol and a carbine so she was not helpless. He and his partner headed to town. Together Wes Bracken and Jace Cousins rode along the dusty street of Lincoln, past the large new adobe house McSween had built for him and his wife, then toward the imposing adobe structure that contained Tunstall's store, the Lincoln County Bank, and McSween's law office. Thick adobe walls and iron shutters gave it the look of a fortress, as if the Englishman was prepared for certain trouble when he challenged the House. Though not as imposing as the two-story store run by Dolan, the one-story Tunstall mercantile stood as a new threat to the crumbling Murphy-Dolan empire. Behind the store towered a corral with an eight-foot adobe fence.

"It appears the Englishman spent plenty on his store," Jace observed.

Wes nodded, aiming his sorrel for the hitching post. "Wonder if he's paid his hands yet?"

Jace drew up beside Wes, and both men dismounted, tying their horses to the rail. Wes unbuttoned his coat and hooked it behind his pistol. He didn't plan on using it, but wanted it visible so the Englishman understood he meant business. Jace yanked his Henry rifle from the saddle scabbard and lowered it to his side. Together the men stepped onto the wooden walk that ran the length of the building and marched inside the double doors.

The store's interior reeked with the newness of fresh paint, newly cut lumber, and goods of all description. For a man who couldn't pay his hands on time, Wes thought, Tunstall sure stocked his store well with leather tack for horses, tinware, canned foods, blankets, a modest selection of firearms, and staples in fifty-pound bags. On the far end of the counter was a metal cage with a sign designating it as the Lincoln County Bank and listing Chisum as president, McSween as vice president, and Tunstall as treasurer.

A clerk wearing wire-rimmed spectacles glanced up from a glossy varnished counter where he was stacking cartons of ammunition behind a glass case. "I'll be right with you gents," he said. Barely had the fellow greeted them than a door in a back room opened and the Englishman emerged, striding around the front of the counter until he saw his customers.

As his gaze settled on Wes, Tunstall showed surprise, biting his lip before speaking. "You're that Wesley Bracken chap, are you not?"

"That's what my momma called me."

Tunstall nodded, stepping to the clerk and whispering instructions in his ear. The clerk nodded, grabbed his coat, shoved it on, and strode out the door.

Once the clerk left, Tunstall turned to Bracken and Cousins. "May I assist you?"

Wes stepped toward Tunstall, who retreated behind the counter.

"We want cartridges for our pistols and our long guns," Jace said. "You can't have too much ammunition in Lincoln County as many skunks as there are running about."

"And," Wes said, "I want to talk to you about spreading rumors of cattle rustling."

Swallowing hard, Tunstall replied, "We don't have any ammunition."

Jace lifted his rifle and pointed to the cartons the clerk had been stacking behind the glass case. "That looks like bullets to me. Why don't you visit with Wes while I pick out the cartridges we need?" Jace stepped to the counter and slid in behind it, walking to the glass case and examining the boxes on display.

Tunstall retreated to the opposite end of the counter where the teller's cage offered a barrier between him and Bracken. Wes followed him across the room.

"I've been told, Tunstall, that you're spreading stories that I stole your cattle." Wes leaned into the counter and propped his hands on the edge. "Is that true?"

"My foreman told me so. I have no reason to doubt Richard Brewer."

"You stole the cattle from the widow Casey."

"I bought the herd at an official auction sanctioned by the County of Lincoln, New Mexico Territory!"

"Over a five-dollar debt that I repaid twice. You knew the House was behind the fraud, and you didn't care since you could get the stock for a fourth of their value."

"It was legal," Tunstall shot back, "and you stole them."

"I didn't steal them, Tunstall. I returned them to their rightful owner."

"That's for the law to determine," the Englishman replied.

"There's no law in Lincoln County."

Tunstall lifted his hand and pointed his

finger at Wes's nose as the door flung open and the clerk ran inside, breathless.

"The sheriff's . . . on his way," the clerk said, heaving for air.

"Excellent," Tunstall replied. "Now run and find Alex."

Once again the fellow darted out the entry, this time without bothering to shut the doors.

Tunstall looked from Bracken to the entry and back, hesitating whether to remain where he was or go shut the doors and turn his back on Wes. He stood motionless for a moment.

"Hey, Wes," Jace called, "he's got our caliber of ammunition. I figure we'll need eight boxes or more before we get out of town." He laughed.

The Englishman flinched and gritted his jaw as Wes listened to heavy footfalls on the plank walk outside. Sheriff Brady barged in, slamming the open doors behind him.

"What's the problem?" Brady called.

"Arrest these brigands for cattle thievery," Tunstall shouted.

Wes let his hand fall to his waist, his fingers resting on the butt of his revolver, as he studied Sheriff William Brady, who stepped toward him, stumbling forward. Bracing his feet and jerking his hands up to stop Brady, who lurched at him, Wes caught the sheriff at the shoulders and stopped his momentum. The sheriff looked up with bloodshot eyes, and Wes detected the aroma of whiskey on his breath.

"Obliged," Brady said as he straightened up, embarrassed over his misstep.

"Arrest these cattle-thieving brigands," Tunstall growled. "Think you can keep them in jail where they belong better than you did Jesse Evans? Evans and his boys stole my horses and now Bracken and his gang rustled my cattle."

Brady took a big breath and thrust out his chest. "You've been stealing business from Jimmy Dolan, that's what's been stolen around here."

"Arrest them," Tunstall demanded.

The sheriff turned to Wes, snickering. "Steal whatever you want of his. The Englishman's nothing but a troublemaker."

Tunstall shook his forefinger at Brady's nose. "And you call yourself the law."

Brady flung open the flap of his jacket and slapped the badge on his chest. "This says I'm the law, and you better not forget it. If you do, I'll throw you in the pit, and you won't be escaping from my jail because you don't have friends like Jesse Evans."

"It's not friends," the Englishman shot

back, "it's graft and corruption."

Brady waved off Tunstall's observation and turned to Bracken. "After Jesse escaped, his gang was ambushed up the Ruidoso. Two men died. You know anything about that?"

"Nothing firsthand, Sheriff. I figured it was you trying to capture the escapees."

Brady coughed, then crossed his arms over his chest. "I had other business to attend to that day and couldn't give chase."

"You were drunk, like today," Tunstall scoffed.

The sheriff ignored the insult and the sound of the door opening behind him. Wes saw the clerk enter the store with Alex McSween at his side.

"Word I've heard," Brady continued, "is that Dick Brewer snuck up on them and ambushed them."

"You can't prove that," cried McSween as he moved to the Englishman.

Brady glanced toward Tunstall and his lawyer, then back at Wes as Cousins moved from behind the counter and called the lawman.

"Sheriff," Jace announced, "it wasn't Dick Brewer. He stayed at the Mirror B the night of the shooting." Cousins drew puzzled looks from Tunstall and McSween and a muddled glare from Brady.

"Who are you?" the sheriff inquired.

"Jace Cousins. I'm partner with Wes Bracken on the Mirror B. Brewer dropped by our spread after Jesse Evans gang visited us. When we told him Jesse's men had ridden west, he feared for his place, but we told him there was too many of them for him to make any difference. He stayed the night with us, though sure enough, Jesse's gang burned his barn to the ground."

Wes realized Jace was covering for Brewer as Brady turned to him. "Is that a fact, Wes?"

"I'd never dispute my partner, Sheriff."

Tunstall stepped toward Brady. "Arrest them, Constable, for stealing my cattle and see if you can keep them in custody until a trial."

Brady glared at the Englishman, hate brimming over in his bloodshot eyes.

"You're as worthless a lawman as ever wore a badge." Tunstall spat the words at Brady.

The sheriff lowered his hand to his holster and lifted his revolver from its nest.

"You damned son of a bitch," he scowled as he pointed the pistol at Tunstall.

McSween leaped between the two antagonists.

"Out of the way, lawyer," Brady cried.

"He's unarmed, Sheriff. John's unarmed."

"Give him a gun," Brady bellowed. "I'm ready to end this and save Dolan the trouble."

"It wouldn't look good in a court of law, you shooting an unarmed man."

Brady laughed. "I've got friends on the court. I'll take the chance."

"Don't do it, Sheriff," McSween pleaded. "It'll solve nothing and get you in trouble with the law."

Brady banged his revolver against the badge on his chest. "I am the law in Lincoln County." He lowered his pistol and shoved it back in his holster. He raised his hand and pointed it square between Tunstall's eyes. "I won't be sheriff forever, Englishman, and you don't have long to run before someone in Lincoln County shoots you. I hope it's me." He spun around and strode for the door, flinging it open and barging into the cold.

"You heard that threat," McSween said, stepping toward Wes and Jace. "If I file a complaint, will you two testify on my client's behalf?"

Wes shook his head. "Not until he stops accusing us of cattle rustling."

Tunstall lifted his nose in the air and

sniffed his disgust. "Never!"

"There's your answer, Alex," Wes said. "The Englishman as much as stole the widow Casey's cattle. All I did was return them to their rightful owner. I didn't make a cent off of the exchange. The Englishman best rein in what comes out of his mouth. I ain't his friend and neither am I his enemy — yet. The day'll come when he'll need every ally he can find."

"John's not a crook like the House." McSween defended his client.

"Maybe not, but he's as greedy as Murphy and Dolan," Wes shot back.

"That's unfair," McSween replied.

"Unfair is not paying your hands what money they're due," Wes responded.

"I can handle myself and my business," Tunstall interjected.

"You two aren't dealing with men that'll settle this in a courtroom."

"I can fend for myself," Tunstall said.

Wes twisted to face him, pointing his finger at his nose. "Maybe so, maybe not, Englishman, but I've told you what happened to your cattle. I better not hear of you calling me a rustler again, or I'll come looking for you." He turned around to Jace. "Let's get out of here."

Jace retreated to the counter where he had

stacked eight cartons of cartridges. He shoved two boxes into each of his two coat pockets, picked up the other four, and held them against his coat as he started for the door.

"Did you settle up on the ammunition?" the clerk called as Wes opened the door.

"Add it to my bill," Jace replied.

"You don't have an account," the clerk answered.

Wes let Jace pass, then stepped on the walk and slammed the door behind them. Jace packed the cartons in his saddlebags, untied his horse, and mounted, his stare lingering on the store.

"How long do you think?" Jace inquired.

Wes knew what Jace was asking even though he had not stated it explicitly. "I give them a year. They don't understand who they're up against. Neither will be alive this time next year."

CHAPTER 17

Sarafina rested in the parlor rocking chair, gently humming as she rocked Roberto to sleep while Luis played at her feet, the flames in the corner fireplace casting his shadow on the opposite wall. Luis chuckled when he realized the shadows mocked his every movement. The more exaggerated his gestures, the more animated the silhouette, the louder he laughed.

As he sat on the floor taking apart and oiling his revolver, Wes smiled at Luis's antics. "There's no prettier music than the laughter of your own child," he said to his wife.

She tilted her head at her husband, her eyes aglow with satisfaction. "It pleases me to hear you talk of Luis that way."

From his stool by the fireplace where he read his Bible by the firelight, Jace looked up. "It's nice to have something to laugh about, even if it's your own shadow. What do you think the New Year holds for us?"

"Eighteen seventy-eight, I fear, will be a dance with the devil," Wes answered.

"Don't say such things," Sarafina chided him.

"It's New Year's Eve," Wes replied, "and I should be outside firing off my pistol and celebrating instead of cleaning it and saving ammunition for whatever may come."

"This was a rough year," Jace answered.

"How can you talk that way, both of you?" Sarafina scolded them. "Roberto Luther Bracken joined our family not six months ago. You look for the bad and ignore the good."

"Oops," Jace responded, hesitating when he heard snippets carried on the winter wind of Nip and Tuck barking from the road.

Wes waited with tight lips for the few seconds the hounds yelped before they fell silent. Only the noise of the stiff breeze followed. "They must've scared off a skunk or other varmint," he said, as he resumed cleaning his gun.

Jace laughed. "There are more varmints on two legs than four in Lincoln County." He yawned and closed his Bible. "Maybe I should head to the bunkhouse before the weather gets any worse, and before I say the wrong thing in front of Sarafina again."

Sarafina smiled. "Please stay. It comforts me when you read the Good Book in our home, even if you do it silently."

"There's too many words I can't say to read it aloud," Jace answered.

As the words left his mouth, a pounding rattled the door.

Wes looked to Jace, whose eyes widened as he dropped his Bible, knocking over his stool when he shot up and bolted to the corner for his Henry.

One, two, three times the door shook from a hammering fist.

Wes glanced at his pistol, now in too many parts to reassemble in time to fight off intruders.

"Friend or foe?" Wes cried, jumping up from the floor and stepping to the barred entry.

"You tell us," came a voice distorted by the wind, followed by a cackle. "I won the bet!"

"Who is it? Answer or we shoot," Wes called as he looked to Jace, who yanked his revolver from his holster and tossed it to his partner.

Luis started crying and Roberto took to wailing. Wes motioned for Sarafina to take the boys to their bedroom. She jumped up from the rocker, grabbed Luis, and disappeared in the back.

Wes tensed as he cocked the pistol and lifted the bar securing the door. "Who is it?" he called out.

Laughter and a confession answered. "It's Billy Bonney and Carlos. Let us in. We're freezing."

Wes looked at his partner and shrugged. "Don't know if I can trust them anymore."

Jace patted the barrel of his rifle. "Mr. Henry'll teach them manners if this is a trick."

Wes tossed the bar aside and yanked the door open. Bonney and Carlos stumbled inside and raced to the fire, holding out their hands to warm them. He slammed the entry shut and barred the door.

"You boys almost got yourselves killed," Jace said, lowering his rifle and pursing his exasperated lips.

Bonney turned around with his bucktoothed grin and explained. "I bet Carlos I could slip past your hounds and knock on your door unannounced."

"You didn't hurt them, did you?" Wes demanded.

"Nope. They like us. We helped a family in San Patricio kill a hog this afternoon, and we brought some innards over in a tow sack to treat them. Right now they're enjoying a finer meal than you feed them."

Sarafina darted into the room, Luis running behind her, bawling for her to pick him up. Instead she raced to her brother and hugged him, kissing him on the cheek. *"Es tan bueno verte,"* she said, as she broke her embrace and inspected him.

"It's good to see you, too," he answered.

"Even in the coat you appear to have lost weight, Carlos. Are you eating?"

"I eat when I can," he replied.

Wes walked over and extended his hand. "Welcome, Carlos."

His brother-in-law hesitated until Sarafina's eyes hardened. Carlos shook Wes's hand.

"I'll fix you both something for supper," Sarafina offered.

"We ate a fine meal in San Patricio," Bonney replied. "Maybe a good breakfast in the morning."

Wes gave Jace's pistol back to him, stepped into the kitchen, and returned to the parlor with a pair of chairs. He squatted on the floor and picked up the parts to his revolver, rapidly reassembling it and sliding it in his holster.

"Dick didn't ride with you this time?" Jace asked.

"He's still working off his mad at you for stealing Tunstall's cattle," Bonney said.

"We took the widow Casey's herd to their rightful owner," Wes replied.

"It's good somebody decent got them," the Kid noted.

"What do you mean, Billy?" Wes asked, as Sarafina escorted her brother to the kitchen.

"The House may get the rest."

"They've been rustling other people's cattle for years, Kid. You know that."

"Now they're trying to steal them legally — well as much as anything that happens in Lincoln County is legal."

Wes motioned for the Kid to take a seat. When he did, Jace grabbed his stool, and Wes straddled a chair, resting his arms on the back rail. "Tell us more," Wes said.

Bonney explained that Dolan had accused the lawyer McSween of swindling money from L.G. Murphy before he bought the store from him. Afterwards Dolan filed a claim on McSween for $10,000. The problem, as Bonney described it, was that since the attorney and the Englishman were business partners, the court was sorting out what belonged to Tunstall, what was McSween's, and what was jointly owned. The horses and mules remained disputed property that Tunstall claimed as his, but that Dolan insisted belonged to them both.

Wes looked at Jace and laughed. "So Tunstall's herd might get attached and sold at auction, the same as the Casey cattle?"

Jace grinned. "The Englishman's scheme has bounced back in his face."

Turning to the Kid, Wes grimaced. "Have you and Carlos received any wages yet?"

Bonney scowled. "We got a month's worth of pay. He owes us another four."

"McSween and Tunstall are headed for trouble, Billy. You should cut and run, find you something else to put food in your belly."

"Tunstall's promised he'll give us back wages plus a bonus when things are resolved."

"Lincoln County's so crooked I doubt it'll ever get set right," Wes said.

Bonney stared from Wes to Jace. "I've got a question for you both. You know much about the ambush of Jesse Evans's gang? Two were killed the night they broke Jesse out of jail."

"Just what we've heard," Wes replied.

"I thought you hated Jesse," Jace said. "Why do you care, Kid?"

"I don't," Bonney replied, "but I know where Brewer was the night Jesse's boys died, and it wasn't here. No reason for you

340

to alibi for Brewer unless you were involved in the shootings."

"We left him in a bind returning the widow Casey's cattle," Wes offered. "Just trying to make amends."

Bonney grinned, pointing to Jace's Henry. "Somebody used a rifle from a long distance, firing two shots and making two kills." Bonney stared at Cousins's face. "Next morning Jesse's boys found two hulls in the rocks. They were forty-four caliber rimfire hulls like a Henry shoots."

Jace shrugged. "I'm not the only man in Lincoln County that carries a Henry or uses forty-four rimfire cartridges."

"Perhaps we should elect you as sheriff, Billy. Then you could bring law and order to the county," Wes offered, uncomfortable that his guest had deduced Jace's role in the killings.

The Kid's eyes narrowed as he waved away Bracken's suggestion. "The next morning Jesse's boys found drops of blood on the rock." His gaze bore in on the right side of Cousins's face. "How'd you get that gash on your cheek?"

"I cut myself shaving."

The Kid's lips widened into his buck-toothed grin. "I reckon you ought to be more careful when you shave. All I need to know is whose side you two are on."

"We're on nobody's side, save our own," Wes replied.

"The House is a den of thieves," Jace added. "Your boss and the lawyer McSween are no better."

"If you're not with us, you're against us," Bonney shot back.

"Get out while you still can, Billy," Jace said.

"And don't drag Carlos into the slop with you," Wes added. "The boy needs a chance for a decent life, not one on the run, always looking over his shoulder for the law."

"The law's crooked here, you know that," Bonney said. "Sheriff Brady threatened to kill my boss. You were there that day in the store, so you understand the danger Tunstall's in, if someone doesn't take the sheriff down a notch or two."

"Don't talk that way, Kid, or it'll lead to more trouble than you can escape."

Jace stood up from his chair, rifle in hand. "Come on, Kid," he said. "It's getting late. Why don't we go to the bunkhouse for some shut-eye out of the cold? Wes can visit with Carlos."

"I'll tend my horse first," Bonney replied.

"Come along," Jace said, slapping the Kid on the back. "We'll stable him in the barn, and I'll take care of Carlos's mount." Jace put on his coat as Bonney buttoned his own, both turning to the door. Wes unbarred and yanked it open so they could exit into the frigid night. He secured the door again, then picked up the two chairs and headed into the kitchen where Carlos sat at the table across from his sister.

Carlos tensed when Wes returned the seats.

"How've you been?" Wes asked.

"Broke," Carlos responded.

"Tunstall still hasn't paid you?"

Clenching his jaw, Carlos shook his head. "We got a month's pay, but *el jefe* said he couldn't afford more because of the cattle you stole."

"Carlos," Sarafina shouted, jumping up from her chair and pointing her finger at her brother's nose, "do not accuse my husband of stealing."

"It's true," Carlos shot back.

Sarafina lunged across the table and slapped Carlos's cheek. Her quickness and anger surprised both Carlos and Wes. "*Mi esposo* has treated me and Luis well, and he'd respect you if you let him, but you're too stubborn."

Her brother rubbed his cheek as he stood

up from the table. "I'll go. I'm unwanted here."

Sarafina dashed around the table and wrapped her arms around Carlos. "That is not true, Carlos. You are welcome here, but you must show respect for my family."

Wes nodded. "Our door's always open to you, Carlos, but you're riding with outlaws who have stolen and killed."

Carlos broke from his sister's grasp and stomped the floor. "I haven't stolen cattle like you have, and I haven't murdered two men like Jace."

"You've no proof of that, Carlos," Wes answered.

"That's what Billy believes, and I trust him more than you," Carlos said, turning to Sarafina. "Or you, *mi hermana!*"

Tears filled Sarafina's eyes, rolling one by one down her cheeks. She crossed the room to Wes, who wrapped his arm around her and pulled her to his chest.

"You ride with ruthless men, Carlos," Sarafina said, her voice breaking. *"Dime con quién cabalgas y te diré quién eres,"* she added, then looked up into her husband's eyes. "I told him to tell me who he rides with, and I'll tell him who he is."

"At least I don't live with rustlers and

murderers," Carlos cried, shaking his fist at Wes.

"That may change in the New Year." Wes stared at him.

Carlos grabbed his coat and started for the kitchen door.

"You're welcome to stay the night with us," Wes offered again.

"I'd rather sleep in the barn with the animals." Carlos shoved his arms in his coat sleeves and unlatched the door, letting himself out but leaving the exit wide open.

Wes released Sarafina and dashed to the door, quickly shutting and securing it with the bar. *"Lo siento, Sarafina. Lo siento."*

"I am sorry too, *mi esposo.* Carlos has lost his bearing, and I will not let him insult you."

Come morning Billy Bonney ate a breakfast of eggs, bacon, and tortillas with Wes and Jace, but Carlos stayed with the horses. After complimenting Sarafina on her cooking and thanking her for her hospitality, the Kid headed for the barn alone. Minutes later, Bonney and Carlos emerged from the shelter, mounted their horses, and started toward the road. Sarafina ran out the front door to say goodbye. She called Carlos's name and waved, but only Bonney turned in his saddle. He took off his hat and wagged it over his head. Carlos never looked back.

Shivering, Sarafina returned to the parlor where Wes wrapped his arms around her to warm her as much as console her. Sarafina wept. "We've lost my brother," she sobbed. "We've lost Carlos."

The bitter weather that had blown in with 1878 continued for two weeks, the valley splotched with the remnants of the periodic snows that accompanied the frigid air. The inclement conditions reduced traffic passing the place to an occasional rider or wagon during the day. On three nights after the turn of the year, Wes had heard gunfire along the road and took it as a signal from Jesse's boys that they intended to fulfill their promise to attack the place. Wes worried that those enemies had deciphered the clues identifying Jace Cousins as the sniper who had killed a pair of their own. Sarafina still fretted about her previous visit with Carlos and how he had ridden away without so much as a parting glance.

Wes and Jace fed and watered the horses, letting them out occasionally to run off their winter boredom, and managed the firewood and other outside chores as the weather allowed. On freezing days or in the evenings, they hauled harnesses and tack into the house, repairing and replacing worn leather. They oiled their guns and sharpened their knives, Wes using his pocket blade to whittle a four-inch block of wood into a little horse for Luis. Before bedtime, Jace read his Bible by the fireplace, succumbing now and then to Sarafina's pleas to recite the scriptures, even if he couldn't pronounce all the words.

Other than the upcoming spring planting and the course Lincoln County events would take, the main worry became their coffee supply. While they had managed well the other staples, they had consumed more than anticipated because of the lingering frigid weather. Wes promised to ride to Lincoln for more when a sunny day broke the hold winter had over the countryside. Jace offered to make the ride instead, but Wes declined the suggestion, worrying that one of Jesse's gang would take a shot at Jace in retribution for the ambush deaths.

By the third week of January, the clouds thinned and the sun finally broke through enough that Wes announced he was heading to Lincoln the next day after breakfast. He had Jace fetch the notarized bill of sale on the Casey place so he could file it at the courthouse during his trip. Wes left on schedule the following morning, mounted on Charlie, and enjoyed the ride as the sun broke over the mountains and offered its warmth to a land that had shivered for days. The patches of snow melted quickly in the road, leaving it muddy in places and puddled in the wheel ruts. Wes searched for riders who might carry trouble with them, but he encountered no horsemen, only Hispanic folks coming out of their modest adobes to enjoy the heat and catch up on chores. Several of them waved at him, and he tipped his hat to each, proud that Sarafina's people respected him. Nearing Lincoln, Wes passed Sheriff Brady's ranch where he had driven Ellen Casey's cattle for the auction. He wondered if Brady was at home or at his office in town and whether or not he remembered his drunken threat to Tunstall.

As he neared town, he smelled the fragrance of piñon burning in the fireplaces and stoves of Lincoln and heard the bleating of a dozen sheep in the road ahead of him as an old Mexican on foot herded them toward town. Wes watched a pair of hogs rooting around in the mud as he passed the first house, a large adobe dwelling with a roof that sagged in the middle. On the opposite end of town stood the House, its thick walls hiding the wickedness that originated inside. Nearer the middle of town was the Tunstall store, a veritable fortress with the eight-foot adobe wall forming a corral behind the building with its thick walls and iron shutters. Though Wes had money to spend, he declined to waste it in those stores because of the problems the owners caused the decent folk of Lincoln County. Instead he planned to stop at the modest store operated by José Montaño in the front room of his home. The store's selection was inferior to the Dolan and Tunstall mercantiles, but the old man carried the essentials, like coffee, flour, cornmeal, and dried beans.

Passing four small adobes on the south side of the street, Wes looked north at the jail and saw a bay gelding hitched to the rack outside. He took the animal to be the sheriff's mount so the sheriff was likely in town. Approaching the Montaño store, he passed Juan Patrón's house, just as his friend exited, his face screened by the newspaper he was reading.

"*Buenos dias, Señor Juan,*" Wes yelled, startling his friend.

Patrón dropped the paper on the damp ground and looked up at the caller. Recognizing Wes, he sighed and nodded his greeting before bending and retrieving the broadsheet, gently brushing the debris from the damp newsprint.

"You're jumpy," Wes called, reining his sorrel toward his friend.

Patrón slapped the paper. "Nothing good'll come of this story."

"I never knew Lincoln had a newspaper," Wes replied.

Shaking his head, Patrón grimaced. "It doesn't. This is the *Mesilla Valley Independent* published south of here near El Paso."

"I don't see what harm a Mesilla paper can cause here."

"That fool Tunstall's written a letter to the *Independent* accusing Sheriff Brady and the House of embezzling fifteen hundred dollars in tax monies from the county."

Wes whistled. "There's enough bad blood between the Englishman and Brady already."

"It's gonna get worse," Patrón said, glancing both ways along the street. "Why don't you come inside where we can talk without being overheard."

Wes directed his horse to the side of the road, dismounted, tied the reins to the rail fence, and followed Patrón inside. His host motioned for Wes to take a seat. As Wes settled in the chair, Patrón offered him the newspaper, opening it to the center and thumping a column of the gray type with his middle finger. "Read that, would you?"

Wes took the paper and held it up to the shaft of light from the window. He found the letter and began reading. The missive started with the previously reported news that Governor Samuel B. Axtell had declared Lincoln County in default of 1877 taxes. Further, the missive said McSween gave to Sheriff Brady in his capacity as tax collector a check later endorsed by James J. Dolan and converted to use by the House. Tunstall blamed the sheriff for the fraud, concluding, "A delinquent taxpayer is bad; a delinquent tax collector is worse." Wes looked up at Patrón. "That's not an accusation you put in print."

Patrón nodded. "Even if the Englishman's right, he's a fool for sending it to any paper, especially a Republican paper. The editor is Albert J. Fountain. He's a reformer, one of the Radical Republicans. Everyone with the House and the ring in Santa Fe hates him. This *Independent* is the worst place this letter could appear." Patrón shook his head, crossing himself. "Young Tunstall best be careful because the House has a long memory. Word is that Dolan and his cronies are in Mesilla now getting the court to attach Tunstall's cattle for a debt his partner McSween owes the House."

"Are we the only ones that care about right and wrong, Juan?"

"It's complicated these days. No one's certain anymore what's truth and what's a falsehood. All I can confirm is Dolan's left town, and Murphy's dying. Cancer, they say. He's in the hospital at Fort Stanton on his deathbed, but I suspect he's too mean to die."

"He's so crooked I doubt they can fit him in a straight coffin," Wes replied, folding the paper back and handing it to Patrón. He arose from his chair. "I best tend my business and get back to the Mirror B. I came to town to handle a matter at the courthouse and purchase coffee at Montaño's. We're getting low."

Grimacing, Patrón wagged his head from side to side. "José's out of everything. What he told me was that Tunstall told José's supplier he'd pay more for the same goods if he'd quit selling to Montaño. That's how bad things are for our people, Wes. You either buy necessities at outrageous prices from the House or Tunstall or make the long ride to Roswell or Mesilla for supplies."

"I can't abide the House. I'll hold my nose and go to Tunstall's." He bade Patrón farewell and retreated outside, untied his horse, and rode over to the courthouse, filing his papers on the Casey place, the clerk and assistant paying him little mind as they gossiped about Tunstall's letter in the *Independent*. Finishing his affairs with the county official, Wes remounted and rode to Lincoln's newest store. He slid off his horse into the goop left by the melting snow and tied his sorrel to the hitching post. He marched inside.

The clerk in wire-rimmed glasses greeted him. "Welcome, mister, be sure and wipe your boots on the doormat."

Wes looked at the mud on his boots and stomped on the mat, flinging chunks of crud onto the floor beyond the rug. He strode to the counter. "I need coffee."

The clerk studied him, pointing a finger at his nose. "I remember you," he said. "You're the one that stole eight cartons of ammunition the day the sheriff threatened my boss."

"That was my partner," Wes answered.

"Mr. Tunstall told me not to sell any more merchandise to you or him until the account was settled."

Wes looked around the store, leaned over the counter, and propped his arms on the top. "Is the Englishman here?"

"He's in the back, but is not to be disturbed."

"You either get him or get me five pounds of coffee."

"It'll be seventy-five cents a pound," the clerk said.

Wes whistled. "That's half again what I've paid when Casey had a store."

"Casey doesn't have a store anymore. Neither does José Montaño. And, that's what Mr. Tunstall charges. But I'm not selling unless you pay for the cartridges, or Mr. Tunstall approves."

Wes smiled, stood up straight, and pulled his pistol from its sheath. "Why don't you fetch your boss?"

The clerk nodded and inched along the counter toward the back room. He rapped on the door. "Mr. Tunstall, I need assistance," he called.

The door finally opened, and Tunstall emerged, looking first at his clerk, then his customer.

"Five pounds of coffee," Wes said. "I've got the three seventy-five to pay for it."

"You didn't pay for the eight cartons of ammunition the last time you visited my store."

"That was my partner, not me. Sack up my coffee, and I'll tell you when you'll get your due."

Tunstall looked at his clerk and nodded.

"Go ahead."

The attendant scurried to the coffee grinder and put in the dried beans, working as fast as he could to grind five pounds.

Wes slid his gun back in its holster and dug into his pocket, counting out three dollars and seventy-five cents in bills and change, slapping the money on the counter and waiting. "Split the coffee between two sacks," Wes ordered.

Tunstall nodded to the clerk again. The fellow measured the grounds into two cloth bags, secured the necks with twine, and then tied the two sacks together. He placed the coffee on the countertop next to the money, picking it up piece by piece to count it. "We're good," the clerk said.

"Now," Tunstall said, "when do I get paid for the ammunition?"

Wes yanked the coffee from the counter, spun around, and marched for the door. "As soon as you pay Carlos and Bonney what wages they're due."

"Because of your theft of my stock," Tunstall challenged, "I had to buy another herd of cattle at twice the cost. You're the reason they haven't been paid."

"You get your money when they get their wages," Wes said over his shoulder, slamming the door behind him.

355

CHAPTER 18

"What do you make of it?" Jace Cousins asked Wes Bracken of the throng of riders stopped on the road. Both men started for the house, their long guns in their hands.

Wes whistled for Nip and Tuck and the dogs came running, falling in step with Jace and Wes as they approached the front of the adobe. The hounds growled at the stationary horsemen as two peeled off and started down the trail toward the dwelling.

"Sheriff Brady's one of them," Wes said. "I don't recognize the other."

Jace looked past the approaching pair. "Best I can make out Jesse Evans, Tom Hill, Buck Morton, and Frank Baker are riding with him."

Nip and Tuck inched away from Wes, the hackles raising on their backs as they snarled at the guests. Wes whistled. "Nip, Tuck, get back here." The dogs retreated toward the house, looking over their shoulders and snarling.

Jace lifted his Henry and rested the barrel in the crook of his left arm.

As the lawman neared, he waved folded papers at him. "We mean you no harm, Bracken," Brady called.

"State your business, Sheriff," Wes answered.

He shook the documents again. "I've got writs of attachment on Tunstall's cattle. We're headed to the Rio Feliz to retrieve the stock and to arrest the Englishman if he resists."

"How does that concern us?" Wes asked.

Brady stopped his horse shy of Wes and bent over, offering him the printed materials.

"I believe you, so keep your papers."

The sheriff sat up in the saddle and shoved the legal documents back in his coat pocket. "This is Billy Mathews," he announced. "I've deputized him. We're gathering a posse to serve these papers. We'd be obliged if you joined us so everyone knows where you stood on these matters."

"I stand on my own, Sheriff, not with either side in this dispute."

Brady laughed. "I heard you bought coffee from Tunstall a while back. If you want any more, buy it from the House because we've attached his store as ordered by the court in Mesilla."

"I'll give up drinking coffee, instead," Wes answered.

Jace cocked his head at Brady. "Tell me, Sheriff, do I see Evans, Hill, Morton, and Baker with your posse? Aren't there federal arrest warrants outstanding for them for stealing government horses and mules on the Mescalero Reservation?"

Brady scowled. "They ain't with the posse, and I ain't seen any warrants."

"Sure looks different to me," Jace shot back. "Wouldn't you agree, Deputy Mathews?"

Mathews shrugged and Brady sputtered, "They ride wherever they want."

Wes toed the ground with his boot, looking up at the sheriff. "Didn't they escape from your jail a couple months ago? Shouldn't you arrest them for that and the horse thieving that put them there in the first place?"

"I was trying to be neighborly with you, Bracken, and give you a chance to get on good terms with the House."

"Sheriff, you've got more men than you need right now for the job," Wes replied.

"We won't ride in any posse that includes Jesse Evans and gang," Jace added. "They'd shoot us in the back, if given half a chance."

Brady's eyes narrowed. "Sorta like the assassin that bushwhacked two of his boys after the jail break. You know anything about that, Jace Cousins?"

Jace grinned. "I'd've shot Jesse first, Sheriff. I always figured it was you or one of your deputies that did it trying to arrest him again."

"*Adiós,* Sheriff," Wes interrupted. "Your business is done on the Mirror B."

Brady nodded. "For today, but not forever, Bracken." The lawman yanked on the reins and turned his horse back to the law band. Mathews followed his boss.

"Nice to meet you, Deputy," Jace called as Nip and Tuck barked at the departing lawmen.

When Brady and Mathews rejoined the others, they advanced in a lope toward San Patricio.

"Looks as if Tunstall's imagined empire is crumbling," Wes offered.

Cousins nodded. "Worse than that, we'll be riding to Roswell to buy coffee henceforth."

The partners returned to their chores as a gentle west breeze blew along the valley with the temperatures hovering in the high forties. Toward dusk Wes finished chopping firewood when he caught the sound of bawling cattle on the move from San Patricio. He called Nip and Tuck and tied them to a corral fence post to keep them from spooking or stampeding the herd. Jace emerged from the barn, Henry in hand, and watched the procession as it snaked down the road, Sheriff Brady in the lead.

"How many cattle?" Wes asked.

"I'd estimate three hundred and fifty, but I'm more interested in the number of men, Wes. There's only half those that were here this morning."

"Maybe Brady was honest when he said Jesse's gang weren't with the posse."

Jace shook his head. "I doubt it. Jesse's boys likely handled his dirty deeds. While you've never spent time in prison, I have, and I'm telling you some men are mean and cruel purely for the enjoyment of being mean and cruel. My gut tells me things are about to worsen."

"You're just tired after so many chores today, Jace. I'll untie the dogs, and we'll see what Sarafina's prepared for supper. After we eat, you can study your Bible."

The men enjoyed bowls of menudo with skillet cornbread, then retired to the parlor where Wes continued whittling the wooden pony for Luis, and Jace sat on his stool by the fireplace reading his worn copy of the Good Book.

As Wes carved the toy, he studied Jace's changing facial expressions as he read, biting his lip, grimacing, and looking at the ceiling before bowing his head and closing his eyelids. Wes granted him his moment of privacy until his eyes reappeared. "What's bothering you, Jace?" Wes asked.

Jace stared at Wes, clenching his jaw before relaxing and speaking. "Do you believe the Bible can speak to you or give signs of things to come?"

"I never much considered it, Jace."

Holding up the Good Book, Jace pointed to a passage. "I went to the Psalms for comfort, but I came to chapter fifty-eight, verse ten. 'The righteous shall rejoice when he seeth the vengeance; he shall wash his feet in the blood of the wicked.' Does that passage speak to us?"

Wes put the carving block in his lap, stroking his mustache. "I don't understand it."

"To me the first part says the righteous can take satisfaction in seeing the wicked punished one day."

"And the rest," Wes asked, "the words about washing his feet in blood?"

Jace pondered the question. "I suppose that when such day of judgment comes the righteous cannot walk without getting blood on their boots."

"That's why I don't discuss religion, Jace, because I can't figure it all out."

"You know what bothers me?"

Wes shrugged. "No, sir?"

"Are we the righteous, or are we the wicked in Lincoln County?"

After such a tiring day of chores, Wes lay in bed, frustrated that he couldn't get to sleep. Jace's question tormented him. He had believed life was choices between black and white, good and evil, but Lincoln County had wrecked those notions. Less than two years earlier, he had denied his brother refuge and then buried him on the land they had hoped to operate together. Wes had killed a man defending Sarafina's people at a dance. He had orchestrated a hanging after a sham execution of Robert Casey's killer. After that he had stolen the Casey cattle that the law said belonged to someone else and returned the livestock to the rightful owner, in his mind at least. Since coming to Lincoln County, Jace had slain four men that Wes knew of, possibly more, and Wes still considered him as decent and honest as any man alive in Lincoln County.

Righteous? Or, wicked? Wes turned, pondering the question, turning again and swatting his pillow in frustration.

"What's bothering you, *mi esposo?*" Sarafina whispered as she snuggled against him.

"I'm tired."

"It's more than that," his wife replied, lifting her hand and stroking his cheek. "You are tired most days from providing for me and our sons."

"Something Jace said from the Bible concerning the righteous and the wicked has got me questioning where I fall on the scale."

"*Mi esposo querido,*" she chided, "you are the most righteous man in Lincoln County."

Wes laughed. "That's not saying much, seeing how many evil men call this place home."

"But I have never been anywhere else so how should I know? I *do* know you are good to me and our boys, even carving a toy horse for Luis. A wicked man would never do that for a boy who does not share his blood."

Wes moved to kiss his wife, but the dogs took to barking and howling. He shot up from his bed and grabbed his gun belt, strapping it around the waist of his woolen long johns. The hounds snarled and barked louder than Wes ever remembered.

"What is it?" Sarafina asked.

"I'm not sure. Where's your pistol?"

"In the kitchen."

"With Jace in the bunkhouse, we may need it unless he gets here, but don't shoot until you're certain it's not him coming to help. Now move!" he cried.

"What about the boys?"

"Leave them in bed." Wes grabbed his Winchester and started for the front door, when a gunshot exploded through the air.

Wes unbarred the door and cracked it an inch to search for the attackers in the darkness.

"Wake up! Wake up!" shouted a rider. "It's us, Brewer, Bonney, and Carlos."

Opening the plank entry wider, Wes stuck his head out. "Is that you, Carlos?" Wes yelled.

"Sí," answered his brother-in-law. *"Hemos tenido problemas, pero no queremos hacer daño."*

Sarafina bolted into the room, holding her revolver with both hands.

"It's Carlos," Wes informed his wife, then yelled at the rider. "Say it again."

"Hemos tenido problemas, pero no queremos hacer daño," Carlos shouted.

"He says they've had trouble but mean us no harm," Sarafina translated.

"Stay here with the boys and close the door after me," Wes said as he slipped outside into the darkness. He whistled for the dogs and looked toward the bunkhouse. "Jace," he called, "don't shoot; it's Carlos with other friends."

"Just the same," Jace answered, "I'll stay here and plug 'em if it's a trick."

"It's no trick," cried another voice Wes recognized as Billy Bonney's.

"Come in slow with your hands high," Wes responded. He whistled for the dogs to hush. Three shadowy forms took shape in darkness as Wes studied the riders, lowering his Winchester after confirming it was just the three. "Jace, you can join us. It's who they said." Wes turned to the door and pushed it open enough to stick his head inside. "Sarafina," he called, "everything is okay. It's Carlos, Bonney, and Brewer. You might light candles."

The trio halted their mounts, slid to the ground, and tied their horses to the hitching post.

Jace walked over. "You fellas trying to get yourselves killed, riding up on us like that?"

"Couldn't help it," Brewer said. "We've had bad trouble."

"Yeah," the Kid interjected. *"Tunstall's dead."*

Though the news was not unexpected, Wes still felt as if he had been kicked in the gut with the announcement. "Come in and tell us." Wes pushed the door all the way open, allowing Brewer, Bonney, and Carlos to enter. Jace followed Wes inside, closing the entrance behind him as Sarafina lit more candles.

"I'll get chairs from the kitchen," Jace offered.

Brewer shook his head. "We can't linger. John Middleton is waiting for us by the road, in case the killers are trailing us. We must ride to Lincoln to inform Alex McSween."

"What happened?" Wes asked.

"Sheriff Brady came out with thirty-five or so men to attach the Englishman's cattle," Brewer continued. "They tried to take nine of Tunstall's horses, but the Englishman talked them out of it, saying we'd drive them to town to stay until the matter was resolved. We waited two hours after they left to start for Lincoln, taking the longer route so not to run into the posse."

"They *murdered* him," the Kid muttered.

"About sundown Billy spotted a turkey, and he and I rode over a rise to shoot him for supper. Carlos and Middleton were riding with the Englishman, when they heard galloping horses racing down the valley toward them."

"*Sí,*" Carlos said. "Middleton shouted to Tunstall to run for it, but he froze in his saddle as the two of us raced after Billy. Last time I saw him ten or so riders surrounded him."

Brewer picked up the story. "When Middleton told us what had happened, we took up positions among the rocks, waiting for them to attack. We heard two, three, maybe four shots, and laughter, lots of it. Minutes later, we heard two more shots, but the killers never came for us."

"After a spell," Bonney added, "I crept up to the top of the rise, but the bastards had cut tail and run."

"We argued whether they were running or baiting a trap for us," Brewer said. "That's why we're here, to ask if you'll retrieve poor Tunstall's body and bring him to Lincoln tomorrow. They're out to kill us, too."

Wes looked at his partner, who nodded. "We'll do it. Where can we find him?"

"Who did it?" Jace asked.

"Middleton said he saw Billy Mathews, Buck Morton, Jesse Evans —"

"Figures Jesse was involved," Jace commented.

"— Frank Baker, Tom Hill, and Buckshot Roberts," Brewer added. "There were more, but those were the riders he recognized."

"Bastards," Bonney interjected. "I'll kill them everyone."

"Mi hermana, ¿podríamos comer algo?" Carlos asked. *"No hemos comido desde el desayuno."*

"Yes, Carlos, I'll share what food I've got if you will join me in the kitchen." Sarafina left the room with her brother. *"Que pobre niño,"* she told him.

Brewer turned to Wes and described where to look for the body come daylight while Jace talked to Bonney. Wes noted Brewer's directions, but kept glancing at the Kid.

Bonney's eyes flared with rage and revenge. "Bastards," he repeated as he vowed retribution. "This was Sheriff Brady's doing," the Kid said, then gritted his teeth. "He threatened the Englishman in front of Wes, didn't he?"

Jace nodded.

"His day will come," the Kid promised.

Sarafina escorted Carlos back into the room. Her brother carried a stack of flour tortillas and a neckerchief tied at the corners and filled with the remaining cornbread from supper.

Brewer saw the food and tipped his hat to Sarafina. "Thank you, ma'am." He turned to the Kid. "We best ride to Lincoln to deliver the news."

"Carlos, would you stay with us?" Sarafina asked.

Her brother shook his head. "These are my people now."

Wes observed regret flashing across his wife's eyes.

Brewer offered his hand to Wes, who pumped it warmly. "Bygones are bygones," he said. "For the moment, I intend to see the Englishman buried proper. After that we'll decide what to do because we expect the law will look the other way."

The three visitors turned and marched outside, mounting and riding to join Middleton for the final leg of the sorrowful trip to Lincoln.

When Wes closed the door, Jace spoke. "We both expected this day to come, though I didn't think so soon. Billy's mad, furious that Jesse's men killed Tunstall before the Englishman paid him and Carlos their wages."

"I warned him Tunstall was playing him and Carlos."

"Billy said he'd get his money if he had to steal everything Tunstall's killers owned."

Wes snickered. "All Jesse Evans owns is a bad reputation."

"And other people's livestock," Jace added.

Wes nodded. "We best get what shut-eye we can as we have a long day ahead of us."

They found Tunstall's body midmorning on a bitterly cold day. First, they had spotted the carcass of the Englishman's horse a hundred yards off the trail. As they left the trail to explore, they observed beyond the dead animal a lump on the ground that was Tunstall. As Wes and Jace dismounted, they both saw the Englishman's hat sitting on the horse's head, a sick joke that the murderers must have thought was funny. They stepped to Tunstall and grimaced at the wounds, one gunshot in the chest and a second in the back of the head, the bullet coming out of the top of his forehead, leaving a pulpy, bloody mess. By Tunstall's side, inches from his holster, Jace picked up his revolver and broke it open. "One, two, three, four live cartridges," he said, "and two chambers empty, not even hulls."

Wes nodded. "That'll ruin any alibi that the Englishman fired first and Jesse's men were defending themselves."

"Murder pure and simple," Jace said as he

tucked Tunstall's pistol in his belt.

Wes stood up and searched for discarded hulls that might help explain how Tunstall had died. Finding none, he shrugged. "I didn't expect to discover his horse here. I suppose we should take the saddle. We can cinch it on the mule and drape the body over it." He unstrapped the saddle and with Jace's help worked it out from under the carcass. He picked up the tack and Jace grabbed the saddle blanket and draped it over the mule's back so Wes could drop the saddle in place and secure it. If the Englishman had carried a carbine or saddlebags, thieves had taken them. Once the saddle was tight on the mule, they moved to the body, Wes grabbing the shoulders and Jace the legs as they draped him over the saddle, then bound him to the mule with rope. Wes took Tunstall's hat from the horse's head but dropped it when he saw the blood-stained back.

Both men mounted and started the journey to town. They reached the Mirror B in the middle of the afternoon, transferring the body to Wes's wagon so Tunstall would receive a more dignified entry to town on his final earthly journey. After hitching up the team and grabbing a quick bite to eat in Sarafina's kitchen, Wes and Jace continued their duty. Wes drove the wagon while Jace rode his dun.

By the time they reached Lincoln two hours before sundown, every citizen in town knew of their cargo. All eyes watched the wagon advance. Hispanics crossed themselves as his body passed down the street. Some Anglo men removed their hats and held them over their hearts, while a couple others with allegiance to the House picked up rocks and tossed them at the rig until Jace yanked his Henry from its scabbard, aiming it at them. Their reverence quickly improved.

"I reckon we deliver the body to his store," Wes said, asking a question as much as making a statement.

Jace shrugged. "Didn't Brady say the store was taken over like the cattle?"

Nearing the Tunstall store, Wes pointed to the mercantile where Sheriff Brady stood outside the front door, holding his carbine across his chest.

"Damn," Jace said. "I reckon the sheriff plans to shoot the Englishman again."

"Well, we won't be leaving him there," Wes answered as he neared the sheriff. He tipped his hat at Brady. "Afternoon, Sheriff."

"You chose the wrong side, Bracken," Brady scowled.

"Tunstall doesn't have a side now." Wes pulled on the reins and stopped the wagon. "Care to inspect the body for your investigation."

"No need, Bracken. It was self-defense. The matter's closed." Brady grinned. "Now the Englishman won't be writing any more letters to the *Independent.*"

Rattling the reins, Wes started the wagon toward McSween's place. Two dozen horses stood tied outside the U-shaped adobe house that was the largest dwelling in Lincoln. He recognized the mounts of Brewer, Bonney, and Carlos, then saw Brewer exit the house with McSween, McSween's wife, the Kid, Carlos, and several men he didn't recognize.

Wes came to a halt, set the brake, and jumped from his rig, lowering the tailgate so others could pull the body from the back. Six men and McSween's wife approached the cart. "Don't let any of the women see his head," Wes said. "It's in bad shape."

Brewer came and shook Wes's hand, nodding to Jace. "Thank you both for delivering the Englishman. Things have been tense in town."

Jace dismounted and walked over to Brewer. He pulled Tunstall's revolver from his gun belt and gave it to the dead man's ranch foreman. "He never fired it. We found four loaded chambers and two empty ones, no hulls or nothing. He didn't shoot a round, and the sheriff doesn't care, telling us it was self-defense."

"The worst indignity of all is the House had the only coffin in town for sale," Brewer said. "They charged us four times its value, but we owed it to Tunstall."

Wes watched as McSween's wife directed the handling of the body as the men pulled the corpse from the wagon. "Damn shame," he said, "and it's a damn shame that nothing will be done about the murder."

Brewer grinned. "I'm not so sure that's the case, Wes. Alex McSween knows the law."

"But McSween knowing the law ain't gonna have any sway with Brady," Jace added.

"We won't need Brady."

"How's that?"

"Squire Wilson here is justice of the peace. McSween says that me, Middleton, Bonney, and Carlos can sign affidavits naming the men in the posse that killed the Englishman, and Wilson can issue warrants for their arrests and even deputize lawmen to capture them."

"Do me a favor, Dick, and don't have

Carlos sign an affidavit. One Mexican kid's word and mark won't mean a thing in this county."

"Okay, Wes, but I'm looking for men that will ride with me to bring Tunstall's killers to justice. Carlos can ride with us if he wants. In fact, I'd count it as a personal favor if you and Jace joined us. That's the only way we'll bring justice to Lincoln County."

Wes shook his head. "I can't speak for my partner, but I'm not picking sides in this."

"Wherever Wes goes, I go with him," Jace said.

"I was hoping we could count on the two of you."

"It's six weeks or fewer until planting time. We've got work to do," Wes answered as he watched the volunteers lug Tunstall's body toward McSween's home.

"The Kid's vowing to kill every man involved in the Englishman's death."

"Sounds as if you are, too," Wes replied.

"If that's what it takes to enforce the law, that's what I'll do," Brewer replied, then followed Tunstall's corpse into McSween's adobe.

Wes stepped to the back of the wagon and latched the tailgate. "It's time to go home, Jace. They can bury the Englishman on their own." Wes climbed into the seat and released the brake.

" 'The righteous shall rejoice when he seeth the vengeance; he shall wash his feet in the blood of the wicked,' " Jace said, quoting the Psalms.

CHAPTER 19

The shock of Tunstall's death hovered over Lincoln County in the two weeks after the Englishman's assassination. News was scarce as men seldom discussed matters for fear of alienating one side or the other, but alliances always shifted so nobody knew who to trust. After awaiting information that never came, Wes Bracken and Jace Cousins received a subpoena from Justice of the Peace Squire Wilson, who was conducting an inquest into the Tunstall murder, to appear before him in two days. They were to testify at ten o'clock, allowing them to leave in the morning and get back in the afternoon. The trip would also allow them to visit Juan Patrón and catch up on the turmoil in Lincoln. Wes encouraged Sarafina to ride with them, but she declined as Roberto had been sickly with a runny nose and general listlessness and she did not care to risk his health by getting him out in the cold. In preparation for the trip, Wes brought in more firewood than Sarafina would need and reminded her of her shooting lessons, making sure she had a revolver and carbine to defend herself. The day before the hearing, the partners moved their breeding stock from the barn to the corral, which had become too crowded for the mules so they let them range free, knowing Nip and Tuck would not allow them to stray. The day of the hearing they saddled their horses and headed for Lincoln on a trail they alone traveled. Any men or women they observed outside their houses scurried inside when Wes and Jace approached. Neighbors could no longer trust one another, even with a simple wave or a spoken howdy.

As the Mirror B men passed Sheriff Brady's place on the outskirts of Lincoln, they saw in the road ahead of them two dozen riders coming their way. Wes and Jace leaned over in their saddles and pulled their long guns, ready to fight. The approaching gang carried their carbines as well. As they drew nearer, Wes recognized Brewer, Billy, Carlos, and even the lawyer Alex McSween among them. Wes and Jace directed their horses to the side of the road and waited for the grim band.

Brewer reined up in front of Wes and Jace, twisting in his saddle and ordering his men. "Keep moving, and I'll catch up with you." Bonney tipped his hat as he rode by, but Carlos ignored Wes and Jace.

Wes nodded as the dour-faced riders passed. "What's going on?" he asked Brewer.

"The sheriff's done nothing about arresting the Englishman's murderers so Justice of the Peace Wilson has deputized me to find the killers and bring them in for a trial. He was planning to subpoena you two as well for additional information." Brewer pulled out a clump of papers from his shirt pocket and unfolded the top one, reading it aloud. "The coroner's jury in the death of John Henry Tunstall finds that said Tunstall was brutally murdered by one or more of the persons whose names are herewith written, to wit: Jesse Evans, Buck Morton, Frank Baker, and Thomas Hill and others not identified by the testifying witnesses. The jury also indicts J.J. Dolan and Deputy Billy Mathews as accessories to said murder." Brewer refolded the indictment and slapped it back in the stack of documents, which he held up for Wes and Jace to inspect. "Here are eighteen indictments, and we intend to serve every one of them.

You're welcome to join us, both of you."

Wes shook his head. "We're scheduled to appear before Justice Wilson. I won't ride with any posse that includes Alex McSween."

"Murphy's men have secured a warrant for Alex. If they catch him, they'll kill him. We are escorting him to John Chisum's place where he'll be safe. We've learned Jesse Evans's gang has split up. The largest group is hugging the Rio Peñasco southeast of here. That's where we're going once we drop off McSween."

"What have you heard on Jesse?" Jace asked.

"Don't know for certain, though he's rumored to be riding with Tom Hill. Some folks say he's still around here, and others report he's headed southwest for Tularosa. A lot of conflicting accounts are being tossed about, likely to throw us off their trail. But I intend to bring them to justice."

"Even if it kills them?" Jace asked.

"Justice Wilson appointed me as a special constable," Brewer answered. "It's legal, not revenge." The constable licked his lips. "I'd deputize you both if you wanted to ride with us. It'll take a lot of us to end the wrongdoings."

"I intend to stay out of this," Wes said.

"Whatever Wes does is what I do," Jace answered.

Brewer nodded. "I figured as much. You two staying in the middle means you'll get caught in the cross fire between both sides." He nudged his horse with his heel, and the animal took out after the posse.

Wes and Jace watched until they rode out of gun range and continued their journey to town. They arrived on time at the adobe of Squire Wilson and answered his questions about the location and condition of Tunstall's body. Wilson then offered to deputize them, but when they declined he thanked them for their testimony and sent them on their way. They found Juan Patrón at his adobe. He invited them inside and apprised them of the Lincoln developments and the countervailing forces at work, the House using the power of the sheriff's office and the McSween faction employing the justice of the peace for their legal authority. After the coroner's inquiry had indicted Dolan's men, Billy Bonney had calmly walked to the House to arrest them all, though he was outnumbered. Quickly subdued and disarmed, the Kid was escorted to jail with his own carbine stuck in his back by Sheriff Brady, who threw him in the pit for incarceration and kept Bonney's carbine for his own.

"The Kid's vowed to get even with the sheriff for that public humiliation and for killing Tunstall. Bonney's mad enough to fight a mountain lion with a spitball," Patrón said. "I've never seen anybody with more nerve."

Patrón related how Wilson had charged the sheriff with theft of hay from the Tunstall store and how Brewer and the other "Regulators," as they were calling themselves, had retaken the mercantile and marched to the jail to free Bonney. When Brady failed to investigate the murder or arrest any of Tunstall's killers, McSween approached Wilson, seeking a special constable appointment for Brewer.

Next Patrón explained how word circulated that Jimmy Dolan had written Governor Samuel B. Axtell seeking help from the army at Fort Stanton to quell the lawless in Lincoln County. That was rumor, Patrón said, but he knew for a fact that McSween had written the secretary of the interior claiming fraud by the House in fulfilling contracts to provide beef and hay to the Mescalero Reservation and Fort Stanton.

"This mess resembles two corrupt grizzly bears stalking each other, looking for an edge before going in for the kill," Patrón said. "Come next month, though, a grand jury will convene here in Lincoln."

"Who'll be the judge and the district attorney?" Wes asked.

"Warren Bristol will preside and William Rynerson will be the prosecutor."

"They presided over the trial of Bob Casey's killer, but I have little faith in them."

"Me neither," Patrón said, "but I have faith in the citizens of the grand jury, assuming they can find enough men to serve without ties to the House or the McSween faction."

"Justice is a forlorn hope for Lincoln County," Wes replied.

"That may be changing," Patrón said. "L.G. Murphy's in bad shape. He doesn't have long to live. Things'll improve when he's gone."

"Dolan's no better," Jace said.

Patrón shrugged. "Murphy was a fox, shrewd in his corruption, letting other people do his meanness. Dolan is a lion, attacking and dirtying his own laundry."

Wes arose from his chair. "We could discuss it for a month and still not solve the county's problems. We best get back to the Mirror B."

Jace stood up. "We found out what we needed to know."

"Please," Patrón said, "let me buy you

lunch at the Wortley."

"Too many from the House eat there," Wes replied.

"Not lately," Patrón answered. "Most are on the run and Sam Wortley could use the business as things have been slow since Tunstall's death. After lunch I'd like to introduce you to Justice Wilson. He's at least trying to do right by the law as justice of the peace."

"We visited the justice before we came over," Wes said.

"That was business," Patrón answered. "This will be social."

Wes looked at Jace. "Stay or go?"

"Your call."

"Okay, Juan. We'll take you up on the offer."

The three men stepped outside, deciding to walk as Patrón had not saddled his horse for the day. Wes and Jace retreated to their mounts and pulled their long guns from the saddle scabbards and started for the Wortley.

Once inside, they found the dining room empty of customers and Sam Wortley delighted to have their business. They exchanged pleasantries, sat, and read the chalkboard menu on the wall, Patrón ordering liver and onions while Wes and Jace went with fried steak and potatoes. Wortley gave them steaming cups of coffee, and they visited while Sam prepared their orders. With no other customers to tend, the proprietor brought their plates and a coffee pot for refills, joining them at the table to gossip about Lincoln County's trials and tribulations. Before they left, Wortley gave them slices of apple pie on the house. Wes and Jace left two bits on the table for Wortley after thanking him for his hospitality. He shook their hands and told them to be careful with so much mischief going around.

Outside the Wortley, Wes stared down the street at the imposing Dolan store. Only one horse stood hitched in front of the place, fewer than he ever remembered. He and Jace followed Patrón back toward his home, passing the house that former Sheriff Ham Mills had abandoned and the dwelling McSween and his wife called home. Wes found the Tunstall store locked and shuttered. Patrón turned off the street and angled through open ground to the southeast toward the flat-roofed adobe dwelling Wes and Jace had just visited. They walked over ground that Wes remembered from the botched hanging of Casey's killer. In front of the house, Wes spotted a bench on either side of the door and beyond the house a small orchard and a fallow plot for a garden.

Nearing the house, Patrón shouted, "Green, you've company coming."

The door opened, revealing a man in his fifties with a graying beard and a thinning head of matching hair. He stepped outside into the sunlight, squinting and hooking his fingers under his suspenders. "Business or pleasure?" he asked.

"Whatever suits you best," Patrón answered. "These are the two fellows that run the Mirror B, Wesley Bracken and Jace Cousins."

A grin cracked the graying whiskers. "Didn't we just visit?" he asked, yanking his right hand from his suspenders and extending it first to Wes and then Jace for a hearty handshake. "My baptismal name is John B. Wilson, though I've gone by Green for years, even though people around here have taken to calling me 'Squire' as it sounds better for a distinguished public servant — that's a fancy alias for a slave — such as a justice of the peace." Wilson laughed, but before Wes or Jace could respond, he continued. "Of course, we know there's no justice and no peace in Lincoln County, though I'm trying to do right by everyone, which is why I subpoenaed you boys. Now that your testimony is done, we can talk as friends. I understand you've been trying to steer between the factions that are tearing this county apart."

"It ain't easy, Squire," Wes replied.

Jace studied the justice of the peace. "You ain't any kin to Willie Wilson are you, the man that killed Bob Casey?"

Wilson's eyes narrowed and his gaze hardened. "Hell, no," he answered. "I'd claim kinship to the devil himself before I'd acknowledge any relation to that saddle tramp." The judge examined Jace and his long gun. "You're the one that's reputed to be good with a Henry rifle, aren't you? Two shots and two kills, isn't that what they say?"

Wes noted a flicker of panic flash across his partner's face.

"Don't give it a second thought," Wilson added. "It's not in my jurisdiction, anyway." He chuckled. "That's another justice's problem."

"You sure talk a lot," Jace said.

"I can rattle on like a freight train when I'm around people I trust, and Juan says you are dependable boys."

Wilson stood for an hour talking and discussing matters, never inviting his visitors to enter his cabin or take a seat on the benches. Patrón, Wes, and Jace remained on their feet listening to him prattle on, sometimes on the machinations of Lincoln County politics and at other times on everything ranging from his service in the Mexican War, where he never fired a shot, to the failed job search that led him to Lincoln, where his ability to read and write made him a fine candidate for justice of the peace against the shills put up against him by Murphy's crowd.

Wes finally informed Squire Wilson that he and Jace had to get back to their place as he didn't want his wife alone when darkness fell. The judge shook his visitors' hands again, invited them to come by anytime they wanted to talk, and sent them on their way.

"He talks faster than I can listen," Jace said as they marched off.

"My ears are exhausted," Wes answered.

"I should've warned you that Green can talk the ears off a stalk of corn, but he's the only law we've got on our side."

"You should lock Squire in a room with Dolan and his allies," Jace suggested "to see if he can talk 'em to death."

Wes laughed with Patrón as they reached his house, returned their long guns to their scabbards, thanked him for lunch, and mounted for the ride back to the Mirror B. They rode past the city cemetery and then Brady's place as the sheriff emerged from his house and stared at them as they passed.

"Well, Brady sure isn't out chasing the Englishman's killers," Jace observed.

"It's a damn shame the law's been corrupted," Wes replied.

Jace laughed. "Not when Wilson knows of my ambush of Jesse's men and looks the other way."

"I guess it depends on whose ox the law is goring."

As they neared the junction of the Rio Bonito with the Rio Ruidoso, Jace stood in his stirrups and pointed toward the low mountain ridge. "Wes," he shouted. "Smoke!"

Wes glanced toward home and saw a tower of black smoke rising above the mountain crest that screened his view of his property. He kicked his sorrel's flank and slapped the reins against his neck, sending Charlie charging down the trail. He looked over his shoulder and saw Jace dropping in his saddle and reaching for his Henry, which he jerked out of the scabbard. Jace then charged after Wes, who left his Winchester carbine sheathed so not to delay his race to check on his wife and boys. The sorrel outpaced his partner's dun, and Wes soon reached the Y in the road and shook the lines so his sorrel galloped toward home. As he made the turn, Wes felt like he had been gutted with a dull knife.

His barn had been torched!

Wes screamed at Charlie to fly ahead. His gut knotted when he spotted the wide-open front door of his home. "Sarafina! Sarafina!" he yelled as he raced homeward, panicked over the safety of his wife, his boys, and his horses.

The barn still flamed, but it had collapsed on itself and was now just a burning pile of debris. Drawing closer to his place, he scanned for his breeding stock, but observed only clumps in the corral, reminding him of Tunstall's dead horse. Wes knew that his breeding horses had been slaughtered, but he could accept their loss if only Sarafina and his boys survived. Terrified over the fate of his family, Wes never thought to look for the attackers, turning off the road toward his house and urging every ounce of energy from the stallion. Charlie dodged one furry lump in the trail, then another, and Wes realized Nip and Tuck had been shot too.

"Sarafina! Sarafina!" he cried.

"I'm right behind you," called Jace. "Find your family. I'll kill the bastards that did this."

Nearing the house, Wes spotted a white form on the ground between the adobe and barn. Realizing it was his Sarafina, he raced to the lump, jerked on the reins, and leaped from the saddle, landing on his feet and running to his wife. "Sarafina, Sarafina, talk to me." He fell to his knees beside her and grimaced at her bloody face and the knot on her forehead. Gently, he slid his arm under her shoulders and lifted her head, uncertain if she was alive or dead.

Jace raced by on his dun, circling the house and the bunkhouse before charging to the demolished barn and riding around the debris. He cursed. "Bastards!" he yelled, galloping to Wes and yanking back on the reins at the same time he jumped to the ground. Landing on his feet, he ran to Wes, tossing his Henry aside and squatting by the couple. "How is she?" he gasped.

"I don't know. God, please let her live."

In an instant, Jace shot up from the earth and raced to his dun, untying the canteen from the saddle horn and yanking the cork from its mouth. He stepped to his partner, pulled his kerchief from around his neck, and doused it with water, offering the wet cloth to Wes, who took it and gently wiped his wife's face.

Sarafina's head twitched, and she tried to lift it, moaning at the effort. Her eyelids fluttered, opened, and then narrowed into slits to limit the bright sunlight prying at her eyes. She seemed to recognize Wes, a slight smile worming its way across her lips, then disappearing. *"Mi esposo,"* she whispered, *"¿dónde están mis hijos?"*

"She's asking about the boys, Jace, where are they?"

Jace handed Wes the canteen and jumped up, retrieving his Henry and brushing the dirt off as he sprinted to the house. "Luis, Roberto, where are you? Boys?" he cried as he ran through the open door.

Wes took the container and tipped it to Sarafina's lips, which parted enough to take a sip.

Jace ran back out the door. "I can't find them," he shouted, before retreating inside again.

"Mis hijos," Sarafina said, choking on her drink of water and coughing.

"Who did this?" Wes asked, pulling the canteen from her lips.

"Mis hijos," Sarafina repeated.

"Who did this?"

Her eyes widening, Sarafina understood. *"A la que llaman Jesús."*

"Jesse? Was it Jesse?"

Sarafina nodded. *"Y otro hombre."*

That other man, Wes knew, had to be Tom Hill.

Jace barged out of the house, carrying the two boys. "I found them, Sarafina. I found your sons. They were hiding under your bed. Luis was protecting little Roberto."

Wes gritted his teeth, vowing to punish those that had done this to his wife, to his boys, to his horses, to his dogs, and to his place.

For two days Wes Bracken and Jace Cousins had tracked Sarafina's attackers. They had let her rest that night in her bed, then had taken her and the boys to San Patricio on the mules that the attackers had ignored when they struck the place. It would've been faster and easier to carry her and their sons in the wagon, but it had burned in the barn. The attack on his family was horrible, but the killing of his horses was pure meanness. They were fine horses with great value, but rather than steal them out of greed, Evans and Hill had shot each — even the colts and fillies — in the head out of evil spite. Wes vowed to remember and avenge the assault on his family and the slaughter of his horses. If he didn't catch the pair on this expedition, he would on a future one.

In San Patricio, Wes and Jace found several families willing to shelter Sarafina and the boys because they remained grateful to

Bracken for driving the racist Horrell brothers from Lincoln County previously. The Hispanic men and women promised to care for and protect his family.

Sarafina begged him to stay and not go on the vengeance trail. "I have lost one husband," she told him. "I could not bear to lose another."

"And I can't live every day in fear of another attack on you and the boys," he answered.

From San Patricio the two men rode west along the Rio Ruidoso, passing Dick Brewer's vacant place and reaching Dowlin's Mill where Paul Dowlin confirmed that Jesse Evans and Tom Hill had passed a day earlier, headed to Tularosa. The Mirror B partners rode each day fast and long, only resting when they couldn't see in the darkness, then starting the next morning before sunrise. Wes and Jace skirted the Mescalero Reservation and stopped at Blazer's Mill come lunchtime, learning from Dr. Joseph Blazer that Evans and Hill had indeed passed by earlier that morning, stopping for a quick breakfast and bragging of shooting some poor man's horses before riding on. Wes grimaced at the account, but the pain was worth the return as they understood they were but three, maybe four, hours behind them. The man hunters ate their lunch of red beans with rice and resumed their trek toward Tularosa, trying to gain as much ground as they could before dark so they could set up a cold camp on a mountain where they might spot the campfire of their quarry. The tall trees of the higher altitudes blocked their view, and they slept as frigid as their camp, arising early and moving on, never spotting Evans or Hill.

Just past noon they came to a high meadow surrounded by tall pines and filled with bleating sheep. Across the grassy field, they observed an odd sight, a wagon unlike any they'd ever seen before. It featured a rounded canvas covering with a stovepipe coming out the top and wisps of smoke wafting from the funnel. While the wagon bed was a common width, the top of the sideboards stuck out with another two feet of lumber where the canvas fastened to the frame. The back of the wagon had two steps leading up to a door big enough for a man to enter.

"Do you reckon that's a sheepherder wagon?" Wes asked. "I've heard of them, but never seen one."

"I've never even heard of one," Jace admitted, "but it looks better than a tent as you don't have to set it up every night and take it down every morning. And I bet it's warmer than sleeping on the ground by a campfire."

Wes grinned. "Wish we'd had it last night."

Jace studied the room on wheels and shook his head. "Sheepmen are scorned in Texas, but I'll be damned if he isn't smarter than a cowboy that sleeps on the ground every night."

"Think we ought to visit and beg for lunch or at least information on Evans and Hill?" Wes asked.

"Might as well," Jace answered, until Wes leaned over and grabbed his arm. He looked at his partner.

"Back up into the trees," Wes whispered. "I see them."

The two men tugged on the reins, pulling their mounts back deeper into the trees until they could barely make out the opposite side of the meadow.

"Now I see them," Jace said. "What do you think?"

"There's too much ground for us to cover to charge them. They'd have time to take a position in the trees and shoot us. As cautiously as they're riding forward, I suspect they plan to rob the poor fellow. Let's circle behind the wagon and surprise them from the trees."

"That's fine, Wes, but one thing," Jace replied. "Jesse's mine."

Like hunters after a big elk, they circled around through the trees, careful not to move too suddenly or act too hastily and ruin their advantage. They lost track of time. It was only minutes, but they were so eager to bag their quarry it seemed like hours. Reaching a spot deep in the woods where they felt it safe to leave their horses, they dismounted and hobbled their mounts. Both men pulled their long weapons. Jace kissed his forefinger, then touched the barrel of his Henry for good luck.

They started through the trees, spreading out fifty feet apart and planning to enter the clearing on both sides of the wagon. As the partners neared the camp, Jesse Evans called the sheepherder.

"Hello, the wagon," he cried. "We're a couple of hands needing something to eat."

As Wes moved closer, he observed the sheepherder had tied his mules to the trees. One of them brayed, then the other. Wes and Jace froze in their tracks.

Jesse shouted again. "We're friends, just in need of a few bites before we move on."

Wes saw the rig vibrate as if a man was moving. Then he heard the door open, but the sheepherder said nothing.

Evans and Hill stationed their horses on either side of the wagon door and dismounted. Wes could see Evans but not Hill as he advanced toward the silent sheepherder. He assumed Jace had Hill in his sight rather than Evans.

"We just need a little to eat, and then we'll go," Evans said, pulling his revolver. The wagon bounced as the herder jumped out of the door and started running for the woods on Jace's side. Evans aimed his pistol and shot the fellow, who stumbled and grabbed his leg. Jesse laughed as the terrified herder scrambled to his feet and limped toward the cover of the trees before being screened from Wes by the wagon.

A shot came from the opposite side of the wagon. By the thud, Wes knew it had struck flesh. He sighted in on Jesse's chest.

"Damnation," Jesse cried, spinning around as Wes squeezed off a shot.

Jesse's sudden movement threw Wes's aim off, but by Jesse's scream, Wes grinned, knowing he had hit the outlaw. Jesse grabbed his left arm, then reached for his mount's reins. Wes fired again. By the sound, Wes knew the bullet had hit flesh again. Behind him the mules brayed. Jace charged by the wagon, firing his Henry one, two, three, four times as Jesse clasped the saddle horn, shoved his foot in the stirrup, and struggled himself aboard. Jesse turned his gun hand enough to fire his pistol blindly at his attackers. His horse bolted forward as Wes and Jace ran for another shot. Each man fired three times, Jesse slumping in the saddle, though Wes remained uncertain if he'd been hit or simply dodged bullets.

"Dammit," cursed Jace. "Jesse's got as many lives as a wicked tomcat."

The outlaw disappeared in the trees.

"How about Hill?" Wes asked.

'He's dead. I dropped him cold, but I couldn't see Jesse."

"Nor me Hill."

"If Jesse'd been on my side of the wagon, he'd be dead instead of Hill, dammit. Are you ready to chase the bastard?"

"No, too many chances for him to ambush us. He may die as is, and we've taken enough risks for today. I don't want him surprising us." Wes turned around and started for the herder, who kept falling every time he tried to get up and dash for the trees.

Wes ran to the man and realized by his dark skin that he was either a Mexican or an Indian. The shepherd looked up at him in fear until Wes lowered his weapon and inspected the wound. The victim grimaced as Wes squeezed and prodded the gash.

"It went through muscle, nothing else," he said to Jace, certain the man didn't understand English.

Jace stepped to Hill and rolled him over with his boot. The front of Hill's shirt and coat dripped with blood. Jace bent and removed the kerchief from Hill's neck and then fetched the canteen from the dead man's horse. He poured water over the cloth and offered it to Wes for treating the herder's wound.

While Wes worked on the man's gunshot wound, Jace stripped Hill of his gun belt and revolver, pulled off his boots, and offered the footwear to the herder, who nodded his acceptance. Wes helped the man to his feet and assisted him to his wagon. The sheepherder grinned with appreciation, though neither said a word the other could understand. By the time Wes got the injured herder situated and stepped outside the wagon, Jace had draped and tied Hill over the saddle of the dead man's gelding.

Wes pointed to the woods. "I'll get our horses." He retreated into the trees and returned with the sorrel and dun. He offered the dun's reins to Jace, who draped

Hill's gun belt over the saddle horn and mounted, taking the reins to Hill's horse and starting back the direction they'd come.

After mounting, Wes called *adiós* to the herder and started after Jace, soon catching his partner. "You planning on burying Hill or taking him back to Lincoln?"

"Neither," Jace answered. "Once we get him beyond smelling distance from the camp, I'm dumping him. A man that would attack your family and shoot innocent horses don't deserve a Christian burial. His horse will be a start to rebuilding our herd."

Wes nodded. "I hope Jesse dies in the woods, too. Now, let's ride for San Patricio."

CHAPTER 20

Approaching San Patricio, Wes saw Charlie's ears flick forward. The sorrel had heard something. Wes motioned for Jace to stop as he reined up his stallion. Tom Hill's trailing bay halted as well. Leaning forward in his saddle, Wes cupped his hand to his ear and listened. He detected distant pops. "Hear that?" he asked Jace.

"Gunfire," his partner answered, "but it's not our fight."

Wes shrugged. "I don't know whose fight is whose in Lincoln County anymore."

Both men pulled their long weapons from their scabbards. Wes nodded, and the two advanced cautiously with Wes concerned that the horse tied to his might slow him if they had to escape. As they rode ahead, the sound of gunshots grew louder until they passed a curve in the road and spotted a mounted gunman on the slope firing a long gun at two men pinned behind a boulder on the down slope by the Rio Ruidoso. The pair answered rifle fire with ineffective pistol fire that lacked the range of their assailant's weapon.

Jace pointed toward the stream. "Isn't that the Kid's dappled gray?"

Wes looked at the river course and observed not only Bonney's gray but also Carlos's gelding. "It's the Kid and Carlos. I reckon this is our fight after all."

"Should we shoot him or scare him away?" Jace asked.

"Let's shoo him off since we don't know who it is. Let's go." Wes nudged his horse forward, with Tom Hill's animal and Jace's dun following.

The partners whistled and shouted as they rode, firing their weapons and scattering hot lead around the assailant who spurred his horse to escape. The gelding angled down the slope, racing for the trail. Wes and Jace fired another shot apiece into the air to hasten the attacker's departure, then reined up as they reached Billy and Carlos, who jumped from behind the boulder, big grins on their faces.

"Gracias," said Carlos.

"Nice to see you," Bonney offered, removing his hat and wiping his brow with his sleeve.

Jace pointed to the stream. "I'll fetch their horses." He rode toward the animals.

"Who was it?" Wes asked.

"Buckshot Roberts," Bonney answered, putting his headgear on. "He was with the gang that killed the Englishman. He got the jump on me and Carlos." The Kid noticed the horse tied to Charlie and walked over to examine it. "That looks like Tom Hill's horse." He rubbed his hand over the saddle, studying the leather seat. "Appears to be bloodstains. Did you get Hill?"

Wes grinned. "Tom had an unfortunate encounter with a sheepherder near Tularosa. He didn't survive the meeting."

"What about Jesse Evans?"

"He took a hit hard, but escaped into the woods. For all we know his ugly carcass may be rotting away among the trees."

"Jesse deserves to die alone," Bonney said, "especially after word I heard in San Patricio about what he did to your wife and horses. That was evil."

"Sarafina did not deserve such treatment," Carlos spat. "I pray that the diablo Jesse dies a miserable death."

"Jesse's the luckiest bastard I've ever been around," Bonney said, spitting on the ground as if the very mention of Evans's name left a bad taste in his mouth.

Wes looked from Bonney to Carlos. "What are ya'll doing here? I thought you were south of here at the Rio Peñasco searching for Tunstall's killers."

Bonney laughed. "We jumped five of them and captured two. As we were escorting Buck Morton and Frank Baker to jail, I'll be damned if they didn't make a run for it. We shot them both."

"Left them for the buzzards," Carlos added.

"Figuring we wouldn't be welcome in Lincoln, we made San Patricio our home and saw what they did to your place when we passed," Bonney said. "When you came along, we were guarding the western approach to town in case someone tries to attack us."

"Jace and I saw no one between Blazer's Mill and here," Wes noted as his partner rode up with the horses. He dropped the reins for each man, and Billy and Carlos took to the saddle.

"Good! Carlos and I'll ride back to San Patricio with you," Bonney said. "I'm dying to know what's been going on in Lincoln. Rumor has it the territorial governor himself is in town, trying to sort out the troubles, not that he'll do any good."

Wes agreed. "I doubt President Hayes

could resolve the matter."

Jace looked from Wes to Bonney. "What about God? You think He'd have a shot at patching things up?"

Bonney pursed his lips, shook his head, and offered a bucktoothed smile. "He doesn't stand a chance. The devil might be the one to fix things, provided he had plenty of cartridges."

As they rode to San Patricio, Wes maneuvered his horse beside Carlos's. "Have you seen Sarafina?"

He nodded.

"How is she and the boys?"

"Luis and Roberto are fine," he answered, then scowled. "You should've been there to protect her." He nudged his gelding ahead of Wes's.

Now his brother-in-law blamed him for Sarafina's humiliation. Maybe Carlos was right, Wes thought. Had he stayed with Sarafina that day rather than riding with Jace to Lincoln for news, things might've turned out better. Those were decisions he could not change, but it tormented him that his wife had been violated as a result.

Entering San Patricio, Wes observed twenty horses and a buckboard outside the cantina, and he knew the Regulators had gathered there. While Bonney led Jace and

Carlos toward the establishment, Wes veered off to the adobe where he had left Sarafina and the boys while he pursued Evans and Hill. In the corral behind the house, he glimpsed his two mules. At least he still had them, even if he didn't have his breeding horses. Riding around the back to tie Charlie and Hill's horse, Wes smiled at the sight of Sarafina bending over a basket and pulling out a damp skirt to hang on the clothesline.

Glancing up and seeing him, Sarafina threw the skirt into the container and ran over to greet him. "My prayers have been answered," she cried. "You're back safe."

Wes slid out of his saddle, tossed the reins aside, and grabbed his wife, hugging and twirling her around. He kissed her cheek and lips.

"I missed, worried, and prayed over you," she said.

"One of your attackers is dead and possibly the other," he told her.

"I don't care as long as you've returned and don't believe I am tainted."

Wes separated himself from her and held her by the arms, studying her bruised cheeks and blackened eyes, which overflowed with tears. "You are my wife, and as beautiful as ever."

"But my face is so ugly now."

"The bruises will go away and the memories will too," he assured her. "Gather your things and the boys, and I'll be back in an hour to take my family home."

Sarafina smiled, breaking from his grip and hugging him even tighter.

He preferred to stay, but knew he should visit the cantina to learn what he could about developments in the county. He extricated himself from her hug, picked up the reins to his horse, and tied the sorrel to a corral post before striding around the house to join the Regulators.

Stepping inside, he found the saloon crowded, every chair taken, and men, both Anglo and Hispanic, standing along the walls listening. Surprised at seeing Juan Patrón in front of the group and speaking, Wes stepped from the doorway. Patrón hesitated for an instant and nodded.

"Glad you made it back, Wes. I was telling the Regulators that Governor Sam Axtell is in Lincoln. The news is not good."

Wes shrugged. "Go ahead."

"The governor has removed Green Wilson as justice of the peace. That means his commission designating Dick Brewer as a constable is invalid. Any actions taken by Brewer and the other Regulators were made without legal authority."

Brewer stood up from a chair by the bar. "What he means is, those of us involved in shooting Morton and Baker are murderers in the eyes of the law."

Wes stepped forward, weaving his way through the crowd. "Juan," he called, "how can we break the corruption if Murphy's and Dolan's cronies are determining what's a crime and what's not? Everyone's tired of the threats, the violence, and the fear for our families."

The men in the room nodded or shouted their agreement.

"I can't answer that, Wes," Patrón replied. "I can say I've been summoned as a grand juror, and I intend to listen to the facts and decide what's right and wrong, not who it hurts."

Bonney stood up and shouted. "That means some of us in this room could be indicted for protecting our own. Any of us could get hung."

"What it indicates, Kid, is you might go to a trial before a jury of your peers," Patrón replied. "That's the only way to receive actual justice instead of vigilante justice."

"I don't like it, not with a crooked sheriff that'd rather watch us die than see us receive a fair trial." Bonney crossed his arms over his chest.

"If we're ever to bring the law to Lincoln County, we've got to abide by it," Patrón answered. "I can't say what the other jurors will do, but I will be fair."

"I don't care for it either," Brewer replied, "but I prefer taking my chances before a fair jury rather than a crooked sheriff, Kid."

"The grand jury convenes on April first," Patrón announced. "That's three weeks from today. Lincoln will be crowded with men testifying and families awaiting the jury's findings. If any of you come to town, don't cause any trouble. That's the last thing we need if we are ever to right the wrongs of the previous decade in Lincoln. I shouldn't even be here telling you this, but I felt I owed it to you as much as you have been wronged in this whole matter. Now I best return home." Patrón picked up his hat from the bar and his coat from the back of a chair, starting for the door as the noise increased from men chattering about his news. Patrón motioned for Wes to accompany him outside, and both men exited together.

Slipping on his hat and coat, Patrón turned to Wes. "Are you coming to Lincoln for the grand jury?"

"Are you saying I need to be there?"

"There's the Casey cattle you stole from Tunstall's place. I can't say whether it will come up, but it might. That aside, you can stay at my place as the Wortley will be full. Bring Sarafina and the boys so you won't have to leave them alone again. I'm devastated about what happened after our last visit. Come the afternoon before the session convenes. Stay as long as you need."

"*Gracias,*" Wes answered. "I'll take you up on that."

"One more thing," Patrón said. "Did you get the men that attacked your wife?"

Wes studied Patrón. "Is this official as a grand juror or unofficial as a friend?"

"I can't say for certain, Wes."

"What I know is Jesse Evans and Tom Hill tried to rob a sheepherder's camp. In the ensuing shootout, Hill was killed and Jesse was wounded before escaping."

"As a friend, I'll tell you that's good to know," Patrón said with a wink. "As a grand juror, I may need to learn the herder's name in case the incident comes up."

"The herder was an Indian, and he didn't understand English, so I never learned who he was. Besides, I'm not sure the fight even occurred in Lincoln County."

"That should make it easier on everyone," Patrón said as he climbed in his buckboard, tugged his hat over his forehead, and untied the reins. "See you in three weeks, Wes." He turned the wagon around in the street for the return home.

An idea struck Wes, and he called to Patrón. "Juan, hold up." Wes chased after the buckboard until the conveyance stopped. When he caught up with Patrón, Wes asked, "Since you're passing our place, would you mind if Sarafina and the boys rode with you? It'd be easier on them than trying to ride the mules home."

"Glad to help, Wes."

Wes climbed in the buckboard and pointed to the dwelling where Sarafina had stayed. Patrón turned the rig in that direction, and Jace followed on his horse. At the house, Wes jumped from the conveyance and started for the door.

Spotting Charlie and Hill's horse, Jace called to Wes. "I'll fetch Charlie, but I'll keep the extra mount and bring it and the mules after you."

Wes nodded as he knocked on the entry. "Sarafina, Sarafina," he called, "get the boys and your things, and we'll start home. Juan Patrón'll give you a ride in his buckboard."

When the door opened, the aged couple that had kept Sarafina stood there, smiling. *"Ella viene,"* the husband said.

"Gracias," Wes answered, reaching into his pocket. "Let me pay you."

The old man looked at his wife and shook his head. *"No dinero,"* he said. *"Eres amigo de nuestra gente."*

"He's telling you he won't take your money," Sarafina translated as she strode to the entry, "because you are a friend of our people." She held Roberto in one arm and the blanket tied with her meager belongings for the San Patricio stay in the other. Luis ran beside his mother.

"Gracias, gracias," Wes said to Sarafina's hosts as Luis saw him at the door and squeezed between the couple, running to Wes and hugging his legs.

Wes picked up his stepson and toted him to the buckboard, tickling his belly and giving him a hug. Luis cackled as Wes sat him beside Patrón. Wes took the bag from Sarafina and tossed it under the seat, then lifted Roberto and kissed him on the cheek.

"Roberto has started walking," Sarafina announced.

With his free hand, Wes helped his wife in the buckboard and handed her Roberto, who squawked for his father as Jace rode up leading Wes's sorrel. As Wes mounted, his partner told him he planned to follow at a distance. Wes nodded, knowing Jace hoped to screen Tom Hill's horse from the grand juror so he wouldn't ask questions.

Astride his horse, Wes maneuvered Charlie beside the buckboard and leaned over with outstretched arms. Roberto reached for him, and Sarafina smiled as she handed her young son to his father. The toddler quit squawking as soon as Wes sat his boy on the saddle in front of him. Roberto grabbed the saddle horn and sang contentedly.

As Patrón shook the reins and started his buckboard moving, Wes rode beside the conveyance, holding his son, looking at his wife and his stepson, and fearing what he would find on the Mirror B. They had left so quickly the morning after the attack that Wes had not evaluated the damage. Reaching home Wes was relieved to see that at least the house still stood. With the barn demolished along with its contents, including his wagon, tack, and tools, he remained uncertain what to do or if he could even make a crop this year. None of that might matter, however, if the grand jury indicted him or Jace.

They arrived at Juan Patrón's home mid-afternoon before the grand jury proceedings were scheduled, Wes riding his sorrel with Roberto on the saddle; Sarafina on a mule with Luis in front of her; and Jace on his dun, his Henry resting in his arms from the time they departed the Mirror B until they reached Patrón's place. Juan and his wife offered the four Brackens their bedroom while the Patróns said they would sleep on pallets in the front room as they had done when Tunstall boarded with them. Jace preferred to bed out back by the corral to watch over their mounts.

For their hospitality, Wes fished two dollars out of his pocket and gave them to the Patróns so they might dine at the Wortley. While Juan and his wife, Beatriz, argued against accepting the gift unless the Brackens accompanied them, Wes and Sarafina declined, insisting their children were too tired. Too, Wes knew he was running out of money for frills.

The Patróns attended supper and came back with interesting news that Judge Bristol and District Attorney Rynerson had not arrived from Mesilla before dark. The pair usually came the day before the jury panel convened, but perhaps they had delayed their arrival because of the bad blood circulating around Lincoln. Sam Wortley, Patrón reported, fretted that he would lose the income from renting out two rooms to the judge and prosecutor. Patrón said dozens of horses were either tethered to hitching posts at the House or running free in the corral behind the store. On the way back to his house, Patrón noted many more men and horses than usual for the past month around the McSween home. He overheard one fellow saying he expected McSween to return from Chisum's place after dark or in the morning. All the principals in the ongoing difficulties were in town, save for the man who had started it all, L.G. Murphy, who had been taken from the hospital at Fort Stanton to Santa Fe with but days to live, so folks said.

Come morning, Wes arose early, anxious for the proceedings to begin. While his wife and boys still slept, Wes joined Patrón and Jace walking the darkened street to Sam Wortley's for breakfast as soon as the dining room opened at six o'clock. Wortley greeted them with a frown.

"Bristol and Rynerson didn't show up," Patrón guessed.

Wortley nodded. "Took money out of my pockets, they did. I could've sold their rooms a dozen times over last night, but I was afraid to release them. If they showed up without a place to stay, they'd indict me first thing and send me to jail for life. Morning, gents, and pardon my foul mood."

"We understand, Sam," Wes answered. "If you'll give us a quick breakfast, we'd like to eat and get out of here before any fellows from the House show up."

"Bacon, eggs, biscuits, and coffee it is," Wortley said. He left and returned ten minutes later with three plates and a pot of coffee. Putting the plates in front of them, he next dispensed coffee.

As Wortley finished filling their cups, Jace dug into his pocket and pulled out enough coins to cover the meal. "You fellas are eating on me this morning."

"I should pay," Wes answered, knowing he didn't have enough to cover the meal cost, "Juan giving us his bedroom, and you sleeping out by the corral."

"Hush up and eat," Jace countered, "so we can leave here before Dolan's boys arrive."

They gobbled down their food and headed back down the street just as the dim morning light was eroding the darkness. Passing the McSween house where several horses were hitched, Wes looked for Bonney's dappled gray or Carlos's mount but missed them. The trio strode by the Tunstall store, which was still shuttered and locked. Wes noticed a lookout standing at the wooden gate at the eight-foot-high adobe-walled corral, which abutted the rear of the mercantile. Wes surmised McSween's men camped there. Again he observed no sign of Bonney or Carlos.

On the opposite side of the street, Wes made out Green Wilson, the former justice of the peace, working with a hoe, preparing his spring garden for planting. They passed the courthouse and the Montaño place before reaching Patrón's home. The men waited outside in the morning cool, letting the women and children sleep undisturbed inside. As daylight washed away the last remnants of the night, Wes slipped into the house to retrieve his carbine, then watched as people emerged on the street, followed by riders and later wagons. The only other time Wes remembered the town being so crowded was for the hanging of Willie Wilson.

By midmorning, Wes was bored, having covered the same topics with Patrón and Jace several times. He yawned and stretched his arms. "Grand jury convenes at one o'clock?"

"If Bristol and Rynerson show up," Patrón said.

"I'll visit with Squire Wilson," Wes said. "He was working his garden earlier."

Jace shook his head. "You've got stronger

ears than I have. If he don't talk you to death, we'll see you next month. We may bore you, but we don't exhaust you."

Wes grinned as he ambled from the Patrón adobe behind the courthouse and to Wilson's dwelling. The old man was spading dirt when he looked up and spotted Wes.

"Howdy, Squire."

"Just call me Green since I ain't justice of the peace anymore. Damned governor replaced me, did you hear?"

"I did."

"It proves I was getting close to the real crooks of Lincoln County, maybe even in all the territory. The governor's a part of the Santa Fe Ring with Tom Catron, you know about him?"

"Can't say I do."

"He's gotten rich on graft and politics, Catron has."

Wilson explained his view on politics and the Santa Fe Ring for an hour and Wes tolerated it because he was killing time until the grand jury convened. A half hour before noon, Wes noticed the street clearing as four men walked down the middle of the dusty road, carbines cradled in their arms. As the quartet passed the McSween house, Wes recognized Sheriff William Brady and Deputies Billy Mathews and George Hindman,

419

but not the fourth lawman.

As the quartet reached the eastern side of the Tunstall store, they angled to the southeast toward the courthouse. At that moment, Wes caught a flash of metal from the sun's reflection on a carbine barrel. He noticed the gate to Tunstall's high-walled corral swing open. Five or six men stood there brandishing revolvers or carbines. Without warning they opened fire on Brady and his deputies. Brady took one of the first bullets, screaming and stumbling forward, the other three deputies scattering like quail, one running down the street, another angling for the courthouse, and the third racing for cover behind a tree between the street and Wilson's place.

Hearing the whiz or thud of bullets passing or striking the ground, Wes lifted his Winchester prepared to shoot back. Behind him, he heard a scream and twisted around enough to see Wilson collapse on his garden's freshly turned dirt, writhing in pain. Another bullet kicked up dust in front of him, and Wes aimed at one assailant. Just as he squeezed the trigger, he realized he was sighted in on Carlos, so he yanked his carbine skyward as the barrel exploded, sending the bullet into the heavens instead of Carlos, who stepped away from the corral's adobe wall and fired at Hindman dashing down the road. The lawman tumbled to the dust, yelping from his wound. Wes watched Carlos dash to Hindman and stand over him as he begged for help and his life. Carlos callously shot him at point-blank range, spun around, and raced to the corral gate.

As Carlos retreated for cover, a second Regulator ran to Sheriff Brady, nudged him with his boot, and leaned over, grabbing the lawman's carbine before fleeing toward Carlos as the two surviving lawmen returned fire, one grazing the assailant's thigh. When the wounded attacker bent to grab his leg, Wes recognized Billy Bonney just before he limped into the corral. Moments later, six horsemen bolted out of the enclosure, Wes recognizing the mounts of Bonney and Carlos but not the other four. Moments later a seventh rider Wes identified as Dick Brewer dashed from the enclosure on his horse and charged after the other riders.

They galloped east along the road fifty yards before cutting north between houses toward the Rio Bonito where they had more cover for their escape. Several townsmen rushed to the downed lawmen in the street, while Wes turned around to check on Wilson.

The old man squirmed on his belly, grasping his buttocks. His pants seat was soaked with blood. "Am I dying?" Wilson cried.

Wes squatted beside him and spotted a fleshy and bloody crease in his britches. "The bullet grazed your butt, Squire."

"It hurts like hell," he answered.

"You'll live," Wes said, jumping up and dashing for the injured lawmen.

Wes joined the dozen men clustered around the sheriff.

"He don't need a doctor," said one. "He needs an undertaker."

Wes noticed Brady held a sheet of paper clenched between his stilled fingers. He squeezed his way between the spectators and squatted, yanking the note from the lawman's lifeless hand.

He read the handwritten notice the sheriff likely planned to post at the courthouse: GRAND JURY POSTPONED FOR ONE WEEK.

CHAPTER 21

The image of Carlos coldly executing the wounded deputy on the street in Lincoln remained etched in his brain as Wes rode to San Patricio, hoping to borrow from one of the Mexicans a harness to plow his fields. He could construct crude handles to replace those burned off his nine-inch steel plowshare in the fire, but making a harness was beyond his skills. Understanding Carlos was impossible for him. Maybe Carlos resented his hard life, especially as a captive among the Apaches. Perhaps the hardships of living with the Indians did not gnaw at him as much as Wes marrying his sister. He could neither decipher Carlos nor convince him that he loved Sarafina and would provide for her and her children.

Wes tried to clear Carlos from his mind because he had more immediate problems if he was to get a crop in the field. He needed a harness, but his money was dwindling, so much so that he couldn't afford to buy a new one and still provide for family essentials. He feared a ride to the store in Roswell would turn out fruitless. With all the chicanery in Lincoln County, no store-keeper wanted to extend credit to a man who might not survive the week. The closer he moved to San Patricio, the more he re-alized he should've gone to Casey's Mill and searched for any tools or gear left behind, assuming that others hadn't already plundered the place. Wes guessed the Casey property was still his, as he had filed the bill of sale with the county clerk. But then again, did filing the papers in a crooked county make any difference at all? Wes had no answer, like he had no harness.

At the edge of the village, Wes passed the cemetery where Sarafina's first husband rested forever and the small chapel where he had married his wife. As he turned down the village's main street, he glimpsed from the corner of his eye a man holding a Winchester emerging from behind the house of worship. Up ahead, he spotted saddled horses, all much better horseflesh than that the villagers rode. He counted fourteen mounts and wondered if they were friend or foe as he swapped the reins to his left hand and let his right fall to his thigh where he might grab his pistol if trouble awaited. He identified Billy Bonney's dappled gray and relaxed a moment until he spotted Carlos's mount. Twisting in his saddle, he looked over his shoulder at the man tailing him. The fellow glared at Wes, his countenance never changing, though he wiggled his Winchester toward Wes, encouraging him to get along or turn and mind his own affairs. Besides the carbine, the lookout wore two gun belts with a revolver on each hip, though the left pistol was worn backward with the grip aimed forward.

As Wes neared the cantina, the man behind him spoke. "Stop in the saloon. I figure the Kid'll want to talk to you."

"Is that a request or a command?" Wes replied.

"You decide," he scowled.

Outside the saloon, Wes halted his sorrel and dismounted. Not finding a space at the hitching rack, he reached in his saddlebags and extracted a set of hobbles he slipped over Charlie's forelegs. Standing up, Wes touched his carbine in its sheath under the saddle.

"Leave it be," the fellow commanded. "You won't need a Winchester inside."

Wes studied the man, wondering if he should try to coldcock him and take his carbine instead, but opted not to create any unnecessary problems. If the ruffian ordered him to remove his revolver, Wes decided to fight back.

"Now get inside," his new pal ordered.

Nearing the door, Wes heard the murmuring from the room. He lifted the handle, then pushed open the entry. As he stepped inside, the room went silent, every set of eyes looking his way and every gun hand reaching for a weapon. Wes recognized many of the same faces that had been in the room when Juan Patrón spoke to the Regulators of the upcoming grand jury. On that occasion, the faces had been hopeful. Now they appeared desperate. Wes turned his back on the crowd long enough to shut the door and search for the gang's leader.

"Where's Brewer?" he asked. The faces darkened, and Wes saw Billy Bonney stand by a table and step up on a chair so that he looked down on Wes. "Where's Brewer?"

"He's dead!" Bonney spewed the words like they were covered in bile. "I'm in charge!"

Wes clenched his jaw and knotted his fists. "What happened, God rest his soul?"

"We jumped Buckshot Roberts at Blazer's Mill. In the fight, Roberts blew the top of Brewer's head off with a buffalo gun."

"Sorry to hear that."

"We gutshot Roberts, and he died the next day after a night of the misery he deserved," Bonney said.

"You Regulators are killers, like in Lincoln when the grand jury planned to meet."

Carlos shot up from a chair, his fingers knotting into a fist he shook at Wes. "I wasn't in Lincoln that day," he cried.

"I didn't say you were," Wes announced, "but I saw you that day and saw what you did."

Carlos stepped toward Wes, but Bonney grabbed him. Carlos yanked his arm free and spun around to the bar, turning his back on Wes and pointing to a bottle of whiskey that the nervous barkeep pushed his way.

"We intended to arrest Buckshot and take him to jail," Bonney replied.

"You arrested Buck Morton and Frank Baker, but they never made it to jail, Billy."

The Kid's eyes narrowed. "Sort of like the sheepherder arresting Jesse Evans and Tom Hill, isn't it, Wes? They didn't make jail either. Everybody's hands are dirty in Lincoln County."

"Some are dirtier than others, Kid."

"I don't need a lecture from someone

that's too yellow to take sides in this dispute."

Wes pointed his trigger finger at Bonney's nose. "I'll stand to protect my family and what's mine, but I'll not align with either side. Tunstall was no better than the House bunch."

"That's a lie."

"Did you ever get all the wages he owed you?"

Bonney scowled, glancing at his scuffed boots, then looking up with fire in his eyes. "We'll take what we're due, one way or another."

"What you'll get is a life on the owlhoot trail, always looking behind your back, never knowing who to trust, always uncertain if your pals might betray you. It's a sorry life, Kid. It wears on you. You can be a curly wolf running from trouble forever, but you can't outrun every bullet that'll come your way."

"Get out of here, Wes," Bonney shouted.

"When the grand jury meets, both the House and the law'll come down on you."

"They're one and the same," the Kid yelled back.

"Perhaps, but it'll get worked out one day. When that day comes, you'll be riding the outlaw trail," Wes answered, pointing his finger at his brother-in-law. "Carlos, I haven't told Sarafina what happened in Lincoln. You're still between hay and grass and don't think you wear big britches just because you killed a man."

Carlos sulked, taking a long swig on the whiskey.

Wes turned to the rest of the Regulators. "You Regulators are no more welcome on my place than Dolan or Jesse Evans and his boys." Wes paused a moment, staring at Sarafina's brother. "Carlos, you're kin so you can visit, but come alone."

Carlos jerked the bottle from his lips and snarled. "If Billy can't visit, you'll never see me again. I don't trust you."

"Bring Bonney then, but nobody else," Wes said, looking around at the other Regulators, whose stunned expressions reflected their disbelief that one man had stood against so many.

"Should I kill him, Kid?" asked a voice behind Wes. "One more death won't matter."

Bonney waved the idea away with the sweep of his arm. "Let him go so he can get out of here, and we can decide our next move."

Wes lowered his finger and turned around, grabbing the handle and opening the door.

He stepped outside, wondering if law would ever reach Lincoln County or if what he had said was a hope rather than a reality. Wes mounted his sorrel and started back toward the Mirror B, dispensing with seeking a harness to borrow as there was no telling how vindictive the Regulators might turn if they took to drinking.

He wondered if Carlos possessed the courage to visit and tell Sarafina what he had done.

When the grand jury convened, Jace Cousins rode to Lincoln that afternoon while Wes stayed at the Mirror B with Sarafina, who felt embarrassed to impose on the Patróns again in Lincoln while Wes refused to leave her alone at home anymore. He ruled out San Patricio as an option since the Regulators frequented the village, making it a target for attacks by the House gang or reprisals by Bonney's men. So, he did chores around the place, clearing rubble from the demolished barn and salvaging what he found in the blackened wreckage. Every piece of debris he discarded diminished his dream of success a fragment at a time. He had left Arkansas to escape violence, only to encounter more sinister bloodshed in New Mexico Territory.

Three days after he departed, Jace returned, grim-faced and wary. So busy and focused was Wes on his chores that his partner rode within seventy-five feet of him before he even realized Jace had come home. Wes looked up startled, wishing Nip and Tuck were still around to guard the place and his family. By Jace's narrow-eyed demeanor, Wes dreaded the news.

"It's been a while, Jace," Wes called. "I feared you'd skipped Lincoln County on me."

"The grand jury had plenty of mischief to cover."

"Were we indicted?"

Jace reined up and dismounted. "No," he replied. "It's worse than that."

"How's that possible?"

"Jesse Evans is still alive."

"Dammit!" Wes exclaimed.

"You winged him good, though, destroying his elbow. He'll have trouble using his left arm for the rest of his life. He's recovering at the Fort Stanton hospital and awaiting trial for stealing government mules from the Mescalero Reservation. The grand jury indicted him in the murder of Tunstall, but no one thinks he'll see a courtroom on that charge. Mules are more important than Englishmen in New Mexico Territory."

"Any word if he recognized us?"

Jace shrugged. "Can't say for certain. He's mentioned the sheepherder from what I'm told, but not us. Whether he knows and just isn't saying or didn't recognize us is up in the air."

"Anything else from the grand jury?"

Jace nodded. "They indicted both Carlos and Bonney for murder, Bonney for killing Sheriff Brady and Carlos for shooting his deputy George Hindman. Six other Regulators were named accessories in that killing. Bonney and Carlos were identified as accessories in the death of Buckshot Roberts."

"Anyone from the House charged?"

"I'll give the ten men on the grand jury credit for having horns aplenty. Besides indicting Jesse Evans in Tunstall's killing, they named seven others as accessories, including Jimmy Dolan and Deputy Billy Mathews. Joe Blazer headed the panel, and served with Juan Patrón. I didn't know the rest of the members, but everybody's tired of the thieving and murdering. From what Juan told me, Judge Bristol and District Attorney Rynerson were furious they indicted men from the House and further enraged when jurors refused to indict Alex McSween for embezzlement."

"I bet they were fit to be roped and

branded."

"Worse than that," Jace replied. "Juan told me that Joe Blazer had overheard Bristol and Rynerson plotting to send John Kinney and his band of outlaws to Lincoln County to clean out the Regulators and anyone associated with them."

"So it continues, does it?" Wes tugged at his mustache. "Did anything good come out of it except more trouble for us?"

"Perhaps," Jace replied. "Rather than George Peppin or Billy Mathews, the other two deputies with Brady when he died, Judge Bristol appointed John Copeland as sheriff."

"Not familiar with him."

"Neither was I," Jace responded. "He operates a ranch on Eagle Creek, eight miles west of Fort Stanton. He's steered clear of the House and McSween, so he's about as impartial a citizen as you can find. While Juan says Copeland's got a reputations for killing Mexicans, his appointment is as good as we could expect from Bristol. If Copeland goes after the Regulators and Dolan's boys both, we come out ahead when the law applies to both factions.

"And," Jace continued, "they're calling a special election for justice of the peace. Under state law, they have to when one is replaced by the governor. Funny thing is, Green Wilson's running for his old job again."

"The Murphy-Dolan empire must be crumbling, and the House's days are numbered."

Jace grinned. "Dolan's suspended business at his store, and it's not just the indictment. Word is Lincoln County's troubles plus Murphy's debts have bankrupted the House, and Dolan's had to mortgage all his properties to Tom Catron of the Santa Fe Ring. Both the House and Tunstall factions aimed to destroy each other and wound up wrecking themselves."

"And Lincoln County," Wes noted, looking around at his scorched dreams. "What are we gonna do about crops, Jace? No plow, no harnesses, no wagon, no nothing, not even money to cover what we need merely to start over. And, there's no market for any of our cattle and no horses other than our mounts and Hill's."

"It's a tough go, Wes. I figure we should visit Casey's Mill and see what's left there we can use. Perhaps we can operate the grist mill and earn some that way, assuming anybody's able to plant and harvest a crop this year."

"Don't know that'll bring in much cash as

everybody is as strapped as us," Wes answered.

"We can barter. It doesn't have to be money long as we can get enough to sustain Sarafina and the boys until next year." Jace took off his hat and slapped it against his britches. "Dammit, I'm prepared to lose this year if Lincoln County is cleaned up. I figure if we can't get the law working, there's no point in staying beyond this year anyway, Wes."

The day had been long as they started for Casey's place at dawn, all of them, Jace, Wes, and, for their own safety, Sarafina and the boys. They arrived at good light and while Sarafina occupied Luis and Roberto, Wes and Jace began to inspect the store, house, barn, tool, wagon shed, bunkhouse, and grist mill on the Ruidoso. They found more goods and tools than they expected and considered moving them back to the house, but that would require too many uncomfortable trips without a wagon.

Wes stopped, scratched his forehead, and looked at Jace. "We've got this backwards. Instead of packing everything to our place, we ought to move to the Casey property, do it on the sly. The fewer people that know we moved, the less chance of another attack on

Sarafina."

"That would sure ease our minds," Jace answered. "Maybe that's the solution for now."

"Let's go home and sleep on it," Wes said as the afternoon drained away.

Back at the Mirror B, Sarafina fixed tortillas smeared with mashed beans. After she prepared supper, cleaned up the kitchen, and put Luis and Roberto to bed it was well past dark when Wes invited her to join him and Jace at the table lit by two candles.

"You look like you have been thinking too much," she said as she sat down.

Wes smiled. "We want to ask you something. Would you consider moving from here?"

"Lincoln County is all I know."

"I mean down the road to the mill. It's abandoned, and Ellen Casey signed papers deeding it to us."

Sarafina frowned. "I like my house, this one you built for me."

"If we moved, it might be safer for you and the boys until the trouble blows over."

"But when that will be?" His wife asked the question everyone in Lincoln County wanted answered.

"It might be a few months or a few years, Sarafina. We don't know."

"Whatever you think is best," she said, "I am for what keeps the boys safest."

Before Wes replied, he heard the sound of horses approaching the back door.

"Trouble?" Jace whispered as each man blew out the candle nearest to him.

Wes pulled his pistol as he jumped up and slipped to the wall while Jace scampered to the corner where he had propped his Henry.

"*Sarafina, es Carlos,*" came a familiar voice.

"Are you alone?" Wes called.

"I want to talk to Sarafina, not you," Carlos answered.

"Did you come alone, Carlos?"

"Billy's with me."

Wes unbarred the door and slowly pulled it ajar. In the darkness he made out three forms, not two.

"Who else is with you?" Wes demanded.

"A friend," Bonney replied.

"Light the candles, Sarafina," Wes whispered.

In a moment a glowing ball grew over the table, and Wes opened the door.

Carlos strode in, moving straight to Sarafina and hugging her. Next Bonney stepped inside followed by the third man. As the fellow walked in, he took off his hat and Wes recognized Alexander McSween.

"He's not welcome here," Wes announced.

"We won't be long," Bonney answered.

"Please," McSween begged. "I have no place to stay. Dolan's men are hunting me."

Wes closed the door as Jace picked up the second candle from the table, touched the wick to the other flame, and lit it. In the growing light Wes saw McSween lower his hat to his waist, his hands rolling and unrolling the brim.

"Carlos wanted to visit his sister," Bonney explained. "I know you said only him and me should visit, so I left a dozen Regulators standing guard up on the road. I didn't think it safe to leave Alex because the House is trying to kill him."

"It's true," McSween acknowledged. "Please have mercy on a hunted man, who hasn't seen his wife in days and can't go home for fear of being assassinated."

Sarafina motioned to Carlos, and she and her brother left the kitchen for the parlor so they might visit in private.

"So, you're working for McSween now, Kid, is that right?"

Bonney nodded.

"Has he paid you and Carlos wages?"

McSween stepped between Billy and Wes. "Times are hard, and I can't get to my money, Mr. Bracken. I'll pay them when I can."

"That's what the late Englishman claimed, and he never gave them their due."

"He was murdered before he could," McSween countered like a lawyer.

"When Tunstall had a chance, he bought the widow Casey's cattle instead of paying Bonney and Carlos. He could afford to buy a second herd when the Casey cattle disappeared. You and Tunstall are branded with the same iron. I don't want you on my property again."

"So you've joined Dolan's gang, have you, Bracken?"

Wes shoved his pistol back in his holster and knotted his fist, ready to punch the lawyer in the face. "I don't work for them now, and I never worked for them in the past like you."

"That was a mistake," McSween admitted.

"A misstep you used to your crooked advantage, seeing how Murphy operated and cheated folks so you could use the knowledge to enrich you and Tunstall at everyone else's expense. You're as corrupt as the House."

Even in the dim candlelight, Wes watched McSween's face redden.

"That's a lie," McSween sighed.

Bonney intervened. "That's a trail that's gone cold, Wes, because the new sheriff is making things hot for us."

"I heard Copeland was as fair as the Regulators could expect."

Bonney growled. "He tried to be fair, but he's no longer sheriff. Governor Axtell replaced him with George Peppin, who's a Murphy-Dolan man, always has been."

Wes licked his lips and nodded. "Peppin and Billy Mathews accompanied Sheriff Brady and Deputy Hindman when they were murdered, didn't they?"

Bonney swallowed hard. "That's what some say."

"Then he's got a grudge to settle with you, Billy, besides whatever Dolan wants out of McSween."

"That's the size of it, Wes. Sure you can't give us a hand?" Bonney asked.

Wes crossed his arms over his chest. "Not as long as McSween is involved!"

Bonney turned to Cousins. "The Regulators need a man as handy as you with a rifle."

"Wes has done right trying to stay out of other men's messes. I'm with him."

"You fellas talk righteous, but your hands have blood on them too, stealing Tunstall's cattle, murdering two of Jesse's gang, assassinating Tom Hill and wounding Jesse Evans."

"We take care of ourselves without hiring people to do our killing," Jace shot back, his gaze fixed on McSween.

"Yeah, but I wouldn't be pious about it," Bonney answered.

"The law's got to sort this out," Wes said.

Bonney scowled at Wes. "The law? We'll see about the law. Jesse goes to Mesilla in two weeks for a trial the first week of May. Bristol's the judge and Rynerson's the prosecutor. We'll watch how that turns out, then you can lecture me on the law and justice, Wes Bracken." Bonney turned toward the door. "Carlos," he called, "let's get out of here and take McSween to Chisum's place for protection." Bonney glared at Wes. "Chisum'll help a man in need."

Carlos reentered the kitchen with Sarafina, who kissed him on the cheek.

"Be careful, my brother," she said. "I am sorry the difficulties have caused you troubles."

Carlos moved behind Bonney. "I'm ready."

"Please visit often, Carlos," Wes said. "You're family."

"Yes," Sarafina reaffirmed, "we're always

glad when you come by."

"Kid, you're even welcome here," Wes continued, turning to the lawyer, "but don't bring McSween back to my place again."

Without another word, the trio opened the door and stepped into the darkness of night and the darkness of the violent morass that was Lincoln County.

As soon as Wes closed and barred the entry, his wife sobbed. "He is in trouble, Carlos is."

"What did he tell you, Sarafina?"

"That he had been wrongfully indicted for murder."

Wes grimaced. He had seen the killing, and he knew better, but perhaps it was best to let Sarafina believe her brother's lie rather than try to correct it.

He offered her a hug and nothing more.

CHAPTER 22

Wes saw the buckboard turn off the road toward the house and recognized Juan Patrón headed his direction. In the two weeks since the nighttime visit of Carlos and Bonney with McSween, Wes and Jace had moved Sarafina and the boys to the old Casey place, taking what belongings they could manage on horseback before dawn or after sunset to disguise their move. If his family's whereabouts remained a secret, Wes would worry less about their safety.

Drawing up in front of the abandoned Mirror B house, Patrón smiled. "Wes, *mi amigo,* Providence has sent us an Angel!"

Wes stood perplexed, uncertain whether an enemy had been dispatched to the pearly gates or whether his visitor had been gnawing on loco weed. "What are you talking about?"

Patrón tied the reins and jumped from the buckboard, grabbing Wes's hand and pumping it. "We have an Angel on our side," Patrón said.

"What side is that?" Wes asked.

"The side of truth, that's what we want. The government has sent an investigator to look into Tunstall's death and Lincoln County's troubles."

"What difference does someone from Santa Fe make? He's surely beholden to the Ring."

"No, no, Wes, you don't understand. Washington, not Santa Fe, sent the investigator. He's a special agent for the U.S. Department of Justice appointed to look into the murder of Tunstall and everything else. His name is Frank Warner Angel, our own guardian angel."

"I doubt much'll come of it."

"But someone in Washington is concerned, Wes. And, as long as Angel is in Lincoln, no one's gonna start any more mischief. In fact, McSween has come out of hiding and is back in Lincoln, helping Angel determine who to investigate. From his time as Murphy's lawyer, Alex knows where to look for fraud."

Wes had become too cynical of the powers in New Mexico Territory and Lincoln County to see much hope. "As soon as he leaves, Juan, things'll go back to their violent ways."

"Angel is looking for the truth in these matters, Wes, and he wanted to interview you next week. That's why I'm here, to extend his invitation."

Wes shook his head. "I've too much work to do."

Patrón glanced around, taking in the demolished barn, the unplowed fields, and the spring weeds that had sprouted in the irrigation ditches. "You're behind in your chores like everyone else, but this is too important for Lincoln County."

"There's something else, Juan, but you've got to promise not to share this information."

"You can trust me, Wes."

"I've moved Sarafina and the boys into the Casey place, but I'm keeping it to myself so Dolan's gang can't find them. I've got to move everything on horseback after dark to keep it secret. Without my wagon, it'll take a while, especially for the furniture."

Patrón nodded. "Agree to meet with Angel, and I'll borrow a wagon to help."

"I'd be obliged, Juan."

"I'll be back in the morning, Wes. Just promise you'll visit the special investigator."

"You have my word."

As agreed, Patrón returned the next day with a wagon and helped Wes load up the table, chairs, bed frames, mattresses, bedding, and other pieces from the house. After delivering that cargo, they returned to pick up the furniture from the bunkhouse and any tools that were salvageable after the arson. Sarafina treated Patrón to supper after they completed the work, and Wes escorted him to the wagon for the return to Lincoln.

Wes grabbed Patrón's hand and shook it. "It would've taken days without the wagon to move everything."

"I won't mention where your family is. Remember that the special investigator wants to see you Friday afternoon at the Wortley."

"I'll be there."

"There's one other thing you should know, Wes. We've got an Angel in town, but a devil has returned as well. They acquitted Jesse Evans in Mesilla for stealing government mules from the reservation."

Wes gritted his teeth as anger pulsed through his veins. "I suppose they released him rather than holding him for trial in Tunstall's murder."

Patrón nodded.

"Nothing's changed with the territorial law."

"It gets worse. Word is that Jesse plans to return to Lincoln, and Sheriff Peppin intends to deputize him."

Wes realized his decision to move his family to the Casey place's mill had been the right one, if he could maintain the secret.

"My prayer for us all," Patrón said, "is that the day is not too distant when we no longer have to fear for our lives in Lincoln County." He climbed into the wagon seat and started the return trip to Lincoln. "See you Friday," he called over his shoulder.

Wes turned and stepped inside what had been the Casey store and house, barring the door behind him and slipping past the counter into the back section of the house, which included the kitchen and three other rooms. Sarafina was washing dishes, something she was comfortable with, though cooking had become a challenge as she had never used a woodstove before, always cooking over open fires or in fireplaces. Bob Casey had built his store dwelling to meet Anglo customs, not those of the native Hispanics, so Ellen had cooked on a cast-iron stove they had left behind. Sarafina had tried to learn the new way of cooking on a stove, and Wes could not complain about her effort, though her results sometimes suffered.

He stepped to her and put his arm around her waist. "Juan enjoyed the stew," he said.

"It was scorched," she said.

"Tasted fine to me." Wes watched a tear roll down her cheek. "It was fine, Sarafina."

"It's not that," she said.

"You hate your new home or the cookstove? Which?"

She grimaced and shook her head. "It's not that. I can make a home wherever I live, as long as I am with you."

He pulled her to him, wrapping his arms around her and looking into her dark, tear-filled eyes. "Tell me what's bothering you, Sarafina?"

"*Estoy con un niño,*" she whispered. "*Estoy con un niño.*"

He smiled. "You are with child again?"

Sarafina nodded, her eyes sad.

His grin faded as Wes realized the implication. Was this baby his or one of her attacker's child? He lifted his right hand to her hair and pulled her head to his chest so she would not question his expression. As Wes held her, she began to sob, and he felt her tears moistening his shirt. "Everything will be fine, Sarafina," he comforted her, hoping he was right.

■ ■ ■ ■

As he rode toward Lincoln, Wes was glad to travel alone. With Jace Cousins staying to protect Sarafina and the boys, he relished the solitary time to consider matters. Though he had never discussed the attack with her, he understood both men had violated her. He had seen it in her eyes. If the child was born with the hair of a reddish tint, he would know it was Jesse's. Wes wondered how to face that possibility or how to treat Sarafina for something that was not her fault. Even so, whoever the father, the baby would be half Sarafina, and he loved his wife. The questions that came to mind were overwhelming, so he was glad when he reached the outskirts of town. He shook his head to rid it of the paternal confusion and focus on the threats in Lincoln.

With Frank Angel in town, the community remained on its best behavior with men and women attending their business. Even children played in front of their homes or in the street, chasing chickens or throwing sticks or playing hide-and-seek. Wes dismounted at Patrón's house long enough to knock on the door and ask his wife to inform Juan he had come to Lincoln to keep his promise. Horseback again, he rode toward the Wortley, passing the location where the bigoted Horrell brothers had shot up a dance and killed four Hispanics eight months after Wes first arrived in Lincoln County. On the south side of the street stood the courthouse where Wes helped hang Willie Wilson for the second time. As he neared the shuttered Tunstall store, he passed the spots where Sheriff Brady and Deputy Hindman had fallen when assassinated by Bonney and Carlos. Next he walked by the spot in the road where Robert Casey had been shot. For all the bloodshed on the street, Wes felt in his bones that more was to be spilled before Lincoln became a law-abiding town and county.

At the Wortley, Wes rode around back of the hotel and tied his sorrel at a hitching post away from the street and the vindictive eyes of any enemies. He walked to the front of the building and entered.

Sam Wortley greeted him. "It's past lunchtime, Wes, so you must be here to see Frank Angel of the Justice Department."

"That's right, Sam."

"He's in room number three."

Wes nodded and backed outside, walking along the porch to the door marked with a numeral three painted on the frame. He knocked. "Wes Bracken to see Frank Angel," he called.

"Enter," came the answer.

Wes went inside, finding a man in his early thirties with great muttonchop sideburns and matching black hair swept back over his head. His face featured a prominent nose, thin lips, and wide, inscrutable eyes. His black suit, black bow tie, black vest, and white shirt with starched collar reflected his task's importance. Wes closed the door and removed his hat. Angel pointed to a chair across the double bed from where he stood. As Wes took a seat, the special agent introduced himself and explained he was trying to get at the root of the violence and fraud in Lincoln County, which might well be the most corrupt in the entire United States.

Like all the lodging at the Wortley, the room was small, barely big enough for the double bed, the two cane-bottom chairs, the chest of drawers, and the washstand. Atop the bed that doubled as his desk, Angel had scattered five notebooks, a writing board, a box of pencils, and two dozen envelopes stuffed with folded papers.

Angel sat, grabbing the writing slat, which he placed in his lap, then took up a pencil and notebook, which he opened to a blank page. He scribbled notes on the paper as he asked questions.

"I'm told by several witnesses you've tried to stay out of the troubles, remain neutral."

"I protected what was mine and avoided involvement in others' dealings."

"Who's responsible for the problems and violence?"

"To me, the Murphy-Dolan gang —"

"You say gang, don't you mean store or associates?"

"— started it all. When I say gang, I mean exactly what I say. The Murphy-Dolan gang ran this county, restraining everyone's business but their own. When Tunstall and McSween got the idea they could take profits away from the House, they turned out to be just as greedy, no better than Murphy and Dolan."

"Which faction was the lesser of two evils?"

"I never cared for Murphy, Dolan, or their gang. Same with Tunstall and McSween, didn't like them, though their men were okay. One of them was my brother-in-law."

"Who's that?"

"Carlos Zamora."

Angel nodded. "His name's come up for killing a deputy on the street. Is it true you were a Lincoln County vigilante that lynched a Will Wilson?"

"I was never a vigilante. I helped hang a fellow that shot a friend of mine. He was condemned to hang, but Sheriff Ham Mills at Murphy's direction tried to make it appear the murderer had been executed, but they'd rigged up a brace to deceive the witnesses. The condemned man wasn't dead. I don't consider that a lynching or me a vigilante."

"Are you a cattle rustler, one that stole a herd from John Henry Tunstall's ranch?"

Wes let out a long, slow breath of air. "Those cattle belonged to the widow of Bob Casey, who L.G. Murphy had killed. The county attached the cattle over a five-dollar debt my friend owed. I paid the debt back twice and returned the herd to their rightful owner."

"Even though Tunstall bought them at a legal county sale."

"Yes, and I'd do it again. The Englishman took advantage of a widow who'd lost her husband. He knew the truth behind those cattle. He and the Murphy-Dolan gang, or the House, were the only ones bidding on the beeves. No one else would stoop so low, even if they could afford it. And Dolan only bid to increase Tunstall's cost. Murphy's men stole whatever livestock they wanted."

Angel turned a page in his notebook and continued recording Wes's answers. "What do you know about the Tunstall killing?"

"Nothing directly, only what I was told. The grand jury indictments covered every name I heard involved, except those that were dead."

"What about the deaths of Buck Morton and Frank Baker?"

"Wasn't there, and I only picked up gossip and speculation."

"What about Jesse Evans?"

Wes's lips tightened. "A despicable bully of a man."

"Do you know details of the assassination of two in his gang west of Dowlin's Mill the evening after he broke out of jail? Or about him and Tom Hill being surprised by a sheepherder?"

"Wasn't at the first killing, though I was glad of it because Jesse had stopped by my place and threatened my family that afternoon. As for the second incident, you should ask the herder."

"Is it true Evans and Hill burned your barn and raped your wife before they encountered the sheepherder?"

Wes grimaced, swallowing hard as he thought of Sarafina's latest pregnancy.

"That's true," Wes answered slowly and deliberately, "but I don't like the details being shared."

"Did you trail the attackers?"

"I did!"

"Alone?"

"I'll let other folks talk about their involvement."

"Are you acquainted with William H. Bonney, also known as Billy Bonney or Billy the Kid?"

"I am."

"Do you consider him a friend?"

"He's a likable kid, though I'm never sure what to make of him as he runs hot and cold."

"He may be the most important witness in my investigation. Bonney saw or was involved in most of the violence over the last six months."

"Maybe you should interview him."

"I've tried, but he won't come. Said he doesn't trust the investigation and that's why I asked to meet you, Mr. Bracken. Bonney says he'll talk to me only if you arrange it."

"What? I'm acquainted with him, but we've had too many run-ins for him to trust me."

"Through his messengers, he's told me

455

you're the only man in Lincoln County he believes trustworthy. Will you help me set up an interview with Bonney?"

Wes considered the offer, then outlined his demands. "I've a few conditions to establish before I'll consider it. First, I don't want Carlos Zamora interviewed or dragged by you any deeper into this than he already is. Second, my partner, Jace Cousins, is not to be questioned or mentioned in your report about anything. Third, if Bonney agrees to visit with me in the middle, he meets you somewhere else in town, a place you won't know about until five minutes before the summit. Fourth, I will name a contact to deliver the time and location you're to meet with him. That's the starting point for me arranging a meeting."

Angel nodded. "I'm uncomfortable with your first two requests."

Wes stood up, grabbing his hat from the bed. "If Bonney's important, and I'm the only one who can get him to you, you will accept my stipulations or we have no more business together."

The investigator scratched his thick sideburns with his right hand. "I find it odd you're protecting your brother-in-law and your partner, but not yourself."

Putting his hat on, Wes stared at Angel,

trying to read the Justice Department agent and determine if he would break. Their gazes locked on one another until Angel looked away. "I'll stand for what I've done and face the consequences. Carlos and Jace wouldn't have been involved in any of this save for me trying to do what's right. It's a damn shame that taking the moral road in Lincoln County can get you in so much trouble with the law."

Angel's eyes focused on Wes. Slowly, he nodded. "I can live with your stipulations."

"All four of them?"

"Every one," the investigator answered.

"When the time is right, you'll be hearing from Jace Cousins; he's my ranching partner. Whatever he tells you, comes straight from me."

"I expect to be here two more weeks. If you don't have Bonney to me for an interview before then, our agreement is null and void. How soon can I expect the meeting?"

"As soon as I can arrange a safe meeting place."

With the dark skies of a moonless night overhead, Wes Bracken stood by the adobe of Squire Wilson, who had agreed that his place would be the rendezvous point for Frank Angel to meet William H. Bonney.

457

Wes carried his Winchester across his chest, ready for any surprise that might disrupt the meeting and the agreement to keep the names of his brother-in-law and his partner out of the Justice Department report. Wes and Jace Cousins had tied their mounts in the apple orchard southwest of Wilson's. There too waited Bonney astride his horse so he could escape in case this requested meeting was a trap. While the Kid and Wes waited, Jace went to the Wortley to roust the special agent.

The garrulous Squire Wilson wanted to relive his victory in the latest election and how the people of Lincoln County had more sense than the territorial governor. And once he covered that topic, he was ready to talk about everything else that came to mind, but Wes had silenced him. Wes focused on linking Bonney with Angel and getting the Kid out of town as soon as possible after that. Wes moved to the corner of the house to await Jace Cousins and the special agent.

An hour before midnight, Wes heard the soft footfall of two men. Jace gave a low whistle, two short tweets, then a long one, the signal he was approaching. Shortly, Cousins and Angel appeared. "I don't think anyone saw us," Jace said.

"Sorry to disturb your sleep, Angel," Wes said, "but that's another cost to visit with Bonney."

"Is he inside?" Angel asked.

"He's nearby. Once you're inside, we wait five minutes to make certain no one followed, then I signal for him to ride in. We'll hold his horse outside in case he has to leave in a hurry."

Wes opened the door and motioned for Angel to enter. "Squire Wilson'll keep you company while you wait," Wes whispered.

"Though you may need four ears to keep up with all the words he'll throw at you," Jace said softly.

As soon as the door closed, Jace and Wes took up positions at opposite corners of the adobe, Wes watching the southern and western approaches with Jace covering the northern and eastern access. Sensing no threats after five minutes, Wes confirmed with Jace that everything was clear from his direction, giving the signal of an owl. *"Hoo, Hoohoo, Hoo, Hoo,"* Wes called.

Bonney answered with the same call, and Wes heard a horse emerging from the orchard. Bonney slid gracefully from the saddle and landed at Wes's feet, handing him the reins. Wes led the dappled gray and Bonney around the house to the door, open-

459

ing it and letting the Kid inside.

When Jace walked over, Wes whispered his plan to stay at the entry with the horse in case Bonney had to escape. He asked Jace to circle the house as a lookout.

"Angel told me what you did, Wes," Jace whispered.

"What are you talking about?"

"Protecting me and Carlos in the report and not covering for yourself. I'm obliged, as Carlos should be, though he'd never admit it."

The door to the adobe opened and Squire Wilson emerged. "He kicked me out of my house," the justice said of Angel. "Guess I'll have to visit with you boys."

"I'll start my watch duty," Jace whispered. "He's all yours, Wes."

Wilson blathered on about how much he disliked the governor for removing him from office and how much smarter the decent people of the Lincoln precinct were to reelect him to the position that he was eminently prepared to handle. Wes just nodded, saying "uh-huh" a few times and reminding him to keep his voice low so not to attract attention.

Bonney spent an hour and a half with Angel, then slipped out the door, thanking Wes for arranging the meeting, Jace for getting the investigator there, and Wilson for allowing them to use his home. Angel emerged from the house and shook Wes's hand. "I got what I needed," he told Wes. "I'm heading back to the hotel."

"You need an escort?" Jace asked.

"No, sir. Be aware I'm leaving town in three days," Angel said.

"There'll be hell to pay when you do," Wes answered.

"Everybody's waiting for you to depart before resuming their vendettas," Jace added.

"I've never seen so much corruption," Angel admitted, "and it goes all the way to the top. If I have any luck with my initial report, you'll hear about a change at the highest levels. Good night and thank you on behalf of the Justice Department." The agent walked away.

"It'll be about time," Jace said.

Wilson chuckled. "Seems Angel's smarter than the governor, too."

"You best keep that to yourself, Squire, so no one has any additional reasons to hate the investigator. Now get to bed."

The old man scurried inside his adobe. When he shut the door, Wes handed the Kid the reins to his gelding. Both Wes and Jace accompanied Bonney to the orchard. The

461

Mirror B partners untied their mounts and rode with the Regulator around Lincoln to the east before reaching the road that led to the Hondo Valley and Casey's Mill.

They rode silently until they were a mile beyond town. "You need to get out, Bonney, while you still can," Wes suggested.

"And let the House win? No, sir, that's not in me."

"Once Angel leaves Lincoln," Jace said, "the dance of death will begin. It won't stop until you're all dead because there's more of them than there are Regulators. The House has political connections you can't fight."

"McSween says all we need is time for the government to come in and clean it up. Angel's the first sign of that," Bonney said.

"Has McSween paid you any wages yet?"

"No," Billy replied, "but he promises he will as soon as we get this straightened out."

"That may never happen," Wes replied.

"And it may be tomorrow," Bonney shot back.

Wes and Jace parted with the Kid at the Ruidoso, him riding west for San Patricio and them east to Casey's Mill.

A week after Angel departed Lincoln, Juan Patrón visited the Casey place with word that President Hayes had relieved Governor

Samuel B. Axtell of his territorial duties.

Jace Cousins snickered at the news. "I suppose that means Squire Wilson's job is safe until the next election."

He, Wes, and Patrón chuckled at the joke, their last laugh for six weeks.

CHAPTER 23

After Frank Warner Angel left Lincoln for Santa Fe as his first stop on the return trip to Washington, D.C., violence and vengeance resumed in Lincoln County as everyone expected. Like roving packs of wild dogs marking their territory, three groups of outlaws scoured the region, hunting for the Regulators and terrorizing honest citizens that didn't kowtow to their demand. Sheriff George Peppin led a posse that often included J.J. Dolan himself and other adherents of the House in search of Alex McSween and the Regulators. Emboldened by the imprimatur of the law, Peppin's men on July Fourth attacked John Chisum's ranch headquarters where McSween and most of the Regulators had holed up. The limp-armed Jesse Evans commanded a reconstituted mob of bad men that roved the countryside, creating havoc wherever they rode. John Kinney's gang arrived from the Doña Ana County and did more of Sheriff Peppin's dirty work, just as District Attorney Rynerson had ordered. Kinney's men terrorized San Patricio three times, pillaging the town and assaulting the citizens in retribution for the refuge they had provided the Regulators. Kinney promised more attacks if the village offered shelter to a single Regulator, especially Billy Bonney. Complicating the already strained animosities of Lincoln County, even the small ranchers from Seven Rivers southeast of Lincoln grew emboldened, banding together to rustle Chisum cattle and settle festering scores with their enemies. The region trembled with fear of vengeance.

Wes Bracken and Jace Cousins stayed close to the Casey place, both to protect Sarafina and the boys and to make certain they didn't stumble into more trouble. Twice Wes returned to the Mirror B to check on land that had overgrown with weeds from inattention and buildings that had suffered from vandalism. The house showed dozens of bullet holes and scorches where hooligans had tried to start a fire and burn it to the ground like the barn. Wes realized he had made the right decision to leave the place because the Casey dwelling stood farther from the road than the

Bracken home and was a stronger building, as it had been constructed more than a decade earlier to fend off Apache attacks. Four times the Mirror B partners prepared to defend the place when they heard gunfire along the road, but each time the running gun battles passed them without swinging toward the house. Wes was thankful they had plenty of ammunition from what the widow Casey had left them and what Jace had taken from the Tunstall store. They would need the cartridges before things settled.

Other than what they observed from their Casey stronghold, Wes and Jace got most of their information from Juan Patrón, who rode out to visit them twice. Instead of coming in his buckboard, he now rode on a saddle horse to improve his chances of escaping any roving gangs he might encounter. Not that he had done anything wrong in his mind, but the ruffians had grown emboldened by their unchallenged reign of terror. The first time he visited, Patrón brought word of the suspected whereabouts of the roaming bands and Dolan's exasperation that the Regulators still ran free. Further, Patrón reported the rumor that Peppin as sheriff had requested help from the Army at Fort Stanton to quell the violence in Lincoln County. Were soldiers to intervene, Wes, Jace, and Patrón understood the troops would act on behalf of Dolan and squash any enemies of the House. On that trip Patrón also offered the expected news that L.G. Murphy had died in Santa Fe. The man who had started the events leading to the county chaos would not be around to see its conclusion or suffer its consequences, if justice was ever achieved.

In mid-July Patrón returned with more news. He was jaunty as he dismounted, and Wes and Jace welcomed him. They tied his horse behind the house to hide it from the road, then stepped inside the kitchen where Sarafina offered the men coffee, and Luis and Roberto played in the corner with the wooden horse Wes had carved.

Patrón sipped at the coffee tin, then spoke. "President Hayes has appointed a new territorial governor. Lew Wallace is his name. He's a former Army general known for honesty."

Wes grimaced. "A Union officer doesn't carry much sway with me."

Jace agreed. "Wallace will have to prove his honesty before I'll believe anything."

"But the president did more," Patrón continued. "He prohibited the Army from getting involved in civilian matters, leaving that up to the local authorities."

"That doesn't help us," Wes answered, his words dripping with frustration.

"That's true," Patrón said, "but at least they can't be used against us."

"The House'll figure out a way to turn them against decent people," Jace said. "They always do."

"Not this time," Patrón offered. "Governor Wallace has orders to clean up this mess."

"That was Frank Angel's job," Wes shot back.

Patrón nodded. "And we're seeing results. We've got to be patient."

"We've been patient," Wes responded, "and it's only gotten worse."

"Things are changing, I tell you. The truth will prevail," Patrón insisted.

Jace scoffed. "Not when killers like Jesse Evans are acquitted for stealing government mules and not even tried for the Englishman's killing."

"I've got hope," Patrón said, "that things'll turn. Lincoln is as calm as I've ever seen it. All the lawbreakers are out of town stalking their enemies."

Wes disagreed. "The House has a hundred or more men doing their dirty work. Best I can figure, the Regulators have thirty men or fewer. I learned in the war that you can't beat numbers, and the House has numbers. I'm doubtful we can ever beat the corruption."

"Have faith," Patrón chided.

"What faith I have," Wes replied, "is strengthened by plenty of ammunition."

Patrón finished his coffee and stood up, saying he must return home as he was uncomfortable leaving his wife alone in Lincoln, even with the wicked men gone. Wes thanked him for bringing the news and offered to ride with him to Lincoln for extra protection. Patrón declined the offer, gave his thanks to Sarafina for the coffee, and went outside, Wes and Jace following him. He climbed aboard his horse and started back for town.

"There'll be more bloodletting before this is done," Wes said, as much to himself as to Jace.

"Hello, the house," came the cry, startling Wes in his bed. He jumped to his feet, grabbed his gun belt, and fastened it around his waist, then picked up his carbine. He shook his head, trying to clear the fog in his brain. Wes nudged Sarafina from her sleep and told her to get the boys. It was midnight or later on that Sunday morning, he thought, as he scurried through the dark kitchen to the store where Jace had set up his bedding. Jace stood at the window, his Henry pointed outside.

"State your name and business," Jace shouted.

Wes cracked a shutter on the opposite side of the door from Jace and tried to gauge the trespassers. There were too many to count, fifty or more. Wes swallowed hard. He feared this was one of Dolan's bands as the Regulators lacked these numbers.

"State your name and business," Jace repeated.

"Is that you, Jace?" answered a familiar voice.

Wes recognized the intonation of Billy Bonney. "Is that you, Bonney?" he cried.

"In the flesh," he replied. "We thought the place was abandoned and planned to put up for the night."

"Can't let you do that," Jace bluffed. "We've over twenty men here as is."

"Mind if I come in and powwow?"

"Just you and Carlos, if he's a mind to," Wes said.

"Give me a moment," Bonney replied.

Wes watched a horseman dismount and took it to be Bonney. The man walked to another rider, visited with him for a moment, then turned around and started for the house.

"I'm coming in alone," Bonney called.

Jace unbarred the door and opened it enough for Bonney to slip in. After the Kid passed into the darkened room, Jace secured the entry.

"What are you doing at the Casey place?" he asked. "We thought it was still vacant."

"Too many attacks on the Mirror B," Wes informed him. "We're living here. It's safer."

"We planned to stop here for the night and ride into Lincoln in the morning. We've ridden most of the day."

"Who's with you?"

"Everybody. Like us, McSween's tired of running. He wants it settled."

"Get to Lincoln tonight, then," Wes told him. "Juan Patrón visited us before noon today and said the town's empty of most of Dolan's men and the other gangs. They've got a hundred or more fellows looking for you."

"There's thirty of us Regulators, but Carlos persuaded more of his people to join us. We've got sixty-five now. You and Jace should come along and end this matter once and for all."

"Can't do it, Bonney. I've got my family

to protect."

"Carlos is part of your family, isn't he?"

Wes shrugged. "He never claims any kinship to me."

"He's turned into a fast gun and a tough fighter, Wes. Stay on good terms with him."

"Carlos doesn't take to me. And I don't want your men hanging around here tonight." In the darkness, Wes failed to read Bonney's expression.

"That's not very neighborly."

"Lincoln's open for the taking if you ride on, Billy. I can't say what it'll be tomorrow."

Bonney paused, finally answering. "I'll accept your word on it 'cause I can still trust you, even though we don't get along on everything."

"Maybe you should just abandon McSween and your vendetta, get out of the territory where you're not known, and start fresh."

"It's not that easy," Bonney said.

"So McSween still hasn't paid you."

"I'm broke," Bonney admitted, "and I'm exhausted from running."

"We're busted, too," Wes acknowledged. "Me and Jace have no prospects of a crop this year. I don't know that we're running, but we're hiding until this blows over."

"If the Regulators bring the pot to a boil, do you think we can end it?" Bonney asked.

Wes let the question linger before shaking his head. "It'll take the law to end this, not the law like we've endured, but a fair and impartial law that seeks the truth."

"I've waited too long for the law to settle matters," Bonney answered. "Nobody's been tried for the Englishman's death. If the law won't settle it, I will."

"Innocent people may die, Billy."

"Innocence remains in short supply in Lincoln County." The Kid turned toward the door. "Like McSween, I'm ready to end it."

Jace opened the door for Bonney.

"Tell Carlos his sister sends her love," Wes called but received no response. Jace followed the Kid outside to the riders.

Wes strode to the open door and watched Bonney climb into the saddle as Jace walked over to another rider that Wes could not make out in the darkness. Jace spoke in low tones, shrugging as he backed away from the horseman. When Jace stepped back from the gang, Bonney turned his gray about. As a path parted among the riders, Bonney rode through the opening to the head of the band, and they started toward Lincoln.

Jace walked to the house, standing outside

the door as he and Wes saw the Regulators disappear into the night.

"Billy's not the carefree kid that I first met," Wes noted. "I miss that bucktoothed grin because he's in over his head, and he knows it."

Jace sighed. "The Kid's bewildered. Carlos is embittered. He blames us for Sarafina's rape. I told him you'd kept his and my name out of Angel's report, trying to help him out of the hole he'd dug for himself, but he didn't care, saying we both deserved to die. He hates all white men."

"All except Bonney," Wes answered.

Jace stepped inside, and Wes shut and barred the door for the night.

By the activity on the road, Wes decided things had heated in Lincoln. Riders raced back and forth delivering messages or seeking allies, he surmised, though he otherwise remained in the dark about the confrontation. Sarafina fretted over Carlos and his fate, while Wes worried over the implications for his family whatever the outcome. In the middle of a scorching July afternoon on the fifth day after the Regulators' night visit to his place, Jace burst into the front and yelled, "There's a buckboard coming at a good clip. I think it's Juan Patrón."

In the kitchen drinking a cup of cool water, Wes grabbed his Winchester and ran through the house. As soon as he stepped outside, he saw the buckboard racing toward him, kicking up plumes of dust from the thirsty trail. Wes realized Patrón carried a passenger, then recognized Beatriz.

"He's brought his wife," Jace said. "Things are bad."

"Sarafina," Wes called, "come here, *pronto por favor.*"

She joined him as Patrón circled the rig in front of Wes and yanked on the reins, his draft horse whinnying at the sudden stop. "Lincoln's gone to hell," Patrón cried out, heaving for breath. "I feared for Beatriz's safety — and mine."

As Jace helped Patrón's wife from the buckboard, Sarafina ran to her, taking her hands and guiding her to the house. "You'll be safe here," she said. "You can have mine and Wes's bed until it's okay to leave."

"Es horrible en Lincoln," Beatriz stated as Sarafina escorted her inside.

Wes studied the horse, its hide glistening with sweat from the hard ride.

Patrón released a deep breath laden with the tension of his ride. He tied the reins and jumped to the ground.

"Tell us what happened," Wes said, "then

we'll tend your horse."

Patrón nodded, stepping toward Wes and faltering as his knees buckled before he regained his balance. He let out another gasp of air. "Sunday morning McSween and the Regulators returned to town, surprising and outnumbering Dolan and Peppin. They took positions in McSween's house, the Tunstall store, and the Montaño place, driving Dolan's thugs to the House. Come Monday Dolan's men began to gather in town and the shooting started, at least one of Dolan's men dying."

"What about Carlos? Is he okay?" Wes asked.

"I'm not sure," Patrón answered, then continued his account of the siege. "Intermittent firing continued on Tuesday and Peppin sent a request to Fort Stanton for the loan of a howitzer. The soldier that brought the reply was fired on, Dolan's men claiming the Regulators did it, but I think it was Peppin's folks that shot over the trooper's head. Another House man was killed and one more wounded." Patrón gasped for breath.

"Take your time, Juan," Wes suggested.

"On Wednesday another one of Dolan's men was killed and one more wounded as shooting continued throughout the day, the

Regulators getting the better of it. That afternoon a second soldier came from the fort with the word that soldiers would come the next day to restore order."

Wes looked to Jace, then back to Patrón. "I thought you told us on your last visit that President Hayes had forbidden military intervention in civilian affairs."

"I did and the President did, but Colonel Dudley's claiming that when his soldier was fired upon, it was an assault on his troops. He claimed the authority to send more soldiers to town to ensure it didn't happen again."

"Wait a second," interjected Jace, scratching his head. "Since one soldier was shot at, but unharmed, the colonel's sending other soldiers to town to make sure none will be fired upon again, is that right? Why doesn't he just keep the soldiers at Fort Stanton?"

"It's a ploy to let the Army assist," Patrón answered.

"Dammit," Wes said. "We knew the law favored the House, but now we know the Army does too."

Patrón nodded. "Today, the soldiers arrived, bringing a howitzer with them and pointing it at the McSween house. The colonel advised those in McSween's that if a single shot was fired toward the soldiers, the troopers would demolish the house with cannon fire. Not only that, Dudley placed his soldiers between McSween's and José Montaño's so the Regulators there could not shoot at Peppin's men without shooting over the heads of the soldiers. Until then, the Regulators had held their own, but the Army tipped the scales to the Dolan bunch. McSween's men had to abandon the Montaño store."

Wes whistled. "And the Kid and Carlos are in the McSween house?"

Patrón shrugged. "As far as I know, but I cannot say for certain. They're surrounded, and I don't hold much hope for those in the lawyer's place. It was so dangerous, I had to get Beatriz out of town. As we are departing Lincoln, I overheard Peppin ordering men to fire the house and send them to hell where they belong. I had to leave, for I could not bear to risk my wife or hear doomed men die so horribly. Please understand."

Wes put his arm over Patrón's shoulder. "You're safe here, Juan."

Patrón lifted his shoulders, then let them fall like his spirits. "I did not see Carlos leave Montaño's place, so he is either in Tunstall's store or McSween's house, where most of the Regulators holed up."

"So he's likely among those they plan to burn out?"

Patrón nodded. "That's my guess."

Wes felt his jaw tighten as his stomach knotted.

Patrón pulled himself from Wes's arm and stared into his narrowed eyes. "You cannot save him, Wes. Don't even try. More than a hundred guns are aimed at that house, not including the howitzer. And the soldiers, they are taking the side of the attackers. You can't rescue him."

"I could at least retrieve his body," Wes replied. "I owe that to my wife." He turned to his partner. "Jace, would you saddle my horse and put a halter on one of the mules? I'm riding to Lincoln."

Jace nodded, "I'll do it, but I'm riding with you."

"You stay with Juan and with the women," Wes answered. "He's my brother-in-law, not yours."

"I ride with you or you can saddle your own damn horse. Nobody'll attack the women, not when they're settling scores in Lincoln."

Juan stepped between the two men. "I'll remain here. I have my carbine in the buckboard."

Wes nodded. "Okay, Jace, get moving."

His partner dashed for the barn as Patrón grabbed his weapon from the cart and accompanied Wes inside, through the front room, both men placing their long guns on the counter, and then into the kitchen where Beatriz sat at the table, bouncing a giggling Luis on her knee, while Sarafina held the jealous Roberto on her hip. Sarafina looked at her husband, her lips quivering in a concerned frown and her eyes moist with fright. "Do you know about Carlos?"

"Not for certain, but Jace and I are riding to town to find out."

Her hand flew to her mouth and tears overflowed her eyes, rolling down her cheeks. "Do not risk your life, *mi esposo,* for my ungrateful brother."

"I am not doing it for him, Sarafina, but for you."

She sobbed and rushed into her husband's arms, still holding her wailing son on her hip. He kissed her on the cheek, then lifted Roberto from her grasp and handed the bewildered boy to Beatriz, who sat him on her other knee and bounced him like his older brother.

Wes hugged Sarafina and kissed her, feeling her warm breath and her moist tears as they reached his lips.

She raised her head. "I could not bear to

480

lose *mi esposo,*" she whimpered.

"Understand, Sarafina, I am not promising to rescue him. It is not our battle, and there are too many of them to fight. If Carlos is wounded, I will see that he is cared for. If he is killed, I will see that he gets a proper burial."

Sarafina sobbed again. "Why did he bring this upon himself — and on us?"

"It's Lincoln County." He hugged her again, then kissed her cheek.

"I shall pray for your safety, *mi esposo.* I do not know what to pray for my unforgivable brother."

Wes broke from her embrace and moved past Patrón toward the front room. "Follow me, Juan." Wes bent behind the empty store counter and pointed to a low shelf. "We keep our extra ammunition there, should you need it. Sarafina can handle a pistol should anyone harass you in our absence." Wes grabbed a carton of ammunition for his Winchester and another for Jace's Henry, then picked up his carbine. "Good luck, Juan," he said as he marched outside.

"And the same to you both," Patrón answered as he shut and barred the door.

Wes jogged to the barn where he gave Jace his box of shells and packed his own in his saddlebags. While Jace finished saddling his dun, Wes put a halter and tether on one of the mules and tied the line to a ring on his saddle. Wes led Charlie outside and mounted the sorrel, which fidgeted and stamped his hooves, angry at being hitched to an inferior mule. Jace emerged from the barn and climbed atop his dun, then nodded he was ready.

Wordlessly, the men started toward Lincoln, riding at an easy gait to save their horses in case they needed to dash for safety. They advanced silently, alert to danger and any sound that signaled a threat. As they approached town near six o'clock, they saw a plume of black smoke ahead and detected the constant popping of gunfire to the west. The battle was still engaged. As they came closer their noses caught the briefest scent of burning wood and then the acrid smell as the hot breeze carried the overpowering odor. Reaching the outskirts of town, they saw a half dozen soldiers standing guard over the road, a white lieutenant and five black soldiers of the Ninth Cavalry. Wes recognized the lieutenant's rank by the uniform. Even thirteen years after the war's end, Wesley Bracken disliked soldiers in blue as the sight brought back so many unpleasant memories.

Rather than be turned away from Lincoln

by the blue bellies, Wes steered his sorrel and the mule off the road and made a wide swing to the north, crossing the Rio Bonito and heading toward the mountainsides that overlooked Lincoln. Jace followed him. Barely had they crossed the stream than his partner called out to him. "Soldiers are coming."

"Ignore them," Wes answered over his shoulder, "and head for the slopes where we can view the McSween house." Wes nudged Charlie into a fast lope, the mule churning after him as he headed higher up the rocky incline that overlooked the back of the McSween property. There he stopped between two juniper bushes and dismounted, untying the mule from the saddle and securing him to one of the scrub plants as he listened to the crackling of the house fire and the popping of the gunshots. He tied Charlie to the same bush as Jace came up and dropped from his dun. As Jace secured his mount to the second shrub, the lieutenant and two cavalrymen arrived.

"What are you doing here?" the officer demanded.

"Watching the show," Wes said, studying the fire that had consumed half of the house.

"You can't do that because you're armed

and a threat to my soldiers."

Wes pointed to the gunfire raging around the McSween place. "They're the ones shooting guns. They're a bigger menace than we are."

"You need to move on," the lieutenant insisted.

Wes turned around and faced the officer. "I'm a civilian, and I damn sure don't take orders from a Yankee."

Uncertain what to do, the young officer moved to lift the flap of his holster.

Jace clucked his tongue and got the officer's attention as he wagged his Henry at the soldier's nose. "I wouldn't do that, soldier boy. Let us be, and we won't cause you or anybody else any trouble. The fellow you're hassling there killed more than a regiment of you fellows during the late unpleasantries so pester him at your own risk."

The lieutenant dropped his hand away from his holster. "What am I to tell the colonel?"

Jace cocked his head and motioned for the officer to back his horse up. "Tell him we were up here enjoying an evening picnic. Now git!"

Deciding it not worth the risk to challenge Jace, the officer turned his mount around and ordered the two cavalrymen to follow him down the slope.

"A whole regiment?" Wes chided.

Jace nodded as he returned his rifle to his saddle scabbard. "I thought a brigade might be stretching it."

Both men sat on the ground and studied the battle before them outside the U-shaped McSween house. It appeared the fire had started at the near end of the west wing, which ran perpendicular to the street, and gradually ate its way to the front wing, which paralleled the road, the blaze having consumed half of the "U." The assailants ringed the house, shooting at it from all directions, drawing only occasional fire from those trapped in the adobe. Wes looked up at the sun and estimated it was past six o'clock, two-and-a-half hours until twilight faded into darkness.

"I'd make a run for it," Jace said. "Nothing's worse than getting roasted to death."

"Not now, Jace. They're waiting for nightfall when they've got darkness for cover. Even then it'll be a long shot."

"You think Carlos is inside?"

"If Bonney is — and Juan was certain of that — Carlos will be with him."

They watched in silence as the fire consumed its way through the front wing of the house, then turned its blazing appetite along the east wing, slowly eating a path to the back.

"I didn't think adobe burned like that," Jace observed.

"They added wooden walls, partitions, and floors inside," Wes replied. "The adobe bricks may survive, but nothing else will."

The blaze raced against darkness. As sunshine faded, the glow of the fire grew greater and the flames cast wicked dancing shadows across the landscape. The more the inferno consumed of the house, the more the assailants concentrated their shots on the back end of the east wing where the kitchen door opened into a fenced yard with an outhouse in the corner. When night draped the entire sky, the red glow of the fire provided the only illumination, and the attackers slipped toward the fence, which had an open gate on the side and another at the back by the outhouse.

From the distance, Wes could just make out several dark forms creeping closer to the ball of light, their positions periodically identified by the flashes of their pistols and carbines. Occasionally, a flare from the adobe showed that the trapped men still had life and ammunition. The blaze inched toward the back door, the flames licking at the wood in the structure, which flared and popped as the inferno grabbed more and more of the building. When the firing stopped, everyone reloaded for the impending escape attempt.

And then it happened.

One, two, three Regulators burst from the building shooting left and right, heading for the side gate. They ran like demons from hell. A fourth and a fifth followed, all firing, all screaming, all running for their lives. One, two, three, four charged out the side gate, then the fifth tumbled to the ground and thrashed on the earth before rolling over lifeless.

Everyone caught his breath. Was that all of the Regulators? Or were there more? The seconds passed like hours. Then more men bolted from the building. Wes counted seven, but it happened so fast he could not be sure of his tally. Guns from all around the enclosure opened fire. Wes heard a scream, "Don't shoot," and the firing stopped but an instant, then a single gunshot was followed by more than he could count. Wes saw four, maybe five men fall, as the gunmen turned their fire from the house toward those escaping in the darkness. A stillness fell across the land, a silent reverence for death, the only noises being the crackling, popping, and hissing of the blaze.

Then by ones and twos, then threes and fours, the assailants converged on the bodies, toeing at them and checking their identities. "Here's McSween," yelled a Dolan adherent, and others gathered around the body, kicking it and mocking it. Many celebrated by firing pistols in the air while others discharged their pistols into the ground or the dead.

Soon other men carrying torches came to inspect and celebrate the carnage, though they carried off one of their own dead. Once that body had been removed, Dolan's men danced among the carcasses, especially after someone brought out a fiddle and played sprightly tunes. In the torchlight the killers cavorted, casting fiendish shadows over the ground. Down the street some of Dolan's other men broke into Tunstall's store and pillaged whatever they wanted, mostly the whiskey that quenched their thirst for revenge. They danced and sang their sick songs as they defiled the deceased at their feet.

Wes turned to Jace. "I've seen war and death," he said, "but never have I seen such depravity."

Jace sighed.

"In the morning," Wes said, "we'll look for Carlos among the dead."

CHAPTER 24

Without their bedrolls, Wes and Jace slept
fitfully, tormented by both the rocky ground
where they tried to rest and the hellish ritual
of death they had watched that evening.
They arose in the morning twilight at the
distant crowing of a rooster in town and
took sips of water from their canteens for
breakfast. They led their mounts and the
mule down the slopes from their perch
toward the smoldering remnants of the
McSween house. At the banks of the Rio
Bonito, both men mounted their horses and
crossed the stream, Jace holding the halter
on the mule as they rode to the back fence
of the demolished home.

Wes dismounted and walked inside the
railing where a dozen hens pecked at the
ground and at the bodies for food. Wes
recognized McSween's bloodstained body
and stepped to inspect it, kicking at a hen
that poked at his lifeless eyes. The hen

cackled and scurried outside the fence. McSween had been shot enough to kill fifty men and his corpse was distorted from the abuse it had taken from his killers. Wes checked two more bodies near McSween, both Mexicans but neither Carlos. He wondered if these were men Carlos had recruited to join the Regulators. Near the side gate he discovered another Mexican he could not identify. Beyond the east fence he found the body of the first man he had seen die. He was an Anglo that Wes did not know.

Satisfied Carlos was not among those dead he mounted his horse and rode around the perimeter of the house close enough to the walls that he could lean into the shattered window openings and look for bodies. He saw one body in the ruins and knew it was not Carlos as the deceased was taller than his brother-in-law. After circling the house, he joined Jace, but instead of turning east toward home, he pointed his horse to Tunstall's store. The doors were ajar, so he jumped off his sorrel and entered. A couple of men lay sprawled on the floor, drunk, asleep, or both. Wes leaned over the counter beside the cage that had been marked as the Lincoln County Bank and saw that all the money drawers had been opened and plundered. He looked around the store.

Though some goods had been pilfered, Dolan's men had focused on whiskey and tins of food in their reverie. In one corner they had cut open a flour sack and dumped the white powder on the floor. Wes walked behind the empty glass ammunition case on the counter. Though the case held no cartons, he squatted and opened a drawer where he found more than two dozen boxes of cartridges. He retreated to the far corner, grabbed the empty flour sack, and returned to the drawer, dumping all the cartons in the sack. Though it was wrong to steal, he knew it was better to pilfer the ammo than to let it fall into the hands of Dolan's men.

As he was exiting from behind the counter, he saw in the leather goods a harness and collar that would replace that lost in the barn fire. He toted the flour sack over to the harness, gathered it and the collar, then started for the door, moving awkwardly under the load. His boot bumped one man on the floor, and he groaned as Wes passed. Back on the street, Wes gave Jace the bag, explaining its heavy and lethal contents, then decided it was easier to fit the harness to the mule than to drape it on his back, so he did that as quickly as he could, then mounted and started east toward home.

They passed the smoldering remains of

the McSween home where a pair of soldiers looked among the bodies for souvenirs. Then they rode by the cavalry encampment where other men were just arising, all accomplices in the foul deed they had allowed to happen by their very presence. Wes had even less regard for men in Yankee uniforms than he had had back in the war. At least back then it was a fair fight; this had been anything but fair.

As they reached the far perimeter of the camp, Wes saw the lieutenant who had tried to stop their picnic the day before walking by the road. He looked up and his eyes focused on Wes. "You should be proud of yourselves for what your officers allowed yesterday," Wes called. The soldier hung his head and marched past. "You might take some Army blankets to cover the bodies so the chickens don't peck and mutilate them more." The lieutenant pretended to ignore him, but Wes knew he heard the stinging words.

Wes and Jace rode quietly, not knowing what to say or how to reconcile the slaughter they had witnessed the evening before with their sense of fair play. As they neared the Casey place, Jace broke the silence. "I'll tend to the mule and the horses so you can tell Sarafina the news."

"I appreciate that, Jace."

Reining up in front of the house, Wes had barely slid out of the saddle when the door flung open and Sarafina raced out, throwing her arms around him and hugging him tightly. "You're safe," she cried. "My prayers have been answered."

Juan and Beatriz Patrón walked out, their gazes filled with curiosity about what had unfolded in Lincoln but their tongues stilled until Wes answered his wife's questions.

"We did not find Carlos," Wes explained, "so I don't think he is dead, though several men died. I have no idea where Carlos is or where any of the other survivors are."

Jace leaned over in his saddle and grabbed the reins of Wes's sorrel, leading the stallion and the mule to the barn.

Patrón stepped to Wes. "We heard riders on the road last night, ten o'clock or so. They were riding fast and didn't stop."

"That would've been about the right time," Wes calculated for their escape. "Let's step inside and I'll tell you what I saw, sickening as it was."

Among the decent folk of Lincoln County, the McSween massacre became known as "the Big Killing." The crime shocked a county accustomed to violence and corrup-

493

tion for more than a decade. From what Wes could pick up from Juan Patrón and other friends, the Regulators had been decimated, not so much by deaths but by desertions of Hispanics and Anglos with no stomach for killing or getting killed. John Kinney and others in his gang had taken part in the Big Killing, just as District Attorney Rynerson wanted, according to rumors, in his vendetta against McSween. After the killings, Kinney and the others had abandoned Lincoln County, returning to their regular haunts in Doña Ana County and stealing as many local cattle as they could on their way out. Though crippled in the left arm, Jesse Evans was said to have fired a bullet or two into McSween's corpse after the mass slaying. Jimmy Dolan still swaggered through Lincoln once they exterminated his competition like vermin, but he had no income from the inflated prices in his store, which now belonged to Thomas B. Catron of the Santa Fe Ring. Even so, some of his gang still roamed the county searching for a declining number of Regulators.

Rumors abounded that the new governor was set on cleaning up Lincoln County and fixing all the problems that had plagued the local government and its citizens. Talk resounded that Lincoln County was such a mess that only universal pardons from the governor could set the county on a straight course and give everyone a fresh start. Wes doubted that the rumor, if true, would be effective because a signature on paper did not wipe out animosities burned in a man's brain over the wrongs that had been done to him. Perhaps Wes was wrong, for the Big Killing had not only shocked Lincoln County but much of the country, which had been following the troubles in hundreds of newspapers.

For Wes Bracken, the biggest mystery from the Big Killing was what had happened to Carlos. He had heard accounts of Bonney's escape and his reemergence in San Patricio or Chisum's place or Fort Sumner or El Paso so the Kid was out there somewhere, though he likely kept moving to stay ahead of Dolan's men or Jesse's band. But no one ever mentioned his brother-in-law.

Further, Wes worried over supporting his family for the coming year. He had lost his horses, barn, wagon, and tools because of Jesse Evans; he had failed to get a crop in the ground in time to beat winter; he had not branded whatever calves had been born to his herd in the spring; and he had a baby — that might or might not be his through no fault of his wife — due in late fall. Wes knew he owed Jesse Evans a debt that could only be paid in lead. Though he intended to settle that debt, the challenges of making do and providing for his family weighed on him and occasionally he would take his rifle and climb the mountains behind the mill to hunt for deer or other game. He walked on those expeditions as it gave him time to think and consider his options for the future as well as reflect on the morality of what had transpired, not just among the feudists but with himself, too. He thought many times of one Bible passage Jace had read during one of their evenings back on the Mirror B. *Vengeance is mine; I will repay, saith the Lord.* He pondered that scripture often.

On an afternoon a month after the Big Killing, he was tracking a buck over the mountain behind the mill when he neared the top and saw a rider sitting on a dappled gray. No honest man climbed this mountain when there were passes and roads that were easier on man and animal. Wes feared he had been stalked while he was trailing the deer, but then realized the horse belonged to the Kid. Bonney sat in the saddle, waiting for Wes to reach the summit.

When he stood on ground level with Bonney's horse, Wes removed his hat and wiped his brow. "How long've you been watching me?"

"Ever since you left the house this morning."

"Why didn't you come to the house?"

"I wanted to talk with you alone."

"First, tell me if Carlos is alive."

Bonney nodded. "He's still with the Regulators because his own people are angered that he persuaded several men to ride with us and a handful got killed in the McSween shootout."

"Was Carlos there?"

"Yep, and he was as brave as they come. I ran out with the first batch, and he charged out with the last group, firing like a madman. If McSween had just followed him out the gate, he might have lived, but he cowarded out."

"Did he ever pay you?"

Bonney laughed. "I'm owed a lot of money by a lot of dead men."

"Do me a favor, Kid. When you see Carlos, tell him to visit his sister. We'll do what we can to help him out of his troubles."

"I'll do it, if you'll help me."

"What do you need?"

"I'm tired of running, Wes. You were right. It wears on a man where he can't sleep at night or bed a señorita without worrying they're coming for you."

"Best thing you can do, Kid, is leave the territory. Go some place where you're not known, say Texas. Start over there."

Bonney grimaced. "Texas is the last place I'd go. You know how many Texans are involved in Lincoln County's troubles? A lot! And, I can't run away from it or people will think I'm yellow."

"If you're set on staying, Bonney, you've got to quit stealing cattle and horses and shooting folks."

"I only do those things when I'm broke or defending myself."

"It don't matter, Bonney. You've got to stop it all."

"Will you help me get out of this?"

"I don't know that there's much I can do, but I'll try what I can. In exchange, I want you to bird-dog Carlos and prevent him from going any farther astray. And one other thing, if you find where Jesse Evans is, I want you to tell me."

"It doesn't sound like you and Jesse'll be sitting down to a game of cards."

"We won't play cards, but he and I'll still be gambling."

Billy Bonney understood the implied stakes in Wes's subtle intent. "I'll do what I can," he answered.

Wes offered his hand to Bonney and both men shook. Then Bonney turned his horse about and headed down the back side of the mountain. Wes started back for the mill, hoping he could help Bonney make things right and one day see the Kid's bucktoothed grin again.

He thought of Carlos and wondered what he could do to save his brother-in-law from the path he had taken. He would do it for Sarafina, if Carlos would just let him.

And then there was Jesse Evans somewhere in Lincoln County creating havoc. Wesley Bracken vowed to kill Jesse himself, regardless of what the scriptures said.

ABOUT THE AUTHOR

Three Rivers Trilogy author **Preston Lewis** is the recipient of two Spur Awards and three Will Rogers Gold Medallion Awards for written western humor and short stories. He is a past president of Western Writers of America and the West Texas Historical Association, which has awarded him three Elmer Kelton Awards for best creative work on West Texas. He is known for his comic westerns in The Memoirs of H.H. Lomax series, which includes the award-winning *Bluster's Last Stand.* Lewis holds degrees in journalism from Baylor and Ohio State Universities and a master's degree in history from Angelo State University. In 2021, he was elected to the Texas Institute of Letters. He and his wife, Harriet, reside in San Angelo, Texas.

CPSIA information can be obtained
at www.ICGtesting.com
Printed in the USA
BVHW090004180322
631830BV00001B/1

9 781432 891213